3/12

PITTSBURGH
SEPTEMBER 30, 1972

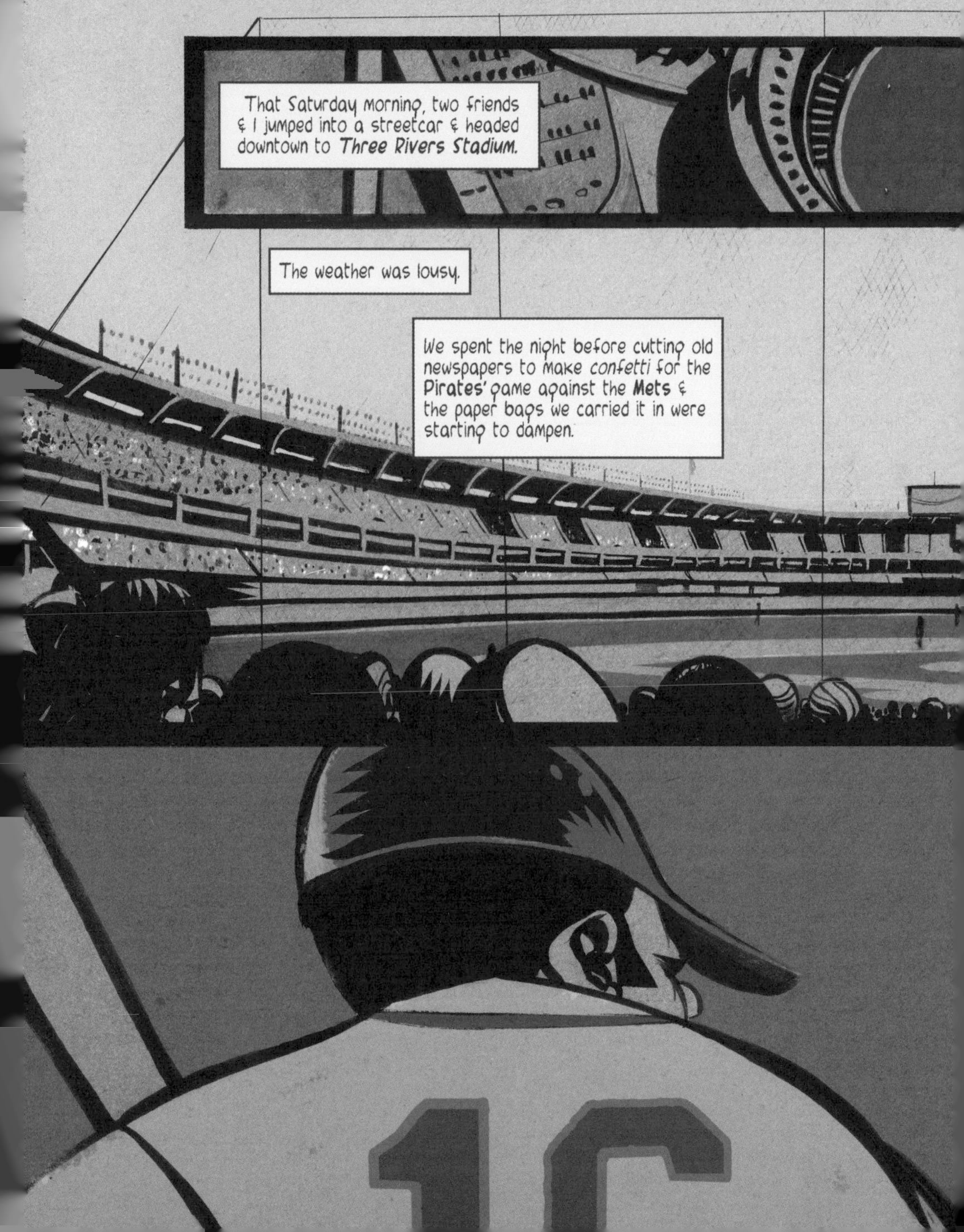
That Saturday morning, two friends & I jumped into a streetcar & headed downtown to Three Rivers Stadium.
The weather was lousy.
We spent the night before cutting old newspapers to make confetti for the Pirates' game against the Mets & the paper bags we carried it in were starting to dampen.

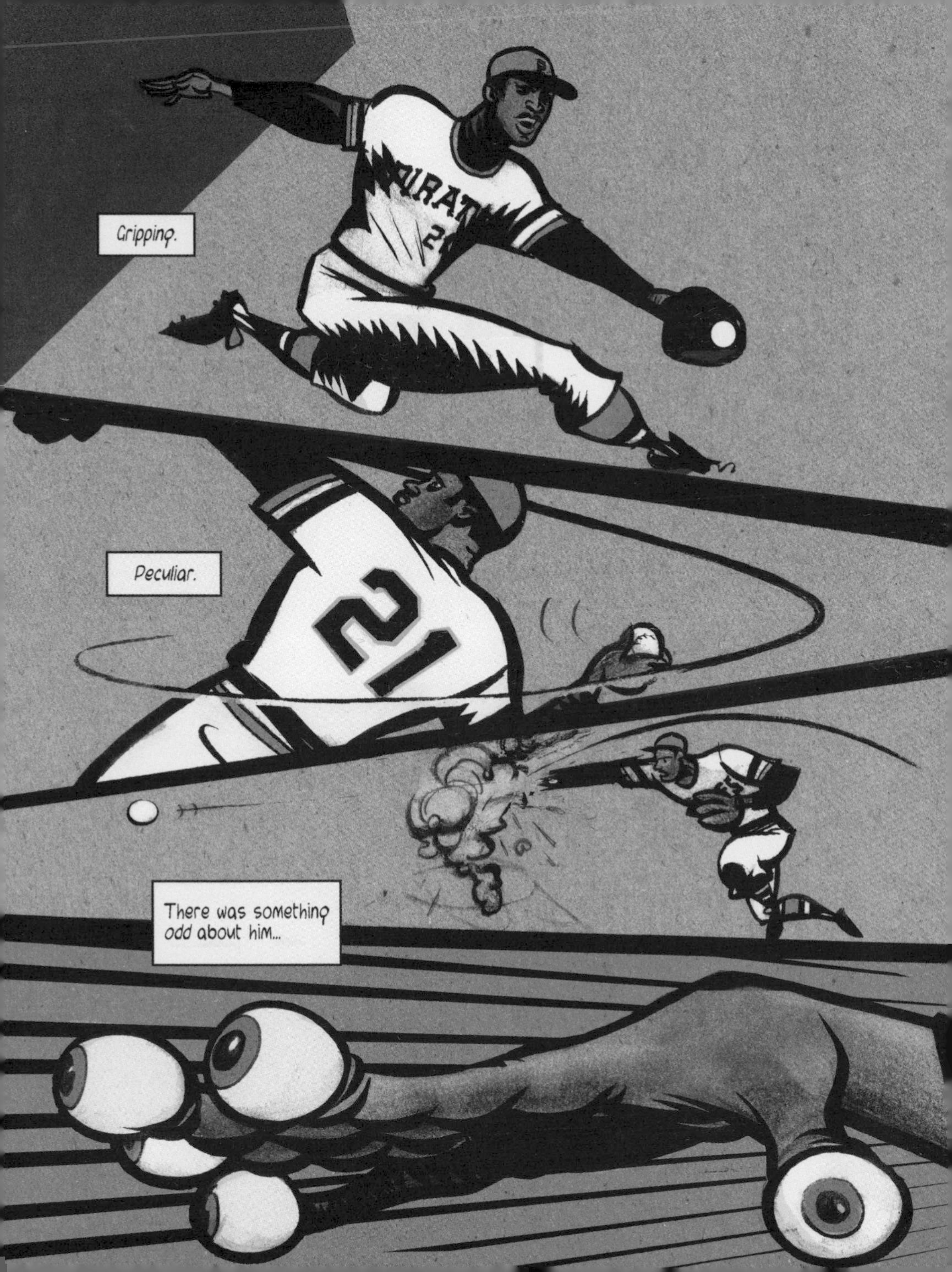
Gripping.
Peculiar.
There was something odd about him...

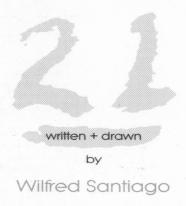

21

written + drawn

by

Wilfred Santiago

F B

FANTAGRAPHICS BOOKS

•

SEATTLE
U S A
since 1976

PUERTO RICO
1942

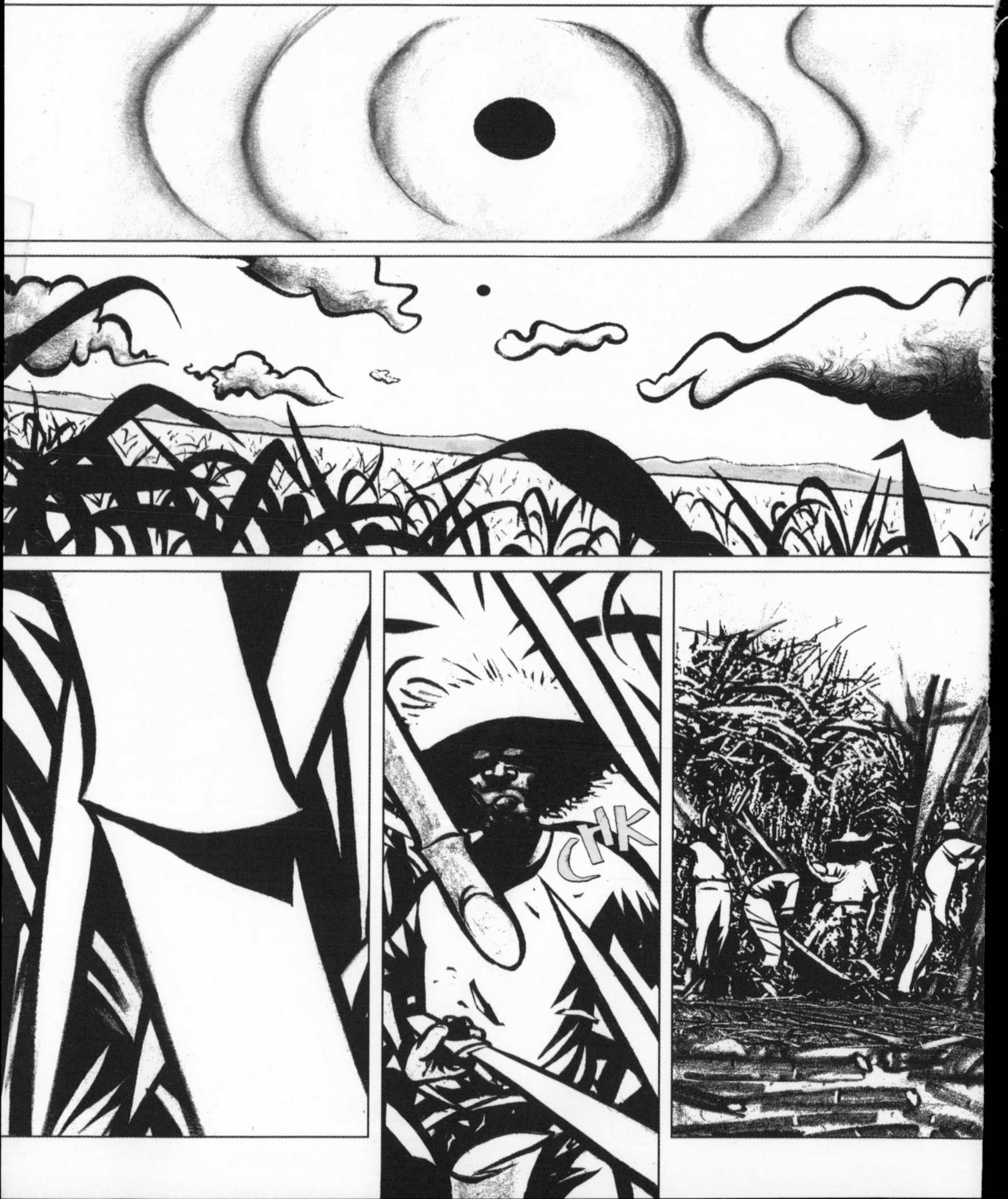
CHK

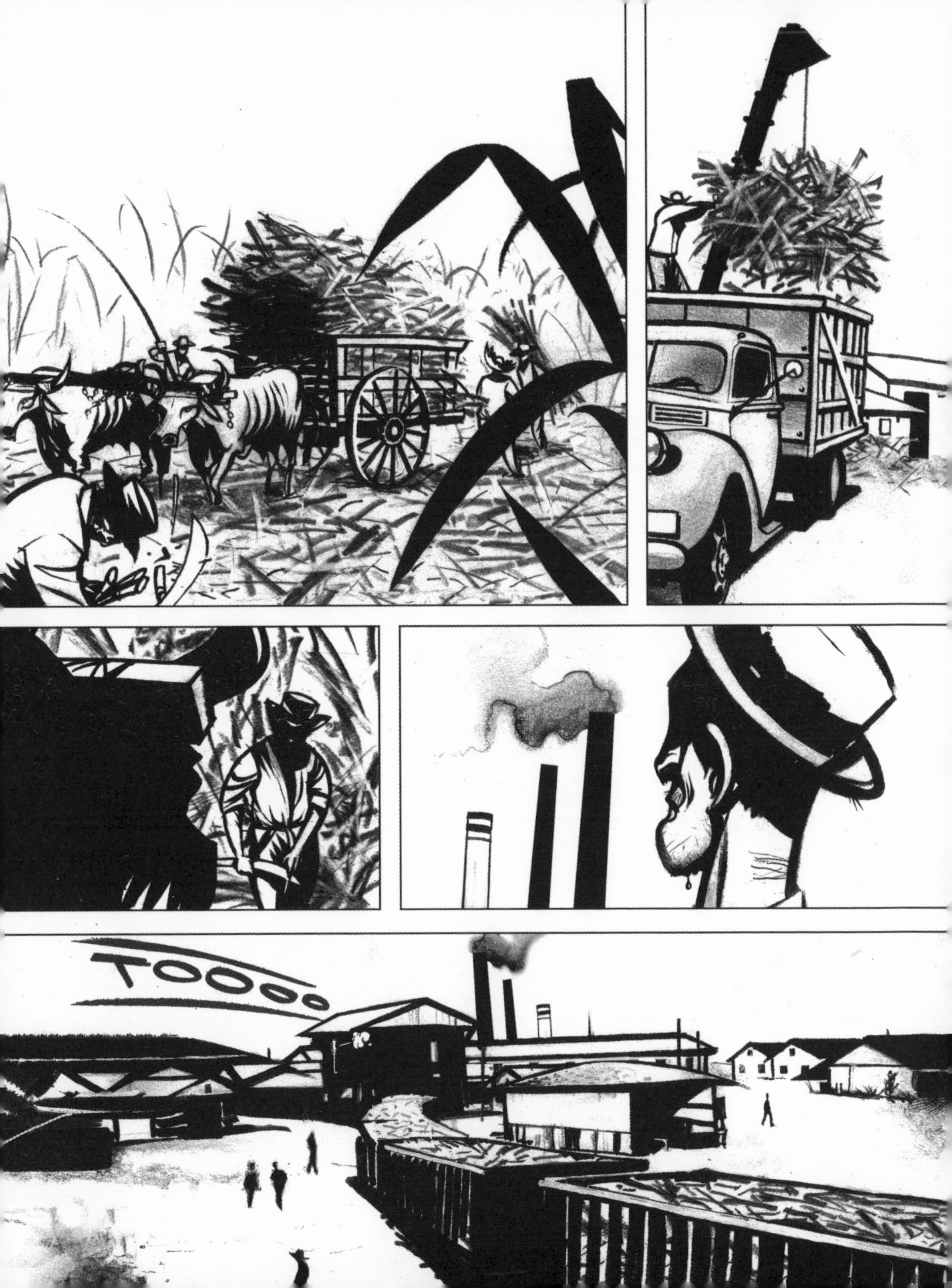
TOOOOO

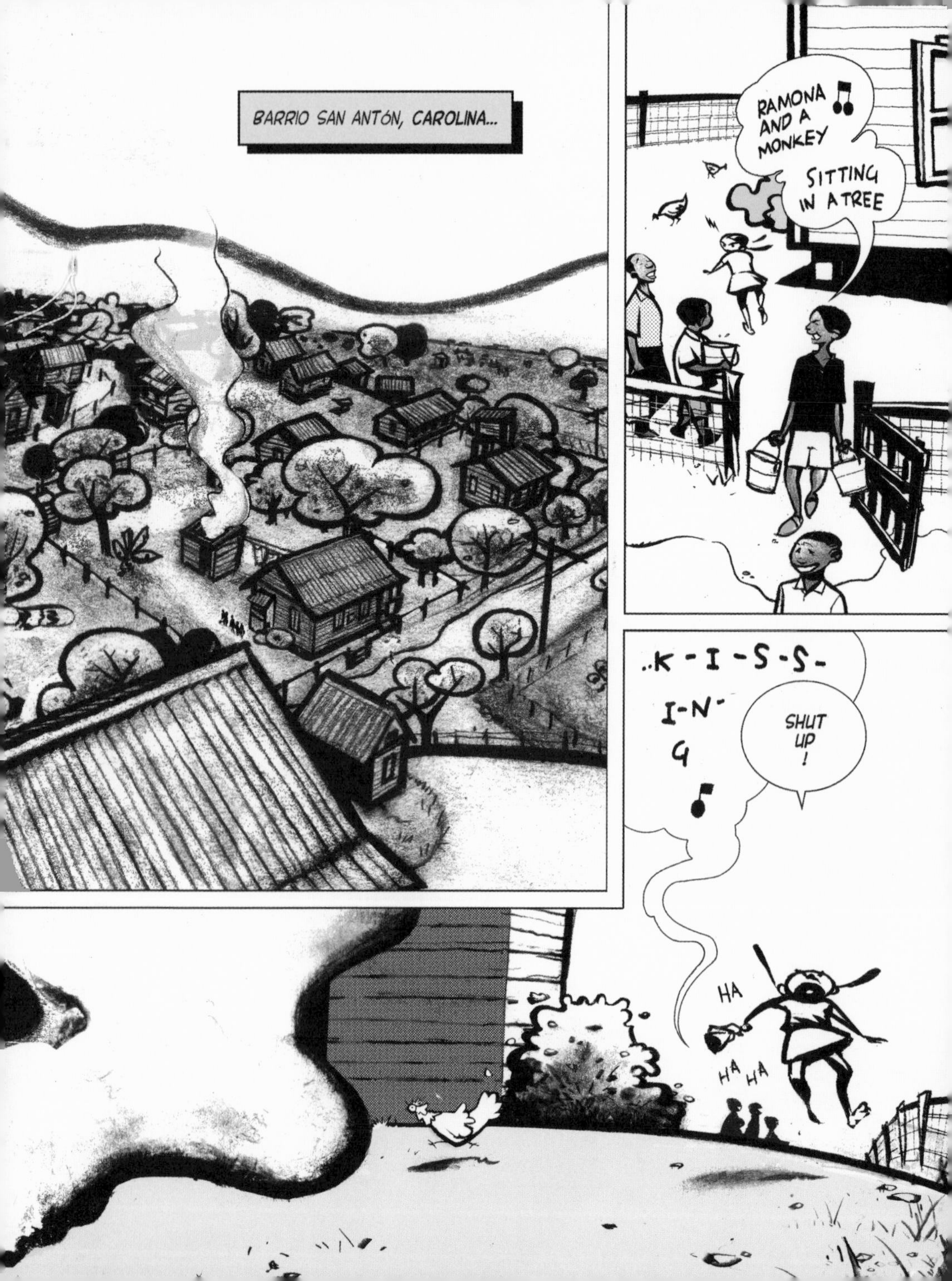
BARRIO SAN ANTÓN, CAROLINA...
RAMONA AND A MONKEY
SITTING IN A TREE
..K-I-S-S-I-N-G
SHUT UP!
HA
HA HA

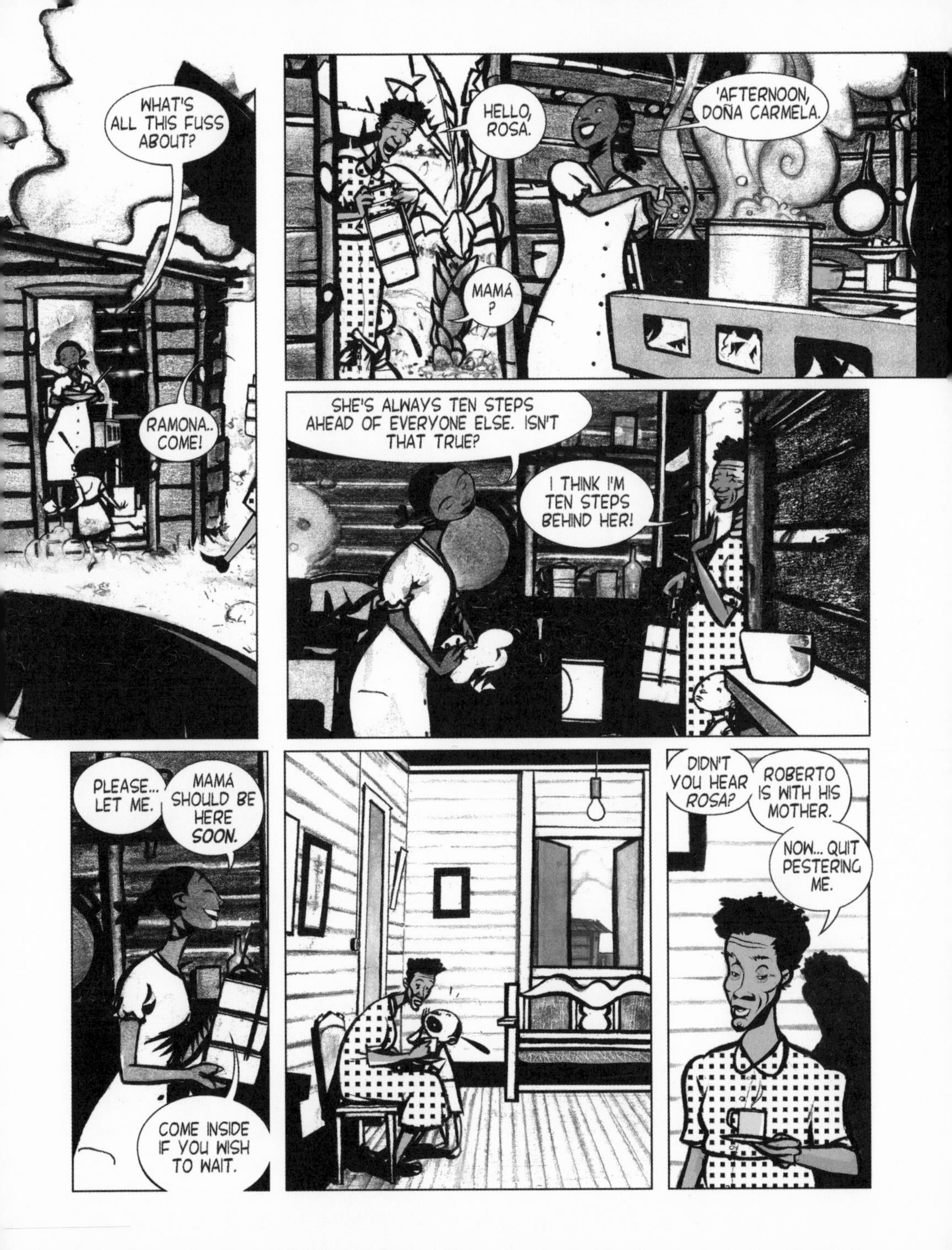
WHAT'S ALL THIS FUSS ABOUT?
RAMONA.. COME!
HELLO, ROSA.
'AFTERNOON, DOÑA CARMELA.
MAMÁ ?
SHE'S ALWAYS TEN STEPS AHEAD OF EVERYONE ELSE. ISN'T THAT TRUE?
I THINK I'M TEN STEPS BEHIND HER!
PLEASE... LET ME.
MAMÁ SHOULD BE HERE SOON.
COME INSIDE IF YOU WISH TO WAIT.
DIDN'T YOU HEAR ROSA?
ROBERTO IS WITH HIS MOTHER.
NOW... QUIT PESTERING ME.

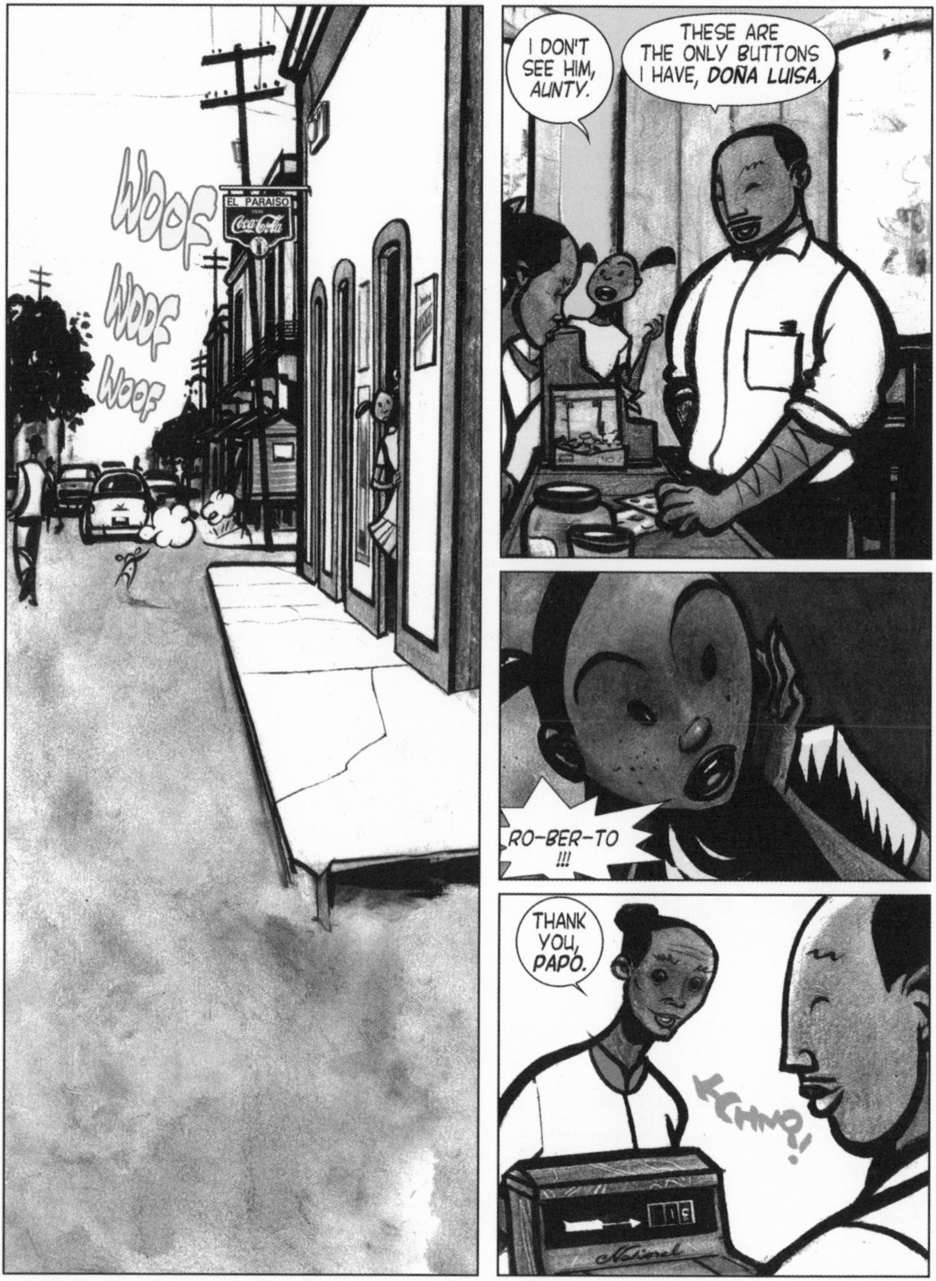
WOOF
WOOF
WOOF
EL PARAISO
Coca-Cola
I DON'T SEE HIM, AUNTY.
THESE ARE THE ONLY BUTTONS I HAVE, DOÑA LUISA.
RO-BER-TO !!!
THANK YOU, PAPO.
KCHING!
National

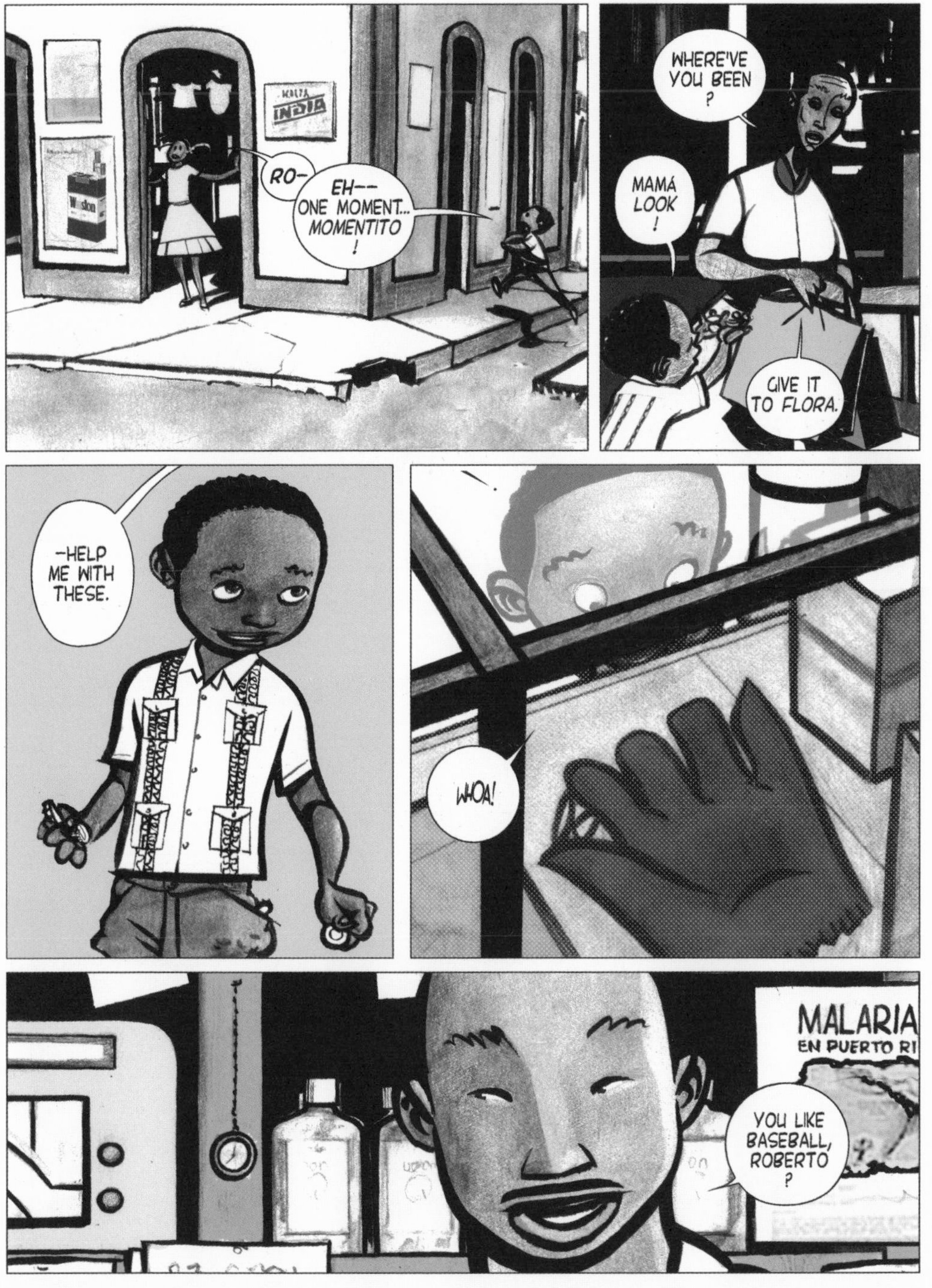
INDIA
RO-
EH-- ONE MOMENT... MOMENTITO !
WHERE'VE YOU BEEN ?
MAMÁ LOOK !
GIVE IT TO FLORA.
-HELP ME WITH THESE.
WHOA!
MALARIA
EN PUERTO RI
YOU LIKE BASEBALL, ROBERTO ?

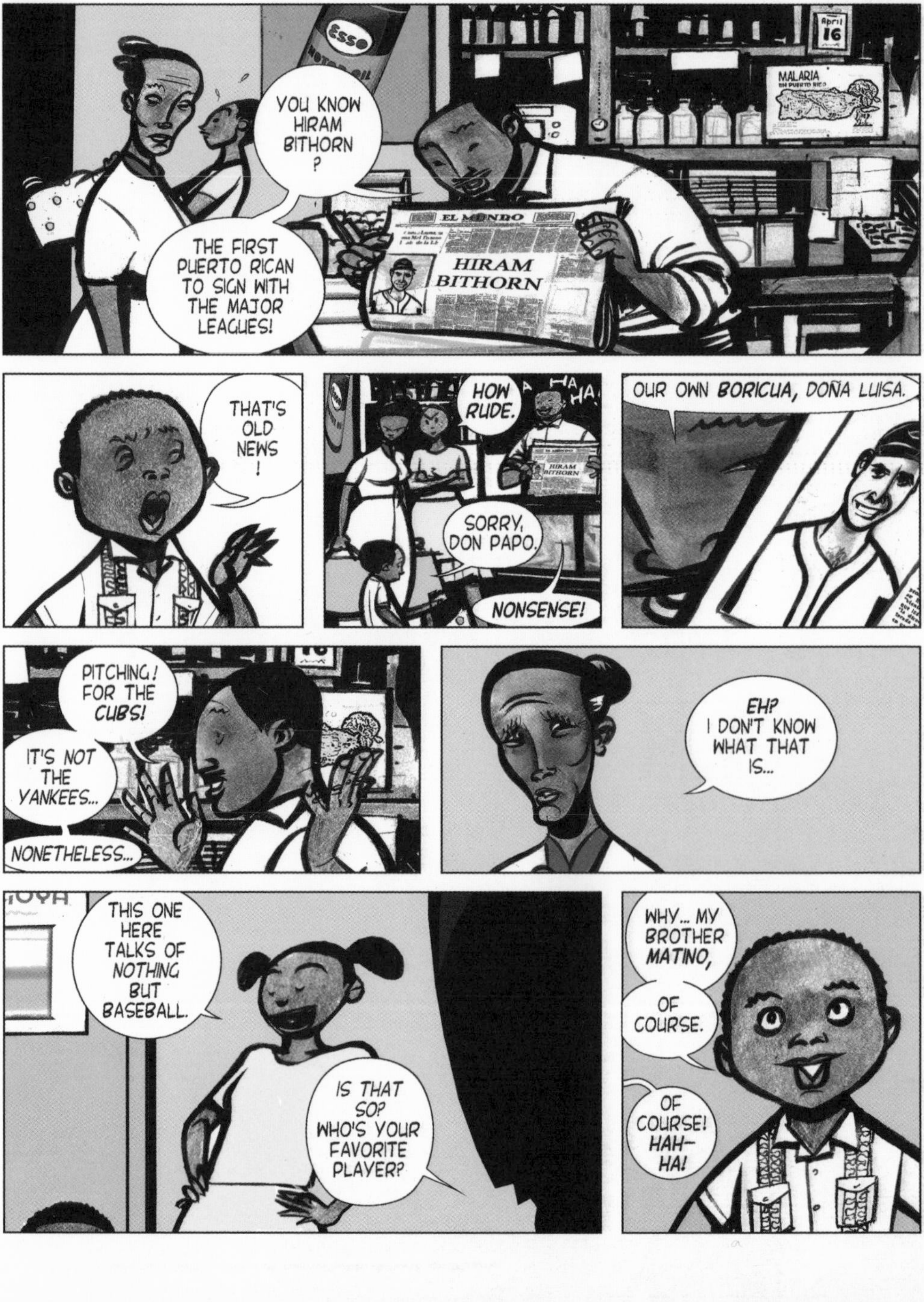
YOU KNOW HIRAM BITHORN ?
THE FIRST PUERTO RICAN TO SIGN WITH THE MAJOR LEAGUES!
EL MUNDO
HIRAM BITHORN
April 16
MALARIA EN PUERTO RICO
THAT'S OLD NEWS !
HOW RUDE.
HA HA HA!
SORRY, DON PAPO.
NONSENSE!
OUR OWN BORICUA, DOÑA LUISA.
PITCHING! FOR THE CUBS!
IT'S NOT THE YANKEES...
NONETHELESS...
EH? I DON'T KNOW WHAT THAT IS...
THIS ONE HERE TALKS OF NOTHING BUT BASEBALL.
IS THAT SO? WHO'S YOUR FAVORITE PLAYER?
WHY... MY BROTHER MATINO,
OF COURSE.
OF COURSE! HAH-HA!

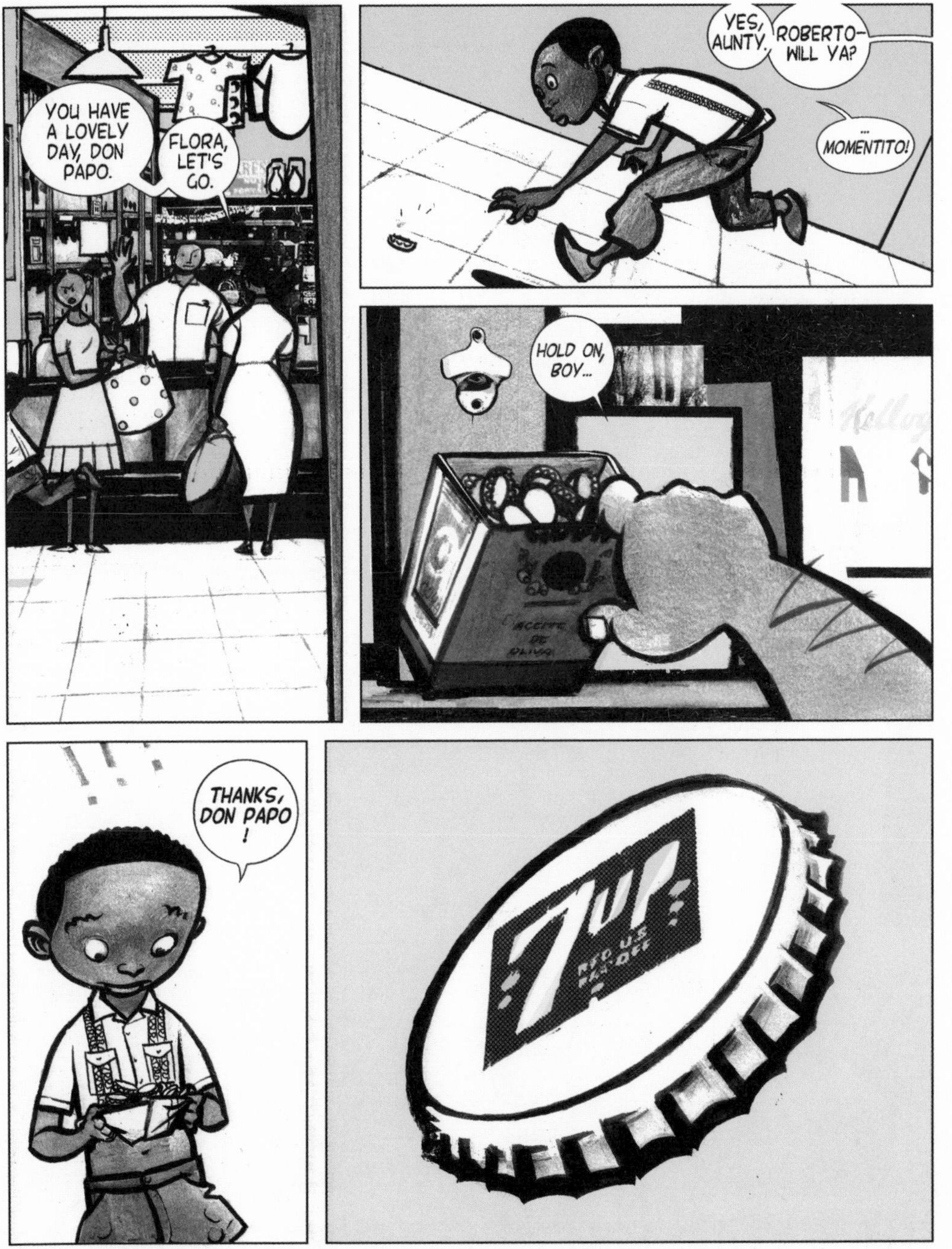
YOU HAVE A LOVELY DAY, DON PAPO.
FLORA, LET'S GO.
ROBERTO— WILL YA?
YES, AUNTY.
... MOMENTITO!
HOLD ON, BOY...
THANKS, DON PAPO!
7UP

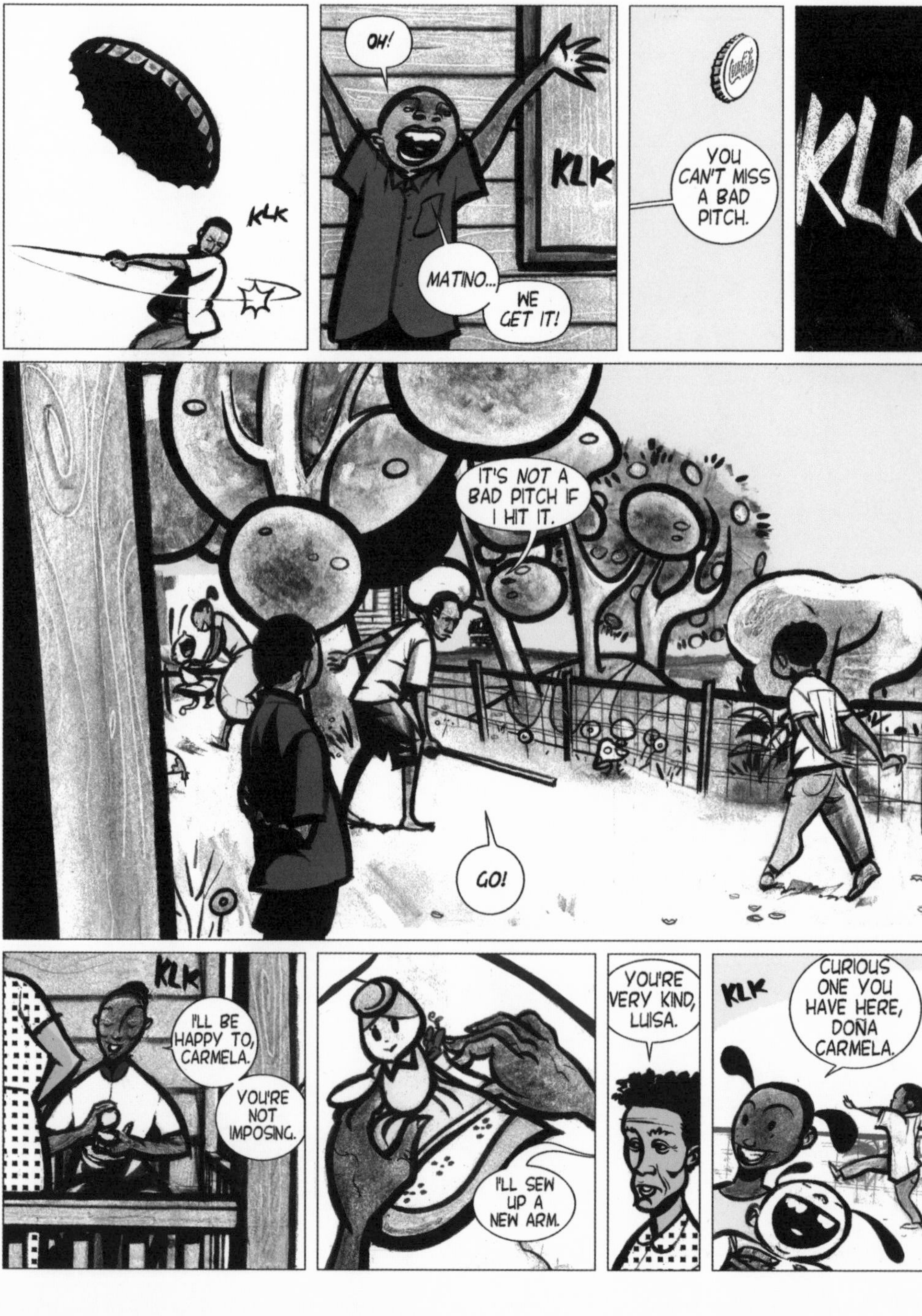
KLK
OH!
KLK
MATINO...
WE GET IT!
YOU CAN'T MISS A BAD PITCH.
KLK
IT'S NOT A BAD PITCH IF I HIT IT.
GO!
KLK
I'LL BE HAPPY TO, CARMELA.
YOU'RE NOT IMPOSING.
I'LL SEW UP A NEW ARM.
YOU'RE VERY KIND, LUISA.
KLK
CURIOUS ONE YOU HAVE HERE, DOÑA CARMELA.

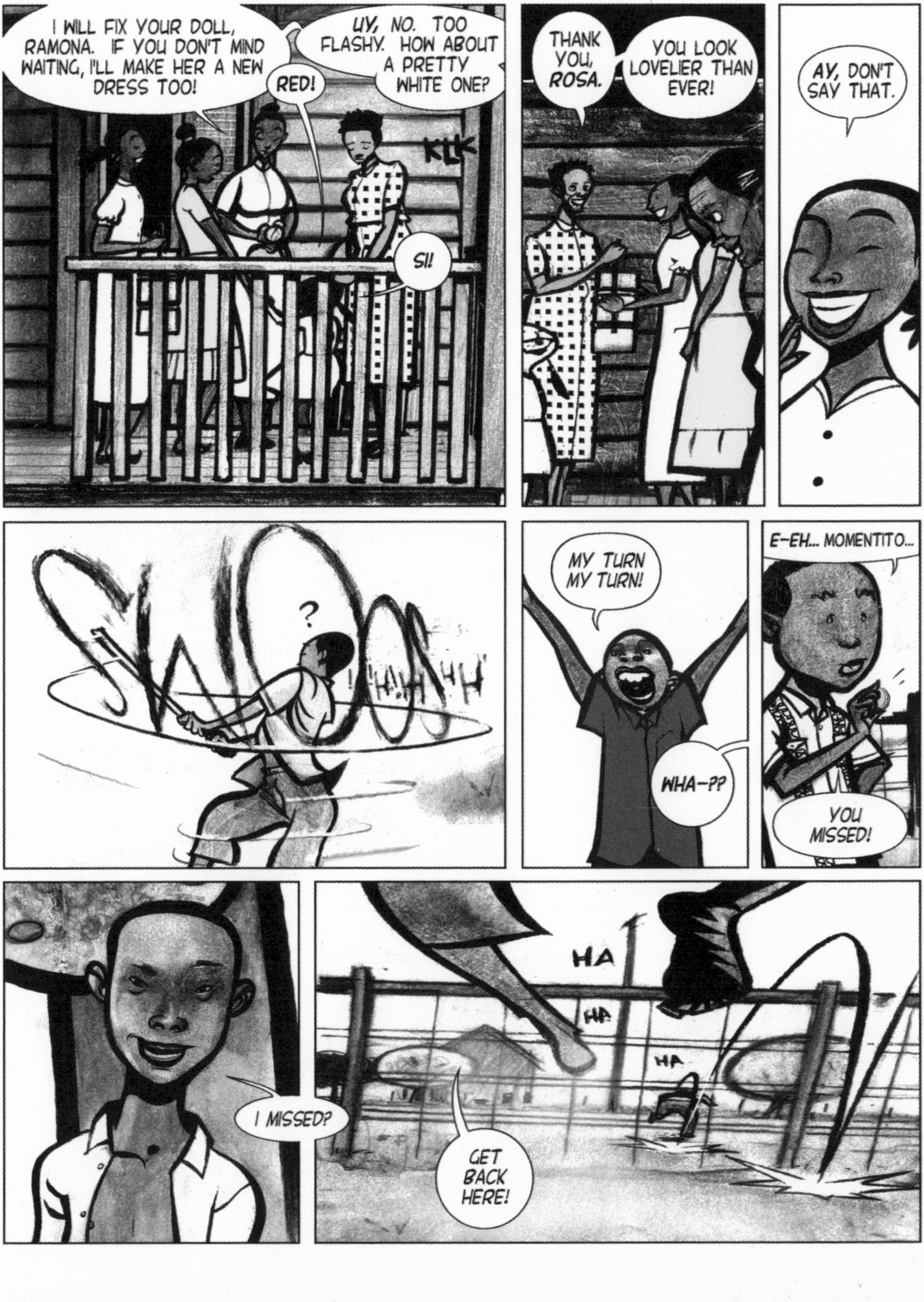

I WILL FIX YOUR DOLL, RAMONA. IF YOU DON'T MIND WAITING, I'LL MAKE HER A NEW DRESS TOO!
RED!
UY, NO. TOO FLASHY. HOW ABOUT A PRETTY WHITE ONE?
KLK
SI!
THANK YOU, ROSA.
YOU LOOK LOVELIER THAN EVER!
AY, DON'T SAY THAT.
SWOOSH
?
HAHAHH
MY TURN MY TURN!
WHA-??
E-EH... MOMENTITO...
YOU MISSED!
I MISSED?
HA
HA
HA
GET BACK HERE!

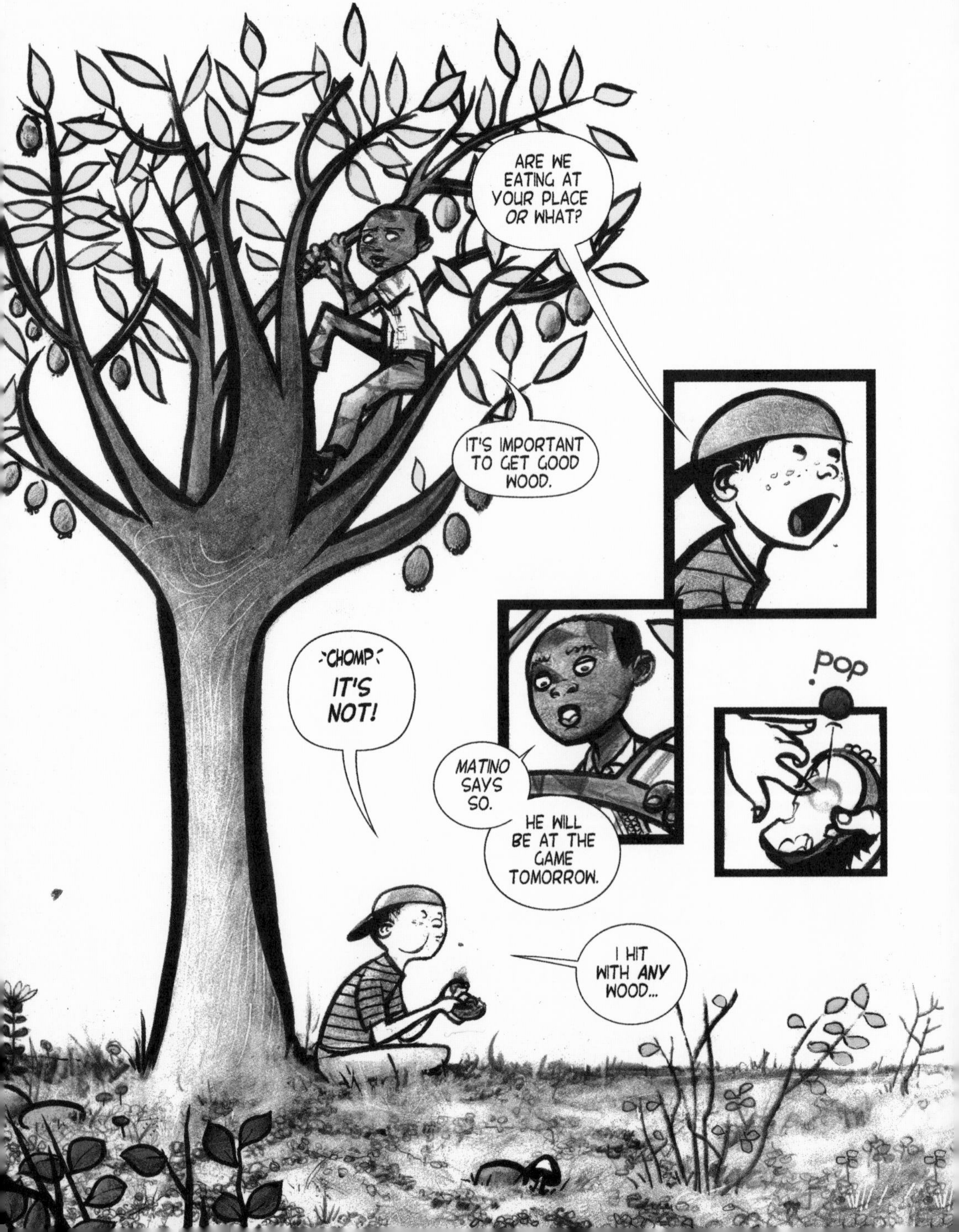

ARE WE EATING AT YOUR PLACE OR WHAT?
IT'S IMPORTANT TO GET GOOD WOOD.
CHOMP
IT'S NOT!
MATINO SAYS SO.
HE WILL BE AT THE GAME TOMORROW.
POP
I HIT WITH ANY WOOD...

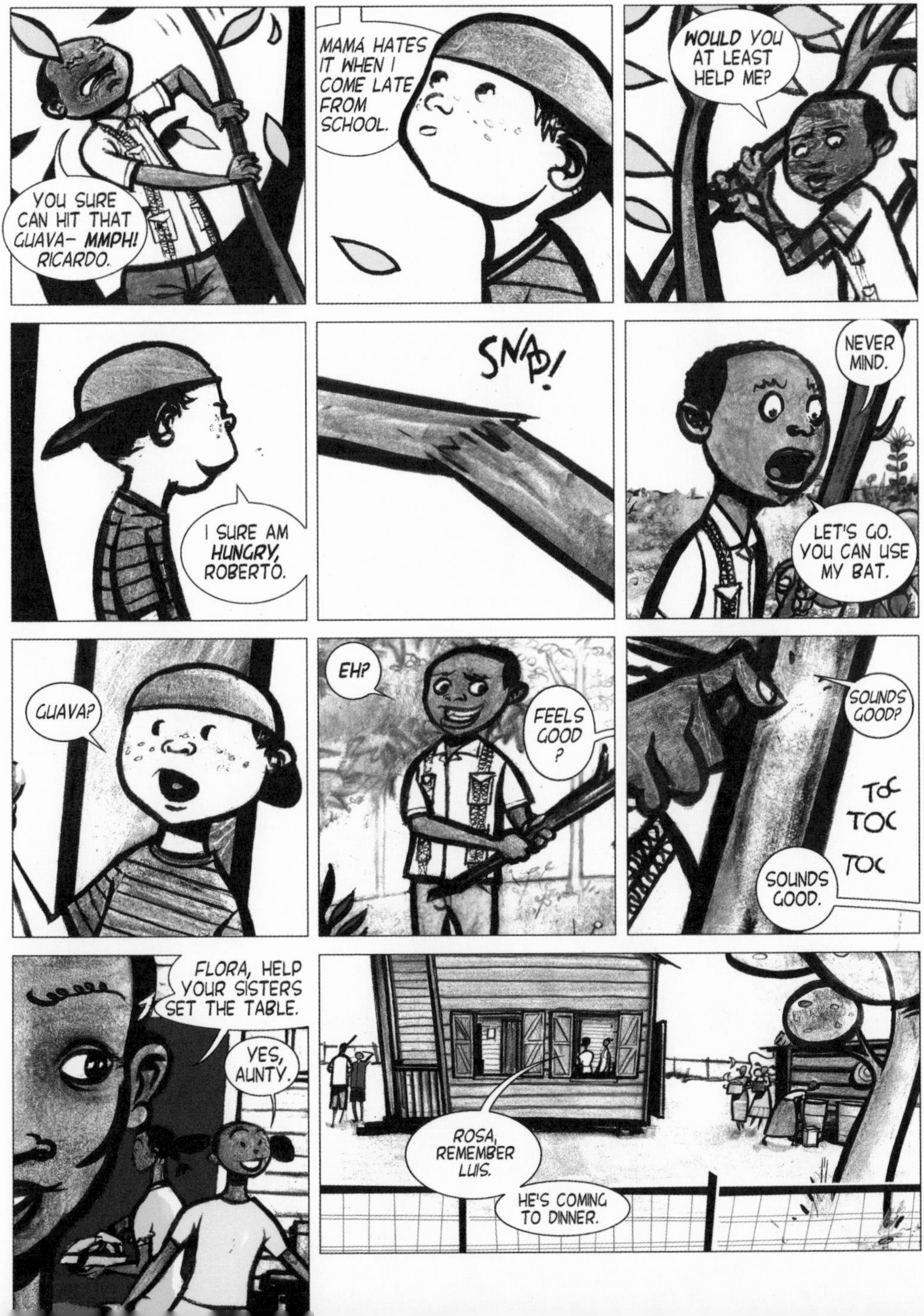
YOU SURE CAN HIT THAT GUAVA– MMPH! RICARDO.
MAMÁ HATES IT WHEN I COME LATE FROM SCHOOL.
WOULD YOU AT LEAST HELP ME?
I SURE AM HUNGRY, ROBERTO.
SNAP!
NEVER MIND.
LET'S GO. YOU CAN USE MY BAT.
GUAVA?
EH?
FEELS GOOD ?
SOUNDS GOOD?
TOC
TOC
TOC
SOUNDS GOOD.
FLORA, HELP YOUR SISTERS SET THE TABLE.
YES, AUNTY.
ROSA, REMEMBER LUIS.
HE'S COMING TO DINNER.

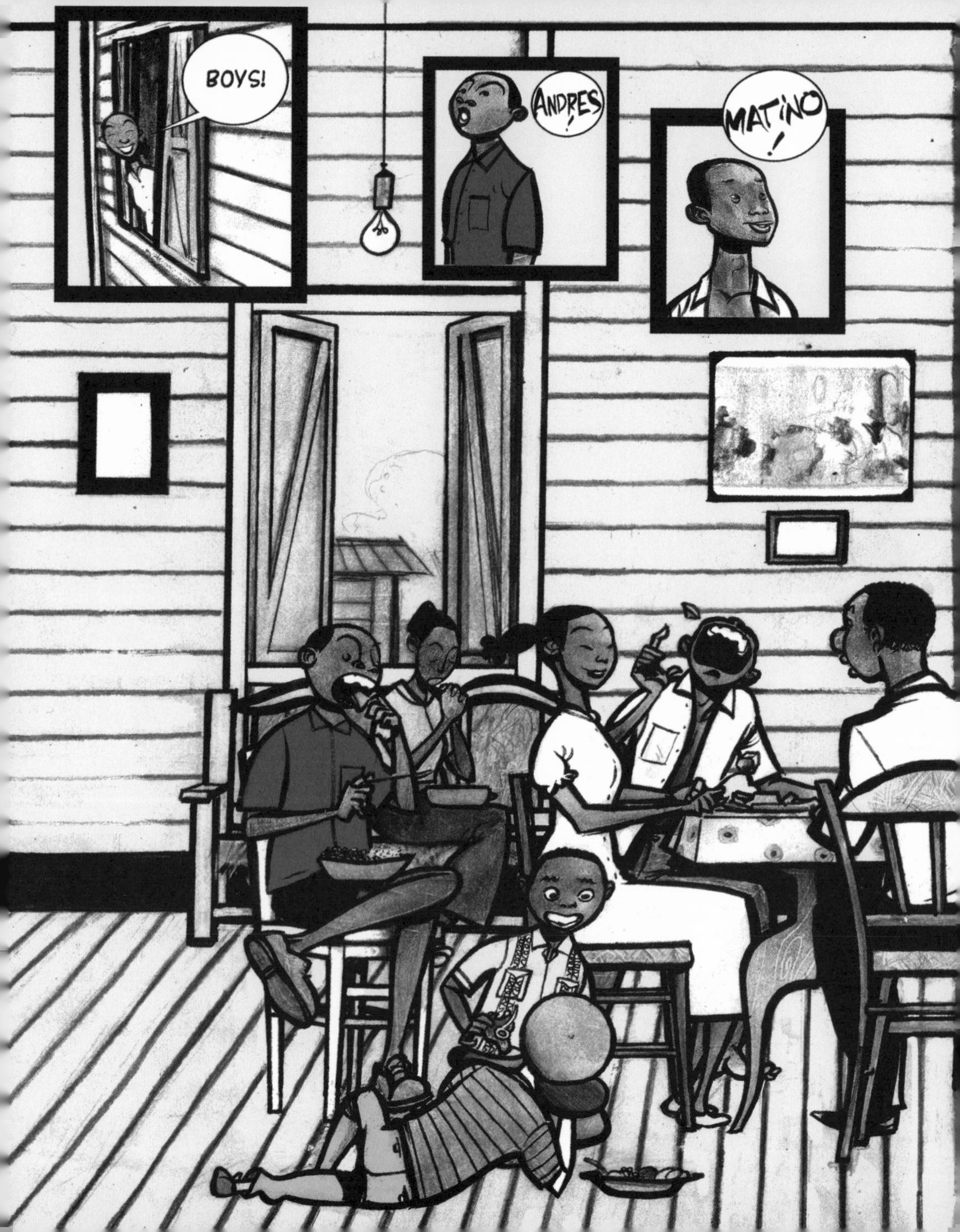
BOYS!
ANDRES!
MATINO!

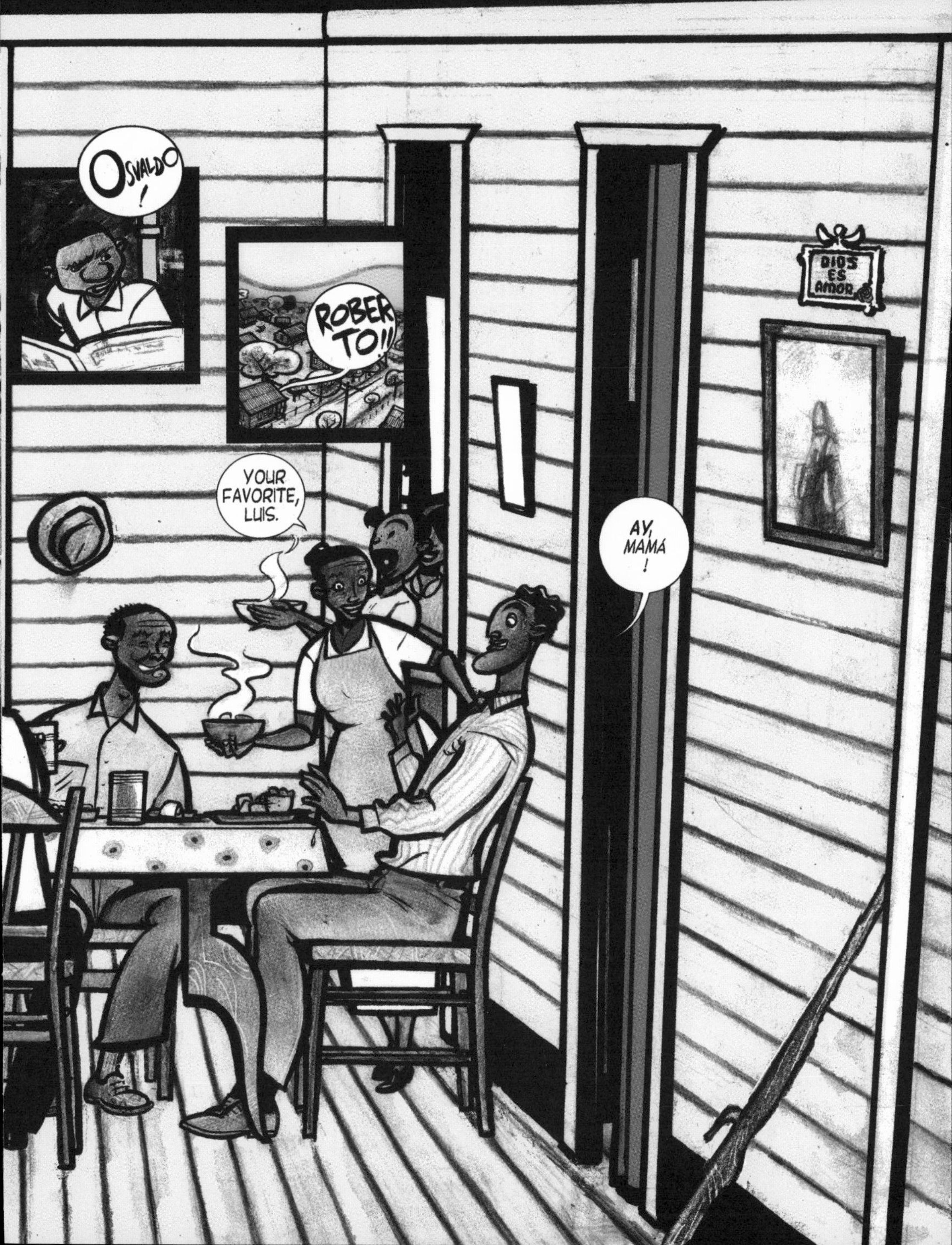
OSVALDO!
ROBERTO!!
YOUR FAVORITE, LUIS.
AY, MAMÁ!
DIOS ES AMOR

THE HEN WENT ALL NUTS OVER RAMONA, AUNTY. SHE WANTED TO KNOW HOW THE CHICKS GET INSIDE THE EGGS!

HA HA!

FOUR EGGS IN THE MORNING, FOUR IN THE EVENING.

PRK

I DO GET TO TASTE YOUR MOTHER'S *PIG FEET* FROM TIME TO TIME.

A BEST SELLER AMONG MY WORKERS.

IT'S THE *RAISINS,* DON MELCHOR! THEY GIVE IT A NICE *JOLT.*

ROBERTO, EAT THIS AND YOU'LL BE STRONG LIKE MATINO.

LIKE ME?

PHSHHH!

YOU ALWAYS SAY THAT, LUIS.

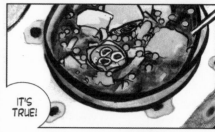

IT'S TRUE!

ANAIRIS ALWAYS DEMANDED EXTRA RAISINS. REMEMBER, DON MELCHOR?

HEE HEE !

NICE STICK. READY FOR TOMORROW'S GAME?

YES.

POC

GOOD JOB.

QUIT IT!

WE GOT IT TODAY—

EH... MOMENTITO.

YEAH... WE...

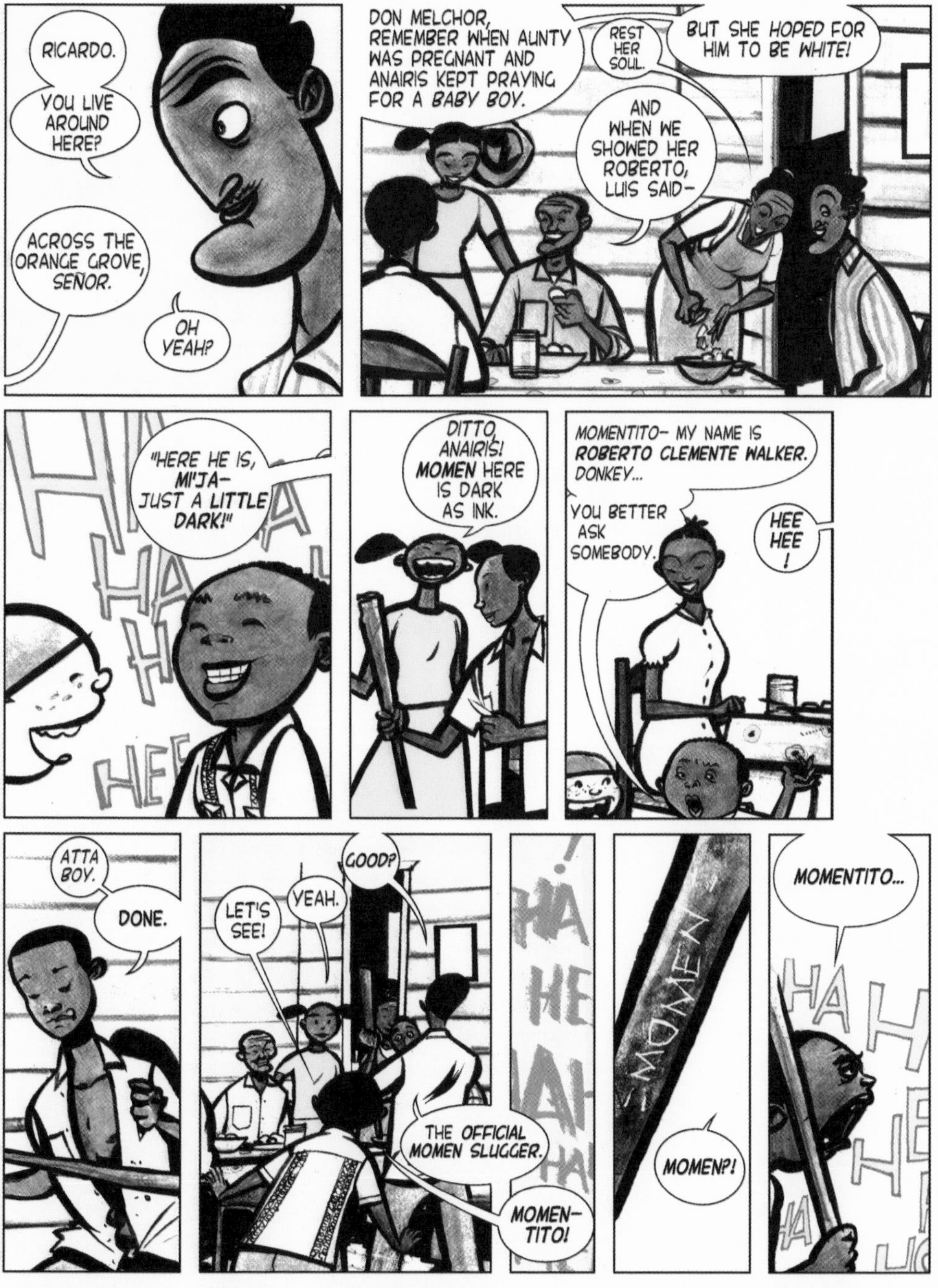
RICARDO.
YOU LIVE AROUND HERE?
ACROSS THE ORANGE GROVE, SEÑOR.
OH YEAH?
DON MELCHOR, REMEMBER WHEN AUNTY WAS PREGNANT AND ANAIRIS KEPT PRAYING FOR A BABY BOY.
REST HER SOUL.
BUT SHE HOPED FOR HIM TO BE WHITE!
AND WHEN WE SHOWED HER ROBERTO, LUIS SAID–
"HERE HE IS, MI'JA– JUST A LITTLE DARK!"
DITTO, ANAIRIS! MOMEN HERE IS DARK AS INK.
MOMENTITO– MY NAME IS ROBERTO CLEMENTE WALKER. DONKEY...
YOU BETTER ASK SOMEBODY.
HEE HEE !
ATTA BOY.
DONE.
GOOD?
YEAH.
LET'S SEE!
THE OFFICIAL MOMEN SLUGGER.
MOMEN-TITO!
MOMEN
MOMEN?!
MOMENTITO...

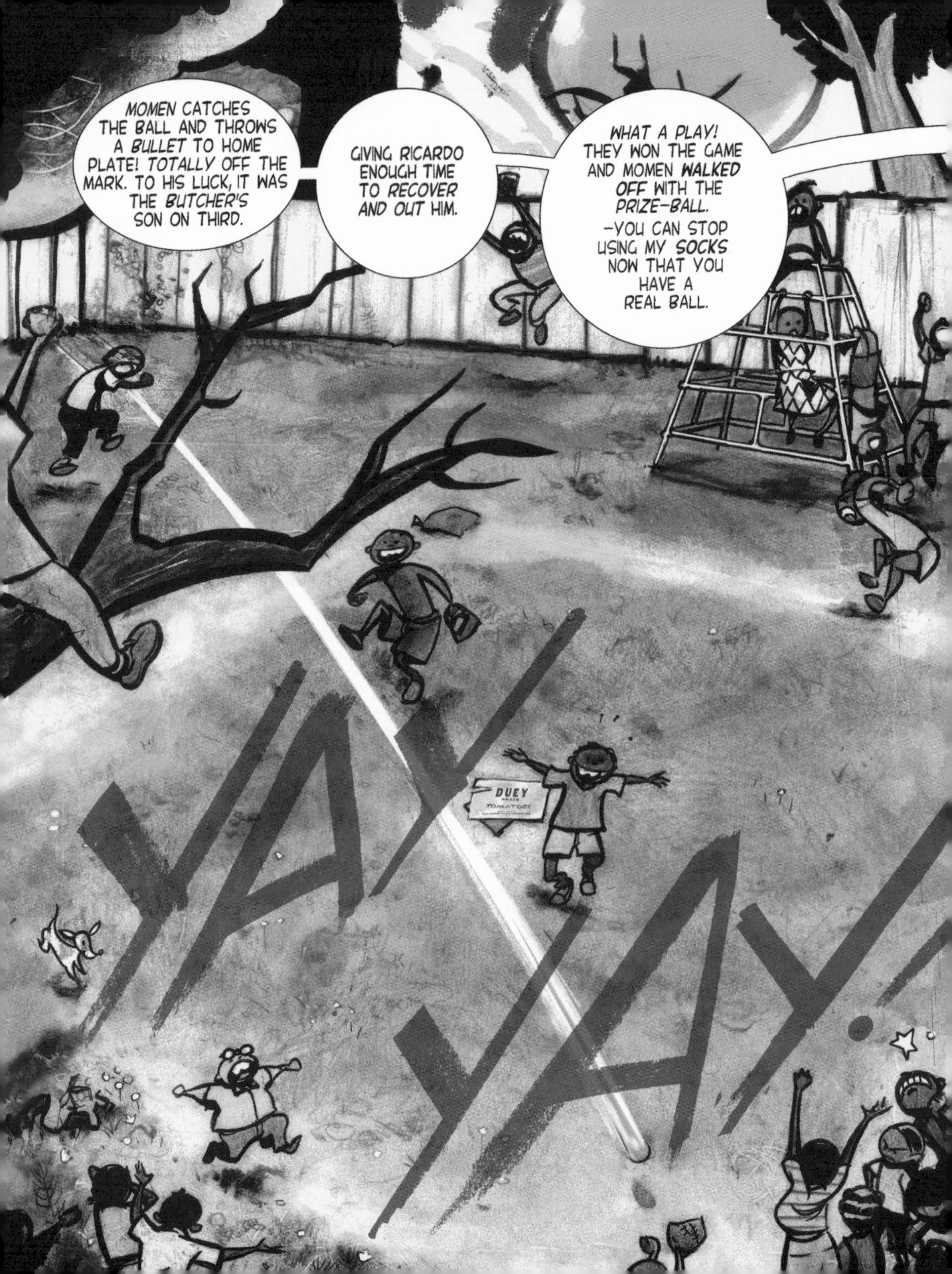
MOMEN CATCHES THE BALL AND THROWS A BULLET TO HOME PLATE! TOTALLY OFF THE MARK. TO HIS LUCK, IT WAS THE BUTCHER'S SON ON THIRD.
GIVING RICARDO ENOUGH TIME TO RECOVER AND OUT HIM.
WHAT A PLAY! THEY WON THE GAME AND MOMEN WALKED OFF WITH THE PRIZE-BALL.
-YOU CAN STOP USING MY SOCKS NOW THAT YOU HAVE A REAL BALL.
DUEY
TOMATOES
YAY YAY!

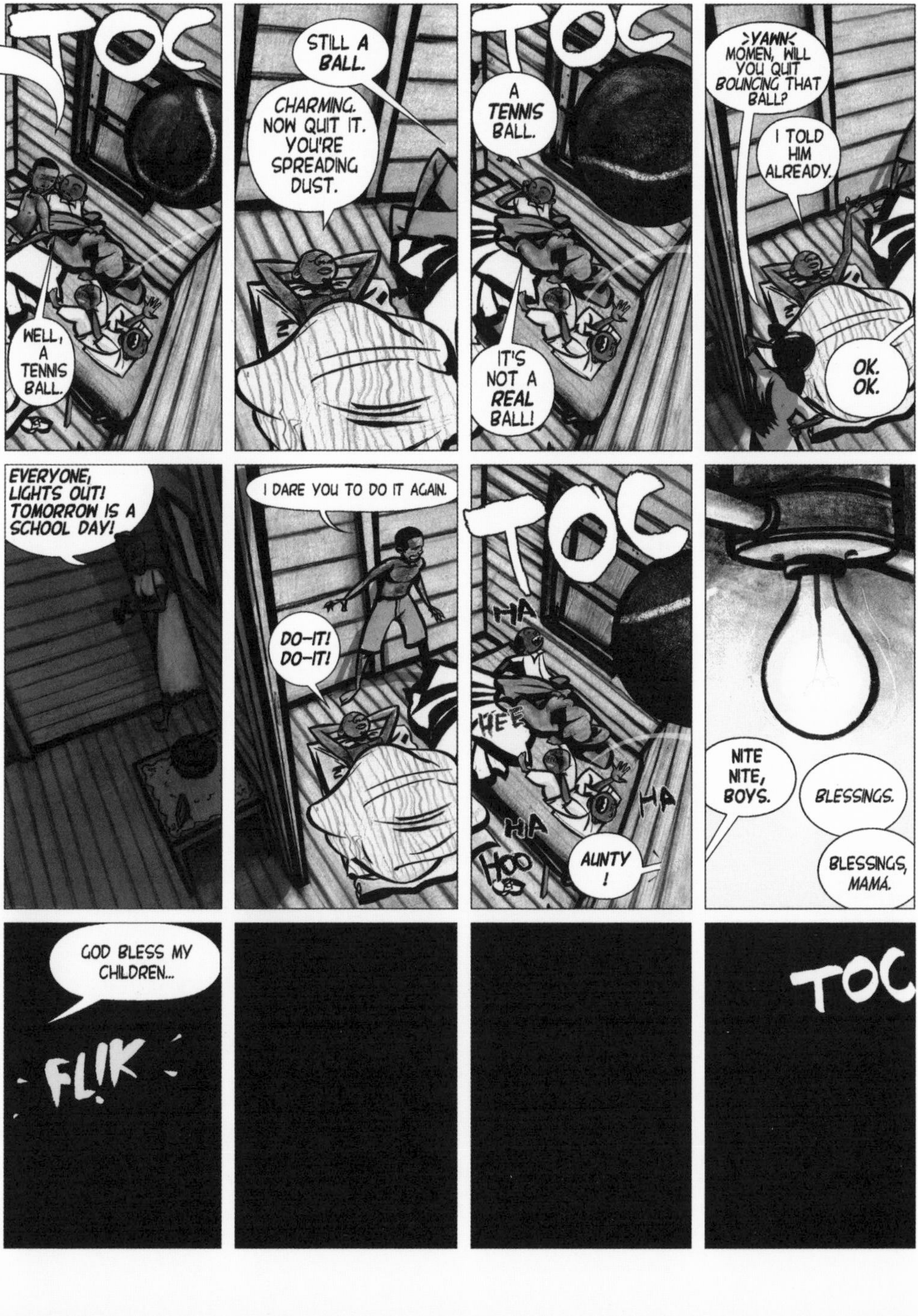
TOC
WELL, A TENNIS BALL.
STILL A BALL.
CHARMING. NOW QUIT IT. YOU'RE SPREADING DUST.
TOC
A TENNIS BALL.
IT'S NOT A REAL BALL!
>YAWN< MOMEN, WILL YOU QUIT BOUNCING THAT BALL?
I TOLD HIM ALREADY.
OK. OK.
EVERYONE, LIGHTS OUT! TOMORROW IS A SCHOOL DAY!
I DARE YOU TO DO IT AGAIN.
DO-IT! DO-IT!
TOC
HA
HEE
HA
HA
HOO
AUNTY!
NITE NITE, BOYS.
BLESSINGS.
BLESSINGS, MAMÁ.
GOD BLESS MY CHILDREN...
FL!K
TOC

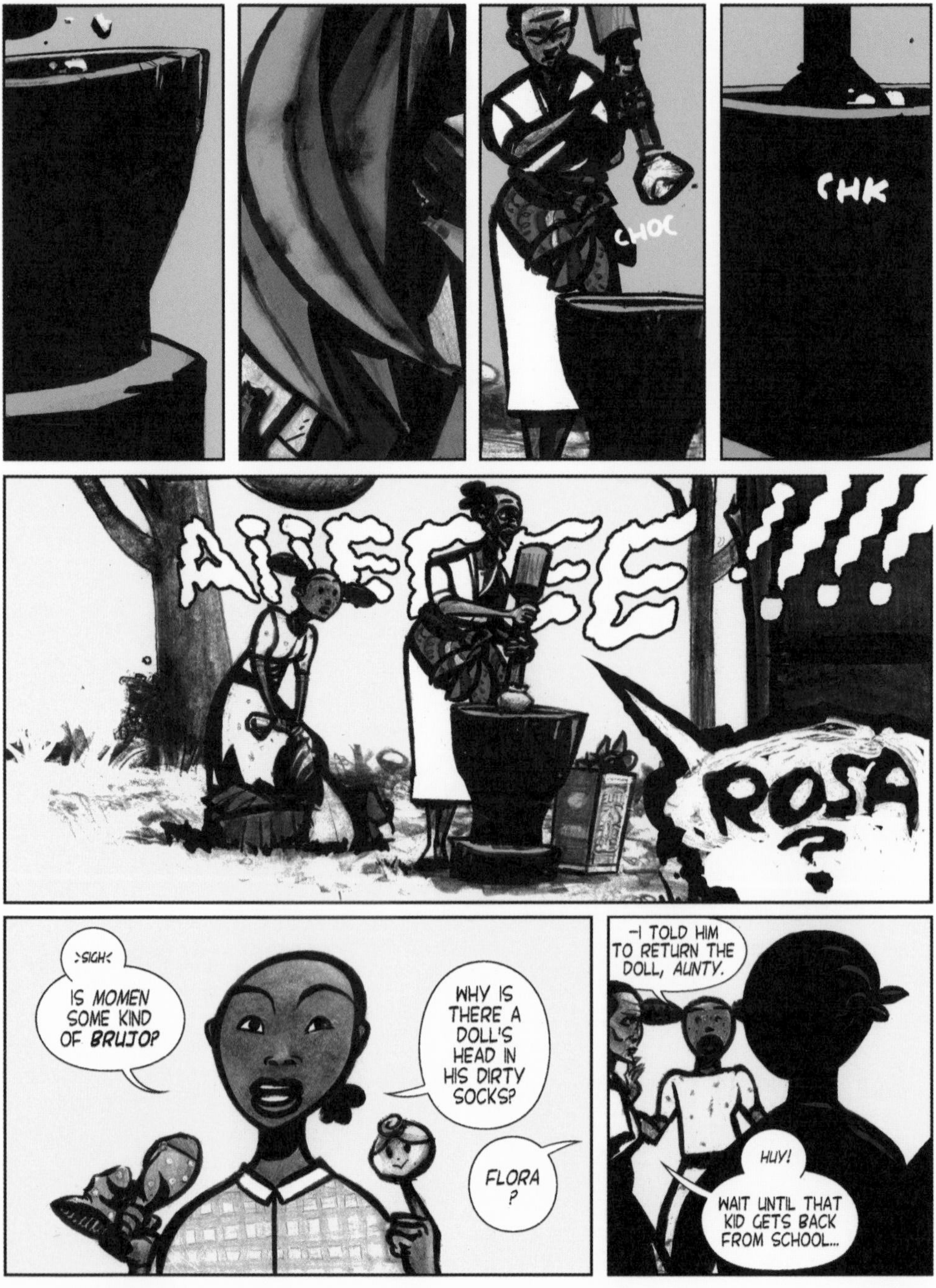
CHOC
CHK
AIIEEEE!!!!
ROSA?
>SIGH<
IS MOMEN SOME KIND OF BRUJO?
WHY IS THERE A DOLL'S HEAD IN HIS DIRTY SOCKS?
FLORA?
—I TOLD HIM TO RETURN THE DOLL, AUNTY.
HUY!
WAIT UNTIL THAT KID GETS BACK FROM SCHOOL...

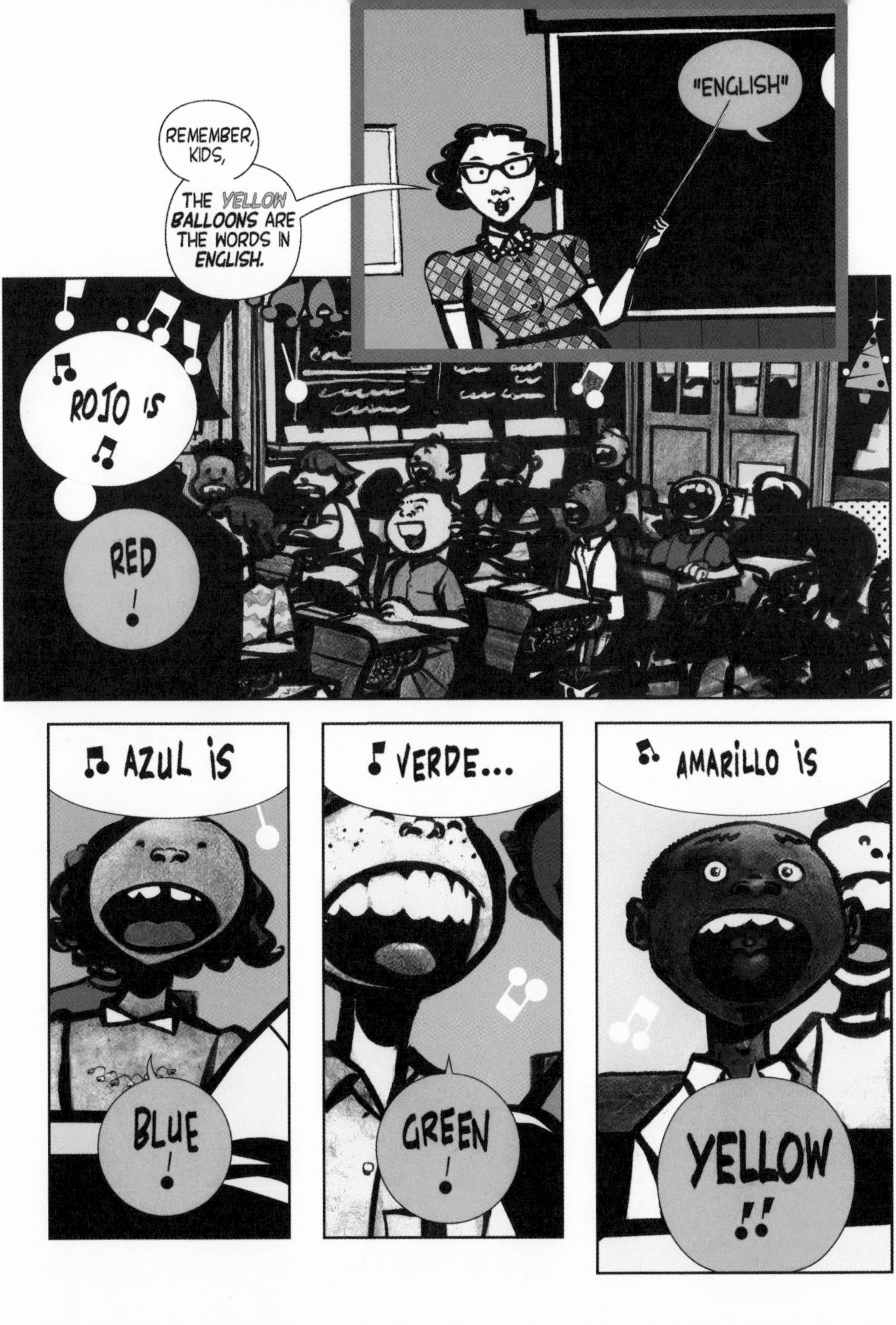

"ENGLISH"
REMEMBER, KIDS,
THE YELLOW BALLOONS ARE THE WORDS IN ENGLISH.
ROJO IS
RED!
AZUL IS
BLUE!
VERDE...
GREEN!
AMARILLO IS
YELLOW!!

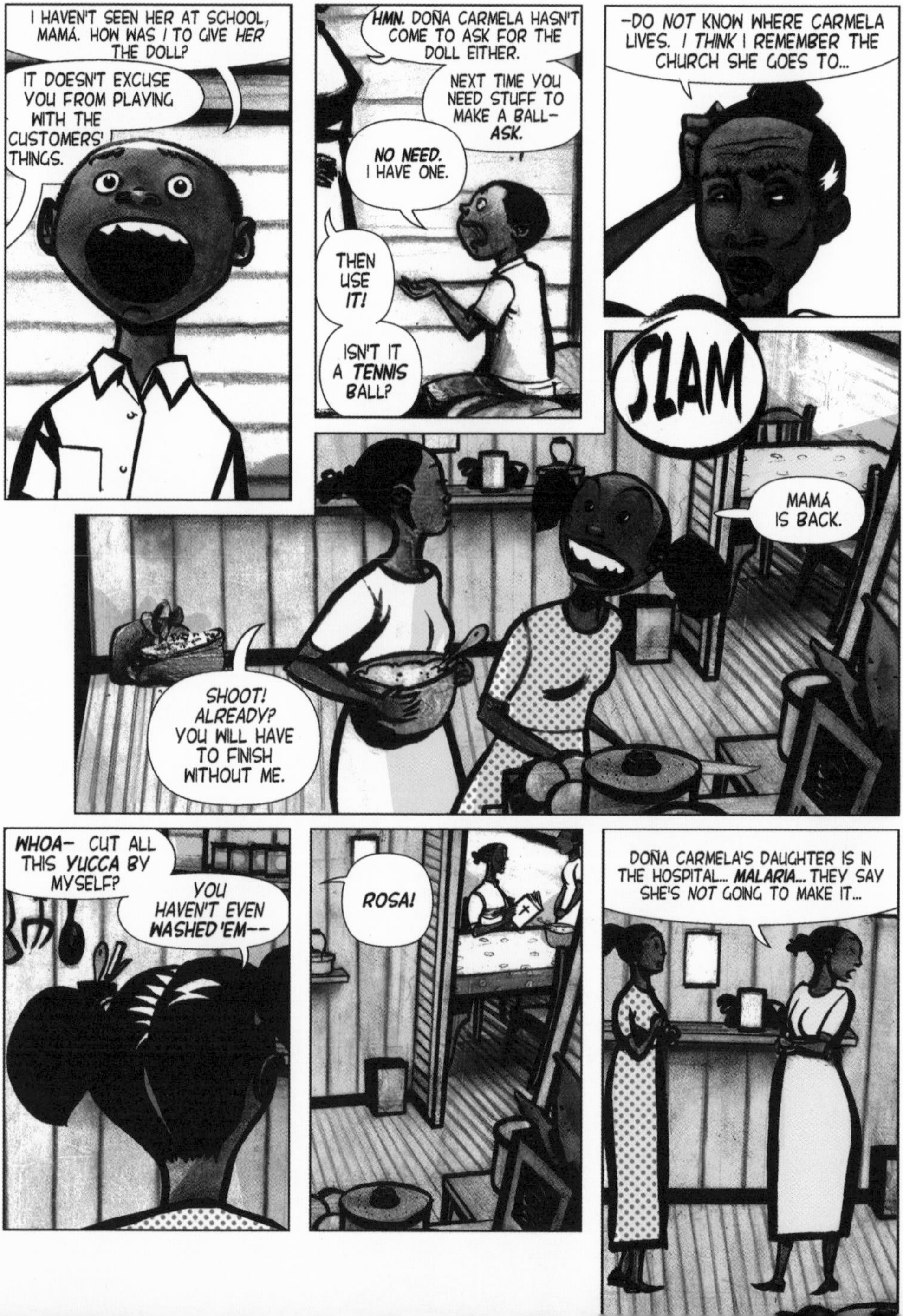
I HAVEN'T SEEN HER AT SCHOOL, MAMÁ. HOW WAS I TO GIVE HER THE DOLL?
IT DOESN'T EXCUSE YOU FROM PLAYING WITH THE CUSTOMERS' THINGS.
HMN. DOÑA CARMELA HASN'T COME TO ASK FOR THE DOLL EITHER.
NEXT TIME YOU NEED STUFF TO MAKE A BALL-ASK.
NO NEED. I HAVE ONE.
THEN USE IT!
ISN'T IT A TENNIS BALL?
-DO NOT KNOW WHERE CARMELA LIVES. I THINK I REMEMBER THE CHURCH SHE GOES TO...
SLAM
MAMÁ IS BACK.
SHOOT! ALREADY? YOU WILL HAVE TO FINISH WITHOUT ME.
WHOA- CUT ALL THIS YUCCA BY MYSELF?
YOU HAVEN'T EVEN WASHED 'EM--
ROSA!
DOÑA CARMELA'S DAUGHTER IS IN THE HOSPITAL... MALARIA... THEY SAY SHE'S NOT GOING TO MAKE IT...

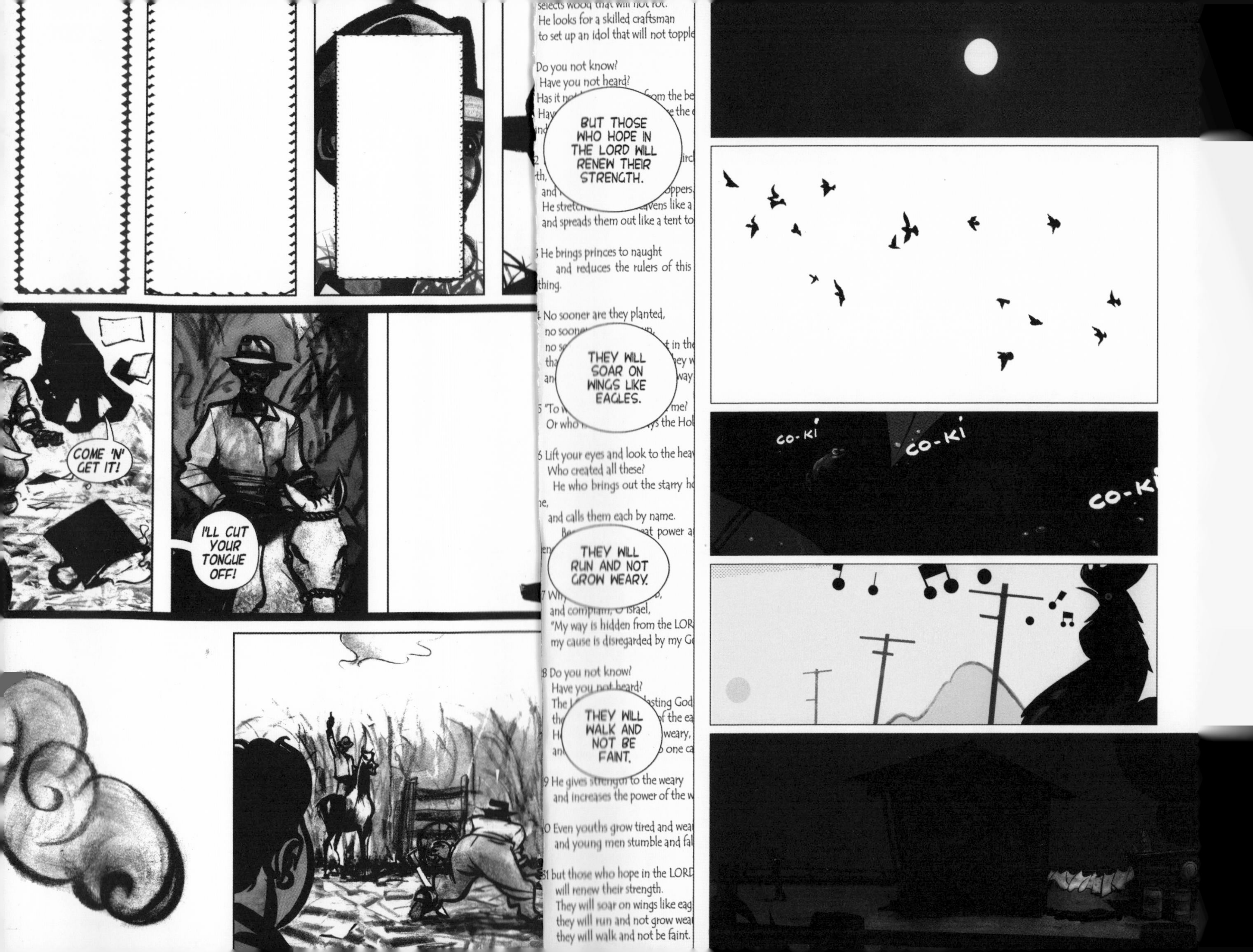

COME 'N' GET IT!
I'LL CUT YOUR TONGUE OFF!
He looks for a skilled craftsman
Do you not know?
Have you not heard?
BUT THOSE WHO HOPE IN THE LORD WILL RENEW THEIR STRENGTH.
and spreads them out like a tent to
He brings princes to naught
and reduces the rulers of this
No sooner are they planted,
THEY WILL SOAR ON WINGS LIKE EAGLES.
Lift your eyes and look to the heav
Who created all these?
He who brings out the starry h
and calls them each by name.
THEY WILL RUN AND NOT GROW WEARY.
"My way is hidden from the LOR
my cause is disregarded by my G
Do you not know?
THEY WILL WALK AND NOT BE FAINT.
and increases the power of the w
Even youths grow tired and wea
and young men stumble and fal
31 but those who hope in the LORD
will renew their strength.
They will soar on wings like eag
they will run and not grow wear
they will walk and not be faint.
CO-KI
CO-KI
CO-KI

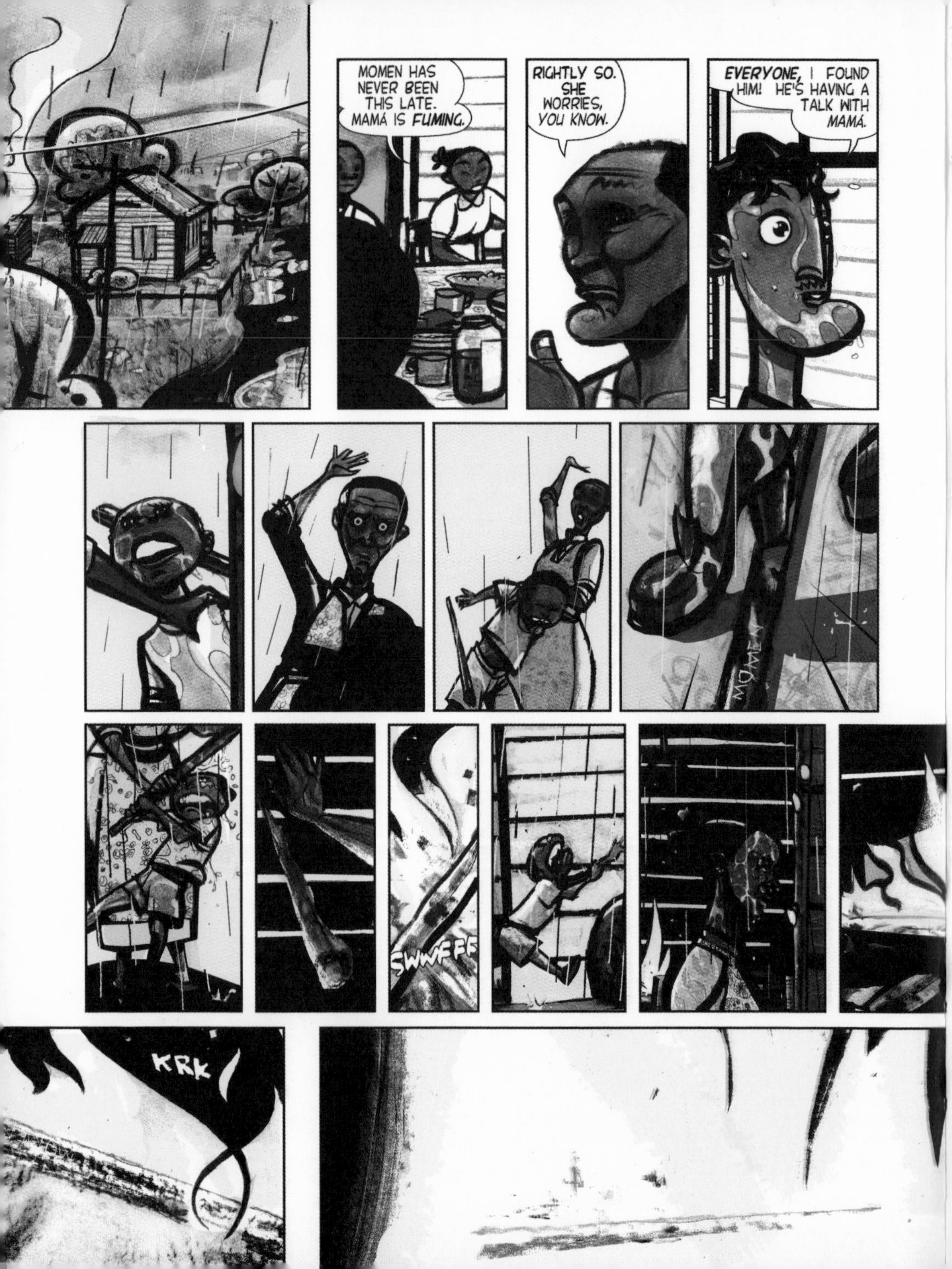
MOMEN HAS NEVER BEEN THIS LATE. MAMÁ IS *FUMING.*
RIGHTLY SO. SHE WORRIES, YOU KNOW.
EVERYONE, I FOUND HIM! HE'S HAVING A TALK WITH *MAMÁ.*
SWWFFF
KRK

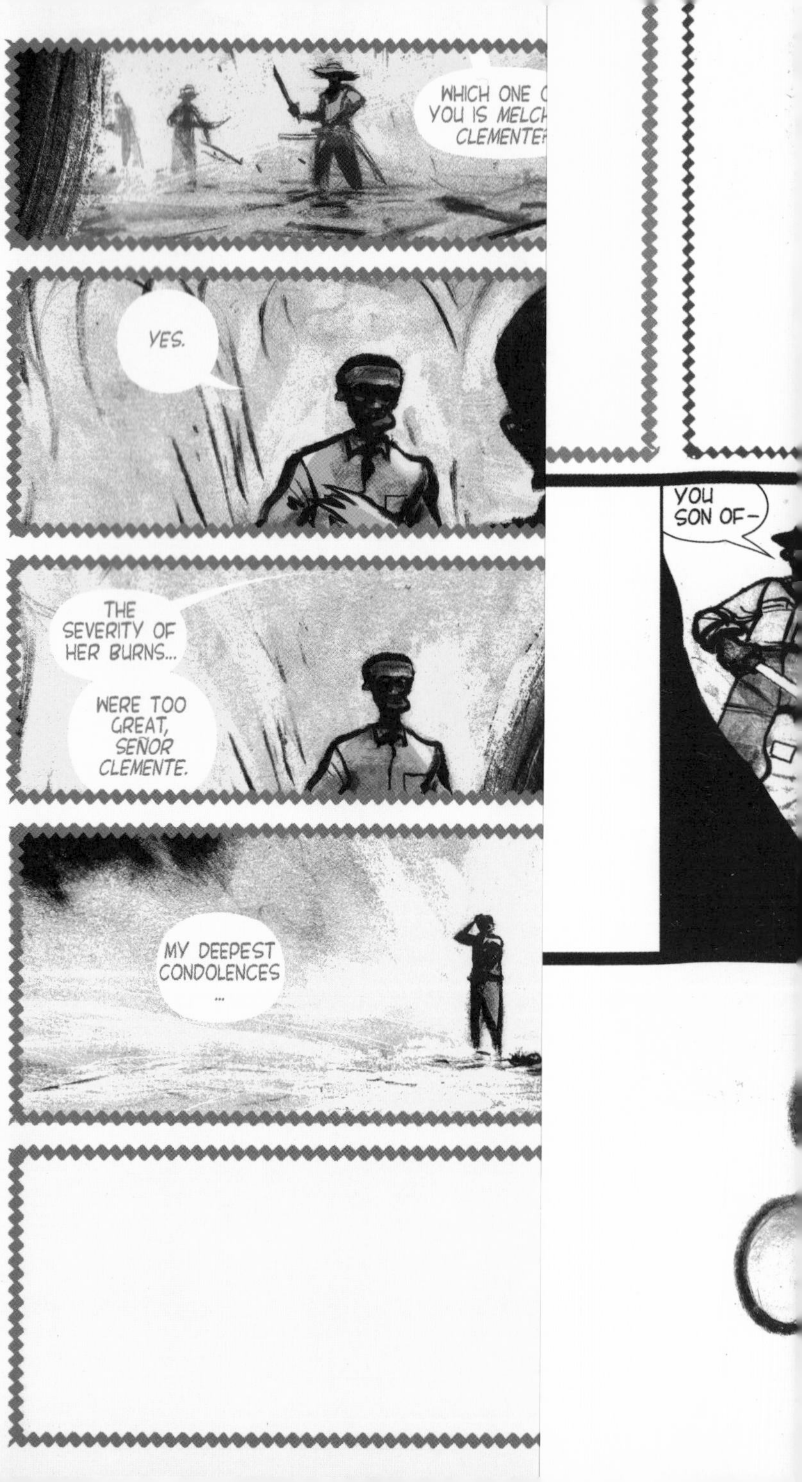
WHICH ONE O
YOU IS *MELCH*
CLEMENTE?
YES.
THE SEVERITY OF HER BURNS...
WERE TOO GREAT, *SEÑOR CLEMENTE.*
MY DEEPEST CONDOLENCES ...
YOU SON OF–

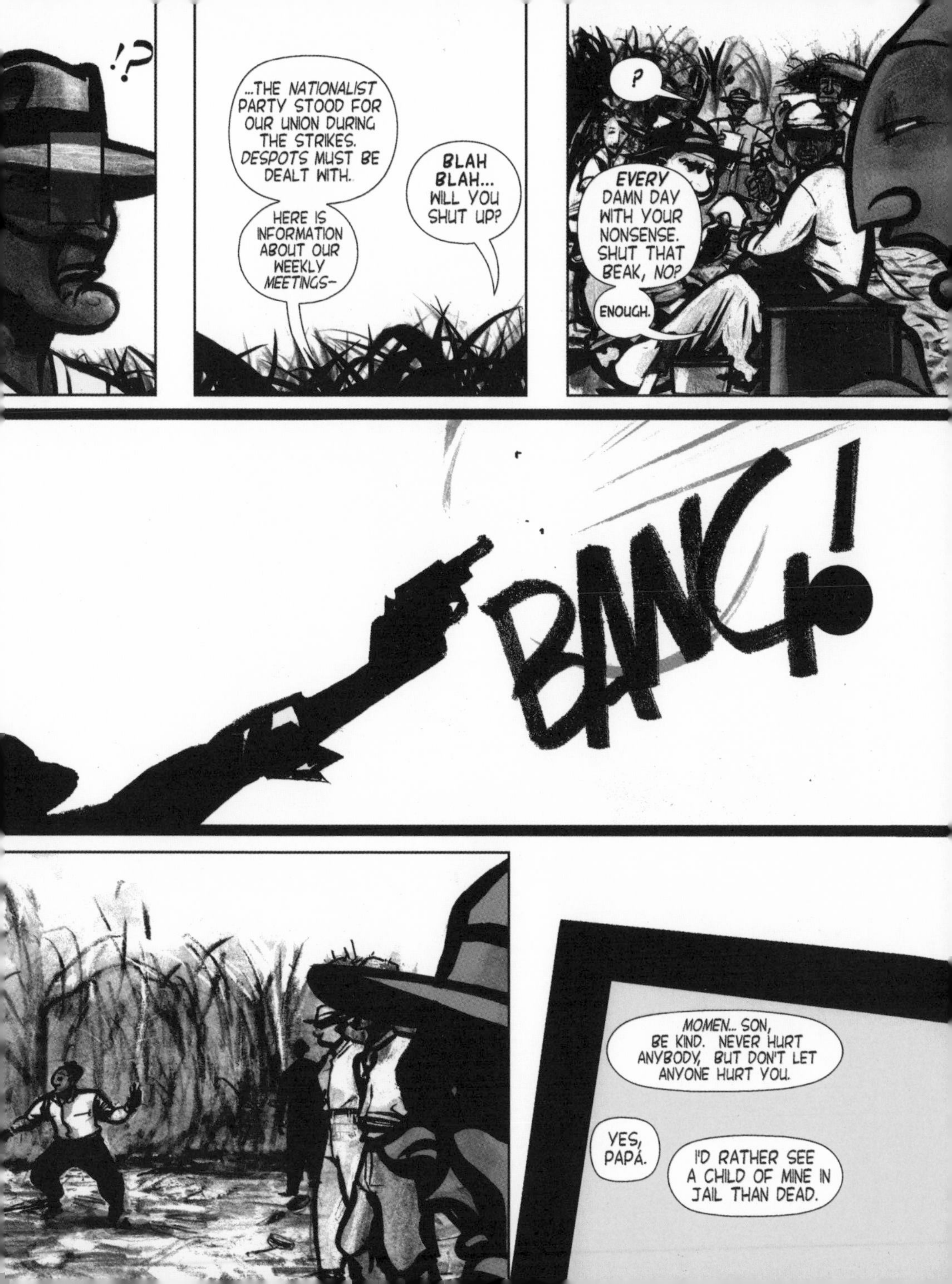
!?
...THE NATIONALIST PARTY STOOD FOR OUR UNION DURING THE STRIKES. DESPOTS MUST BE DEALT WITH.
HERE IS INFORMATION ABOUT OUR WEEKLY MEETINGS-
BLAH BLAH... WILL YOU SHUT UP?
?
EVERY DAMN DAY WITH YOUR NONSENSE. SHUT THAT BEAK, NO?
ENOUGH.
BANG!
MOMEN... SON, BE KIND. NEVER HURT ANYBODY, BUT DON'T LET ANYONE HURT YOU.
YES, PAPÁ.
I'D RATHER SEE A CHILD OF MINE IN JAIL THAN DEAD.

ROBERTO...

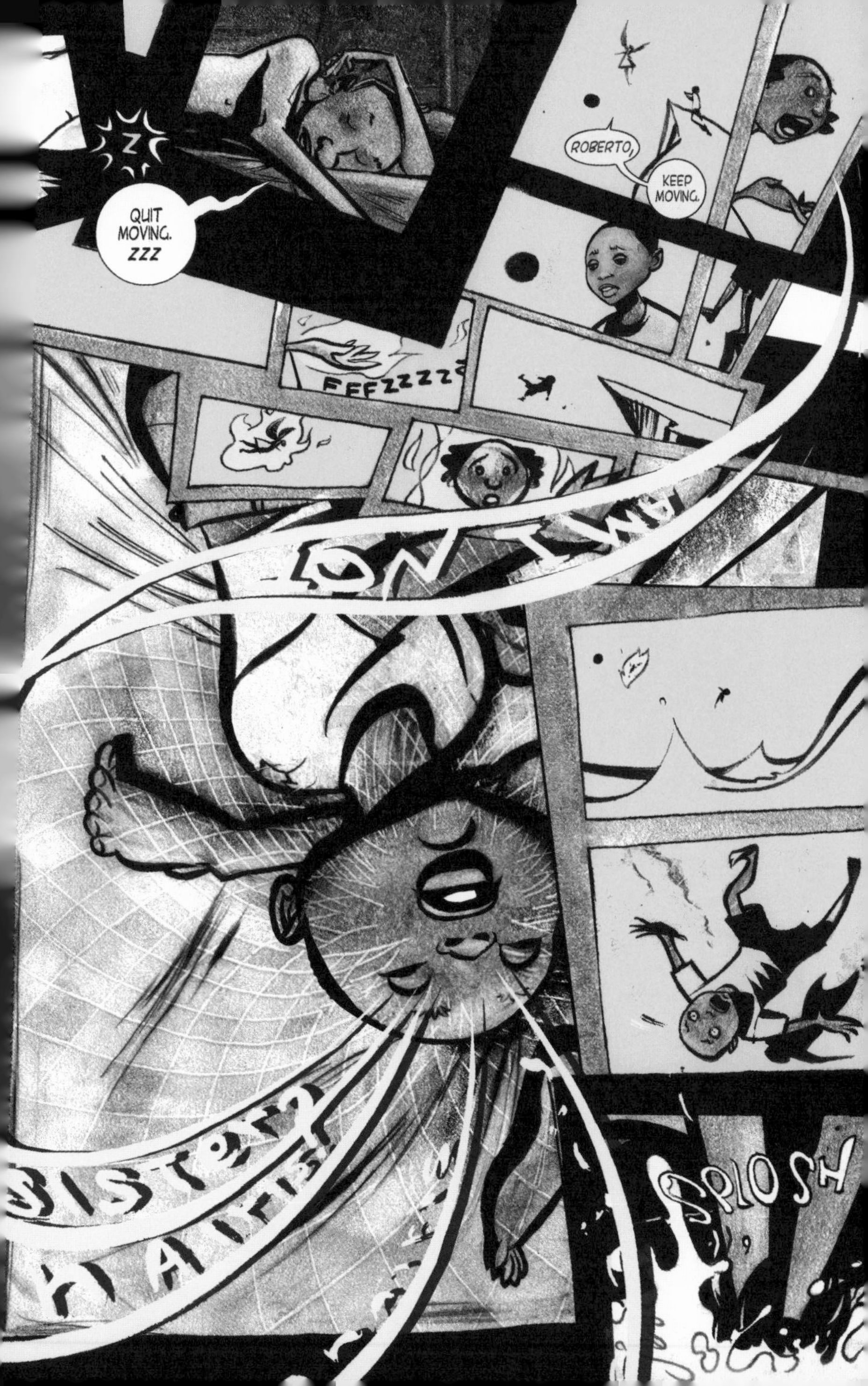

QUIT MOVING. ZZZ
ROBERTO,
KEEP MOVING.
SPLOSH

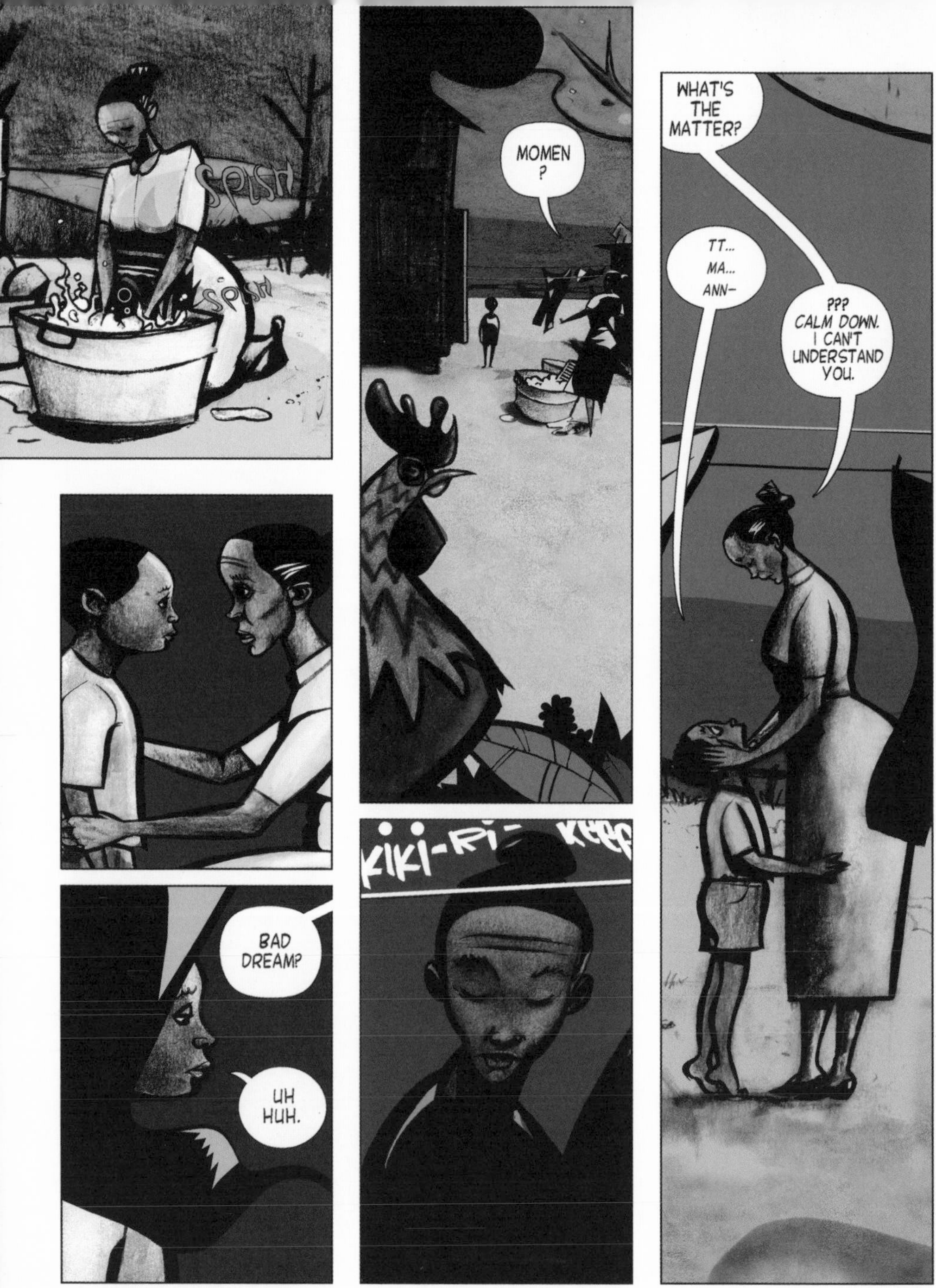
SPLSH
SPLSH
BAD DREAM?
UH HUH.
MOMEN ?
KIKI-RI-
WHAT'S THE MATTER?
TT... MA... ANN–
??? CALM DOWN. I CAN'T UNDERSTAND YOU.

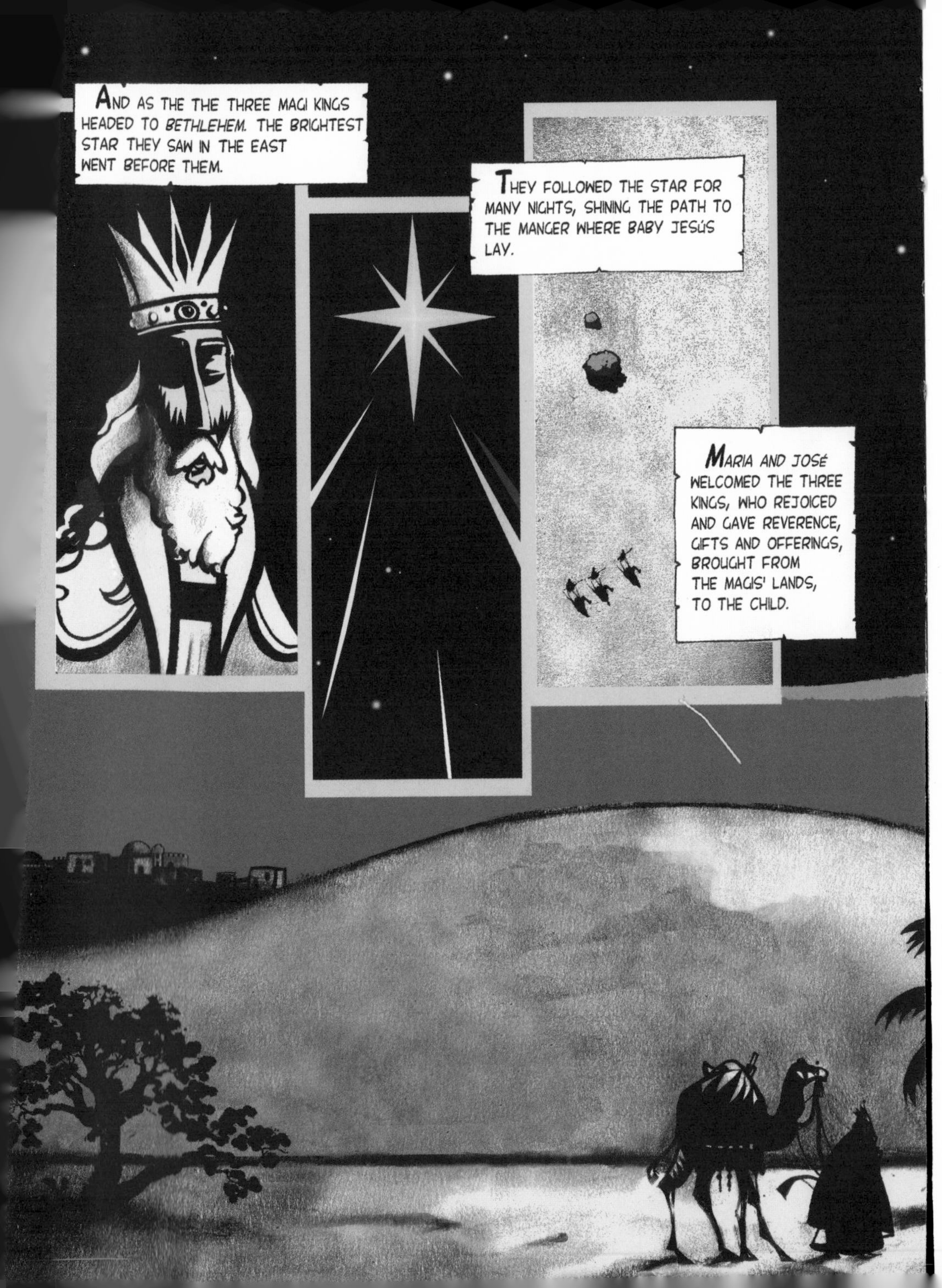
AND AS THE THE THREE MAGI KINGS HEADED TO BETHLEHEM. THE BRIGHTEST STAR THEY SAW IN THE EAST WENT BEFORE THEM.
THEY FOLLOWED THE STAR FOR MANY NIGHTS, SHINING THE PATH TO THE MANGER WHERE BABY JESÚS LAY.
MARIA AND JOSÉ WELCOMED THE THREE KINGS, WHO REJOICED AND GAVE REVERENCE, GIFTS AND OFFERINGS, BROUGHT FROM THE MAGIS' LANDS, TO THE CHILD.

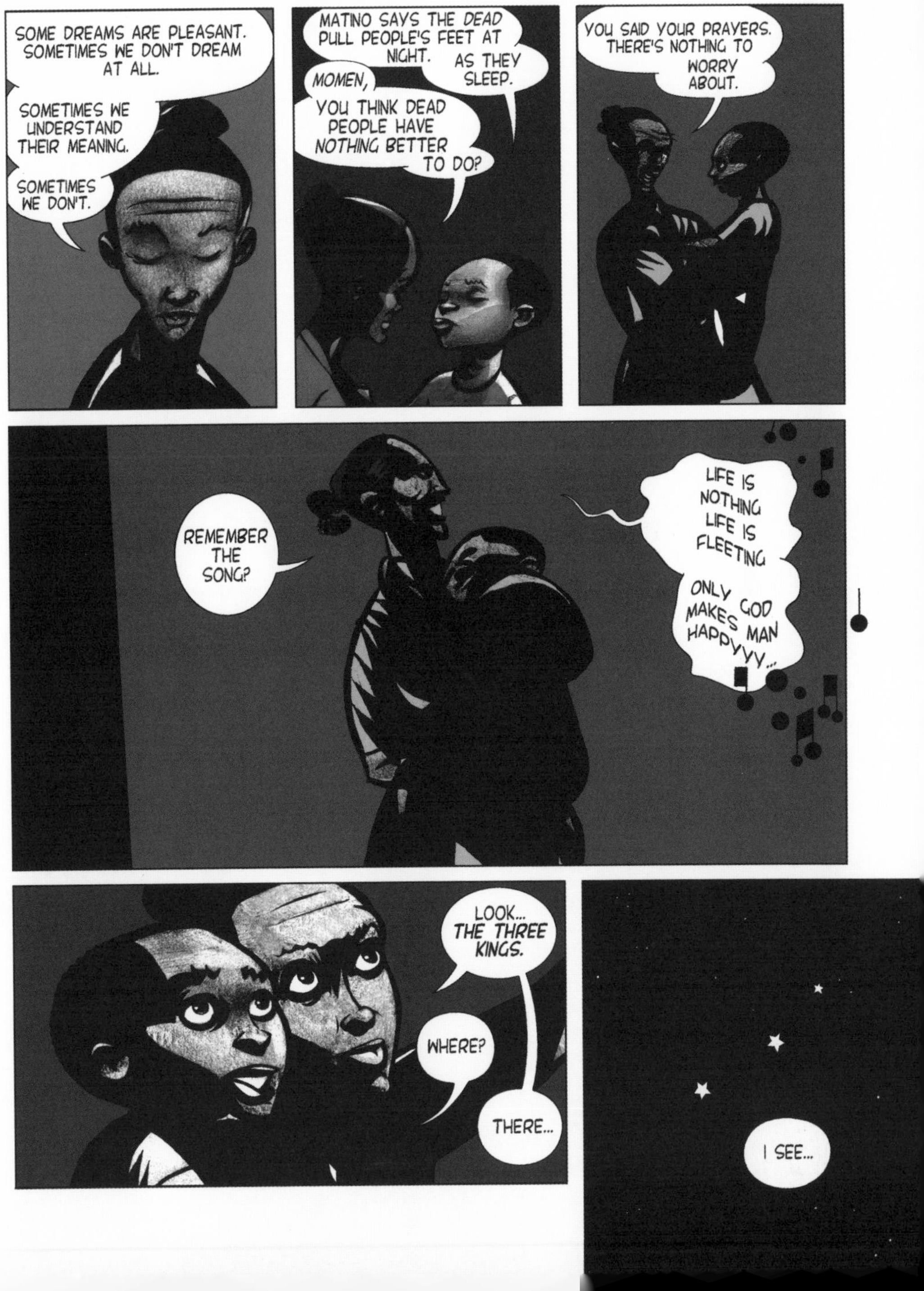
SOME DREAMS ARE PLEASANT. SOMETIMES WE DON'T DREAM AT ALL.
SOMETIMES WE UNDERSTAND THEIR MEANING.
SOMETIMES WE DON'T.
MATINO SAYS THE DEAD PULL PEOPLE'S FEET AT NIGHT.
AS THEY SLEEP.
MOMEN, YOU THINK DEAD PEOPLE HAVE NOTHING BETTER TO DO?
YOU SAID YOUR PRAYERS. THERE'S NOTHING TO WORRY ABOUT.
REMEMBER THE SONG?
LIFE IS NOTHING LIFE IS FLEETING
ONLY GOD MAKES MAN HAPPYYY...
LOOK... THE THREE KINGS.
WHERE?
THERE...
I SEE...

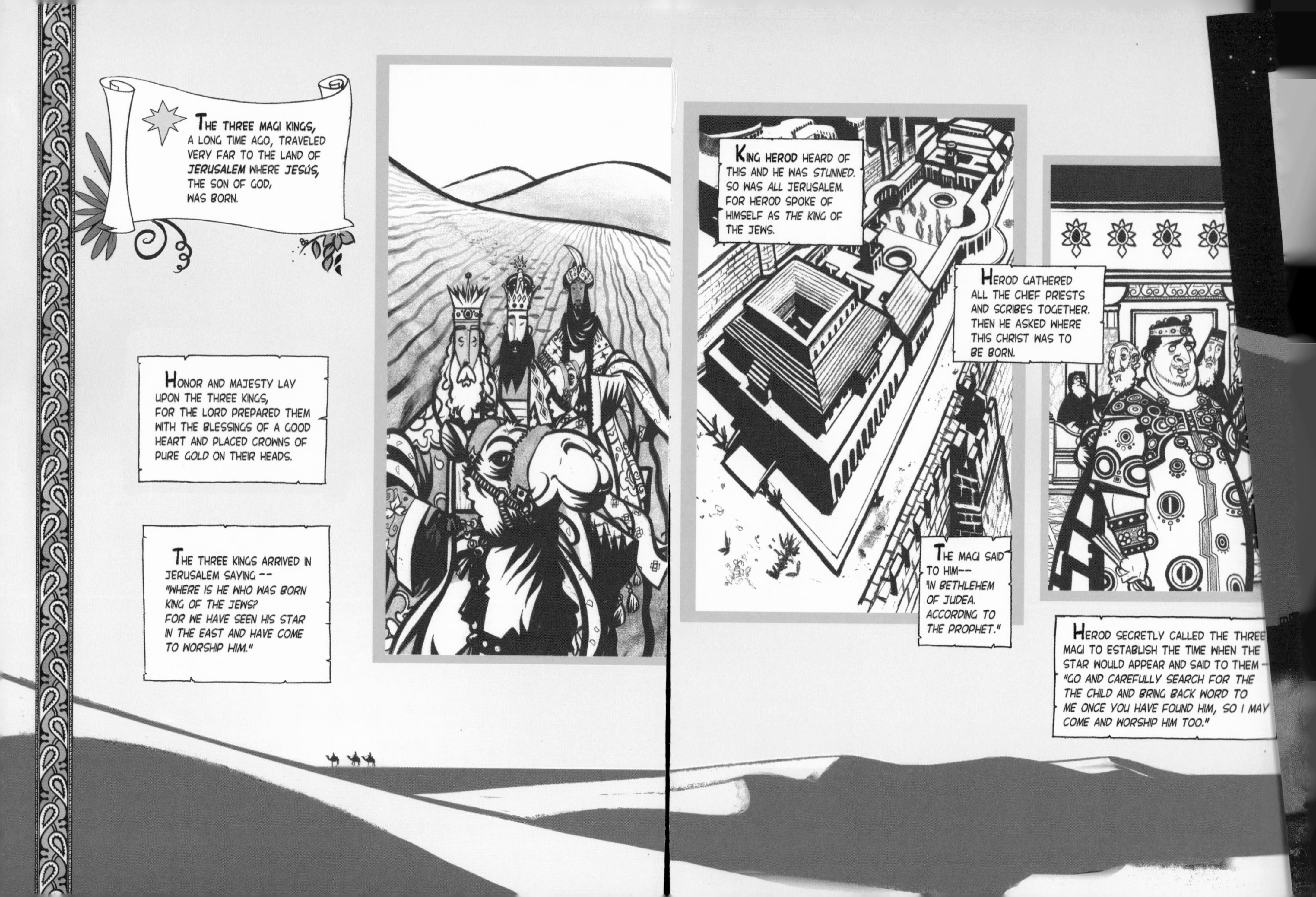
THE THREE MAGI KINGS, A LONG TIME AGO, TRAVELED VERY FAR TO THE LAND OF JERUSALEM WHERE JESÚS, THE SON OF GOD, WAS BORN.
HONOR AND MAJESTY LAY UPON THE THREE KINGS, FOR THE LORD PREPARED THEM WITH THE BLESSINGS OF A GOOD HEART AND PLACED CROWNS OF PURE GOLD ON THEIR HEADS.
THE THREE KINGS ARRIVED IN JERUSALEM SAYING -- "WHERE IS HE WHO WAS BORN KING OF THE JEWS? FOR WE HAVE SEEN HIS STAR IN THE EAST AND HAVE COME TO WORSHIP HIM."
KING HEROD HEARD OF THIS AND HE WAS STUNNED. SO WAS ALL JERUSALEM. FOR HEROD SPOKE OF HIMSELF AS THE KING OF THE JEWS.
HEROD GATHERED ALL THE CHIEF PRIESTS AND SCRIBES TOGETHER. THEN HE ASKED WHERE THIS CHRIST WAS TO BE BORN.
THE MAGI SAID TO HIM-- "IN BETHLEHEM OF JUDEA. ACCORDING TO THE PROPHET."
HEROD SECRETLY CALLED THE THREE MAGI TO ESTABLISH THE TIME WHEN THE STAR WOULD APPEAR AND SAID TO THEM-- "GO AND CAREFULLY SEARCH FOR THE THE CHILD AND BRING BACK WORD TO ME ONCE YOU HAVE FOUND HIM, SO I MAY COME AND WORSHIP HIM TOO."

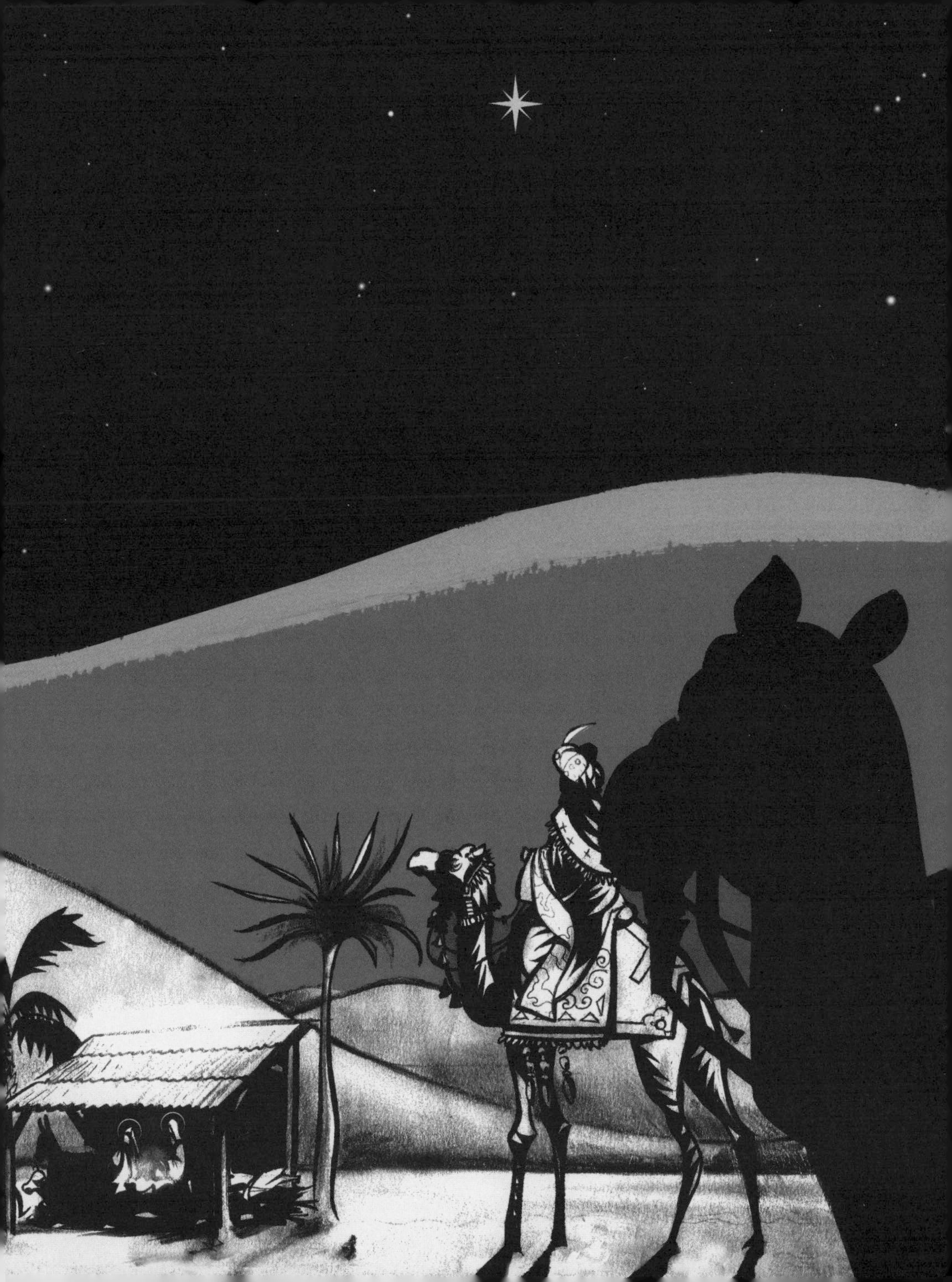

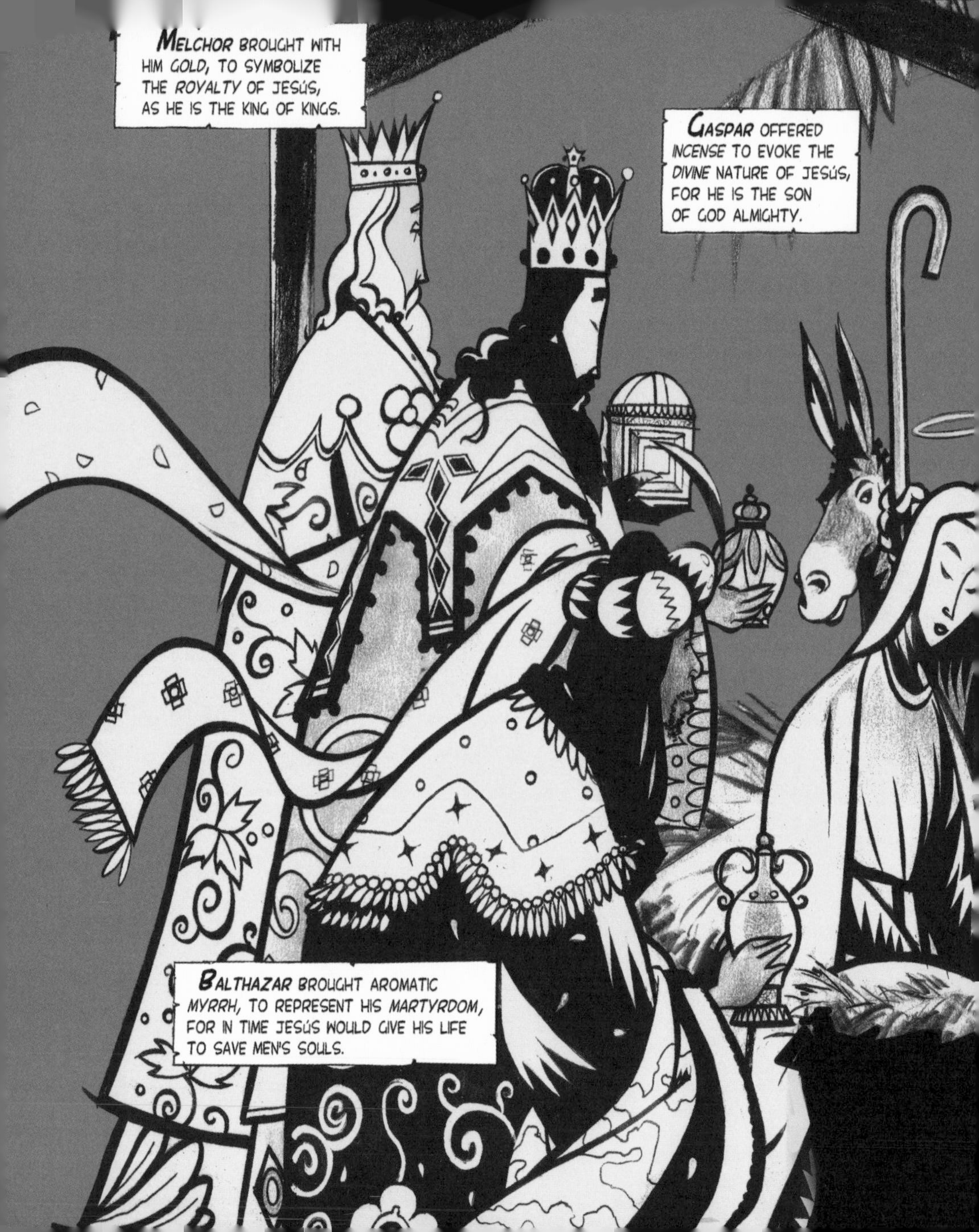
MELCHOR BROUGHT WITH HIM GOLD, TO SYMBOLIZE THE ROYALTY OF JESÚS, AS HE IS THE KING OF KINGS.
GASPAR OFFERED INCENSE TO EVOKE THE DIVINE NATURE OF JESÚS, FOR HE IS THE SON OF GOD ALMIGHTY.
BALTHAZAR BROUGHT AROMATIC MYRRH, TO REPRESENT HIS MARTYRDOM, FOR IN TIME JESÚS WOULD GIVE HIS LIFE TO SAVE MEN'S SOULS.

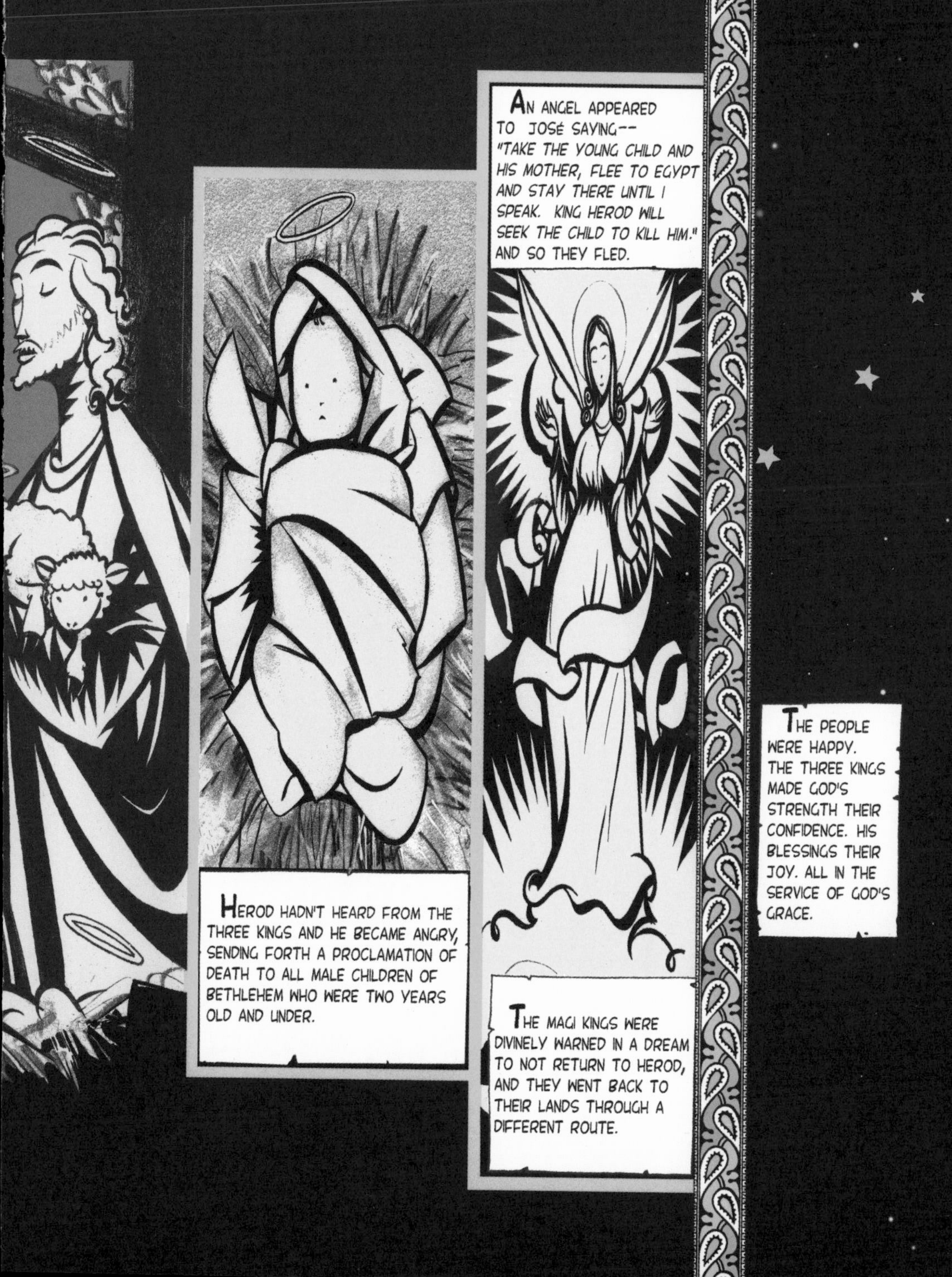
AN ANGEL APPEARED TO JOSÉ SAYING--
"TAKE THE YOUNG CHILD AND HIS MOTHER, FLEE TO EGYPT AND STAY THERE UNTIL I SPEAK. KING HEROD WILL SEEK THE CHILD TO KILL HIM." AND SO THEY FLED.
HEROD HADN'T HEARD FROM THE THREE KINGS AND HE BECAME ANGRY, SENDING FORTH A PROCLAMATION OF DEATH TO ALL MALE CHILDREN OF BETHLEHEM WHO WERE TWO YEARS OLD AND UNDER.
THE MAGI KINGS WERE DIVINELY WARNED IN A DREAM TO NOT RETURN TO HEROD, AND THEY WENT BACK TO THEIR LANDS THROUGH A DIFFERENT ROUTE.
THE PEOPLE WERE HAPPY. THE THREE KINGS MADE GOD'S STRENGTH THEIR CONFIDENCE. HIS BLESSINGS THEIR JOY. ALL IN THE SERVICE OF GOD'S GRACE.

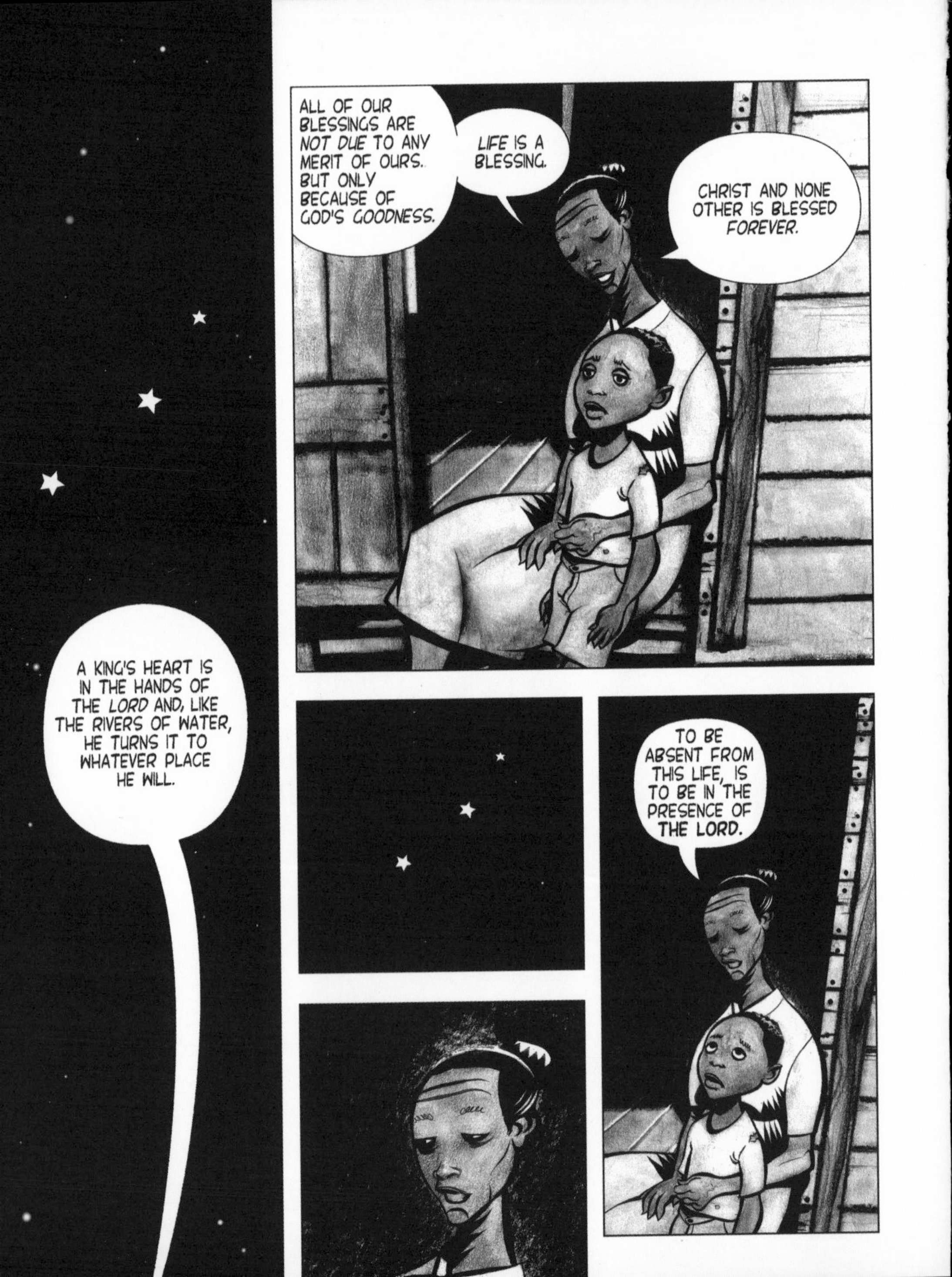

ALL OF OUR BLESSINGS ARE *NOT DUE* TO ANY MERIT OF OURS. BUT ONLY BECAUSE OF GOD'S GOODNESS.
LIFE IS A BLESSING.
CHRIST AND NONE OTHER IS BLESSED *FOREVER.*
A KING'S HEART IS IN THE HANDS OF THE *LORD* AND, LIKE THE RIVERS OF WATER, HE TURNS IT TO WHATEVER PLACE HE WILL.
TO BE ABSENT FROM THIS LIFE, IS TO BE IN THE PRESENCE OF **THE LORD.**

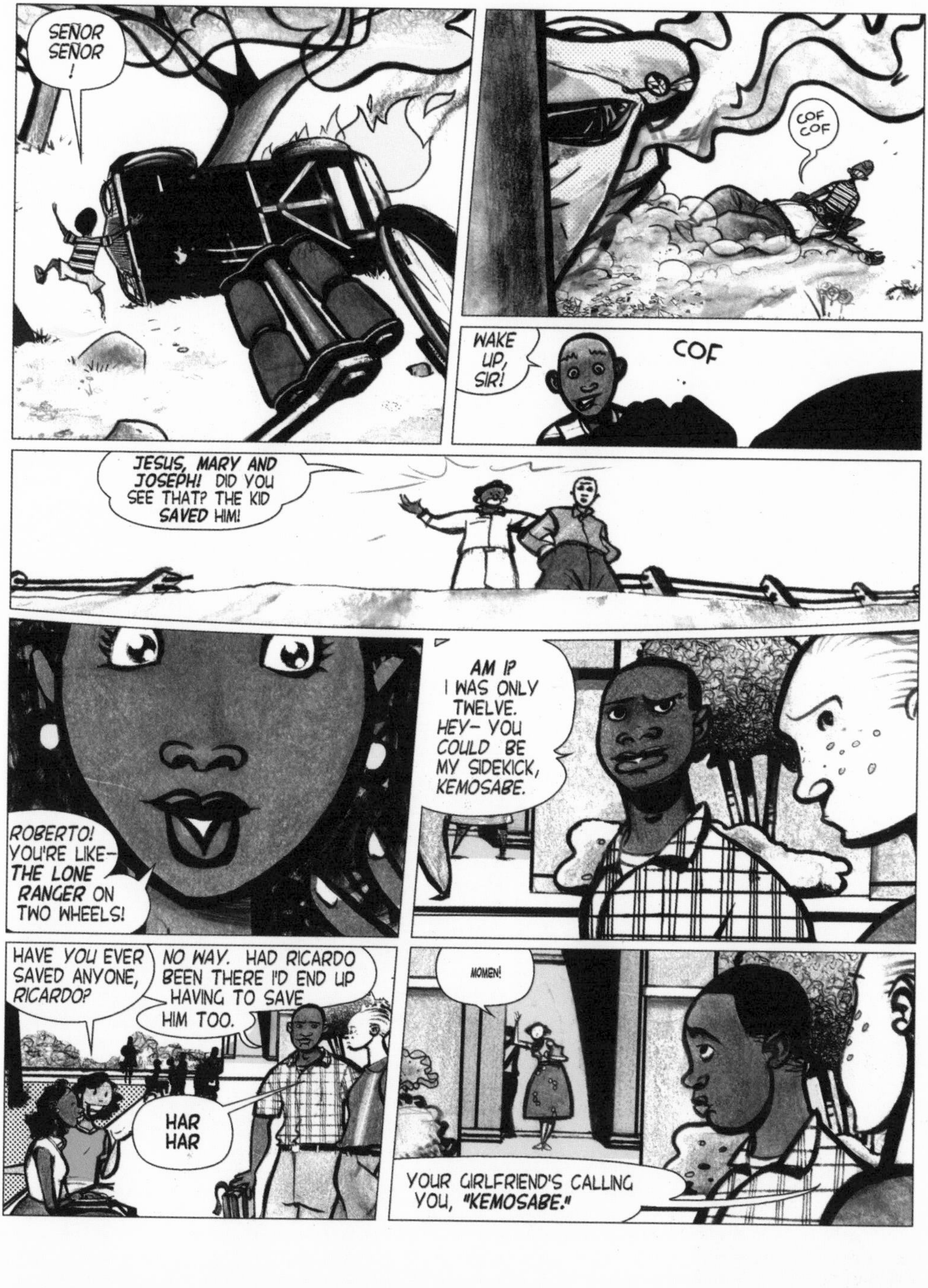
SEÑOR SEÑOR !
COF COF
WAKE UP, SIR!
COF
JESUS, MARY AND JOSEPH! DID YOU SEE THAT? THE KID SAVED HIM!
ROBERTO! YOU'RE LIKE– THE LONE RANGER ON TWO WHEELS!
AM I? I WAS ONLY TWELVE. HEY– YOU COULD BE MY SIDEKICK, KEMOSABE.
HAVE YOU EVER SAVED ANYONE, RICARDO?
NO WAY. HAD RICARDO BEEN THERE I'D END UP HAVING TO SAVE HIM TOO.
HAR HAR
MOMEN!
YOUR GIRLFRIEND'S CALLING YOU, "KEMOSABE."

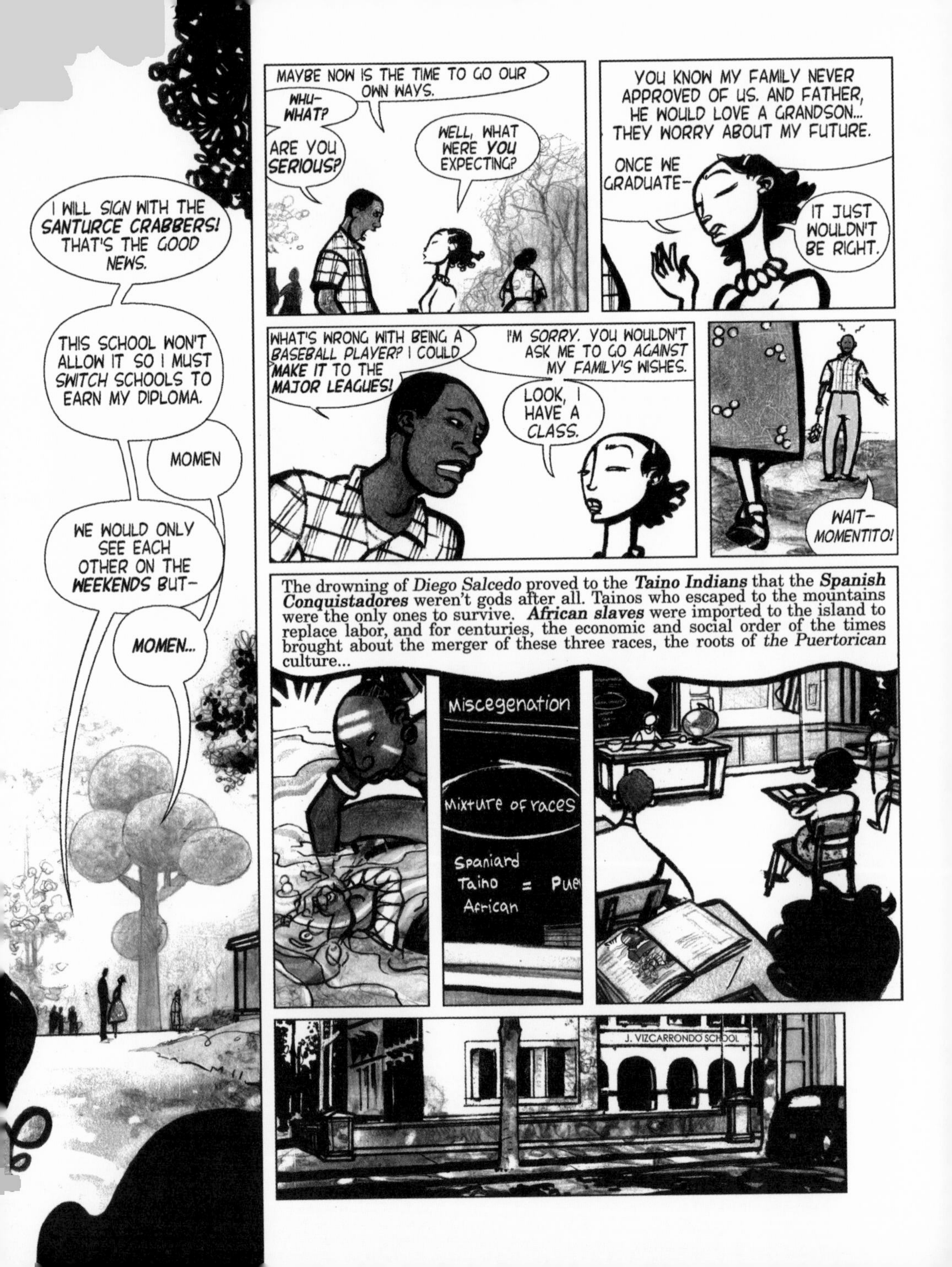
I WILL SIGN WITH THE SANTURCE CRABBERS! THAT'S THE GOOD NEWS.
THIS SCHOOL WON'T ALLOW IT SO I MUST SWITCH SCHOOLS TO EARN MY DIPLOMA.
MOMEN
WE WOULD ONLY SEE EACH OTHER ON THE WEEKENDS BUT–
MOMEN...
MAYBE NOW IS THE TIME TO GO OUR OWN WAYS.
WHU–WHAT?
ARE YOU SERIOUS?
WELL, WHAT WERE YOU EXPECTING?
YOU KNOW MY FAMILY NEVER APPROVED OF US. AND FATHER, HE WOULD LOVE A GRANDSON... THEY WORRY ABOUT MY FUTURE.
ONCE WE GRADUATE–
IT JUST WOULDN'T BE RIGHT.
WHAT'S WRONG WITH BEING A BASEBALL PLAYER? I COULD MAKE IT TO THE MAJOR LEAGUES!
I'M SORRY. YOU WOULDN'T ASK ME TO GO AGAINST MY FAMILY'S WISHES.
LOOK, I HAVE A CLASS.
WAIT– MOMENTITO!
The drowning of Diego Salcedo proved to the Taino Indians that the Spanish Conquistadores weren't gods after all. Tainos who escaped to the mountains were the only ones to survive. African slaves were imported to the island to replace labor, and for centuries, the economic and social order of the times brought about the merger of these three races, the roots of the Puertorican culture...
Miscegenation
Mixture of races
Spaniard
Taino = Pue
African
J. VIZCARRONDO SCHOOL

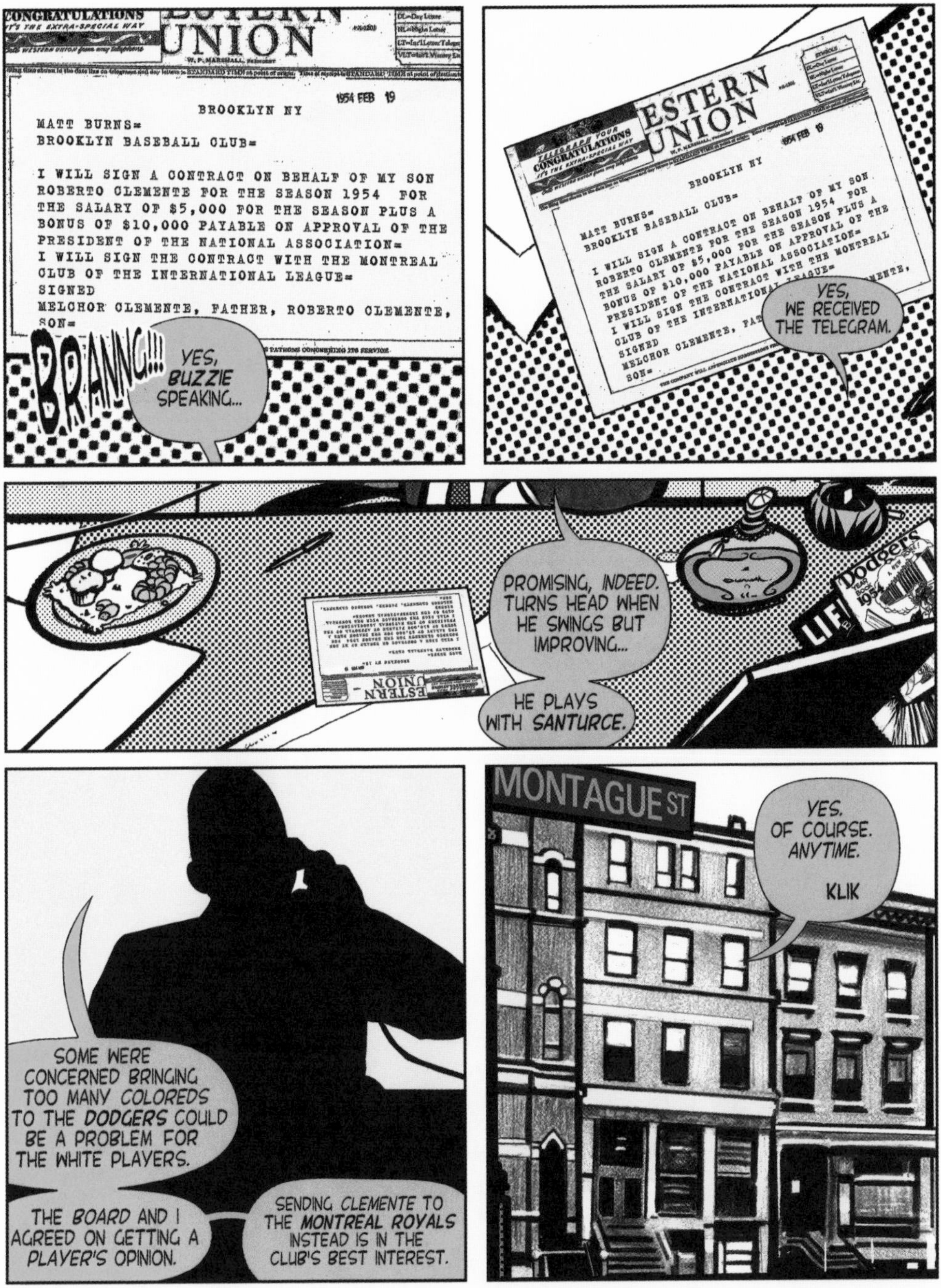
CONGRATULATIONS
IT'S THE EXTRA-SPECIAL WAY
UNION
W. P. MARSHALL, PRESIDENT
1954 FEB 19
BROOKLYN NY
MATT BURNS=
BROOKLYN BASEBALL CLUB=
I WILL SIGN A CONTRACT ON BEHALF OF MY SON ROBERTO CLEMENTE FOR THE SEASON 1954 FOR THE SALARY OF $5,000 FOR THE SEASON PLUS A BONUS OF $10,000 PAYABLE ON APPROVAL OF THE PRESIDENT OF THE NATIONAL ASSOCIATION=
I WILL SIGN THE CONTRACT WITH THE MONTREAL CLUB OF THE INTERNATIONAL LEAGUE=
SIGNED
MELCHOR CLEMENTE, FATHER, ROBERTO CLEMENTE, SON=
BRANNG!!!
YES, BUZZIE SPEAKING...
YES, WE RECEIVED THE TELEGRAM.
PROMISING, INDEED. TURNS HEAD WHEN HE SWINGS BUT IMPROVING...
HE PLAYS WITH SANTURCE.
Dodgers
LIFE
SOME WERE CONCERNED BRINGING TOO MANY COLOREDS TO THE DODGERS COULD BE A PROBLEM FOR THE WHITE PLAYERS.
THE BOARD AND I AGREED ON GETTING A PLAYER'S OPINION.
SENDING CLEMENTE TO THE MONTREAL ROYALS INSTEAD IS IN THE CLUB'S BEST INTEREST.
MONTAGUE ST
YES. OF COURSE. ANYTIME.
KLIK

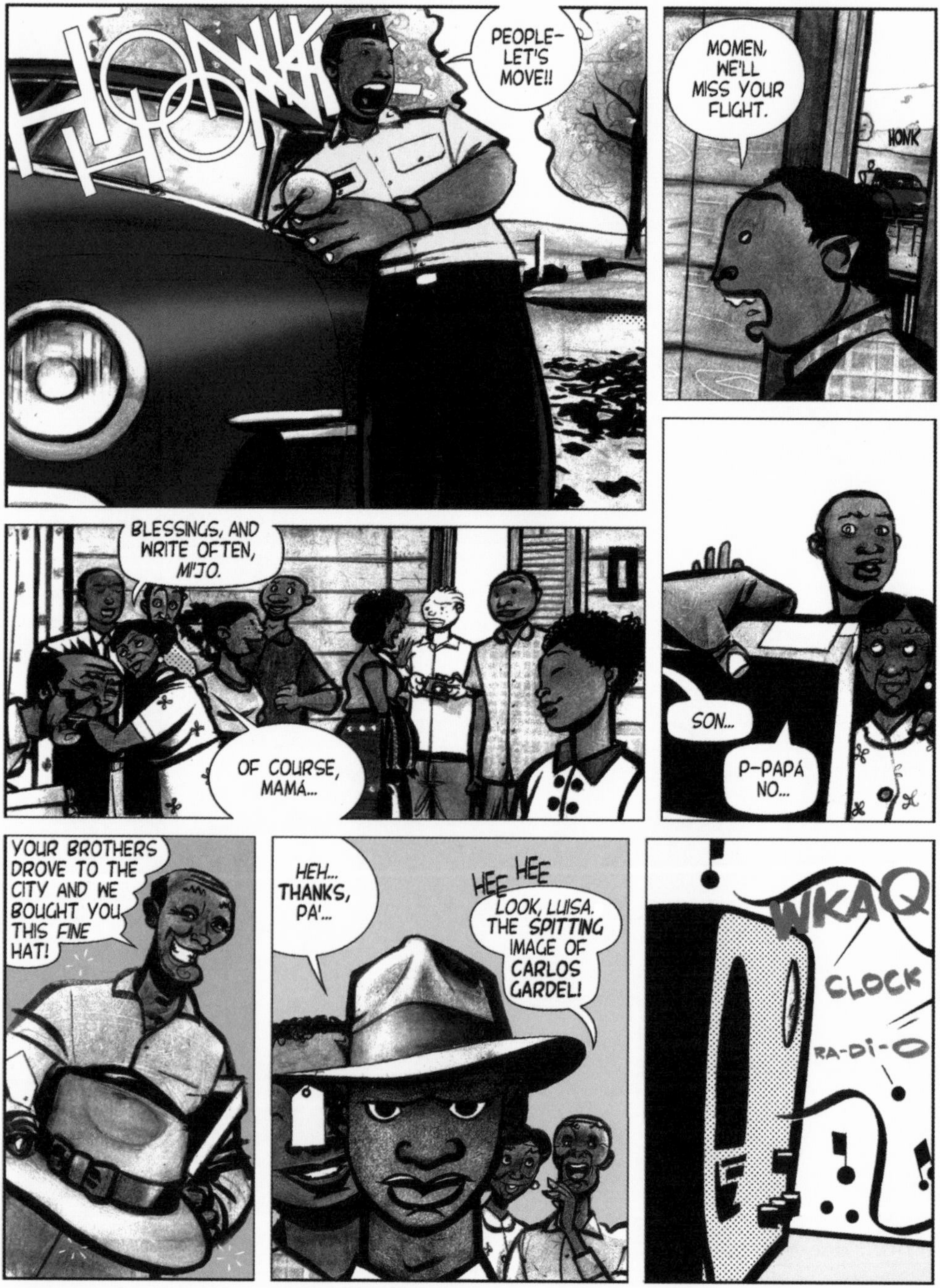
HONK HONK
PEOPLE-LET'S MOVE!!
MOMEN, WE'LL MISS YOUR FLIGHT.
HONK
BLESSINGS, AND WRITE OFTEN, MI'JO.
OF COURSE, MAMÁ...
SON...
P-PAPÁ NO...
YOUR BROTHERS DROVE TO THE CITY AND WE BOUGHT YOU THIS FINE HAT!
HEH... THANKS, PA'...
HEE HEE
LOOK, LUISA. THE SPITTING IMAGE OF CARLOS GARDEL!
WKAQ
CLOCK
RA-DI-O

· THE TIME ·
3:35

Governor Luis Muñoz Marin will welcome
the 65th Infantry Regiment. *"Our men
have gallantly defended alongside fellow
US citizens, common ideals against those
who subvert freedom and this is
something of profound meaning for
us,"* said the Governor.
The 65th arrived in Korea in 1950.

The continuing decline of
malaria cases is being
attributed to the rapid
economic & infrastructure
expansion under the
program,
Operation Bootstrap.

Tax concessions for foreign
investors under the program
have caused manufacturing
jobs to edge ahead of
farming as Puerto Rico's
major source of income...

while the migration to
the United States by
thousands of job
seekers has brought
balance to the
unemployment rate.

In 1953 a record number
of 69,000 migrated to
the mainland, &
similar numbers are
expected this year.

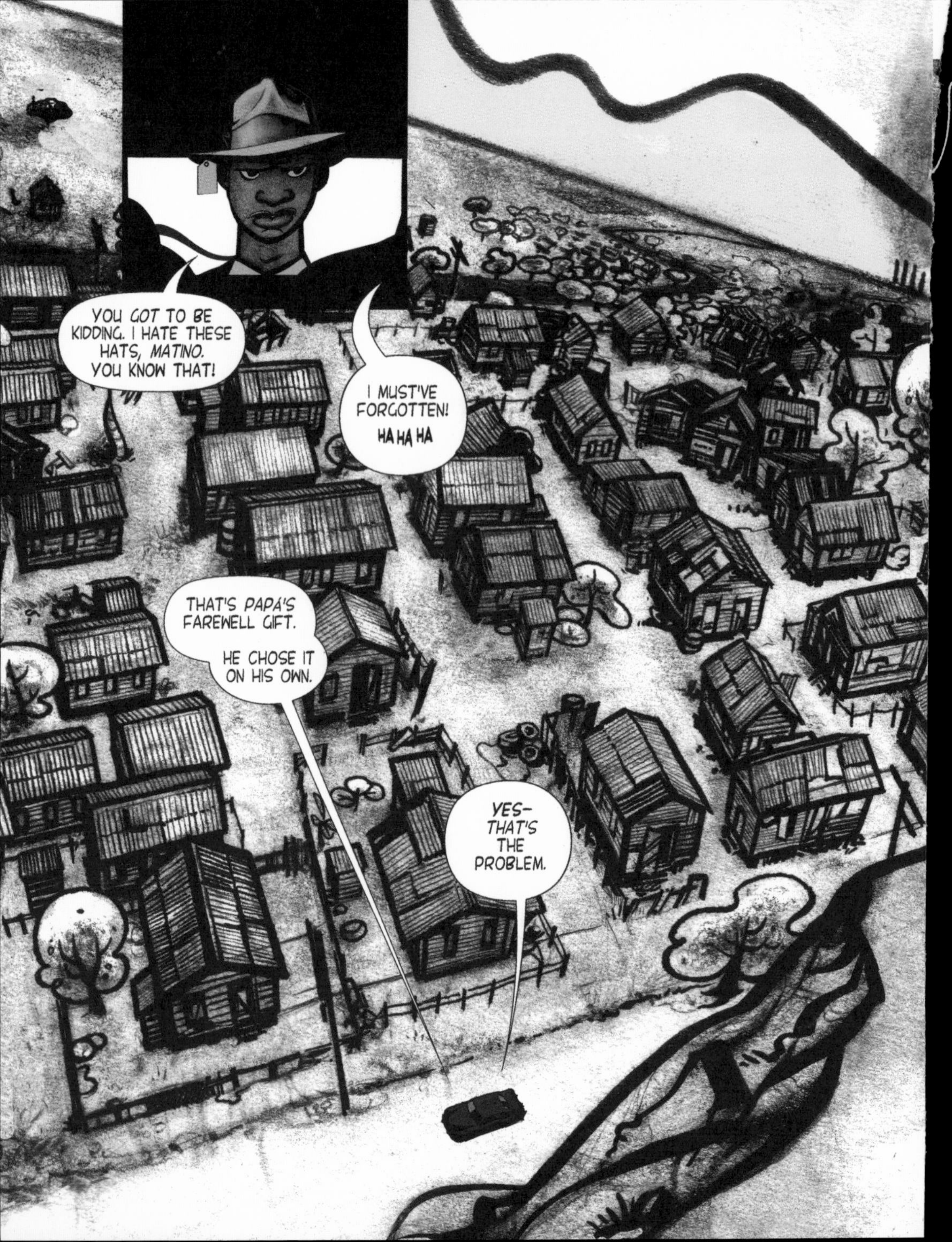

YOU GOT TO BE KIDDING. I HATE THESE HATS, *MATINO*. YOU KNOW THAT!
I MUST'VE FORGOTTEN!
HA HA HA
THAT'S *PAPÁ'S* FAREWELL GIFT.
HE CHOSE IT ON HIS OWN.
YES—THAT'S THE PROBLEM.

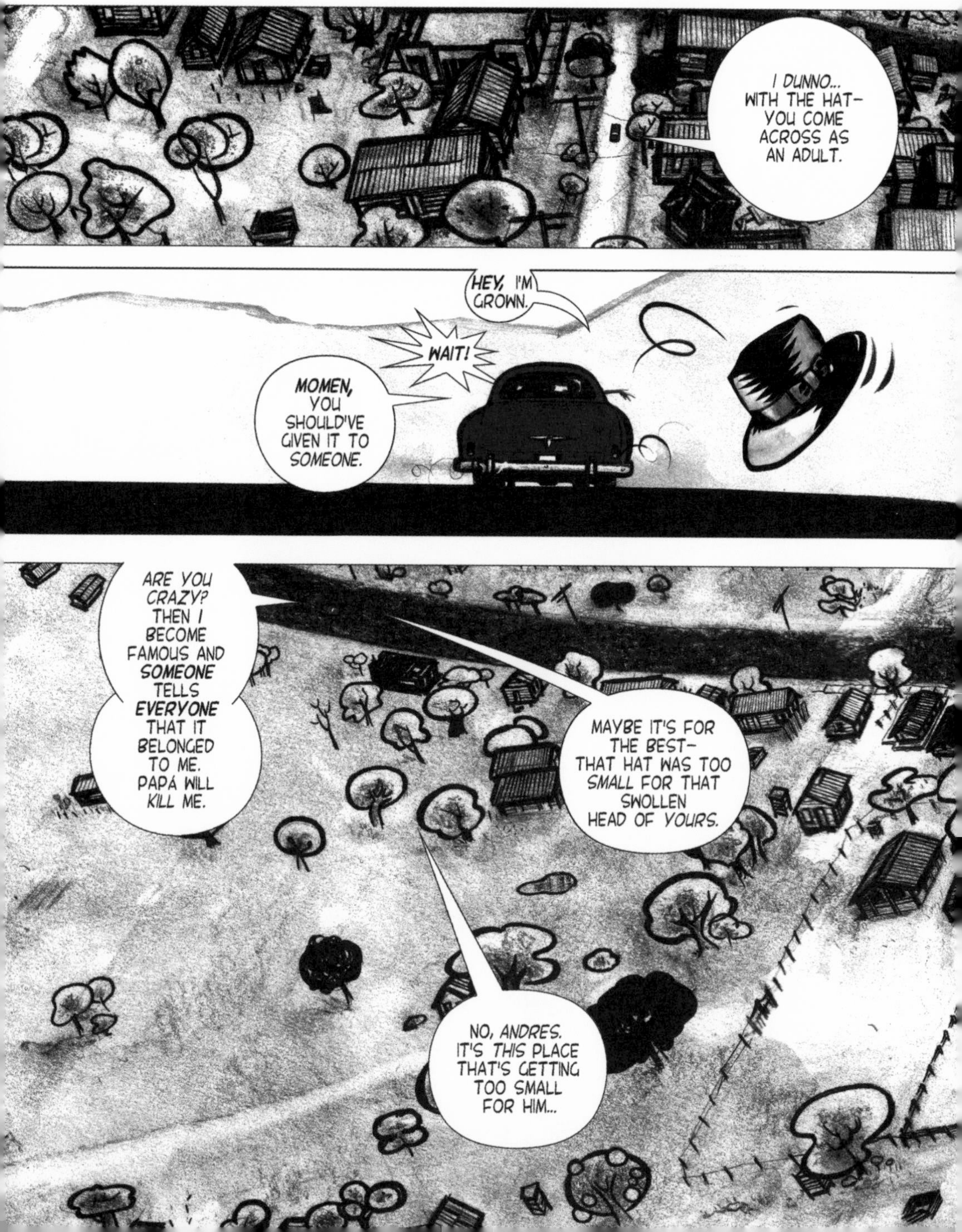

I DUNNO... WITH THE HAT– YOU COME ACROSS AS AN ADULT.
HEY, I'M GROWN.
WAIT!
MOMEN, YOU SHOULD'VE GIVEN IT TO SOMEONE.
ARE YOU CRAZY? THEN I BECOME FAMOUS AND SOMEONE TELLS EVERYONE THAT IT BELONGED TO ME. PAPÁ WILL KILL ME.
MAYBE IT'S FOR THE BEST– THAT HAT WAS TOO SMALL FOR THAT SWOLLEN HEAD OF YOURS.
NO, ANDRES. IT'S THIS PLACE THAT'S GETTING TOO SMALL FOR HIM...

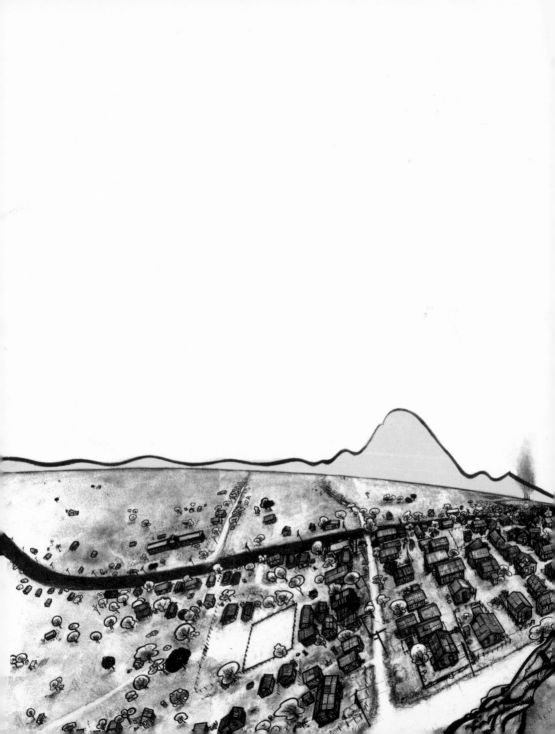

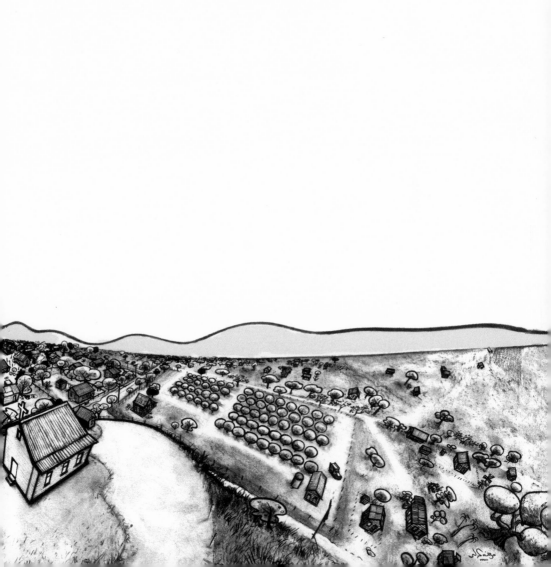

TROPICVS CANCRI.

In the beginning, the earth was a dry desert, no water, no vegetation, only a mountain stood tall and proud amid the vast plain and on this mountaintop, all the people lived. A child walked the land below one day in search of food. When a seed flowing through the winds was caught by the child, within days the child went to collect enough seeds to fill his pouch. He then planted the seeds atop the mountain. In the morning, large, green trees sprouted from the ground, higher and higher, until a forest reached the clouds. And from its tallest tree, the most beautiful golden flower came to be. From this flower, a sphere grew, bright as the sun, its light could be seen from a far distance. Strange sounds could be heard coming from the sphere day and night, and for a time, people stayed away from it. One day, a man decided that possessing the dazzling sphere could bring him the power of the sun and so he began to climb the mountain. On the other side of the mountain, another man wanted the sphere too, so he climbed the mountain, until both men reached the forest and at the bottom of its tallest tree, they discovered that the sphere was a giant pumpkin. The golden flower fruit. The two men fought and struggled over the pumpkin, when its vine finally broke. The pumpkin rolled down the mountain at a great speed crashing against the rocks, splitting open and releasing the oceans and all the creatures in it, covering the whole land. The people ran to the highest spot of the mountain, taking shelter above in the forest, but when the tides reached the forest's edge, the rise of the water stopped. They came out of the forest to see that the oceans brought the fish for the people to feed. Streams of sweet water ran through the forest for everyone to drink. The people were happy, and they named their paradise, Boriken, the land of the brave lord.

-Taino Myth (C. 300 B.C.)

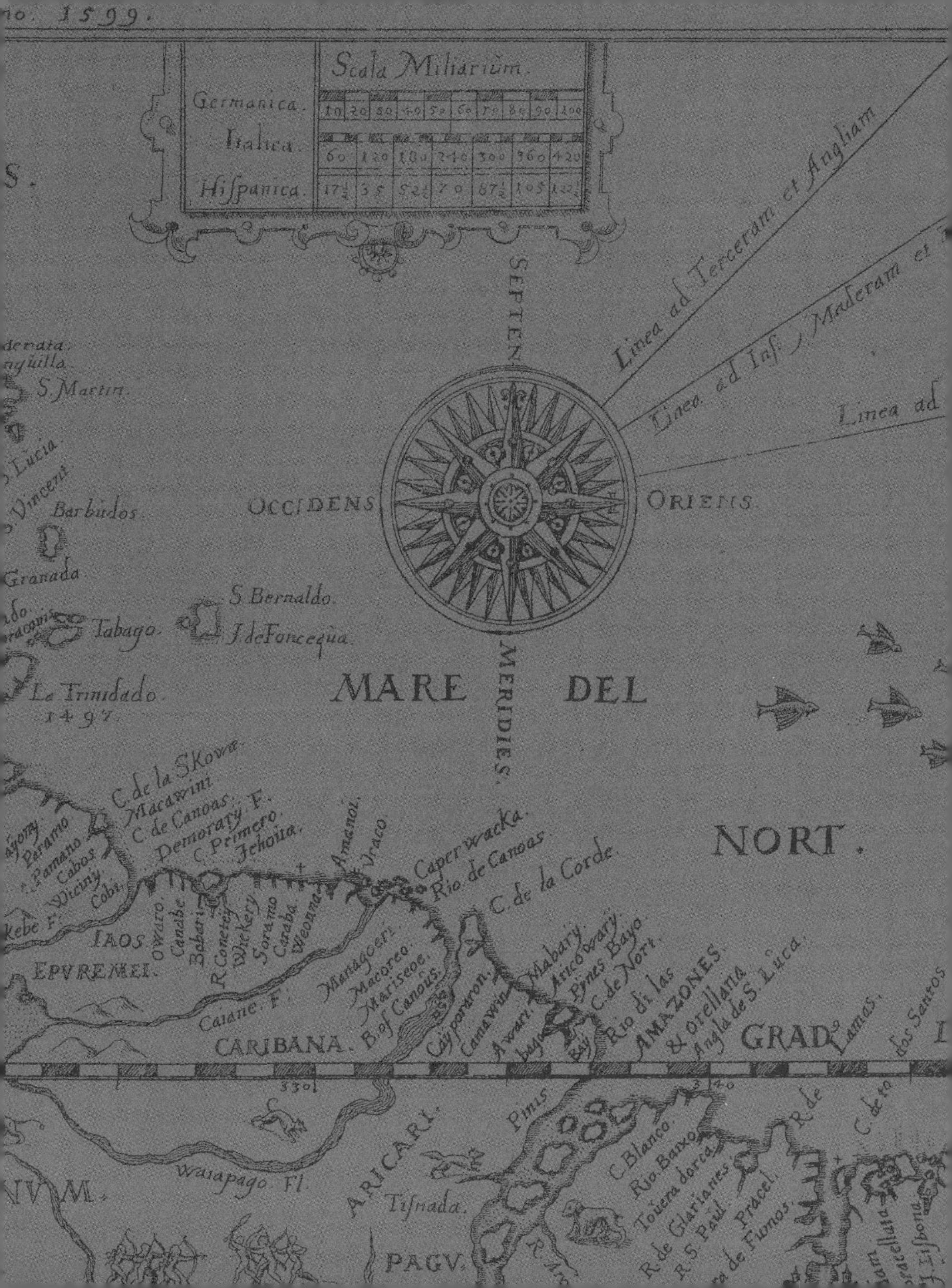

S.

Scala Miliarium.

Germanica.											
	10	20	30	40	50	60	70	80	90	100	
Italica.											
	60	120	180	240	300	360	420				
Hispanica.	$17\frac{1}{2}$	35	$52\frac{1}{2}$	70	$87\frac{1}{2}$	105	$122\frac{1}{2}$				

SEPTENTRIO

Linea ad Terceram et Angliam

Linea ad Insf: Maderam et

Linea ad

OCCIDENS

ORIENS

denata.
nquilla.
S. Martin.

S. Lucia.
S. Vincent.
Barbudos.
Granada.

S. Bernaldo.
do.
racovi.
Tabago.
J. de Foncequa.

Le Trinidado.
1497.

MERIDIES.

MARE DEL

NORT.

C. de la S. Kowre.
Macawini.
C. de Canoas.
Demoratȳ. F.
C. Primero.
Jehoua.

Caperwacka.
Rio de Canoas.

C. de la Corde.

Sgony
Paramo
Pamano
Cabos
Wiciny
Cobi.
Kebe F.

Owiaro.
Canabe.
Bobari.
R. Conetig.
Wickery.
Sorano
Caaba
Weonna.
Amanoi.
Iraco.

Mabary.
Aticowary.
Pymes Bayo.
C. de Nort.
AMAZONES.
& Orellana.
Angla de S. Luca.

GRAD
dos Lamas.
dos Santos

IAOS.
EPVREMEI.

Caiane. F.
Managoeri.
Macoreo
Mariseoe.
B of Canous.

Caypararon.
Canawini.
A vari.
bayu.

Ri

R. de

C. de to

Rio di las

CARIBANA.

330

ARICARI.

Pinis

C. Blanco.
Rio Banxo.
Tonera dorcas.
R. de Glarianis.
R. S. Paul.
de S. Pracel.

NVM.

Waiapago. Fl.

Tisnada.

PAGV.

R. An

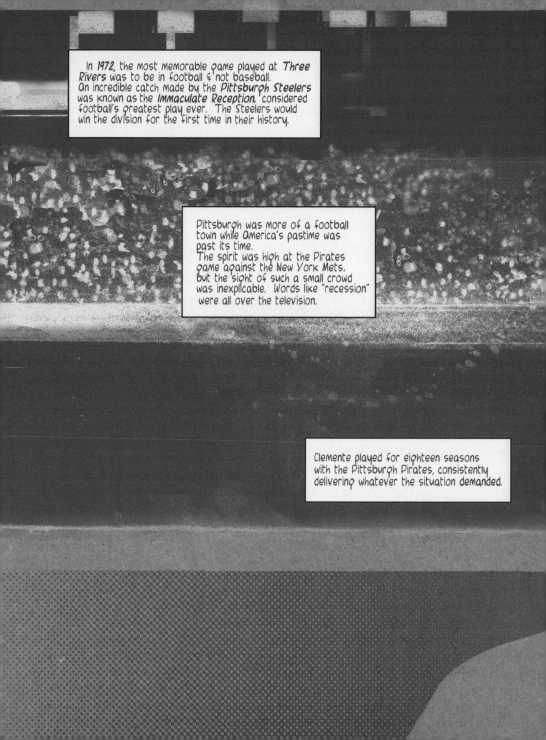

In *1972,* the most memorable game played at *Three Rivers* was to be in football & not baseball. An incredible catch made by the *Pittsburgh Steelers* was known as the *Immaculate Reception,* considered football's greatest play ever. The Steelers would win the division for the first time in their history.

Pittsburgh was more of a football town while America's pastime was past its time. The spirit was high at the Pirates game against the New York Mets, but the sight of such a small crowd was inexplicable. Words like "recession" were all over the television.

Clemente played for eighteen seasons with the Pittsburgh Pirates, consistently delivering whatever the situation demanded.

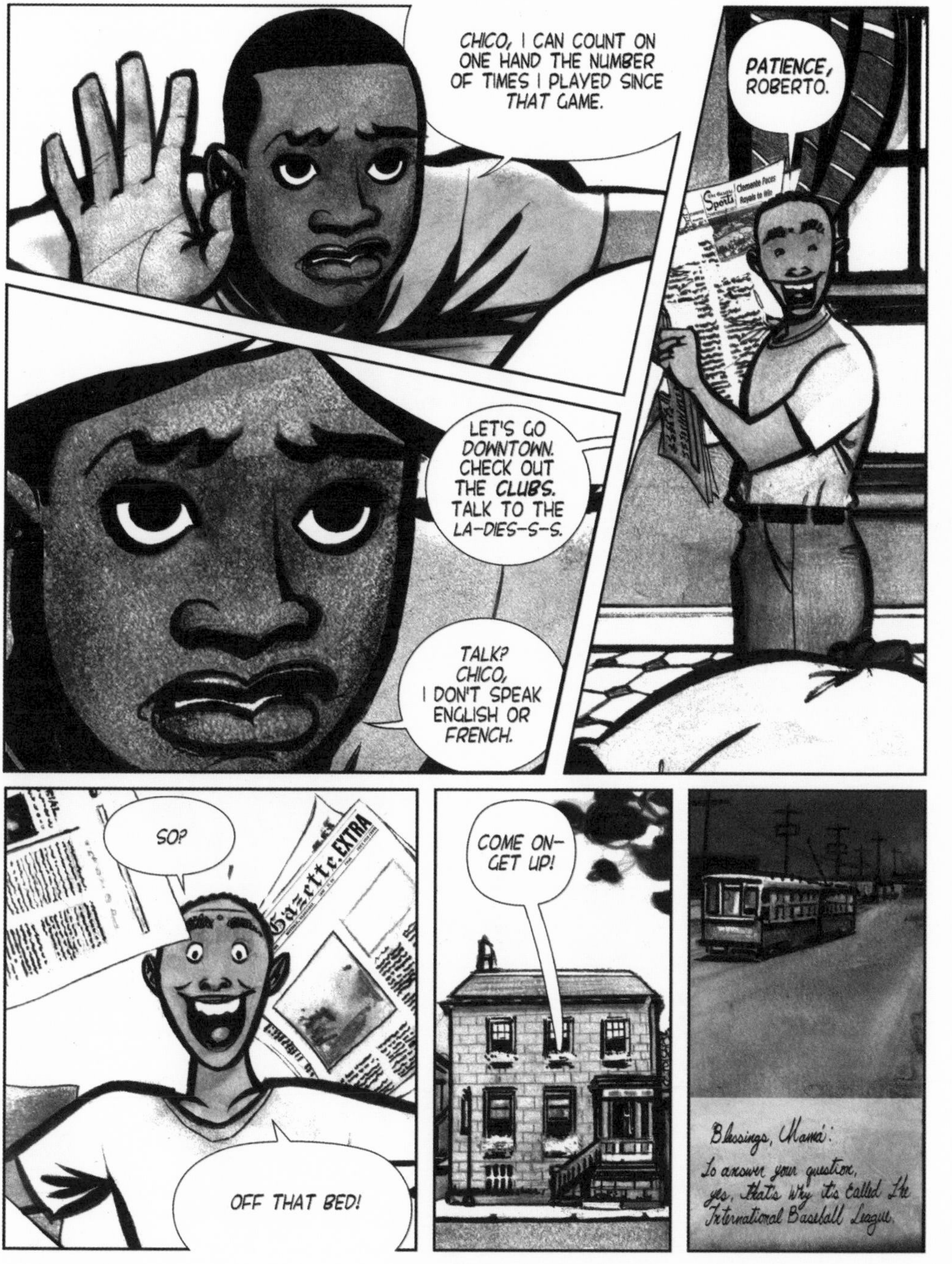
CHICO, I CAN COUNT ON ONE HAND THE NUMBER OF TIMES I PLAYED SINCE THAT GAME.
PATIENCE, ROBERTO.
Clemente Paces Royals to Win
LET'S GO DOWNTOWN. CHECK OUT THE CLUBS. TALK TO THE LA-DIES-S-S.
TALK? CHICO, I DON'T SPEAK ENGLISH OR FRENCH.
SO?
Gazette EXTRA
OFF THAT BED!
COME ON- GET UP!
Blessings, Mamá:
To answer your question, yes, that's why it's called the International Baseball League.

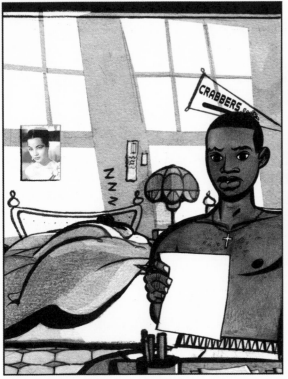

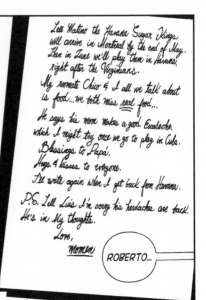

Los Mateo the Havana Sugar Kings will arrive in Montreal by the end of May. Then in June we'll play them in Havana, right after the Virginians.

My roomate Chico & I all we talk about is food...we both miss real food.

He says his mom makes a good Escabeche, which I might try once we go to play in Cuba.

Blessings to Papá.

Hugs & kisses to everyone.

I'll write again when I get back from Havana.

P.S. Tell Luis I'm sorry his headaches are back! He's in My thoughts.

Love,
Momen

ROBERTO...

GOOD MORNING, CHICO!

"GOOD"?

AHH... NEVER DRINK SOMETHING YOU CAN'T PRONOUNCE.

LET'S GET SOME COFFEE.

DE LORIMIER
Restaurant

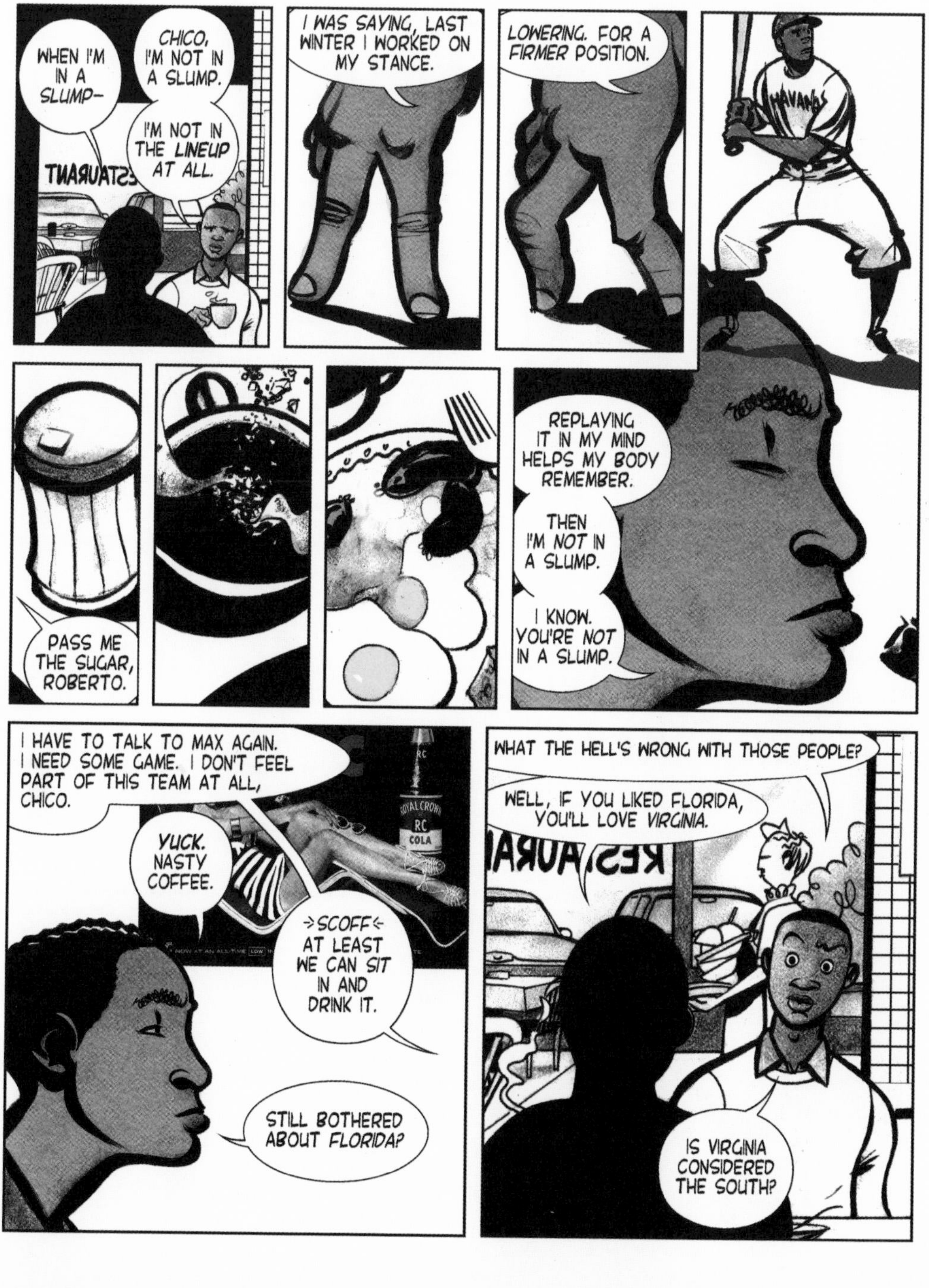
WHEN I'M IN A SLUMP—
CHICO, I'M NOT IN A SLUMP.
I'M NOT IN THE LINEUP AT ALL.
I WAS SAYING, LAST WINTER I WORKED ON MY STANCE.
LOWERING. FOR A FIRMER POSITION.
HAVANAS
PASS ME THE SUGAR, ROBERTO.
REPLAYING IT IN MY MIND HELPS MY BODY REMEMBER.
THEN I'M NOT IN A SLUMP.
I KNOW. YOU'RE NOT IN A SLUMP.
I HAVE TO TALK TO MAX AGAIN. I NEED SOME GAME. I DON'T FEEL PART OF THIS TEAM AT ALL, CHICO.
ROYAL CROWN RC COLA
YUCK. NASTY COFFEE.
→SCOFF← AT LEAST WE CAN SIT IN AND DRINK IT.
STILL BOTHERED ABOUT FLORIDA?
WHAT THE HELL'S WRONG WITH THOSE PEOPLE?
WELL, IF YOU LIKED FLORIDA, YOU'LL LOVE VIRGINIA.
IS VIRGINIA CONSIDERED THE SOUTH?

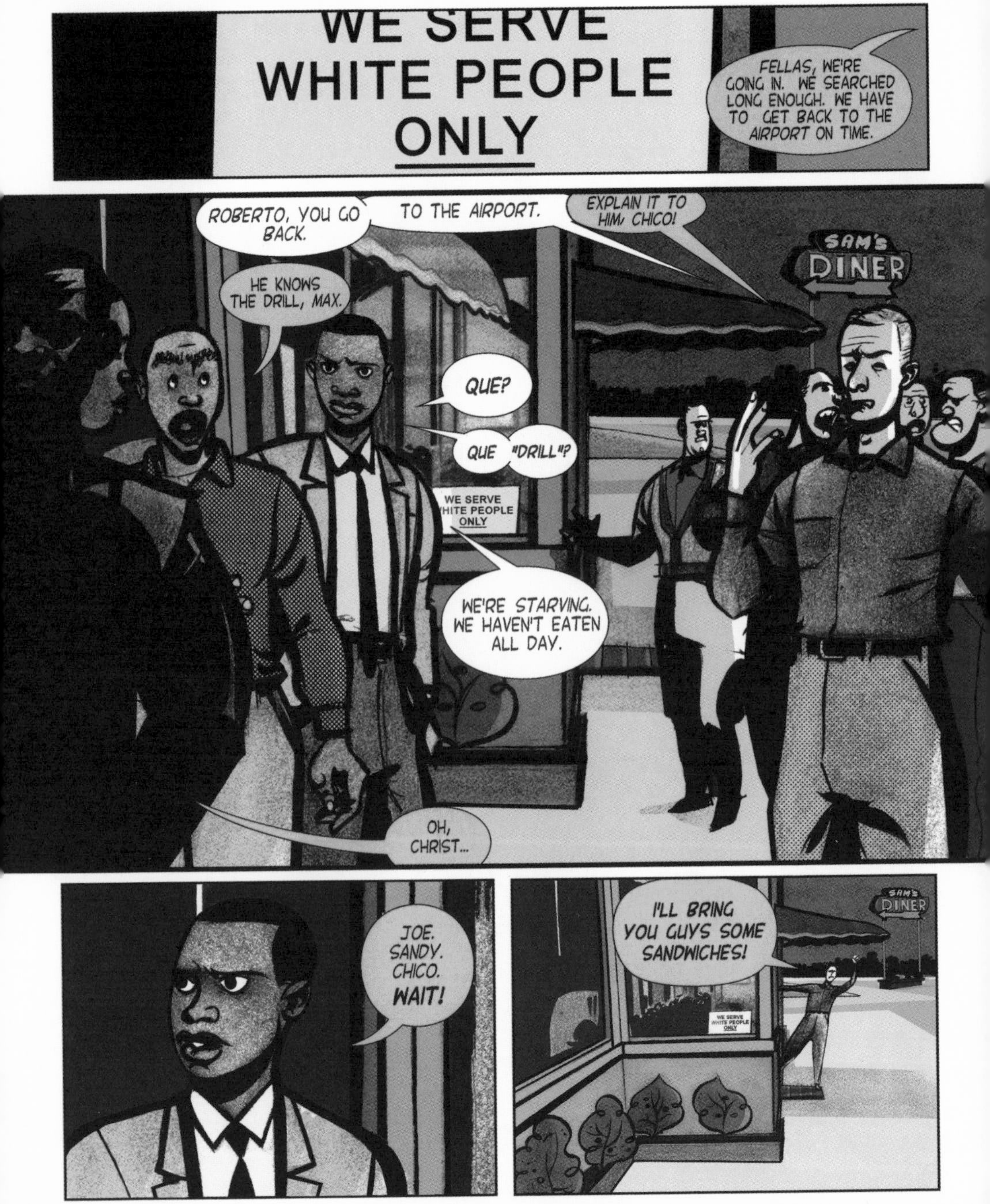
WE SERVE WHITE PEOPLE ONLY
FELLAS, WE'RE GOING IN. WE SEARCHED LONG ENOUGH. WE HAVE TO GET BACK TO THE AIRPORT ON TIME.
ROBERTO, YOU GO BACK.
TO THE AIRPORT.
EXPLAIN IT TO HIM, CHICO!
SAM'S DINER
HE KNOWS THE DRILL, MAX.
QUE?
QUE "DRILL"?
WE SERVE WHITE PEOPLE ONLY
WE'RE STARVING. WE HAVEN'T EATEN ALL DAY.
OH, CHRIST...
JOE. SANDY. CHICO. WAIT!
I'LL BRING YOU GUYS SOME SANDWICHES!
SAM'S DINER
WE SERVE WHITE PEOPLE ONLY

WHAT'S TAKING THEM SO LONG WITH THE DAMNED SANDWICHES?
AND WHERE'S JOE AND SANDY?
LET ME GUESS...
I'M TIRED OF SANDWICHES.
THEY'RE AT THE COLORED RESTROOM.
THIS IS RIDICULOUS.
YAWN
I NEED SOME SLEEP.
VISIT CUBA!
BZ... PASSENGERS: FLIGHT 207 TO HAVANA, CUBA HAS BEEN DELAYED. BZ... PLEASE REPORT THE
FLIGHT.
OH, GREAT!
WE'RE NEVER GETTING OUT OF HERE.

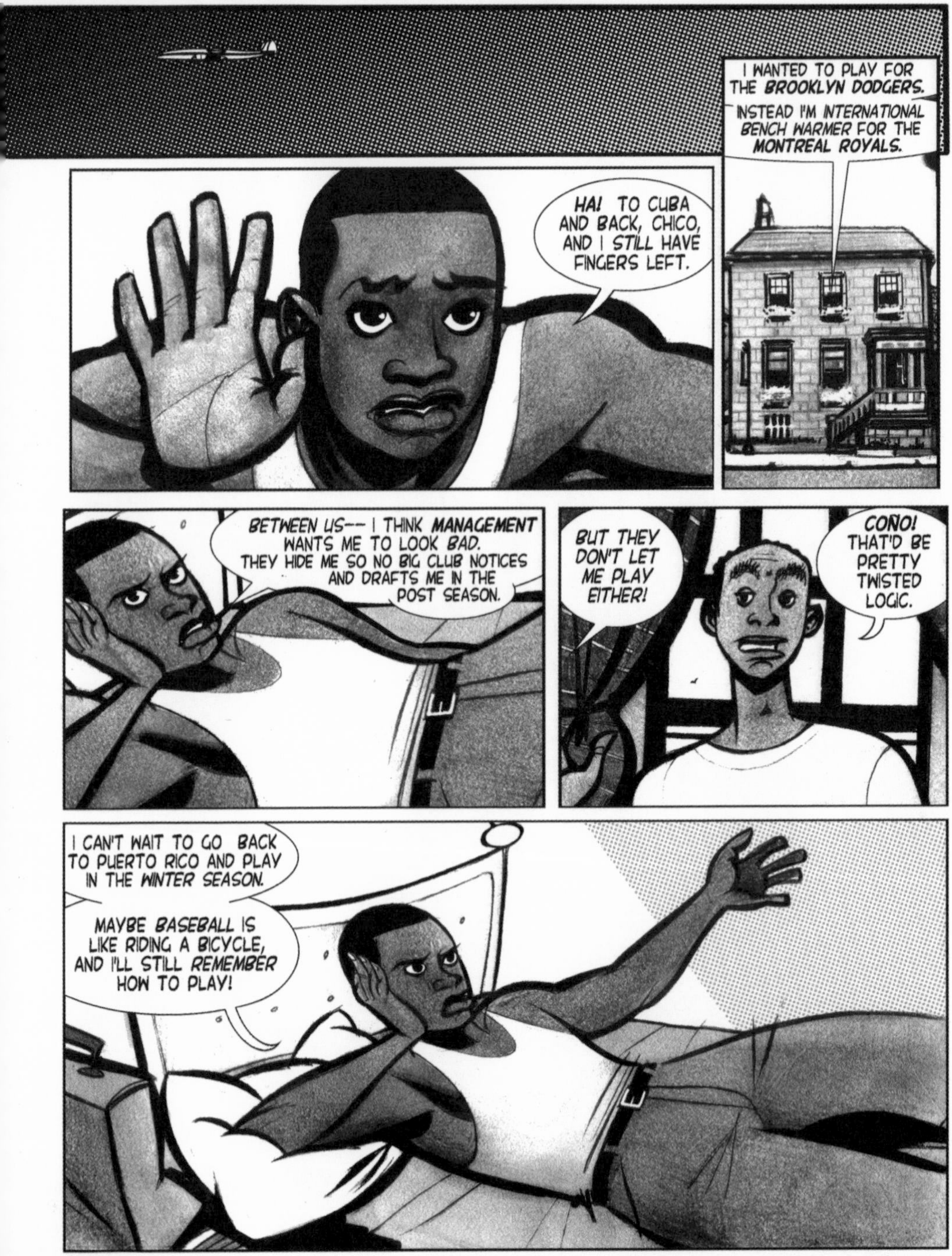
I WANTED TO PLAY FOR THE BROOKLYN DODGERS.
INSTEAD I'M INTERNATIONAL BENCH WARMER FOR THE MONTREAL ROYALS.
HA! TO CUBA AND BACK, CHICO, AND I STILL HAVE FINGERS LEFT.
BETWEEN US-- I THINK MANAGEMENT WANTS ME TO LOOK BAD. THEY HIDE ME SO NO BIG CLUB NOTICES AND DRAFTS ME IN THE POST SEASON.
BUT THEY DON'T LET ME PLAY EITHER!
COÑO! THAT'D BE PRETTY TWISTED LOGIC.
I CAN'T WAIT TO GO BACK TO PUERTO RICO AND PLAY IN THE WINTER SEASON.
MAYBE BASEBALL IS LIKE RIDING A BICYCLE, AND I'LL STILL REMEMBER HOW TO PLAY!

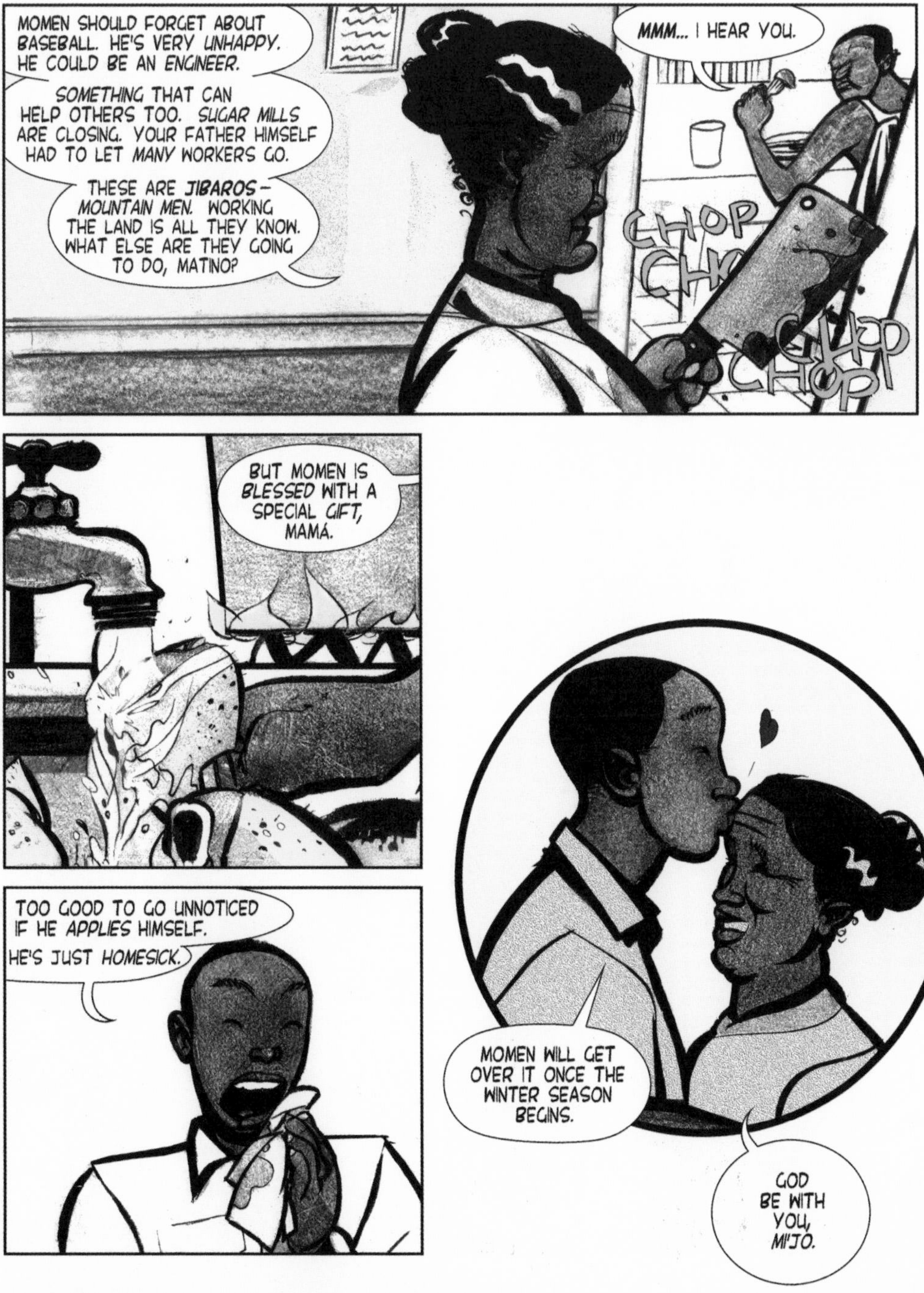
MOMEN SHOULD FORGET ABOUT BASEBALL. HE'S VERY UNHAPPY. HE COULD BE AN ENGINEER.
SOMETHING THAT CAN HELP OTHERS TOO. SUGAR MILLS ARE CLOSING. YOUR FATHER HIMSELF HAD TO LET MANY WORKERS GO.
THESE ARE JIBAROS— MOUNTAIN MEN. WORKING THE LAND IS ALL THEY KNOW. WHAT ELSE ARE THEY GOING TO DO, MATINO?
MMM... I HEAR YOU.
CHOP CHOP
CHOP CHOP
BUT MOMEN IS BLESSED WITH A SPECIAL GIFT, MAMÁ.
TOO GOOD TO GO UNNOTICED IF HE APPLIES HIMSELF.
HE'S JUST HOMESICK.
MOMEN WILL GET OVER IT ONCE THE WINTER SEASON BEGINS.
GOD BE WITH YOU, MI'JO.

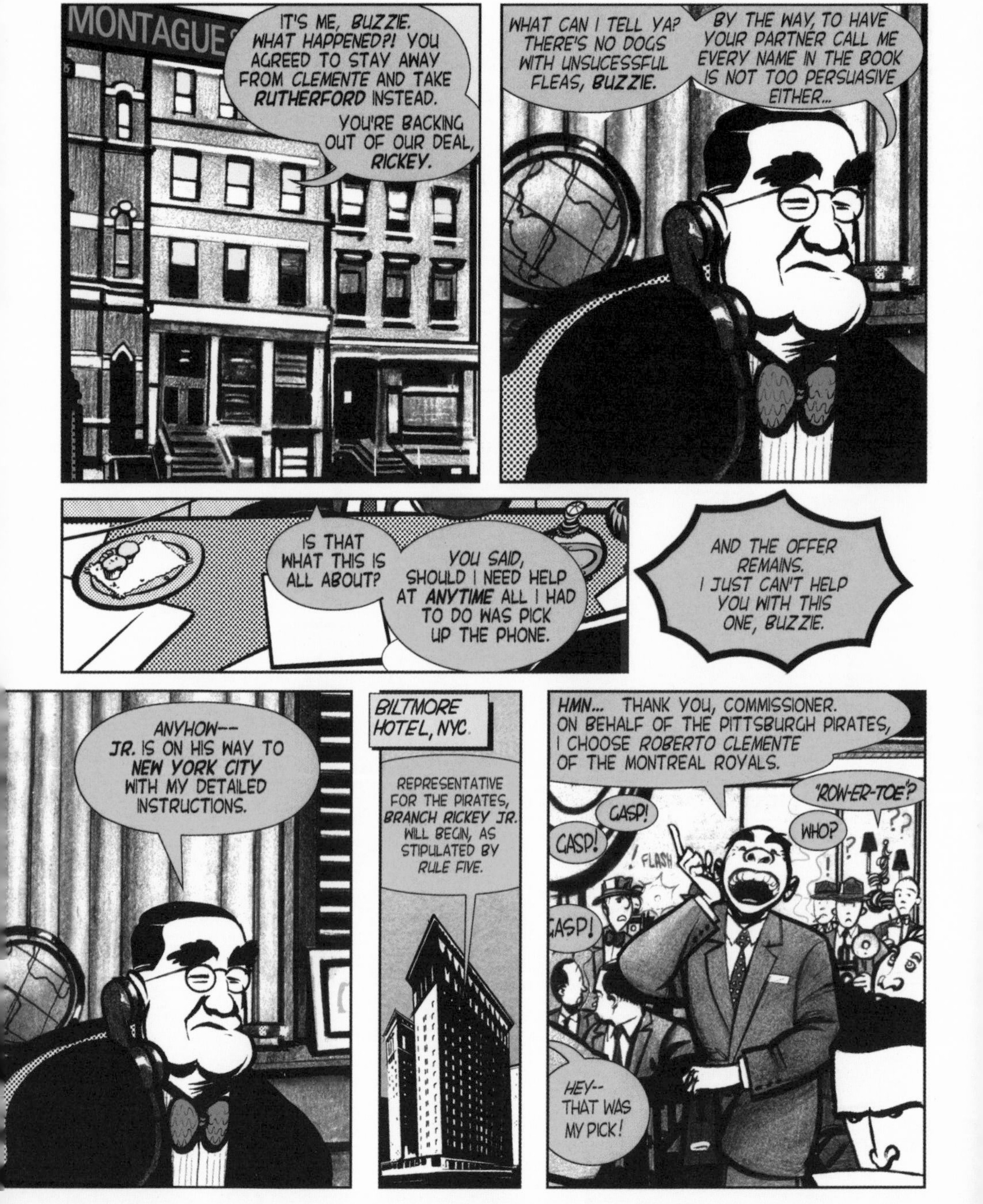
MONTAGUE
IT'S ME, BUZZIE. WHAT HAPPENED?! YOU AGREED TO STAY AWAY FROM CLEMENTE AND TAKE RUTHERFORD INSTEAD.
YOU'RE BACKING OUT OF OUR DEAL, RICKEY.
WHAT CAN I TELL YA? THERE'S NO DOGS WITH UNSUCESSFUL FLEAS, BUZZIE.
BY THE WAY, TO HAVE YOUR PARTNER CALL ME EVERY NAME IN THE BOOK IS NOT TOO PERSUASIVE EITHER...
IS THAT WHAT THIS IS ALL ABOUT?
YOU SAID, SHOULD I NEED HELP AT ANYTIME ALL I HAD TO DO WAS PICK UP THE PHONE.
AND THE OFFER REMAINS. I JUST CAN'T HELP YOU WITH THIS ONE, BUZZIE.
ANYHOW-- JR. IS ON HIS WAY TO NEW YORK CITY WITH MY DETAILED INSTRUCTIONS.
BILTMORE HOTEL, NYC.
REPRESENTATIVE FOR THE PIRATES, BRANCH RICKEY JR. WILL BEGIN, AS STIPULATED BY RULE FIVE.
HMN... THANK YOU, COMMISSIONER. ON BEHALF OF THE PITTSBURGH PIRATES, I CHOOSE ROBERTO CLEMENTE OF THE MONTREAL ROYALS.
"ROW-ER-TOE"?
GASP!
GASP!
WHO?
FLASH
GASP!
HEY-- THAT WAS MY PICK!

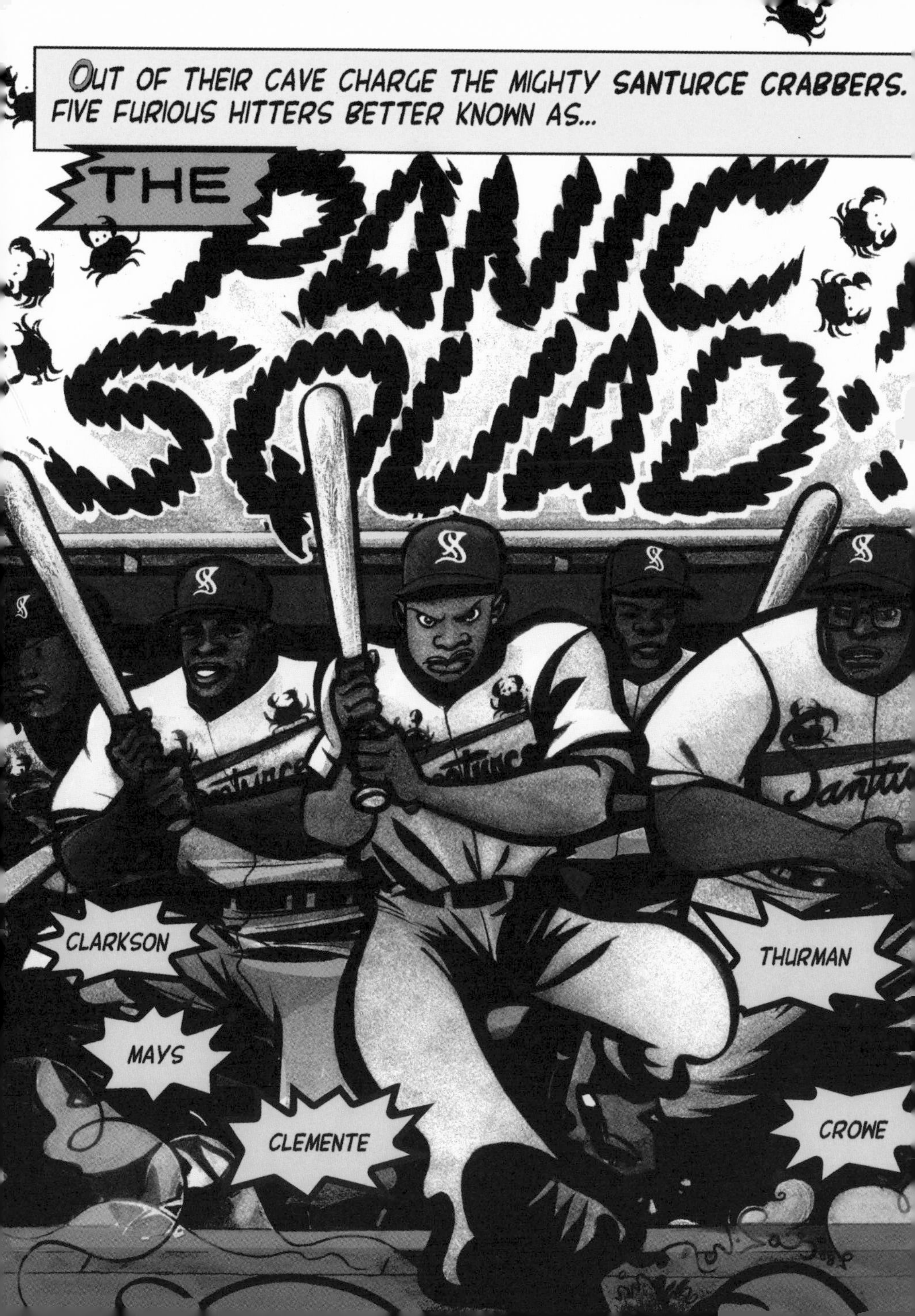
OUT OF THEIR CAVE CHARGE THE MIGHTY SANTURCE CRABBERS. FIVE FURIOUS HITTERS BETTER KNOWN AS...
THE
PANIC SQUAD!
CLARKSON
THURMAN
MAYS
CLEMENTE
CROWE

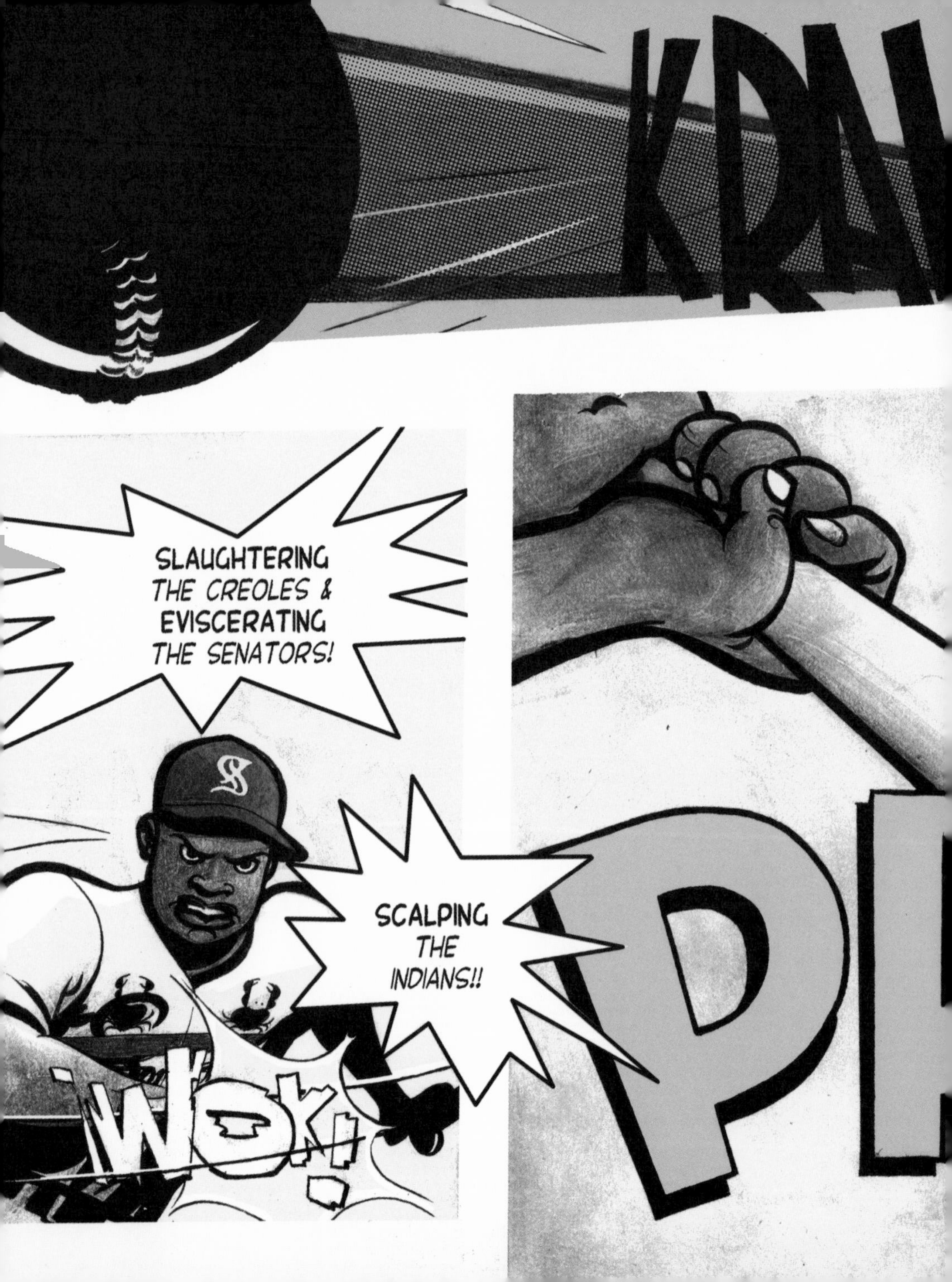
KRA
SLAUGHTERING THE CREOLES & EVISCERATING THE SENATORS!
SCALPING THE INDIANS!!
WOK!

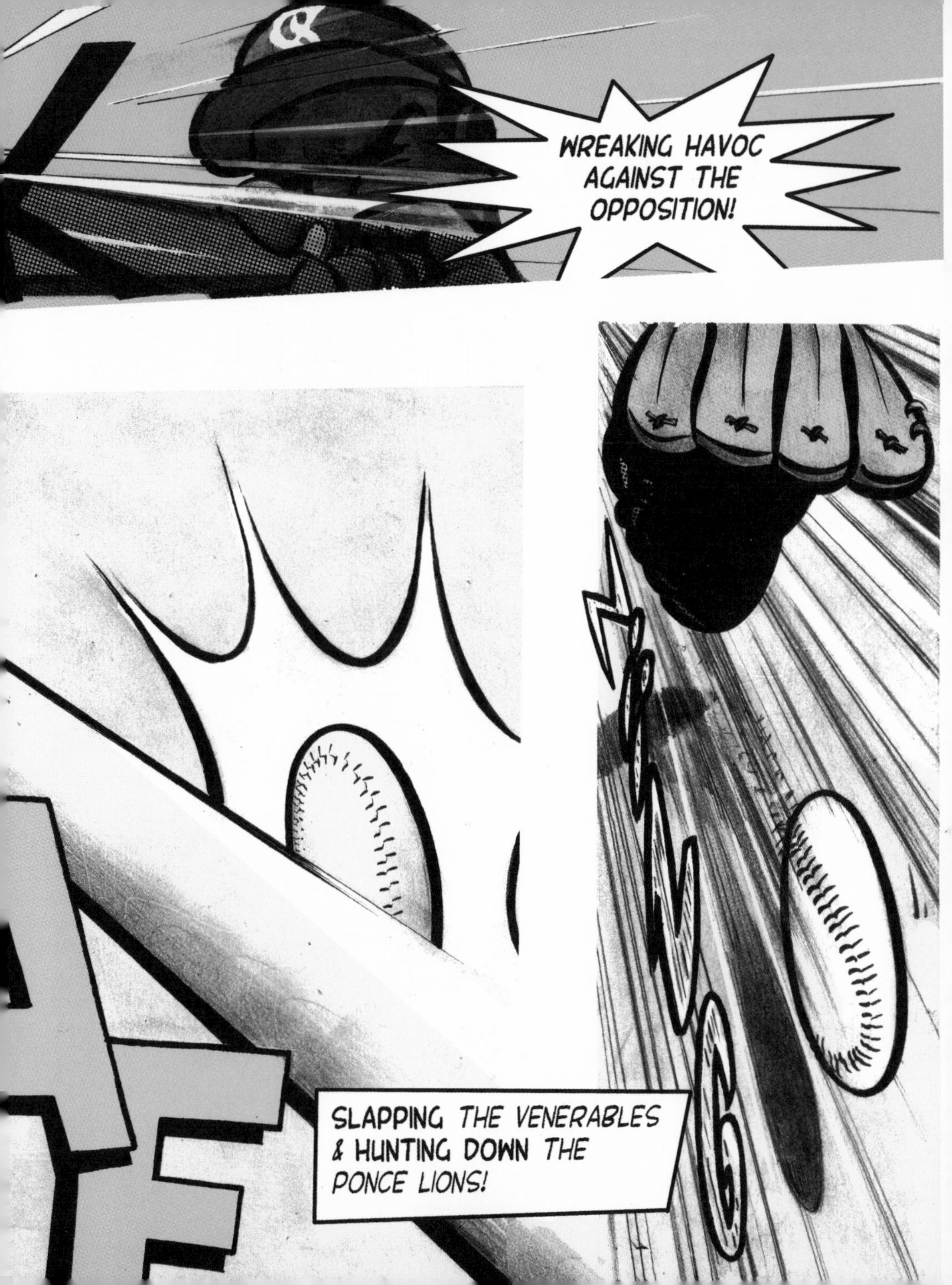
WREAKING HAVOC AGAINST THE OPPOSITION!
SLAPPING THE VENERABLES & HUNTING DOWN THE PONCE LIONS!

PONCE, PUERTO RICO.

MATINO— WHAT ARE YOU DOING HERE?

THE DOCTORS AREN'T SURE WHETHER THE TUMOR IS MALIGNANT. LUIS DECIDED TO LET THEM OPERATE ON HIM.

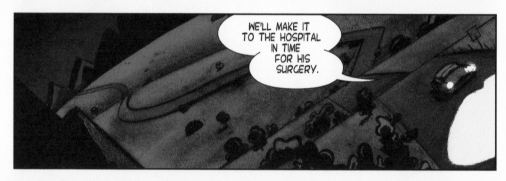

WE'LL MAKE IT TO THE HOSPITAL IN TIME FOR HIS SURGERY.

NORTH

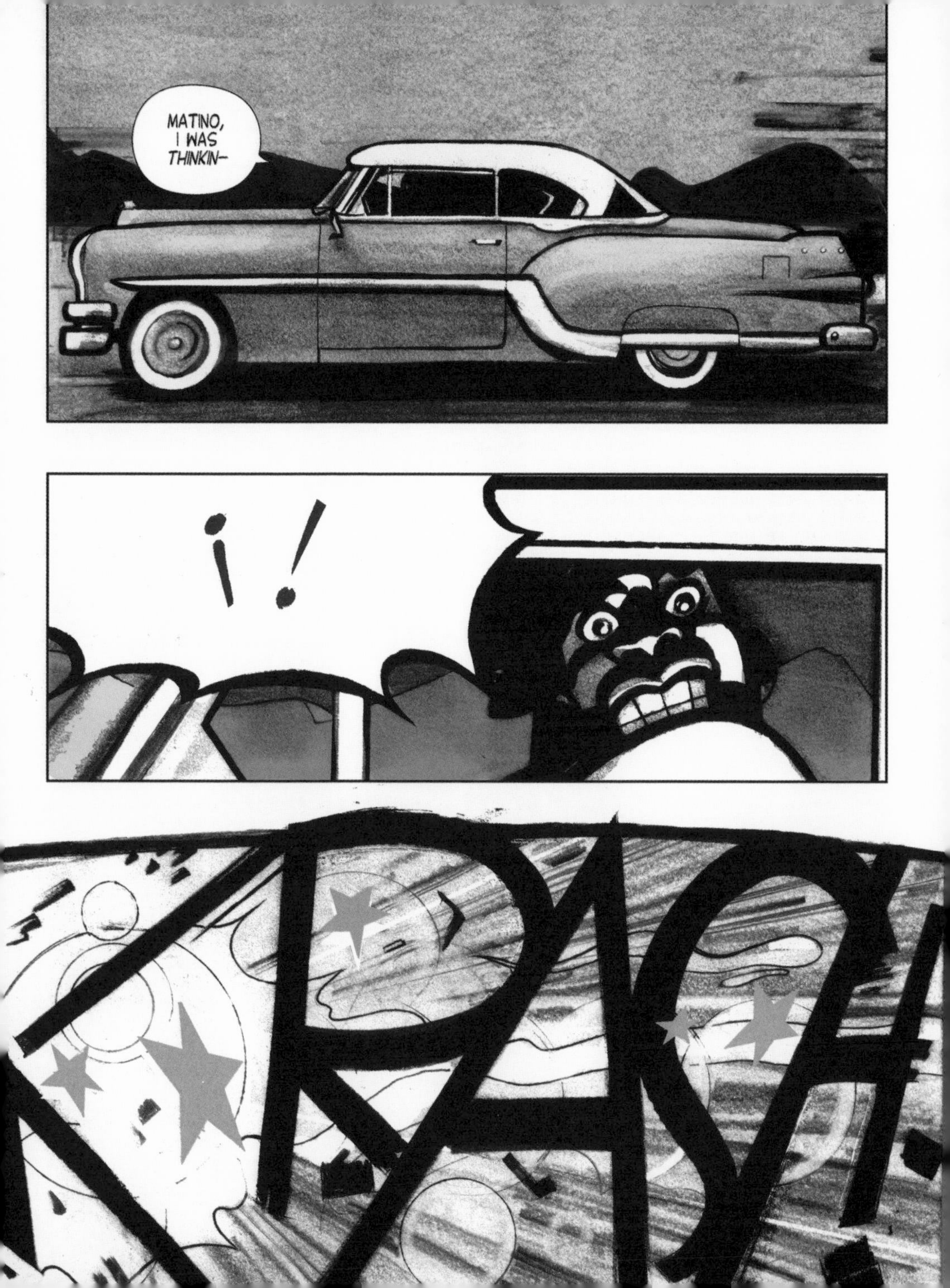
MATINO, I WAS *THINKIN*–
¡!

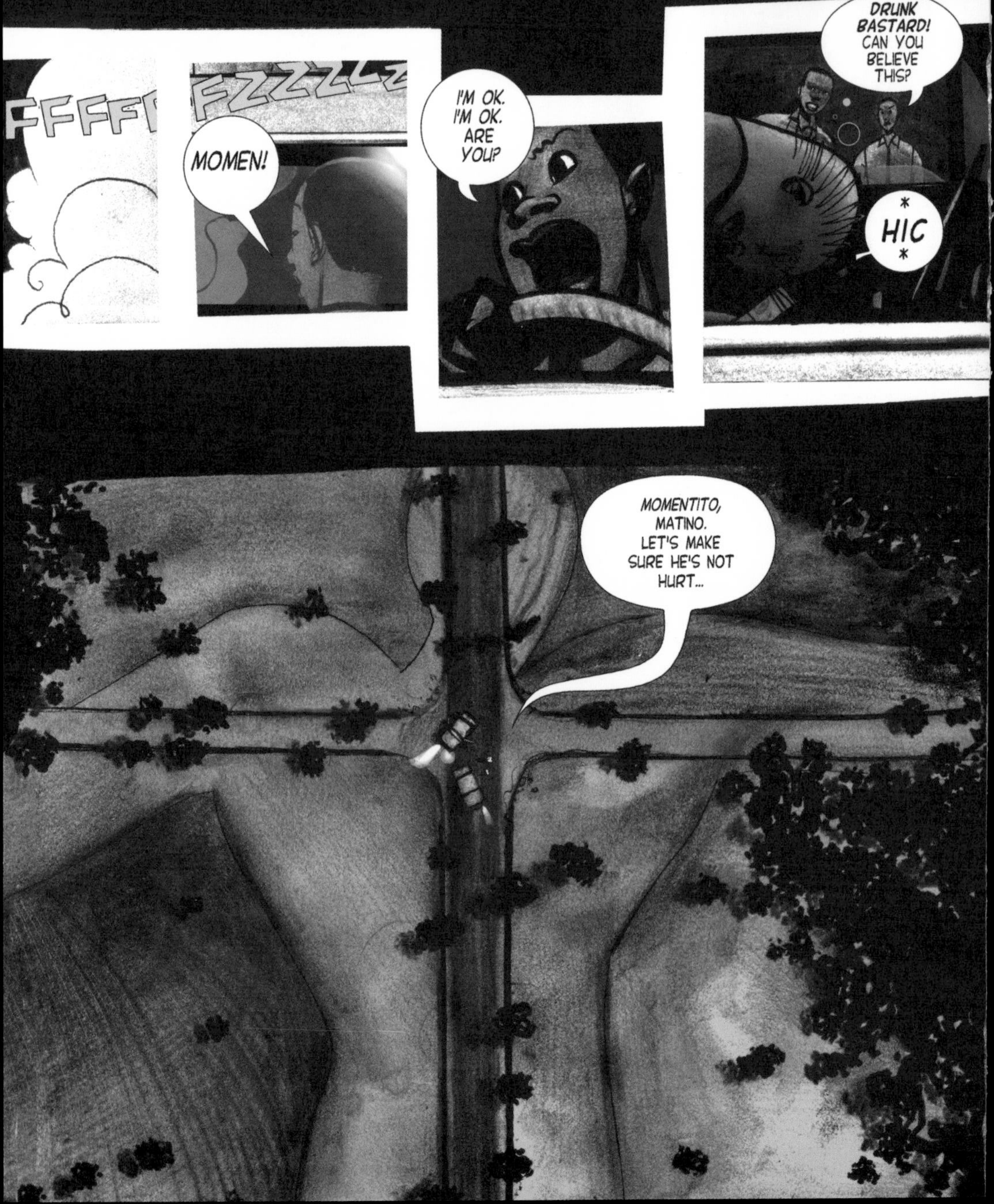
FFFFF
FZZZZZ
MOMEN!
I'M OK. I'M OK. ARE YOU?
DRUNK BASTARD! CAN YOU BELIEVE THIS?
* HIC *
MOMENTITO, MATINO. LET'S MAKE SURE HE'S NOT HURT...

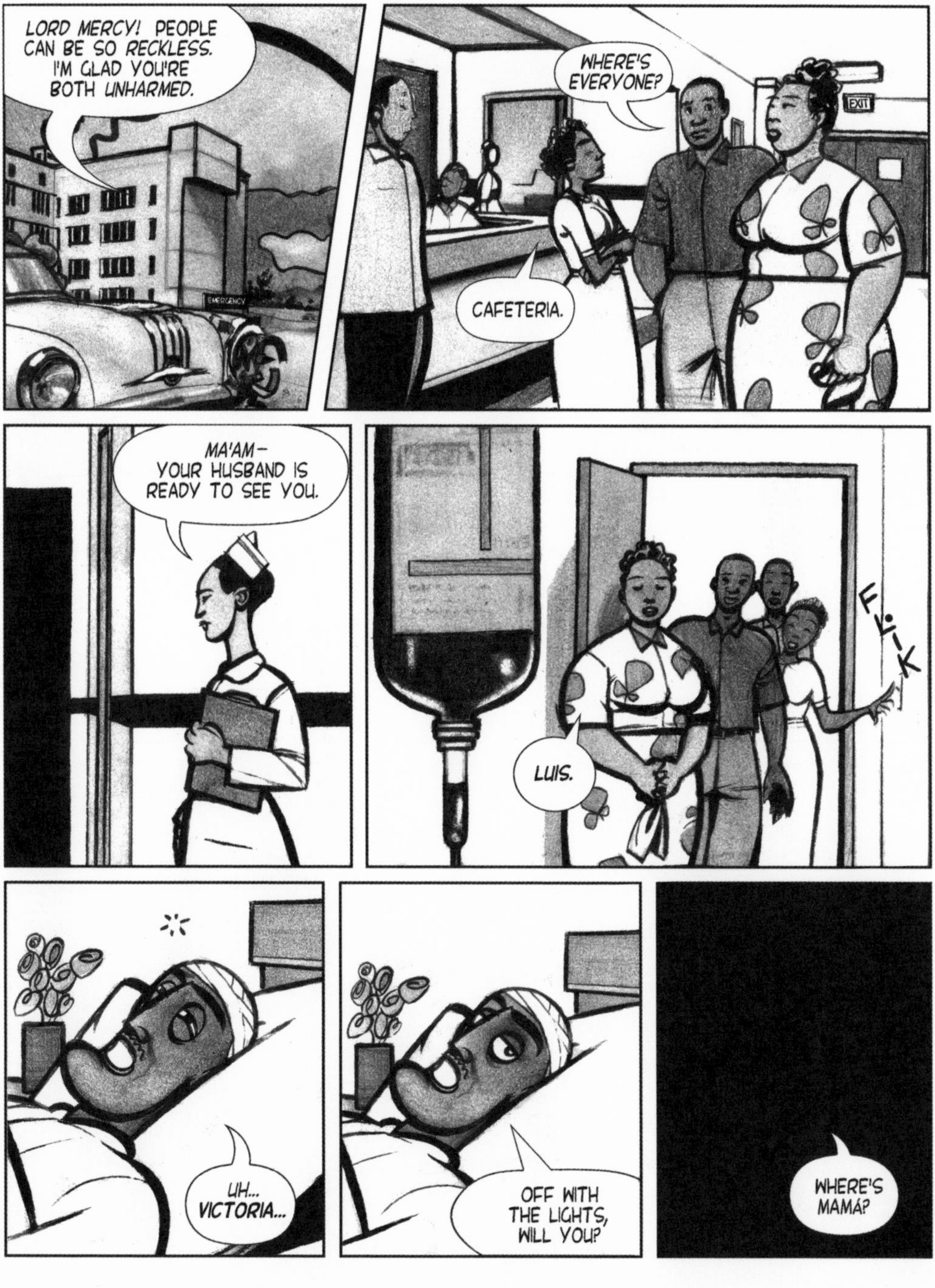
LORD MERCY! PEOPLE CAN BE SO RECKLESS. I'M GLAD YOU'RE BOTH UNHARMED.
EMERGENCY
WHERE'S EVERYONE?
EXIT
CAFETERIA.
MA'AM— YOUR HUSBAND IS READY TO SEE YOU.
LUIS.
FLIK
UH... VICTORIA...
OFF WITH THE LIGHTS, WILL YOU?
WHERE'S MAMÁ?

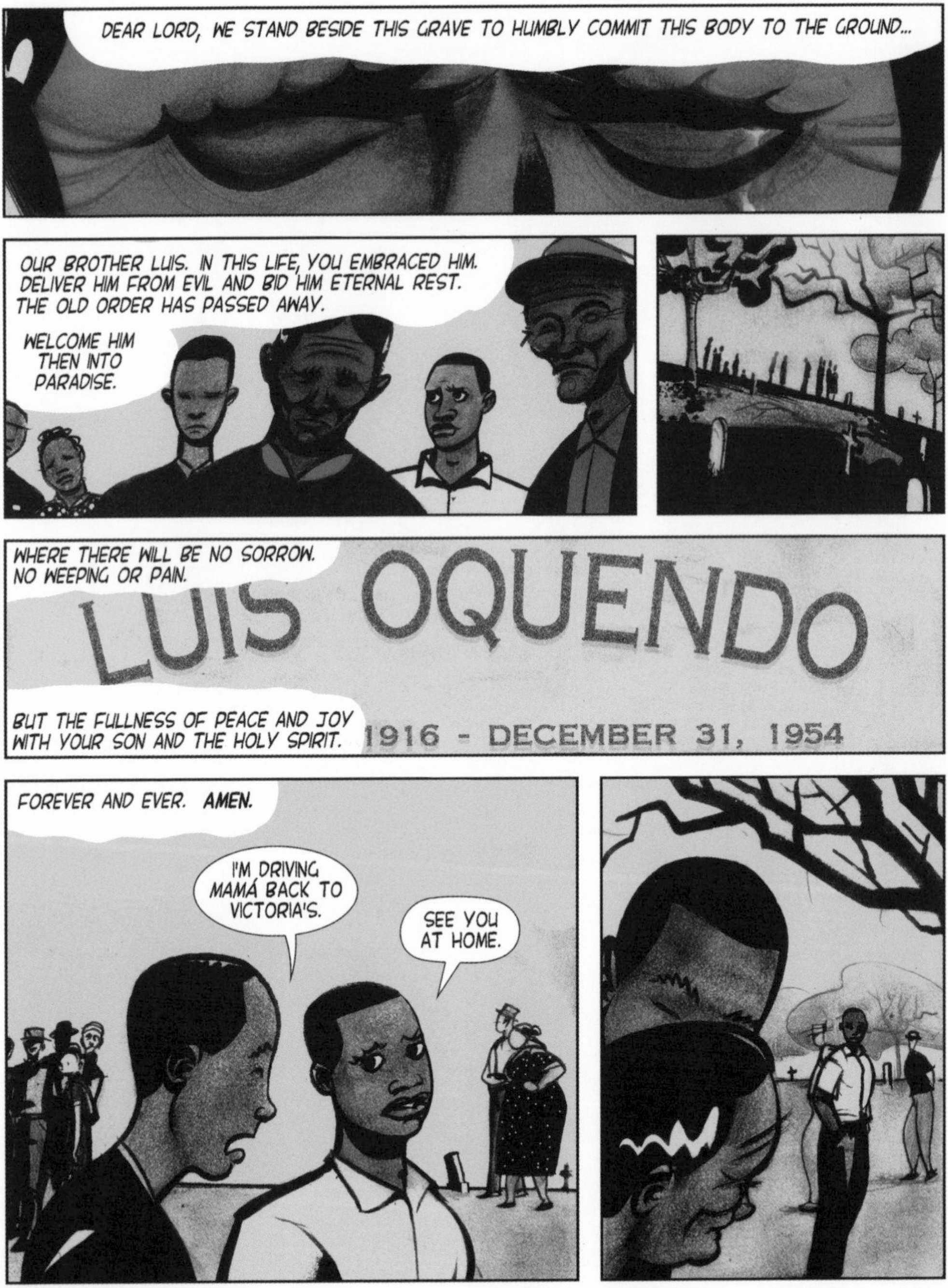
DEAR LORD, WE STAND BESIDE THIS GRAVE TO HUMBLY COMMIT THIS BODY TO THE GROUND...
OUR BROTHER LUIS. IN THIS LIFE, YOU EMBRACED HIM. DELIVER HIM FROM EVIL AND BID HIM ETERNAL REST. THE OLD ORDER HAS PASSED AWAY.
WELCOME HIM THEN INTO PARADISE.
WHERE THERE WILL BE NO SORROW. NO WEEPING OR PAIN.
LUIS OQUENDO
BUT THE FULLNESS OF PEACE AND JOY WITH YOUR SON AND THE HOLY SPIRIT.
1916 - DECEMBER 31, 1954
FOREVER AND EVER. AMEN.
I'M DRIVING MAMÁ BACK TO VICTORIA'S.
SEE YOU AT HOME.

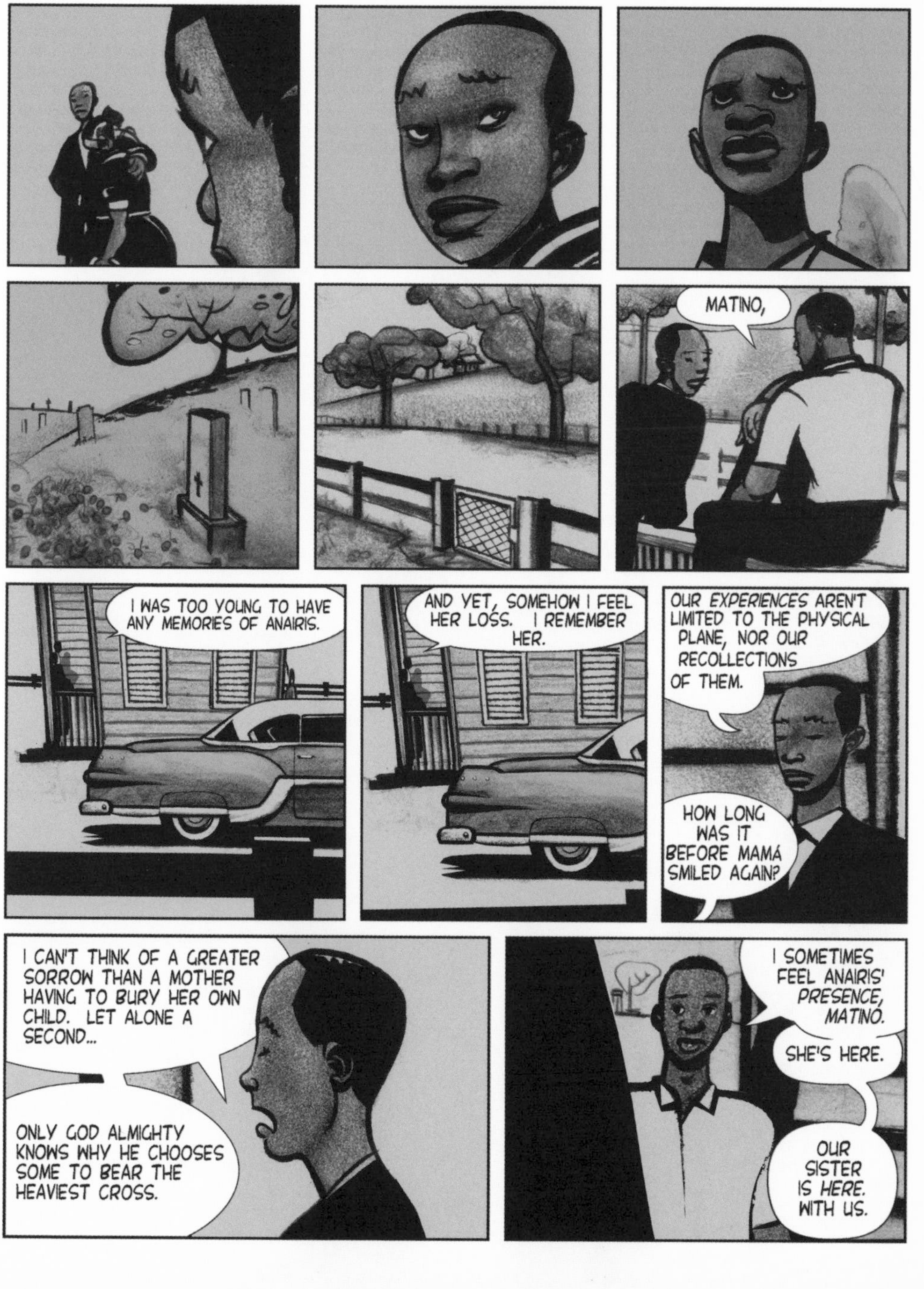
MATINO,
I WAS TOO YOUNG TO HAVE ANY MEMORIES OF ANAIRIS.
AND YET, SOMEHOW I FEEL HER LOSS. I REMEMBER HER.
OUR *EXPERIENCES* AREN'T LIMITED TO THE PHYSICAL PLANE, NOR OUR RECOLLECTIONS OF THEM.
HOW LONG WAS IT BEFORE MAMÁ SMILED AGAIN?
I CAN'T THINK OF A GREATER SORROW THAN A MOTHER HAVING TO BURY HER OWN CHILD. LET ALONE A SECOND...
ONLY GOD ALMIGHTY KNOWS WHY HE CHOOSES SOME TO BEAR THE HEAVIEST CROSS.
I SOMETIMES FEEL ANAIRIS' *PRESENCE, MATINO.*
SHE'S HERE.
OUR SISTER IS *HERE.* WITH US.

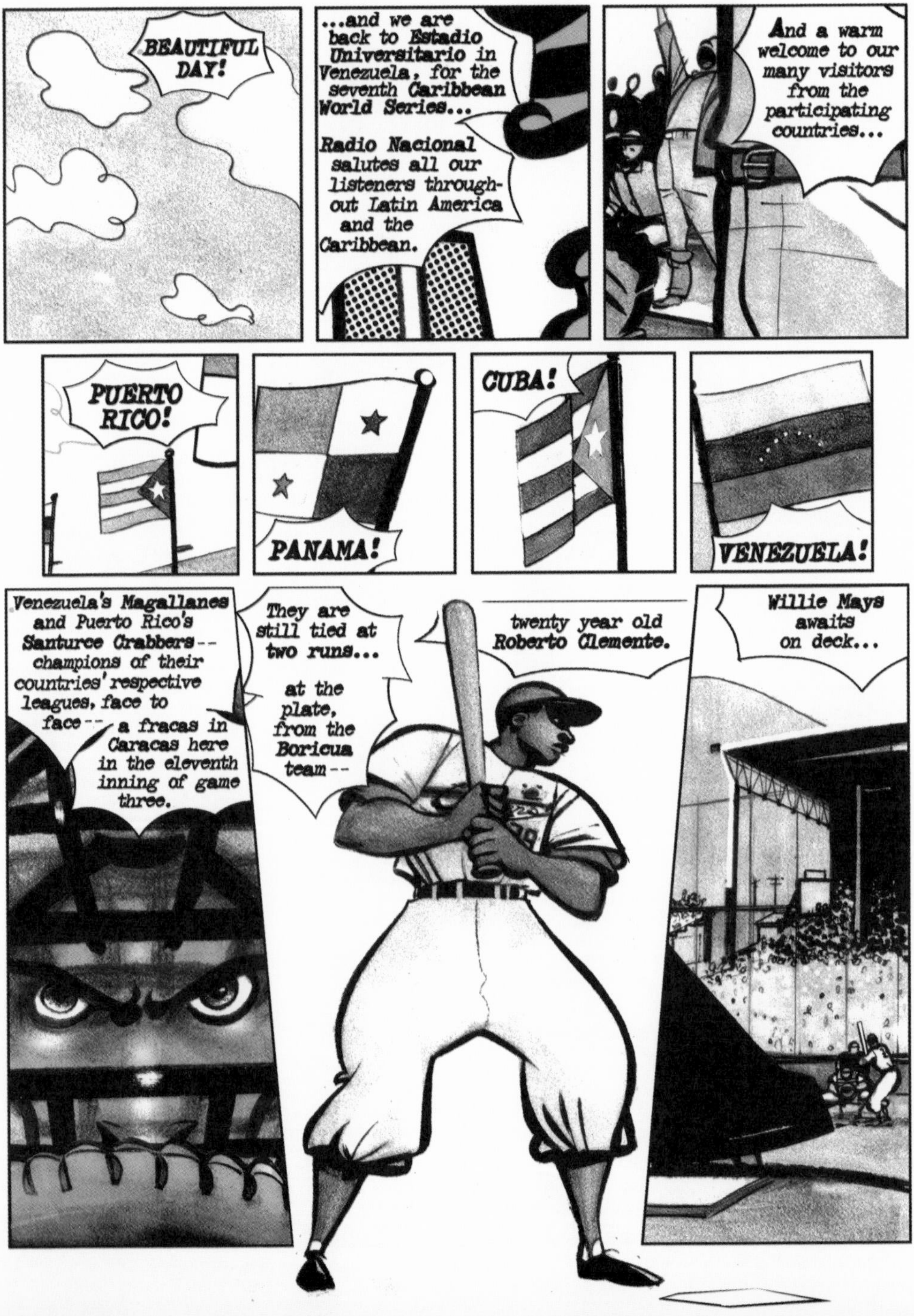
BEAUTIFUL DAY!
...and we are back to Estadio Universitario in Venezuela, for the seventh Caribbean World Series...
Radio Nacional salutes all our listeners throughout Latin America and the Caribbean.
And a warm welcome to our many visitors from the participating countries...
PUERTO RICO!
PANAMA!
CUBA!
VENEZUELA!
Venezuela's Magallanes and Puerto Rico's Santurce Crabbers--champions of their countries' respective leagues, face to face--a fracas in Caracas here in the eleventh inning of game three.
They are still tied at two runs...
at the plate, from the Boricua team--
twenty year old Roberto Clemente.
Willie Mays awaits on deck...

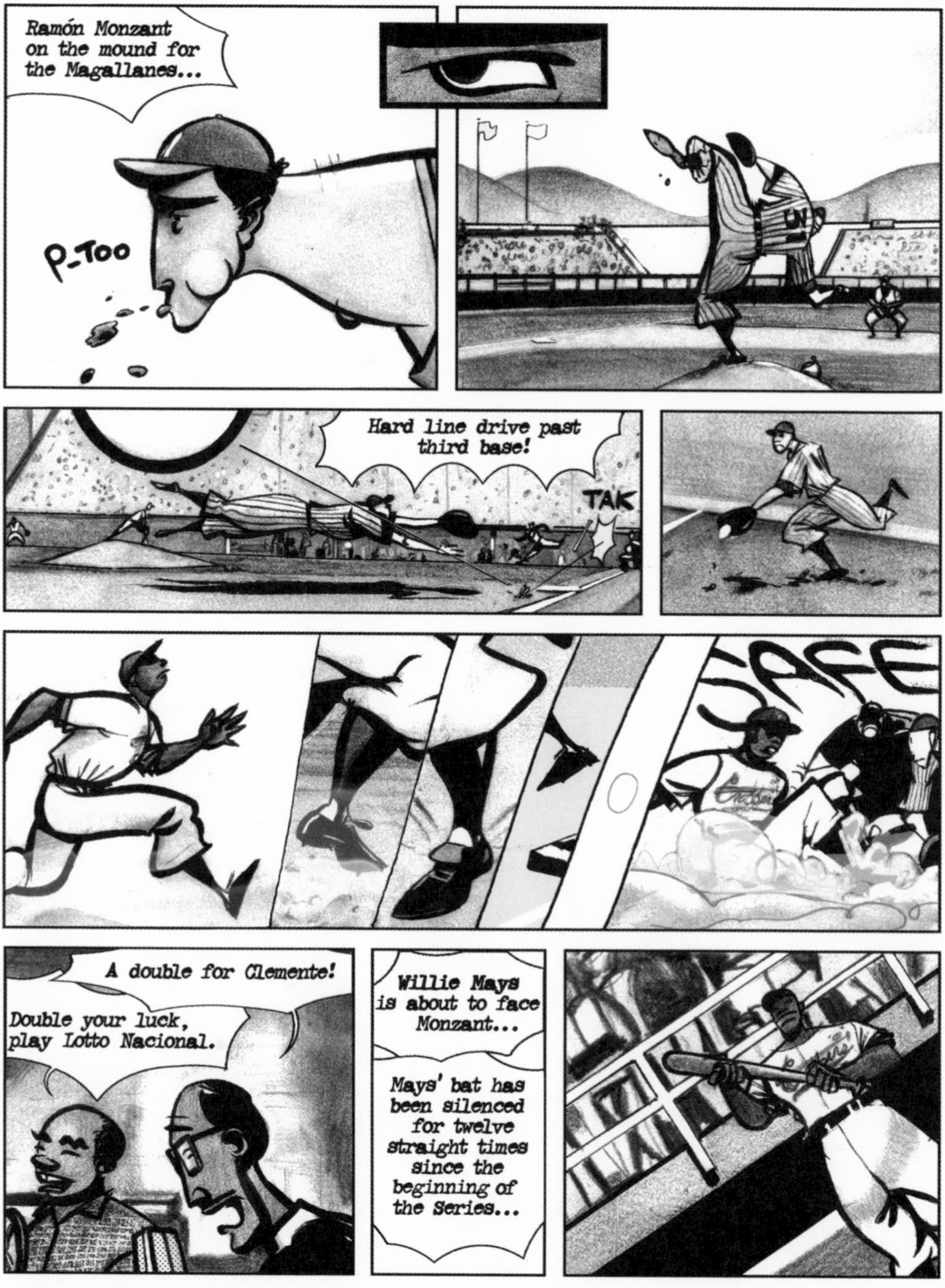
Ramón Monzant on the mound for the Magallanes...
P-TOO
Hard line drive past third base!
TAK
SAFE
A double for Clemente!
Double your luck, play Lotto Nacional.
Willie Mays is about to face Monzant...
Mays' bat has been silenced for twelve straight times since the beginning of the Series...

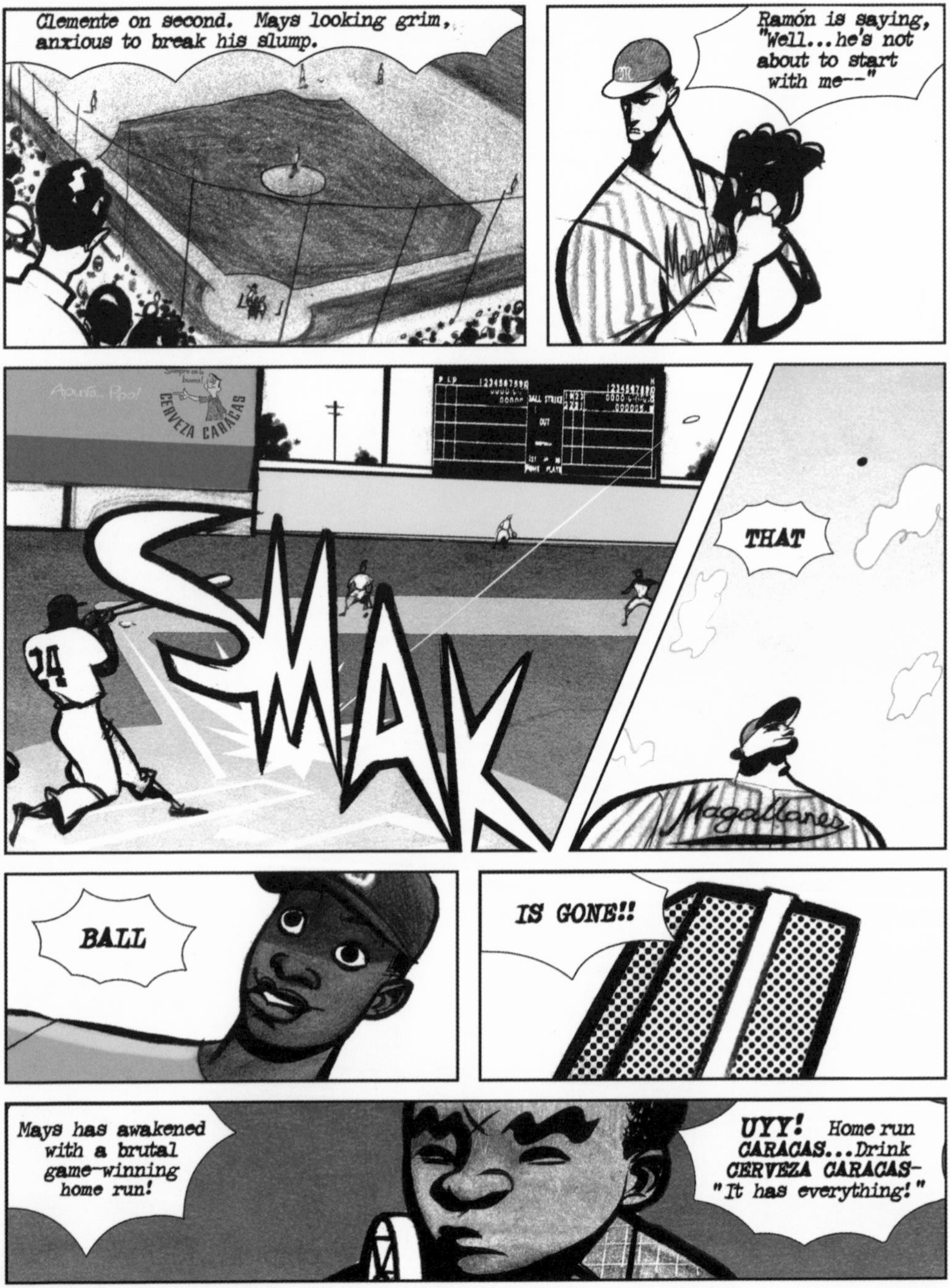
Clemente on second. Mays looking grim, anxious to break his slump.
Ramón is saying, "Well...he's not about to start with me--"
CERVEZA CARACAS
SMAK
THAT
Magallanes
BALL
IS GONE!!
Mays has awakened with a brutal game-winning home run!
UYY! Home run CARACAS...Drink CERVEZA CARACAS- "It has everything!"

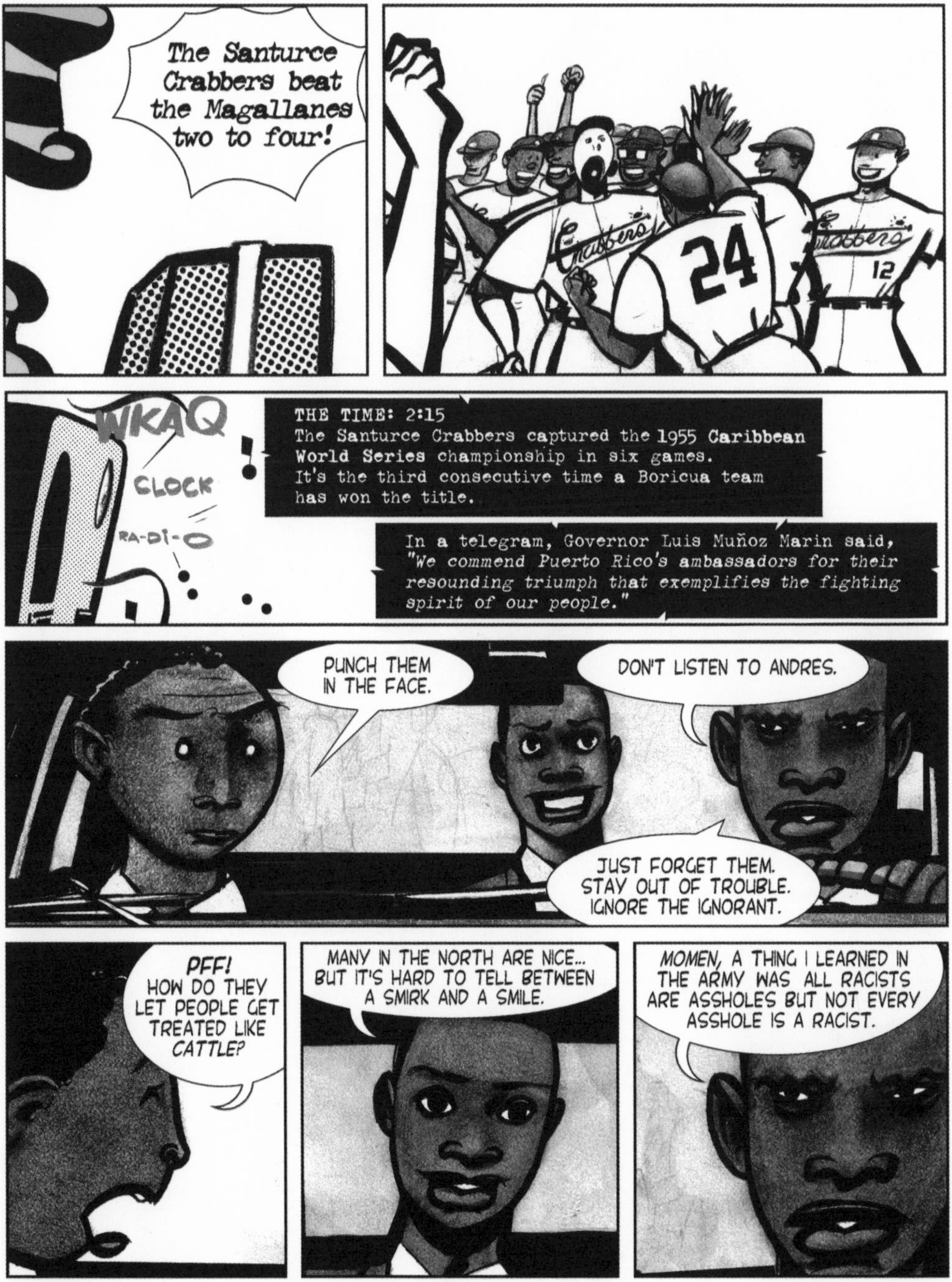
The Santurce Crabbers beat the Magallanes two to four!
Crabbers
24
Crabbers
12
WKAQ
CLOCK
RA-DI-O
THE TIME: 2:15
The Santurce Crabbers captured the 1955 Caribbean World Series championship in six games.
It's the third consecutive time a Boricua team has won the title.
In a telegram, Governor Luis Muñoz Marin said, *"We commend Puerto Rico's ambassadors for their resounding triumph that exemplifies the fighting spirit of our people."*
PUNCH THEM IN THE FACE.
DON'T LISTEN TO ANDRES.
JUST FORGET THEM. STAY OUT OF TROUBLE. IGNORE THE IGNORANT.
PFF! HOW DO THEY LET PEOPLE GET TREATED LIKE CATTLE?
MANY IN THE NORTH ARE NICE... BUT IT'S HARD TO TELL BETWEEN A SMIRK AND A SMILE.
MOMEN, A THING I LEARNED IN THE ARMY WAS ALL RACISTS ARE ASSHOLES BUT NOT EVERY ASSHOLE IS A RACIST.

FORT MYERS,
FLORIDA.

WELCOME TO
TERRY PARK

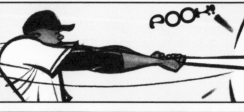

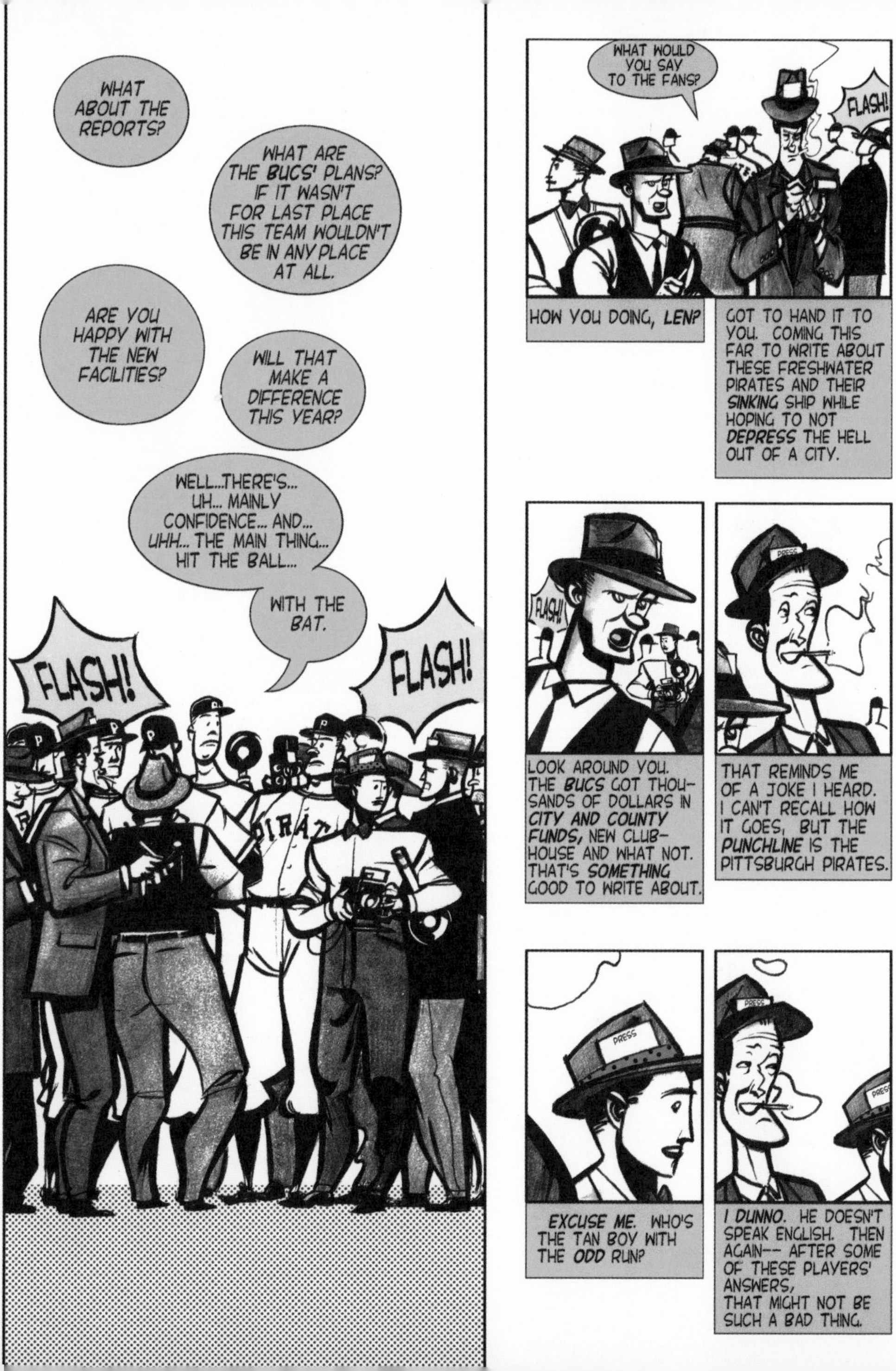
WHAT ABOUT THE REPORTS?
WHAT ARE THE BUCS' PLANS? IF IT WASN'T FOR LAST PLACE THIS TEAM WOULDN'T BE IN ANY PLACE AT ALL.
ARE YOU HAPPY WITH THE NEW FACILITIES?
WILL THAT MAKE A DIFFERENCE THIS YEAR?
WELL...THERE'S... UH... MAINLY CONFIDENCE... AND... UHH... THE MAIN THING... HIT THE BALL...
WITH THE BAT.
FLASH!
FLASH!
WHAT WOULD YOU SAY TO THE FANS?
FLASH!
HOW YOU DOING, LEN?
GOT TO HAND IT TO YOU. COMING THIS FAR TO WRITE ABOUT THESE FRESHWATER PIRATES AND THEIR SINKING SHIP WHILE HOPING TO NOT DEPRESS THE HELL OUT OF A CITY.
FLASH!
LOOK AROUND YOU. THE BUCS GOT THOUSANDS OF DOLLARS IN CITY AND COUNTY FUNDS, NEW CLUBHOUSE AND WHAT NOT. THAT'S SOMETHING GOOD TO WRITE ABOUT.
PRESS
THAT REMINDS ME OF A JOKE I HEARD. I CAN'T RECALL HOW IT GOES, BUT THE PUNCHLINE IS THE PITTSBURGH PIRATES.
PRESS
PRESS
PRESS
EXCUSE ME. WHO'S THE TAN BOY WITH THE ODD RUN?
I DUNNO. HE DOESN'T SPEAK ENGLISH. THEN AGAIN-- AFTER SOME OF THESE PLAYERS' ANSWERS, THAT MIGHT NOT BE SUCH A BAD THING.

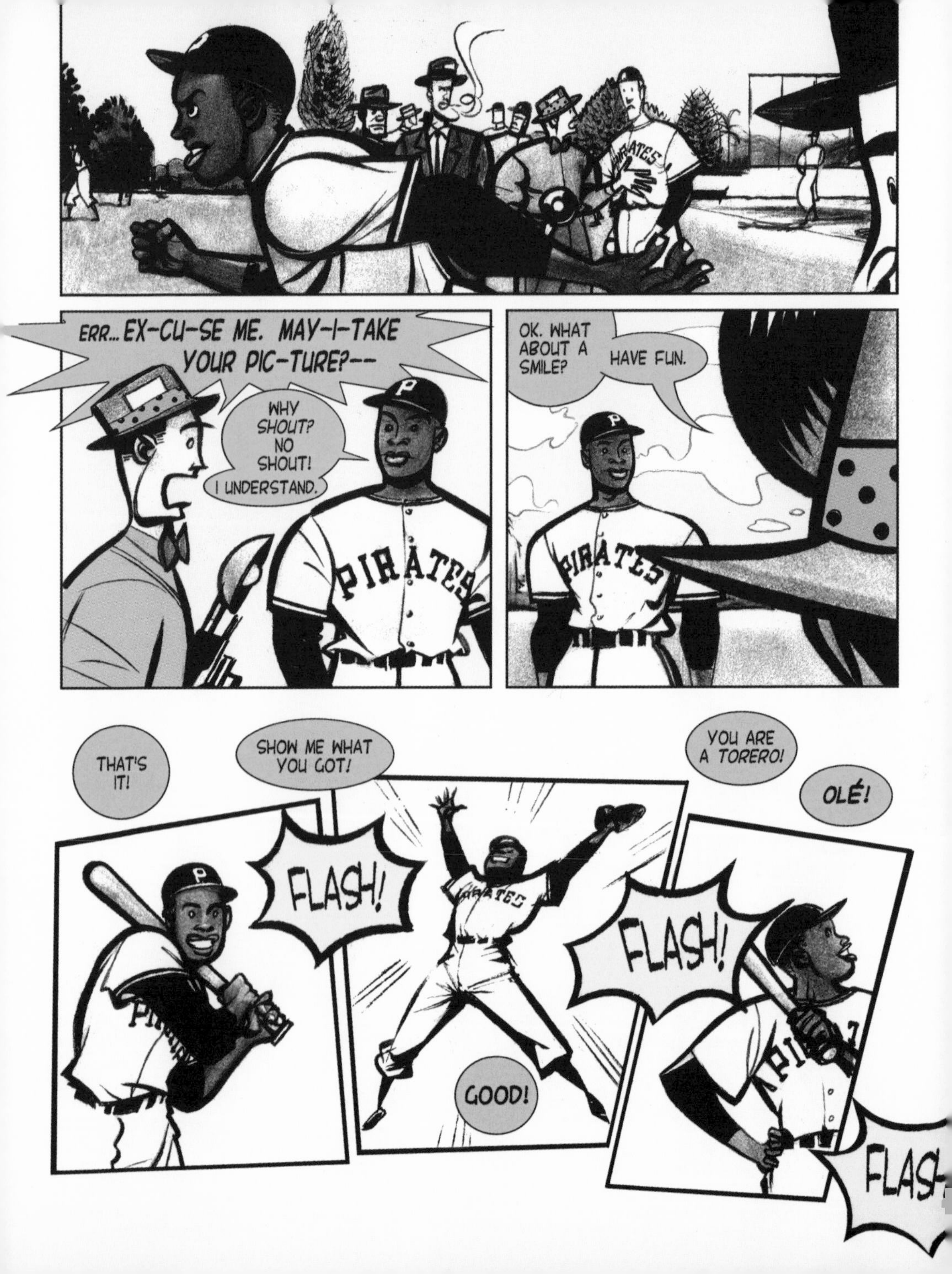
ERR... EX-CU-SE ME. MAY-I-TAKE YOUR PIC-TURE?--
WHY SHOUT? NO SHOUT! I UNDERSTAND.
OK. WHAT ABOUT A SMILE?
HAVE FUN.
THAT'S IT!
SHOW ME WHAT YOU GOT!
YOU ARE A TORERO!
OLÉ!
FLASH!
GOOD!
FLASH!
PIRATES

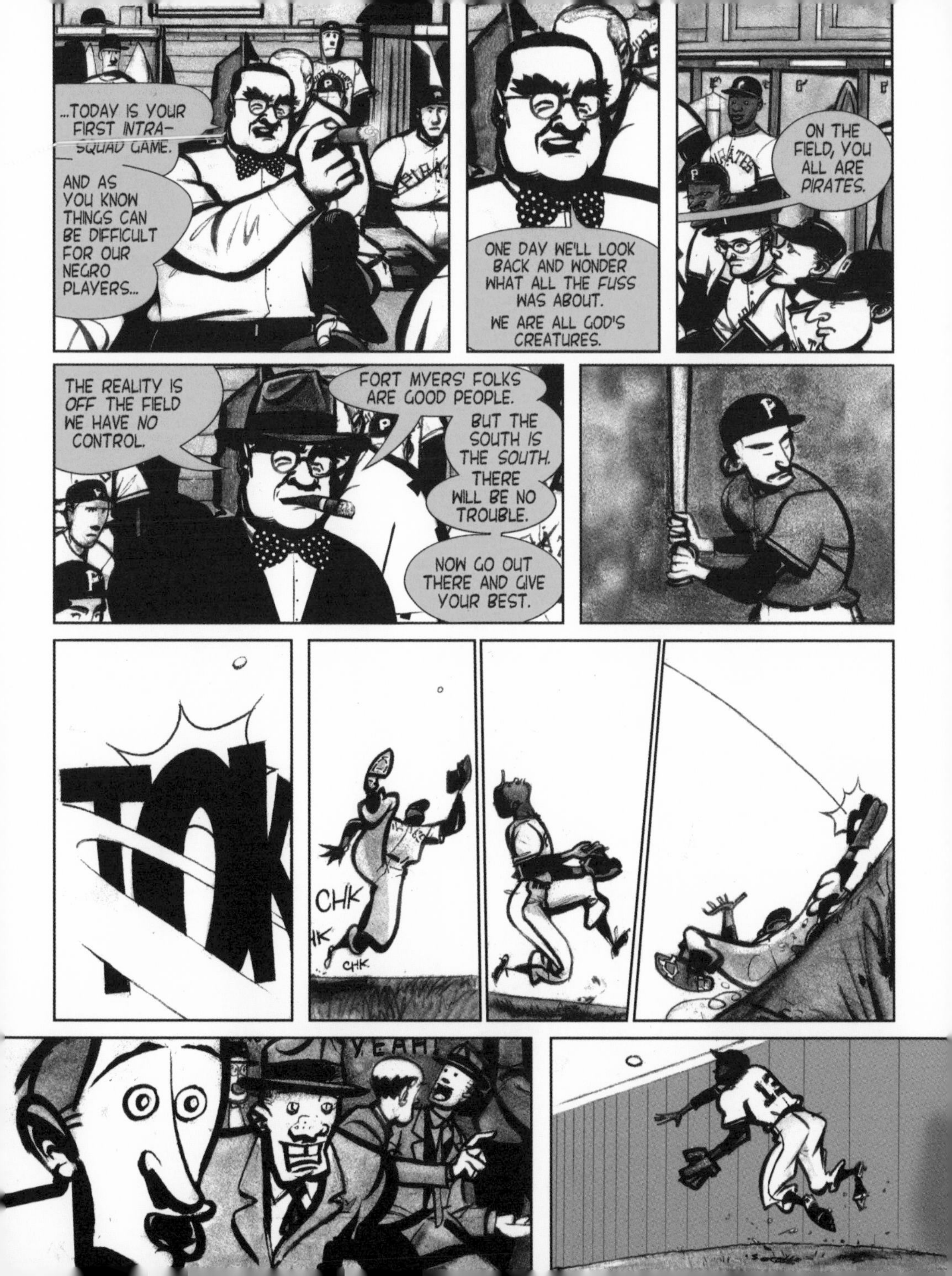

...TODAY IS YOUR FIRST INTRA-SQUAD GAME.
AND AS YOU KNOW THINGS CAN BE DIFFICULT FOR OUR NEGRO PLAYERS...
ONE DAY WE'LL LOOK BACK AND WONDER WHAT ALL THE FUSS WAS ABOUT.
WE ARE ALL GOD'S CREATURES.
ON THE FIELD, YOU ALL ARE PIRATES.
THE REALITY IS OFF THE FIELD WE HAVE NO CONTROL.
FORT MYERS' FOLKS ARE GOOD PEOPLE.
BUT THE SOUTH IS THE SOUTH.
THERE WILL BE NO TROUBLE.
NOW GO OUT THERE AND GIVE YOUR BEST.
TOK
CHK
HK
CHK
YEAH!

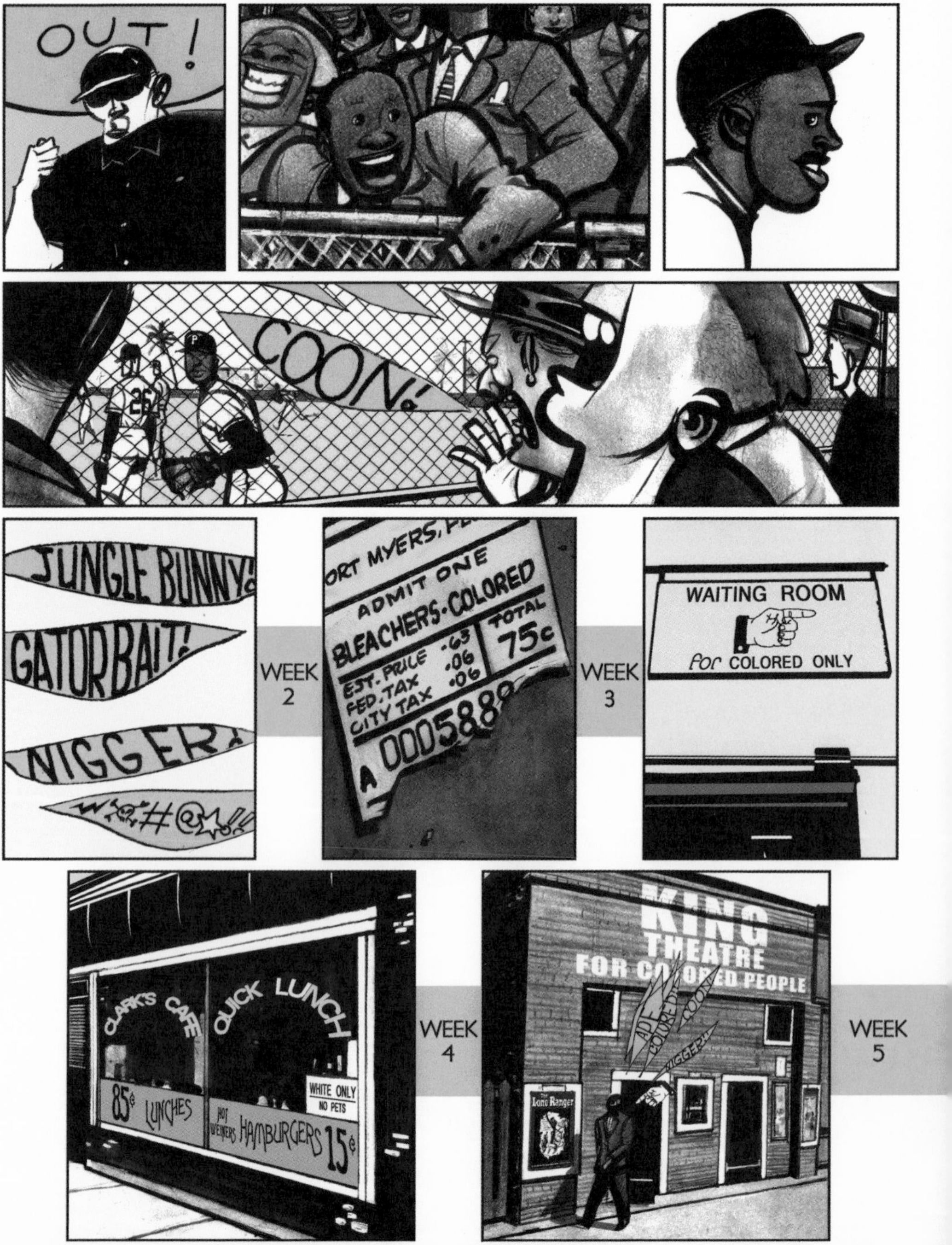
OUT!
COON!
JUNGLE BUNNY!
GATOR BAIT!
NIGGER!
ADMIT ONE
BLEACHERS-COLORED
TOTAL 75¢
EST. PRICE .63
FED. TAX .06
CITY TAX .06
A 00058
WEEK 2
WAITING ROOM
for COLORED ONLY
WEEK 3
CLARK'S CAFE
QUICK LUNCH
85¢ LUNCHES
HOT WEINERS HAMBURGERS 15¢
WHITE ONLY
NO PETS
WEEK 4
KING THEATRE
FOR COLORED PEOPLE
The Lone Ranger
NIGGER!!
WEEK 5

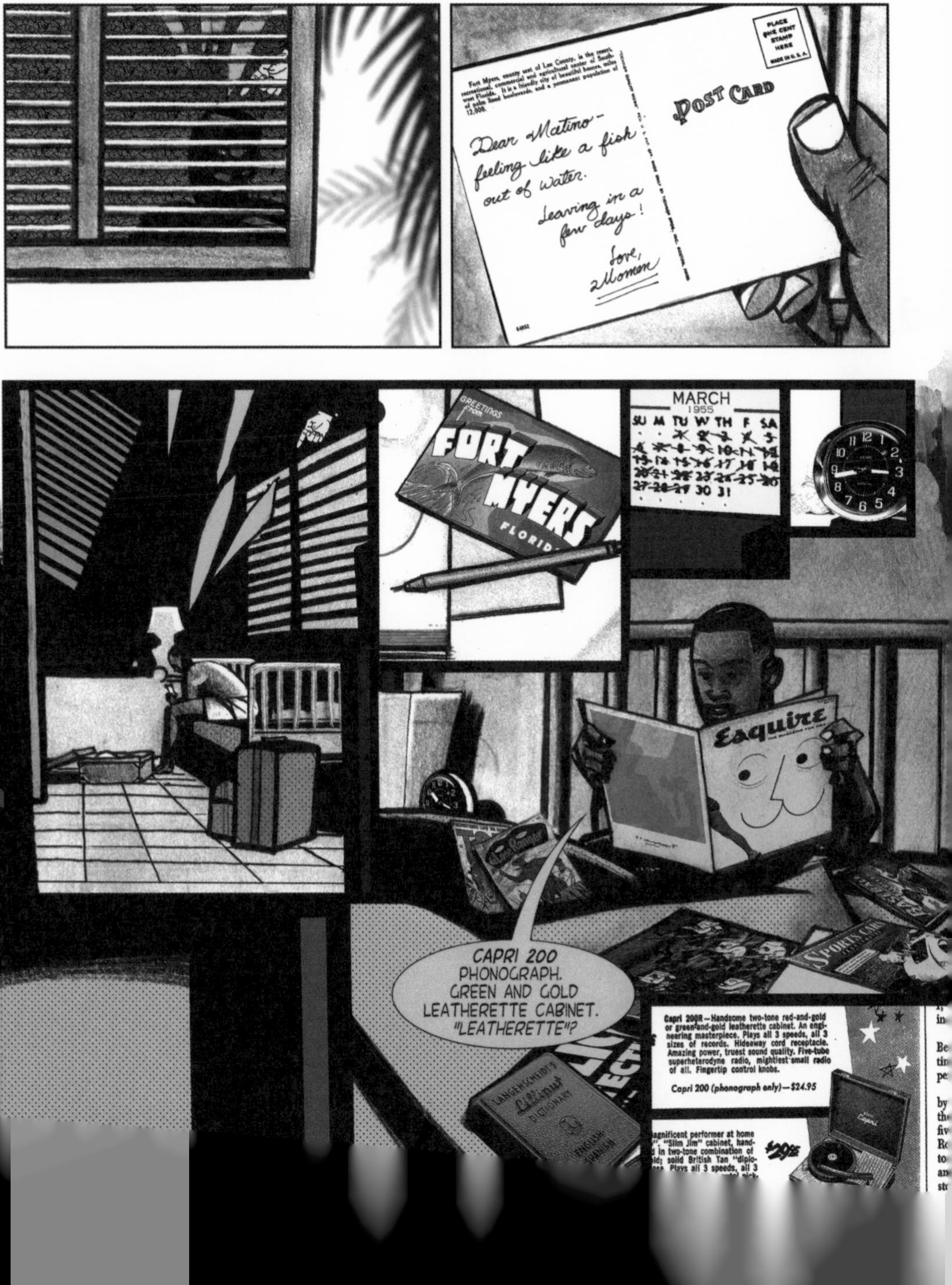

Fort Myers, county seat of Lee County, is the resort, recreational, commercial and agricultural center of Southwest Florida. It is a friendly city of beautiful homes, miles of palm lined boulevards, and a permanent population of 12,000.
PLACE ONE CENT STAMP HERE
MADE IN U. S. A.
POST CARD
Dear Matino—
feeling like a fish out of water.
Leaving in a few days!
Love,
2Momen
GREETINGS FROM FORT MYERS FLORIDA
MARCH 1955
SU M TU W TH F SA
30 31
Esquire
CAPRI 200
PHONOGRAPH.
GREEN AND GOLD
LEATHERETTE CABINET.
"LEATHERETTE"?
Capri 200R—Handsome two-tone red-and-gold or green-and-gold leatherette cabinet. An engineering masterpiece. Plays all 3 speeds, all 3 sizes of records. Hideaway cord receptacle. Amazing power, truest sound quality. Five-tube superheterodyne radio, mightiest small radio of all. Fingertip control knobs.
Capri 200 (phonograph only)—$24.95
LANGENSCHEIDT'S Lilliput DICTIONARY ENGLISH-SPANISH
SPORTS CARS

HOW TO LEARN BY EAR. AWAKE AND ASLEEP. LEARN A LANGUAGE. CORRECT YOUR SPEECH-- OHH!
squire
THE MAGAZINE FOR MEN
ers, Inc.
$H^2 = A^2 + B^2$
N Science
ws you how to
rn by "EAR"
ladies & gentlemen...
YOU CAN LEARN AWAKE AND ASLEEP
at last, science gives you an easy shortcut to learning. With this
ing new tool, you "start" to learn while awake—then the university-
d Dormiphone takes over, continues the learning process for you while
o off to sleep. Do you want to learn a language—Memorize a speech
important facts, figures, formulae—Correct your speech—
UNIVERSITY TESTED DORMIPHONE...
7-0830
ST
We g
text
Libr
law
the
eas
"L
WAT
Swea
shop
prev
ONE GREAT ENTERTAINER SALUTES ANOTHER!
"It's ENGLISH for Me Every Time... Everywhere!"
says BOB HOPE
Color by TECHNICOLOR
ALL-NEW Sonic
the city
The ENGLISH
though
ourg's
Wlour great
tou
giant inflatable toys of pre-historic monsters
ENGLISH!
DINOSAU
$1
4 fee
these fun-
monsters to
always lan
Made of m
quality l
pletely infla
genuine toss
action, Thrill to
cinating names
Plateosaurus -
Protocerat
Tritasnapa
Sphenacondon -
Ceratosau
Each set contai
DINOSAURS for
plus 25c pos
handling per set.
child can receiv
different
-historic
nsters
exciting gift a
Back Guarantee. In ordering plea
name and address.
ENGLISH!
ENGLISH!
Paratroopers! Sportsmen!! If you want the last word in comfort and foot protection, wear genuine Corcoran Paratroop Boots
.95 pr. ppd.
Blancey St., NYC
9.95
for HEALTH and FIGURE
ENGLISH!
acquire the "secrets" of fluent conversation.
words are the tools of thought.
amazing personal achievements.
FREE BOOKLET
Good English pays off
No salesman will call—
no obligation.

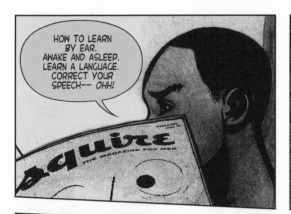

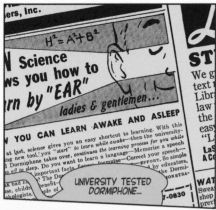

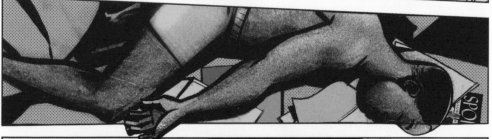

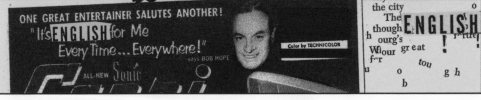

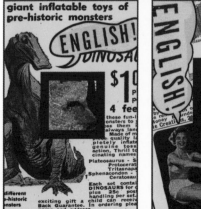

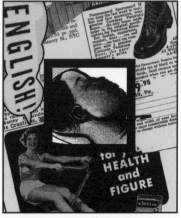

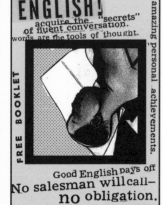

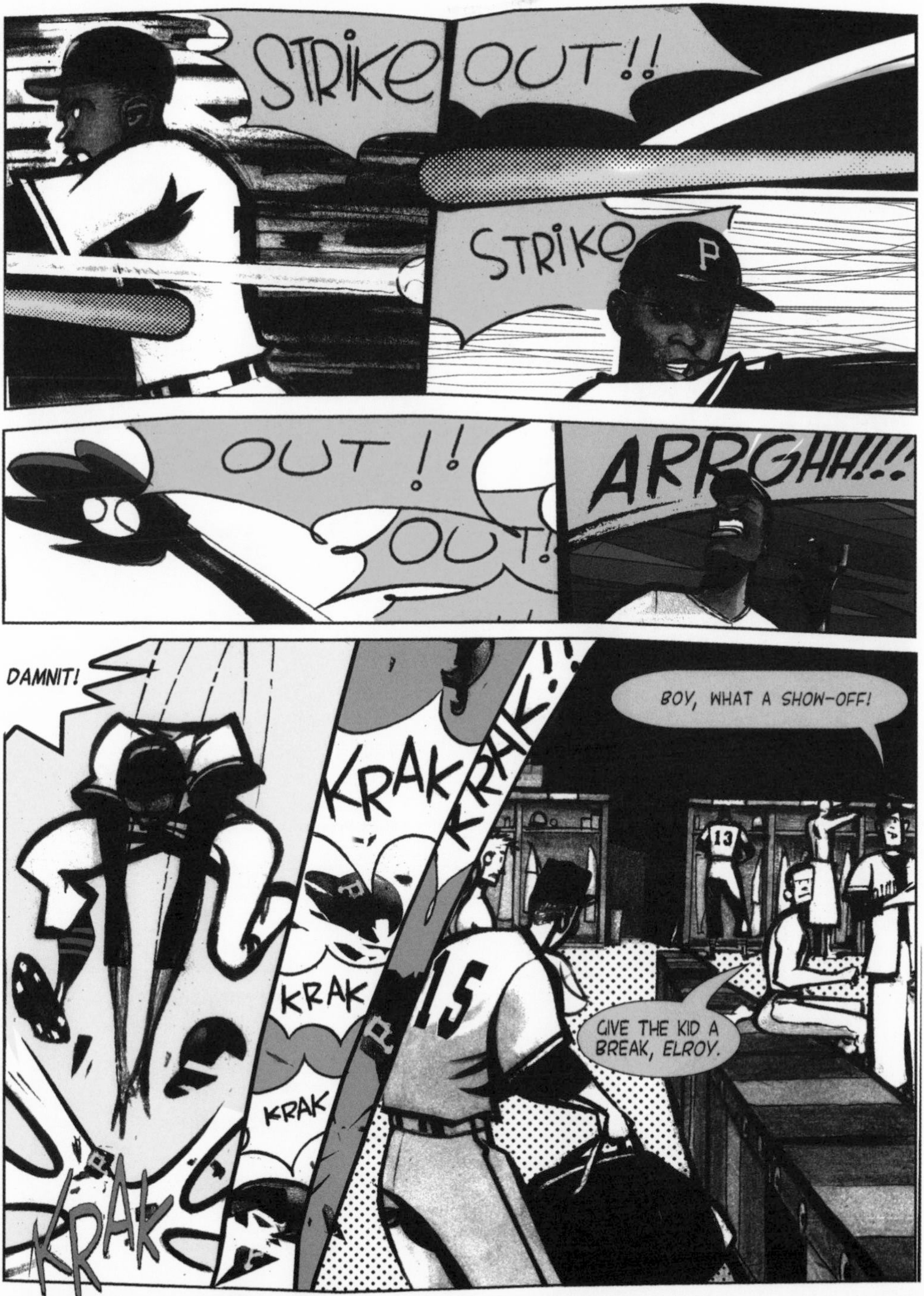
STRIKE OUT!!
STRIKE
OUT!!
OUT!
ARRGHH!!!
DAMNIT!
KRAK
KRAK
KRAK
KRAK
KRAK!!
BOY, WHAT A SHOW-OFF!
GIVE THE KID A BREAK, ELROY.

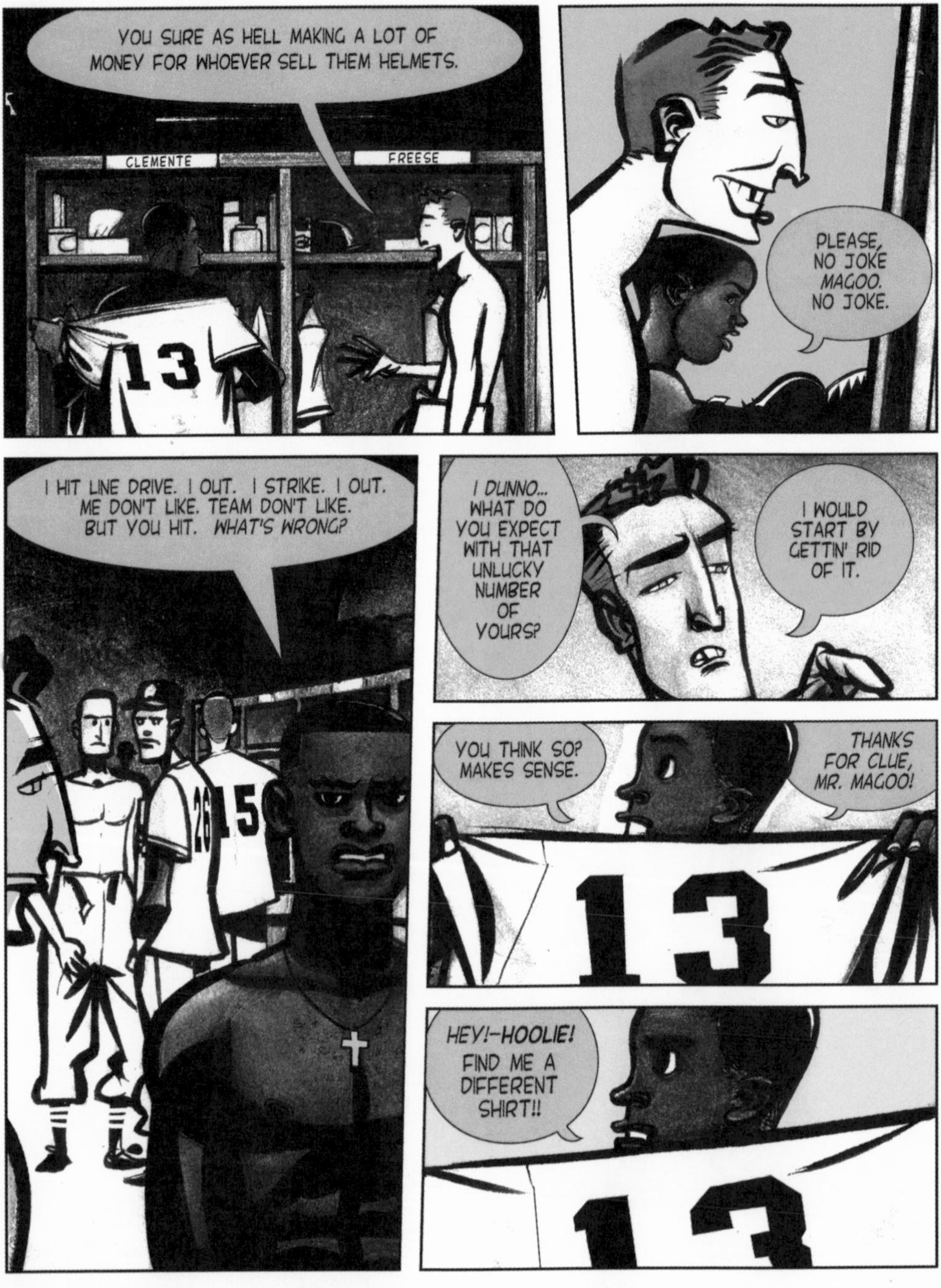

YOU SURE AS HELL MAKING A LOT OF MONEY FOR WHOEVER SELL THEM HELMETS.
CLEMENTE
FREESE
13
PLEASE, NO JOKE *MAGOO.* NO JOKE.
I HIT LINE DRIVE. I OUT. I STRIKE. I OUT. ME DON'T LIKE. TEAM DON'T LIKE. BUT YOU HIT. *WHAT'S WRONG?*
26
15
I DUNNO... WHAT DO YOU EXPECT WITH THAT UNLUCKY NUMBER OF YOURS?
I WOULD START BY GETTIN' RID OF IT.
YOU THINK SO? MAKES SENSE.
THANKS FOR CLUE, MR. MAGOO!
13
HEY!–HOOLIE! FIND ME A DIFFERENT SHIRT!!

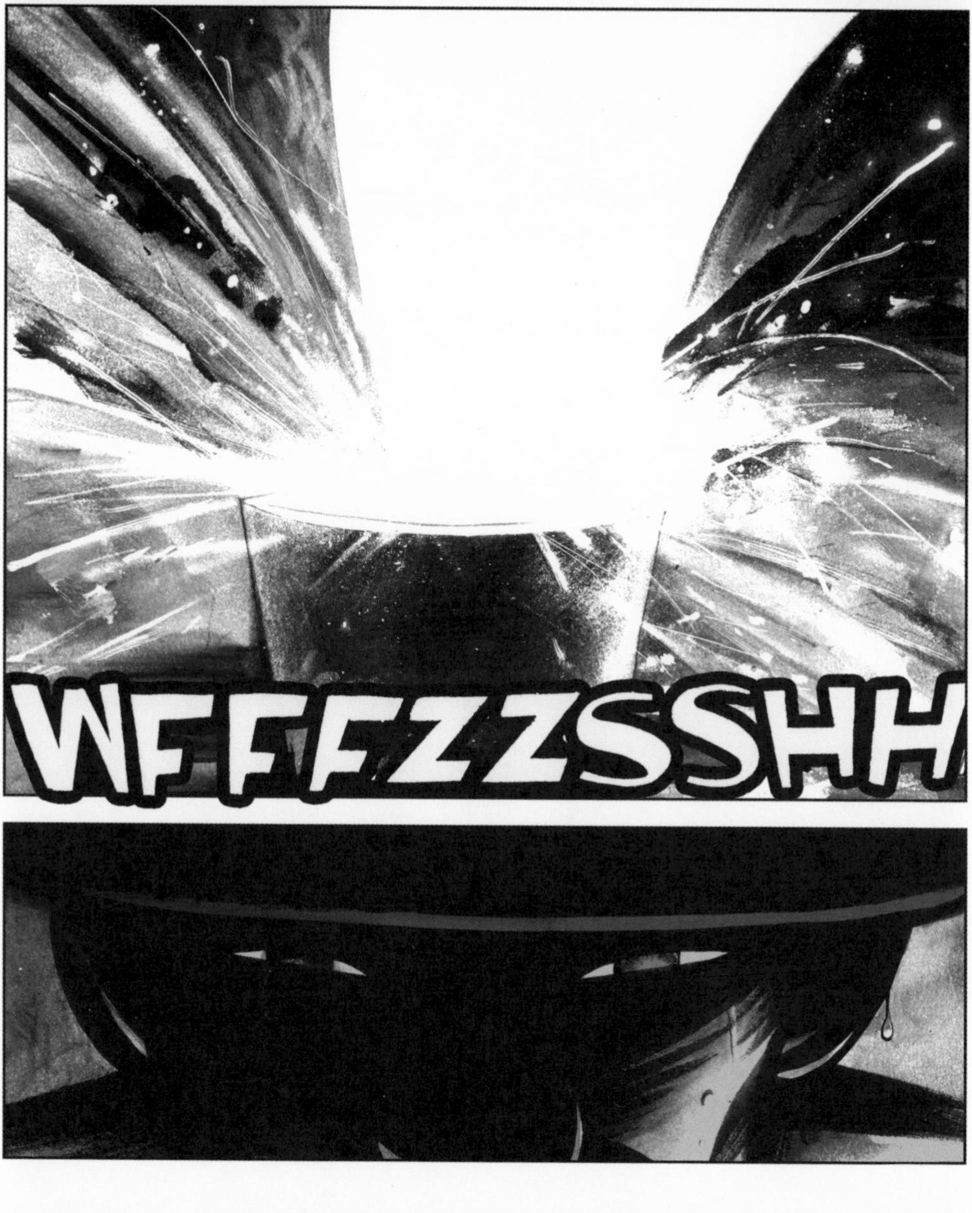
WFFFZZSSHH

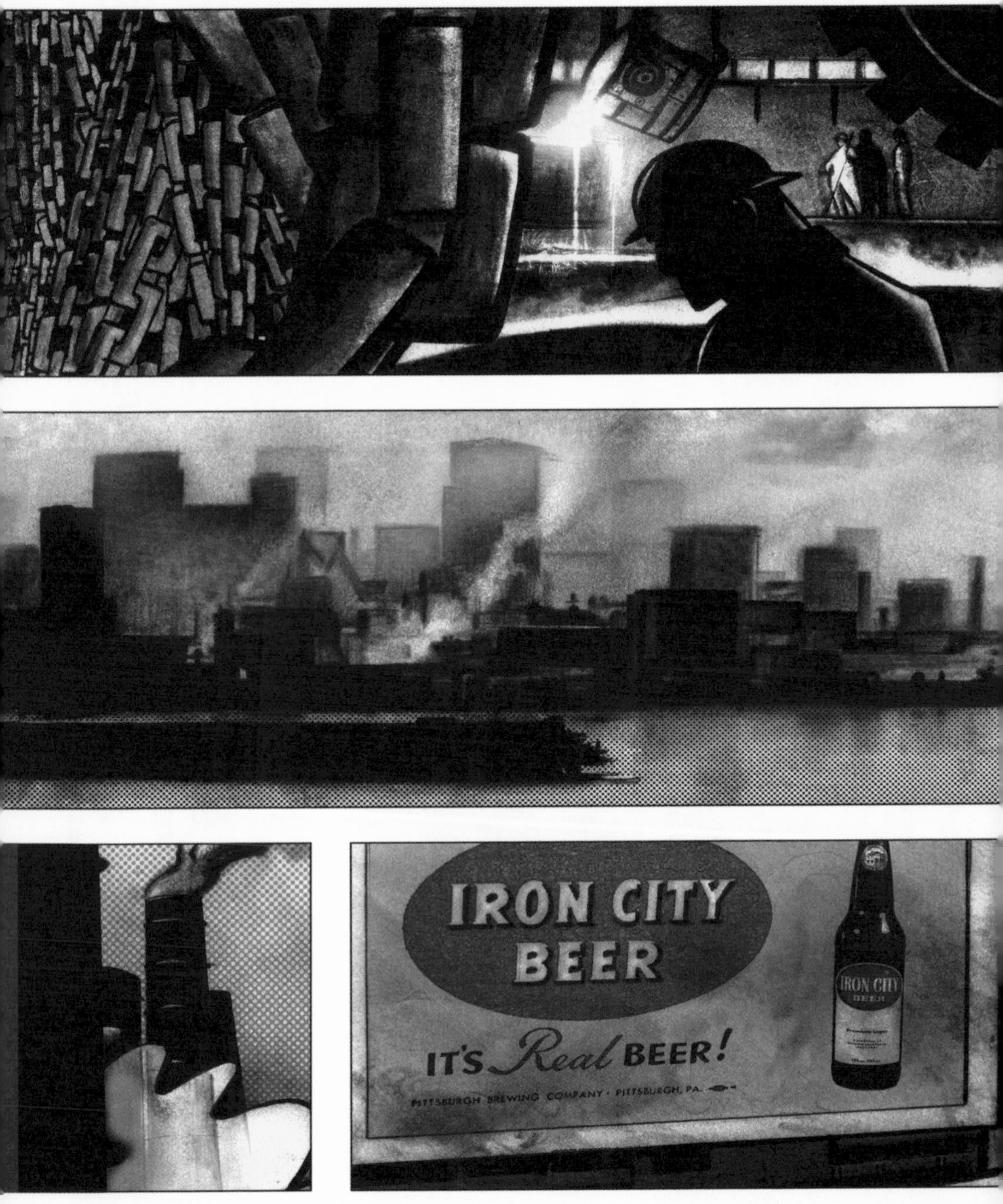
IRON CITY
BEER
IT'S Real BEER!
PITTSBURGH BREWING COMPANY · PITTSBURGH, PA.
IRON CITY
BEER

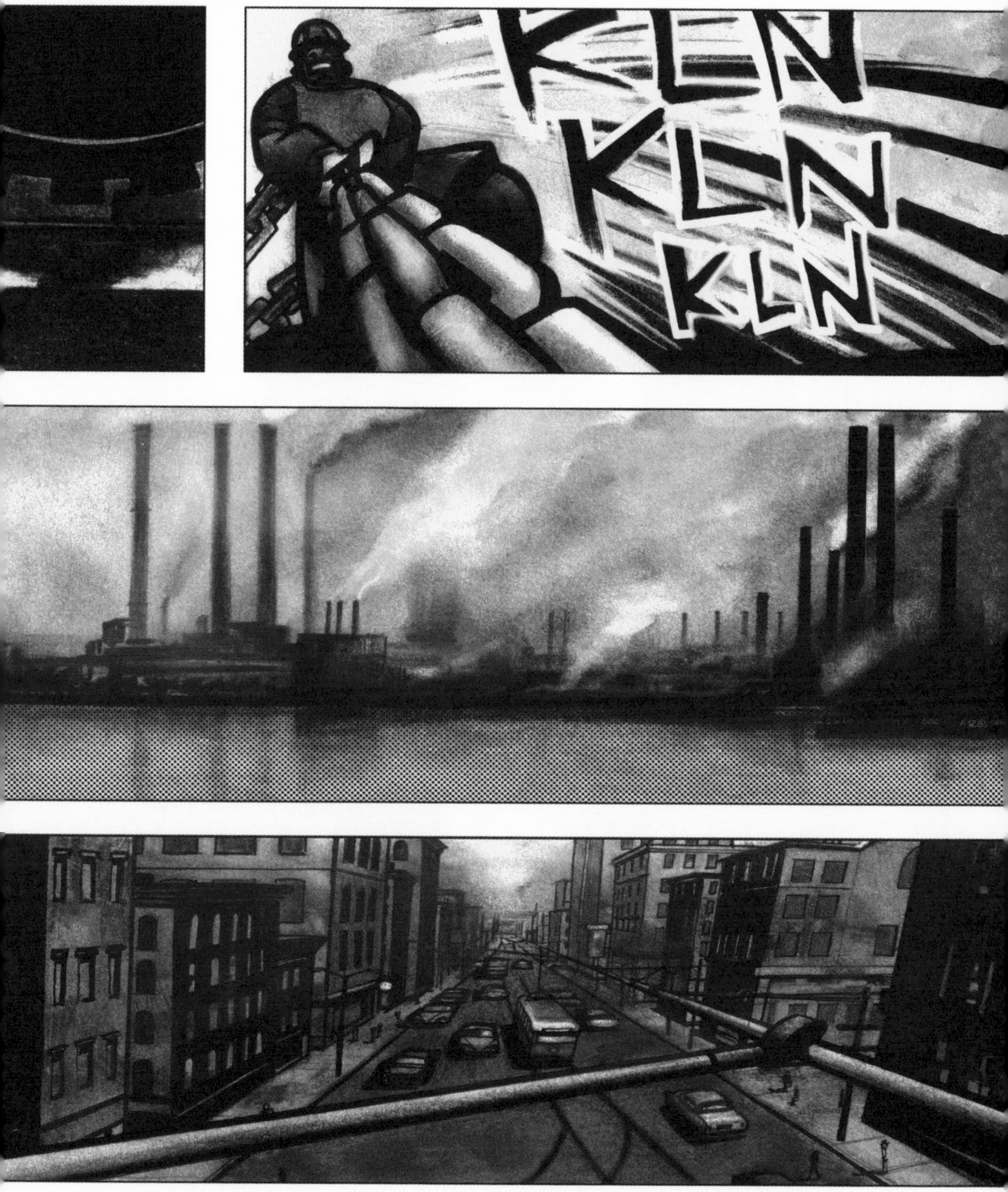
KLN
KLN
KLN
KLN

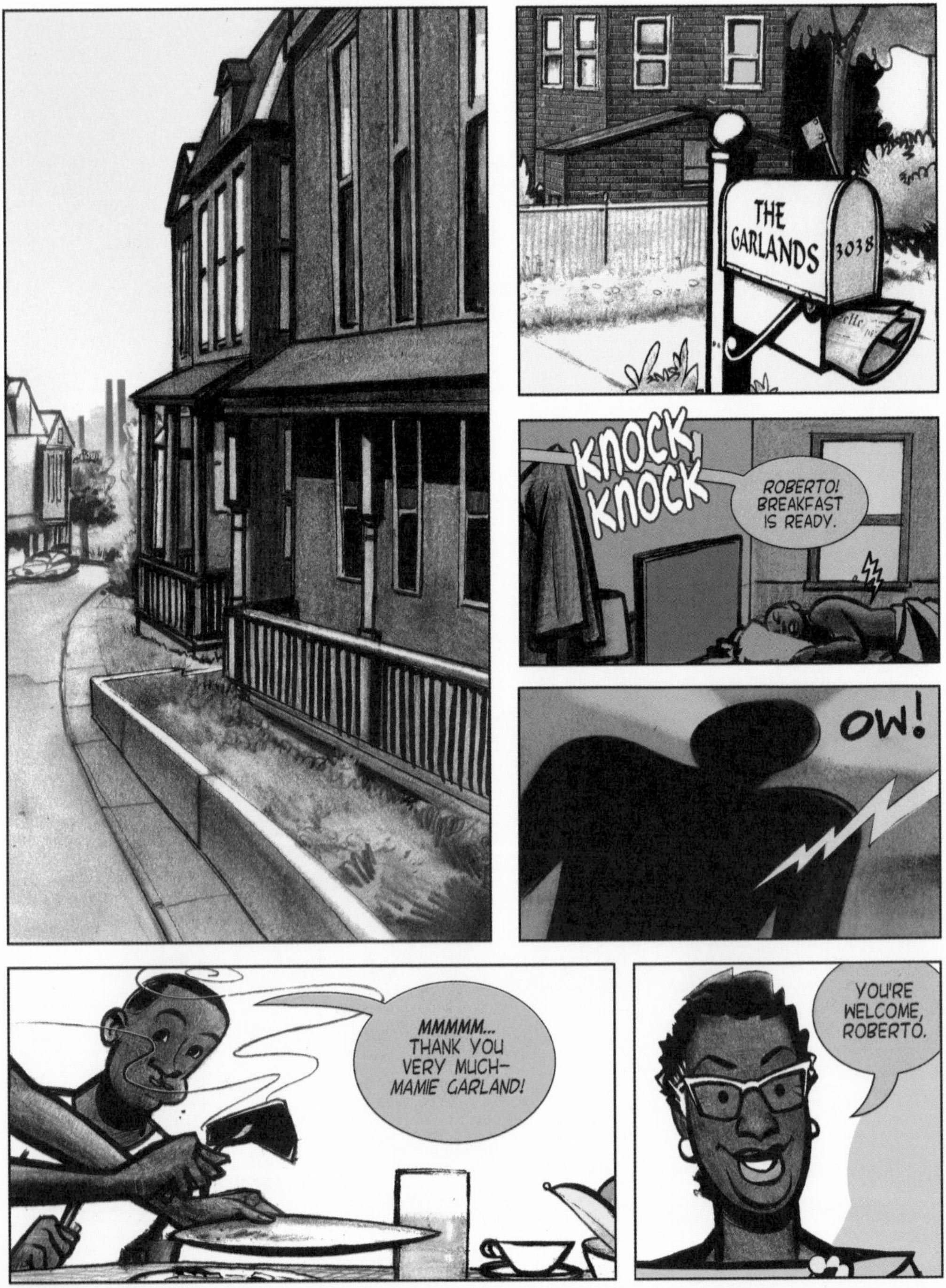
THE GARLANDS
3038
KNOCK, KNOCK
ROBERTO! BREAKFAST IS READY.
OW!
MMMMM... THANK YOU VERY MUCH– MAMIE GARLAND!
YOU'RE WELCOME, ROBERTO.

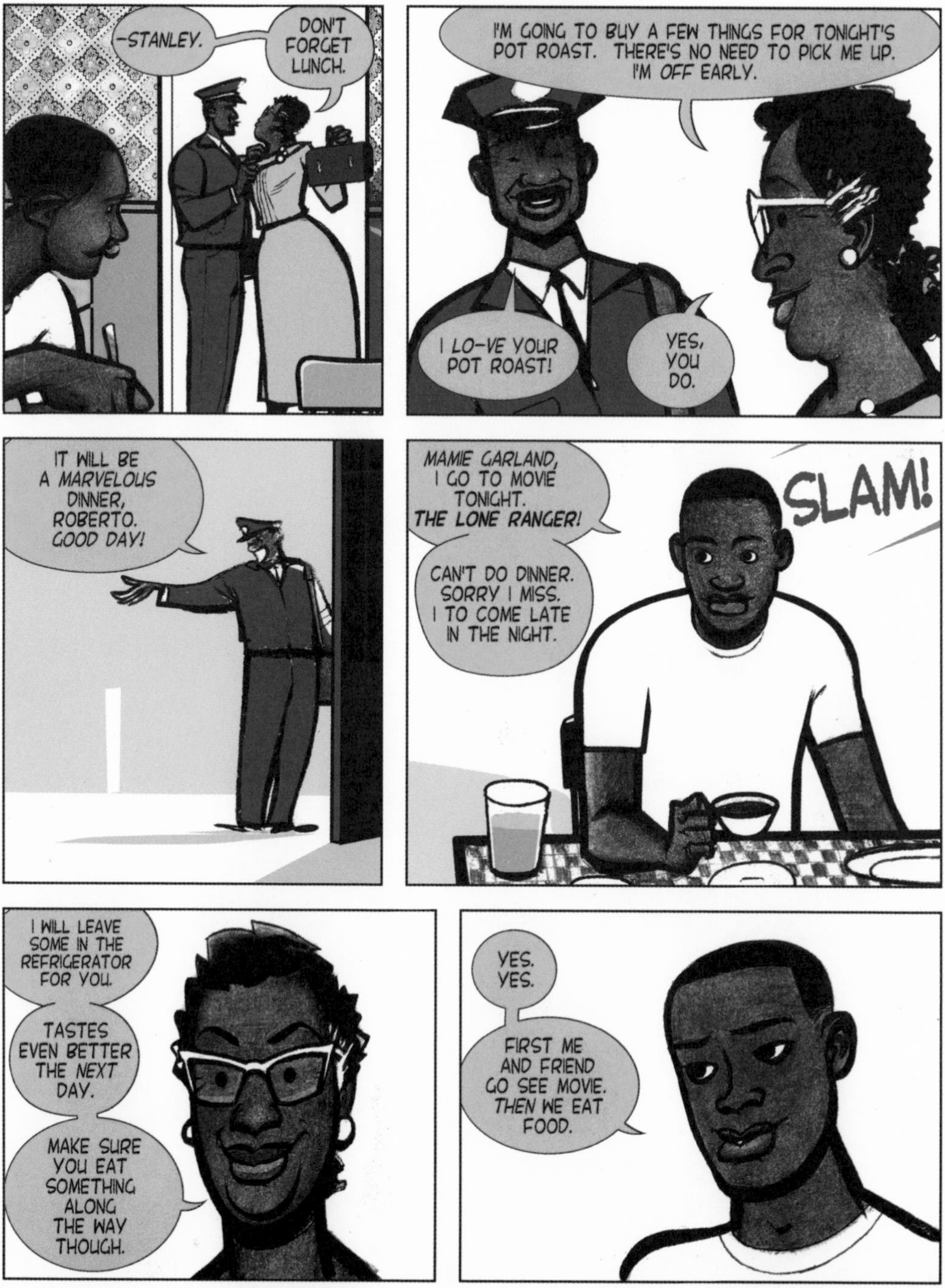
-STANLEY.
DON'T FORGET LUNCH.
I'M GOING TO BUY A FEW THINGS FOR TONIGHT'S POT ROAST. THERE'S NO NEED TO PICK ME UP. I'M *OFF* EARLY.
I *LO-VE* YOUR POT ROAST!
YES, YOU DO.
IT WILL BE A *MARVELOUS* DINNER, ROBERTO. *GOOD DAY!*
MAMIE GARLAND, I GO TO MOVIE TONIGHT. ***THE LONE RANGER!***
CAN'T DO DINNER. SORRY I MISS. I TO COME LATE IN THE NIGHT.
SLAM!
I WILL LEAVE SOME IN THE REFRIGERATOR FOR YOU.
TASTES EVEN BETTER THE *NEXT* DAY.
MAKE SURE YOU EAT SOMETHING ALONG THE WAY THOUGH.
YES. YES.
FIRST ME AND FRIEND GO SEE MOVIE. *THEN* WE EAT FOOD.

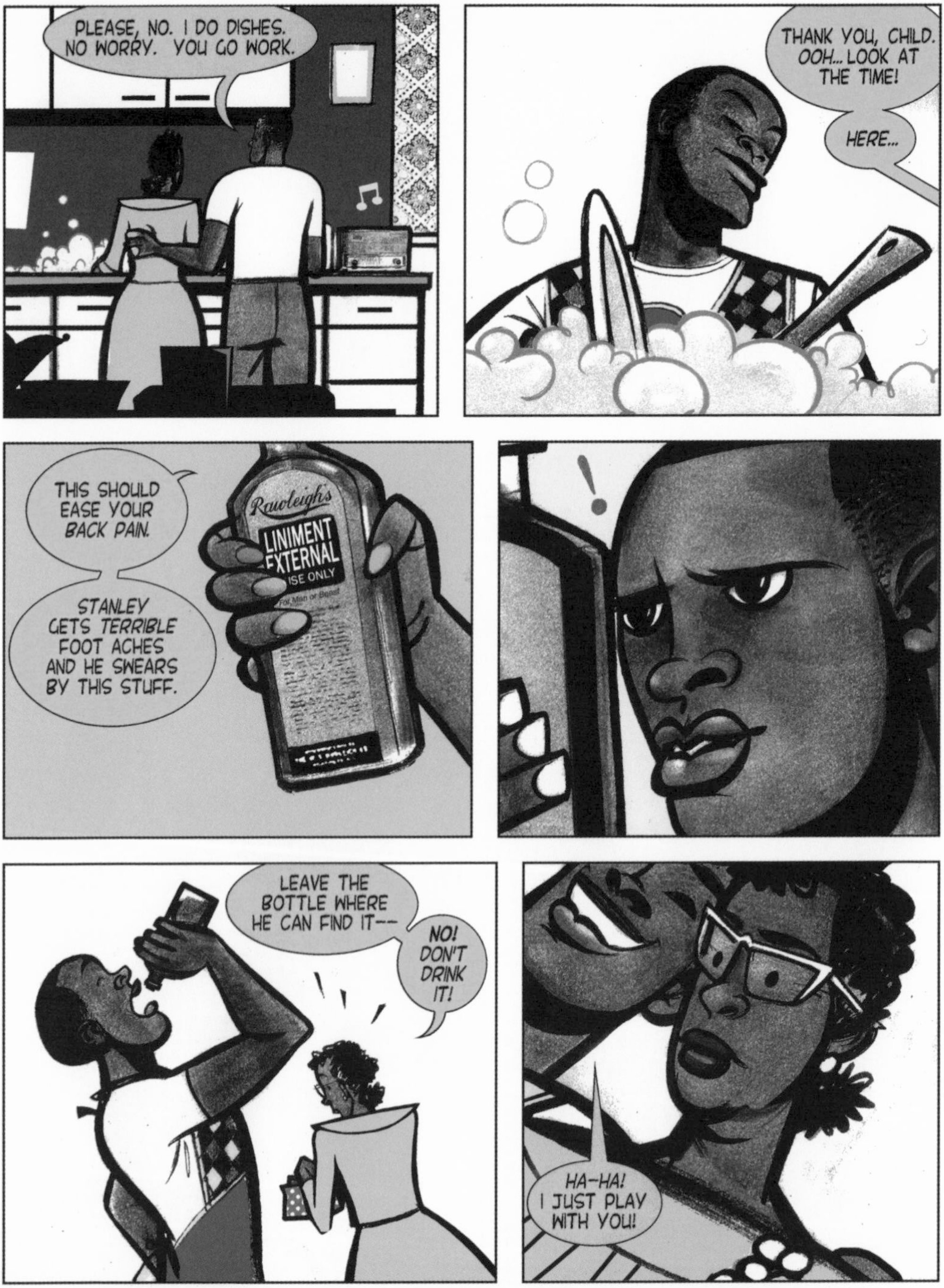
PLEASE, NO. I DO DISHES. NO WORRY. YOU GO WORK.
THANK YOU, CHILD. OOH... LOOK AT THE TIME!
HERE...
THIS SHOULD EASE YOUR BACK PAIN.
STANLEY GETS TERRIBLE FOOT ACHES AND HE SWEARS BY THIS STUFF.
Rawleigh's
LINIMENT EXTERNAL USE ONLY
For Man or Beast
!
LEAVE THE BOTTLE WHERE HE CAN FIND IT--
NO! DON'T DRINK IT!
HA-HA! I JUST PLAY WITH YOU!

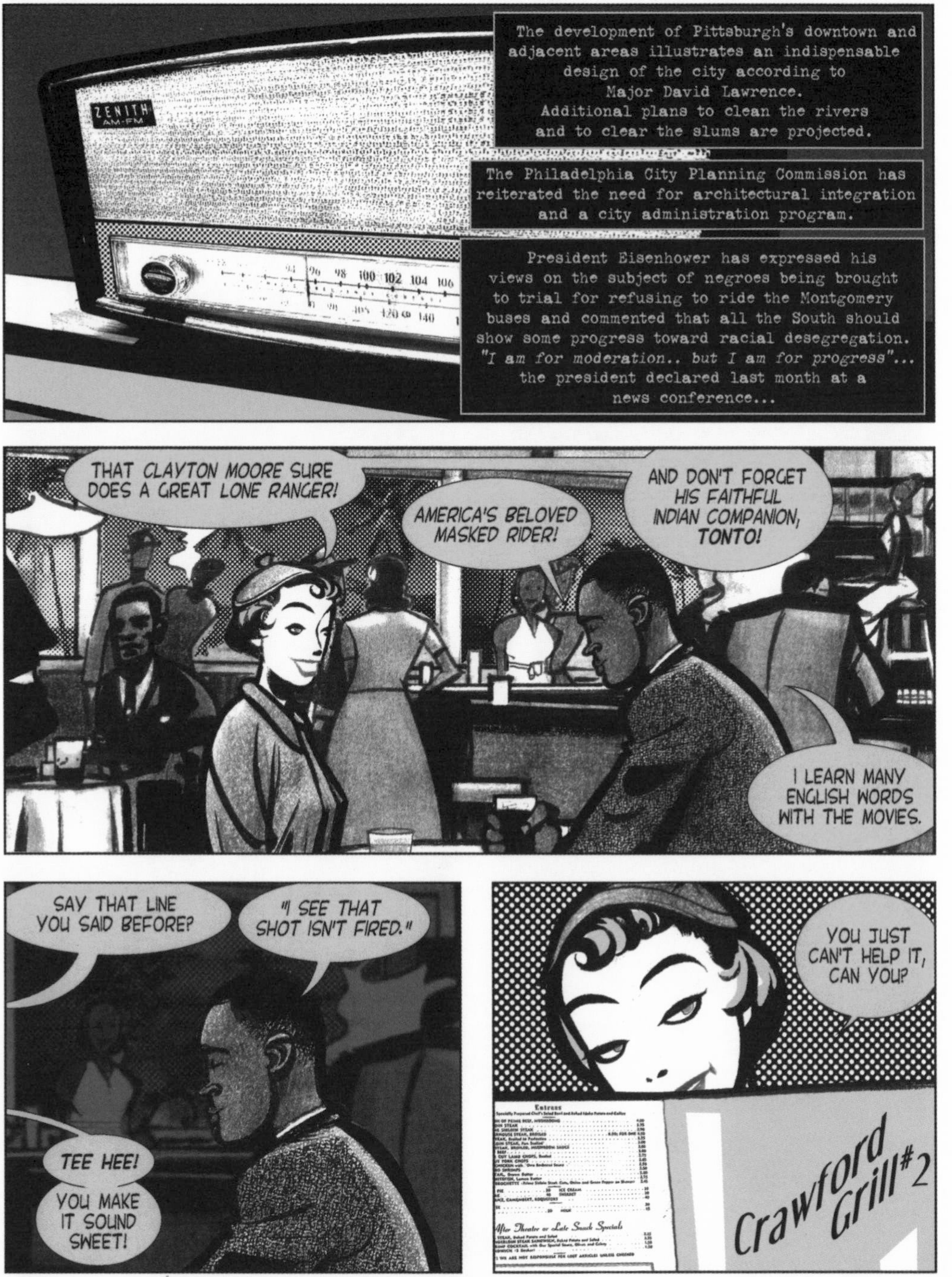

The development of Pittsburgh's downtown and adjacent areas illustrates an indispensable design of the city according to Major David Lawrence. Additional plans to clean the rivers and to clear the slums are projected.
The Philadelphia City Planning Commission has reiterated the need for architectural integration and a city administration program.
President Eisenhower has expressed his views on the subject of negroes being brought to trial for refusing to ride the Montgomery buses and commented that all the South should show some progress toward racial desegregation. "I am for moderation.. but I am for progress"... the president declared last month at a news conference...
ZENITH AM-FM
THAT CLAYTON MOORE SURE DOES A GREAT LONE RANGER!
AMERICA'S BELOVED MASKED RIDER!
AND DON'T FORGET HIS FAITHFUL INDIAN COMPANION, TONTO!
I LEARN MANY ENGLISH WORDS WITH THE MOVIES.
SAY THAT LINE YOU SAID BEFORE?
"I SEE THAT SHOT ISN'T FIRED."
TEE HEE!
YOU MAKE IT SOUND SWEET!
YOU JUST CAN'T HELP IT, CAN YOU?
Entrees
After Theatre or Late Snack Specials
Crawford Grill #2

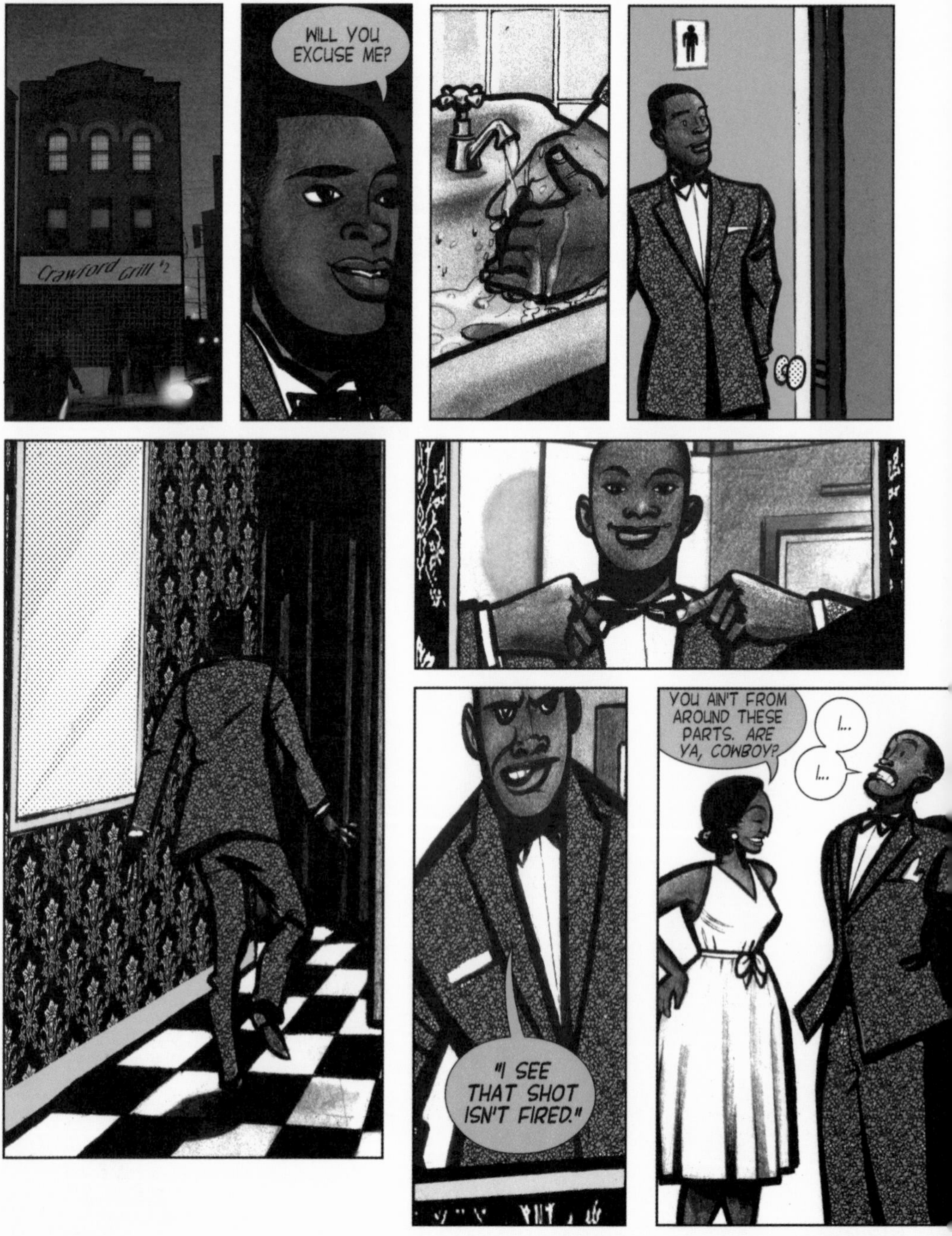
Crawford Grill #2
WILL YOU EXCUSE ME?
"I SEE THAT SHOT ISN'T FIRED."
YOU AIN'T FROM AROUND THESE PARTS. ARE YA, COWBOY?
I...
I...

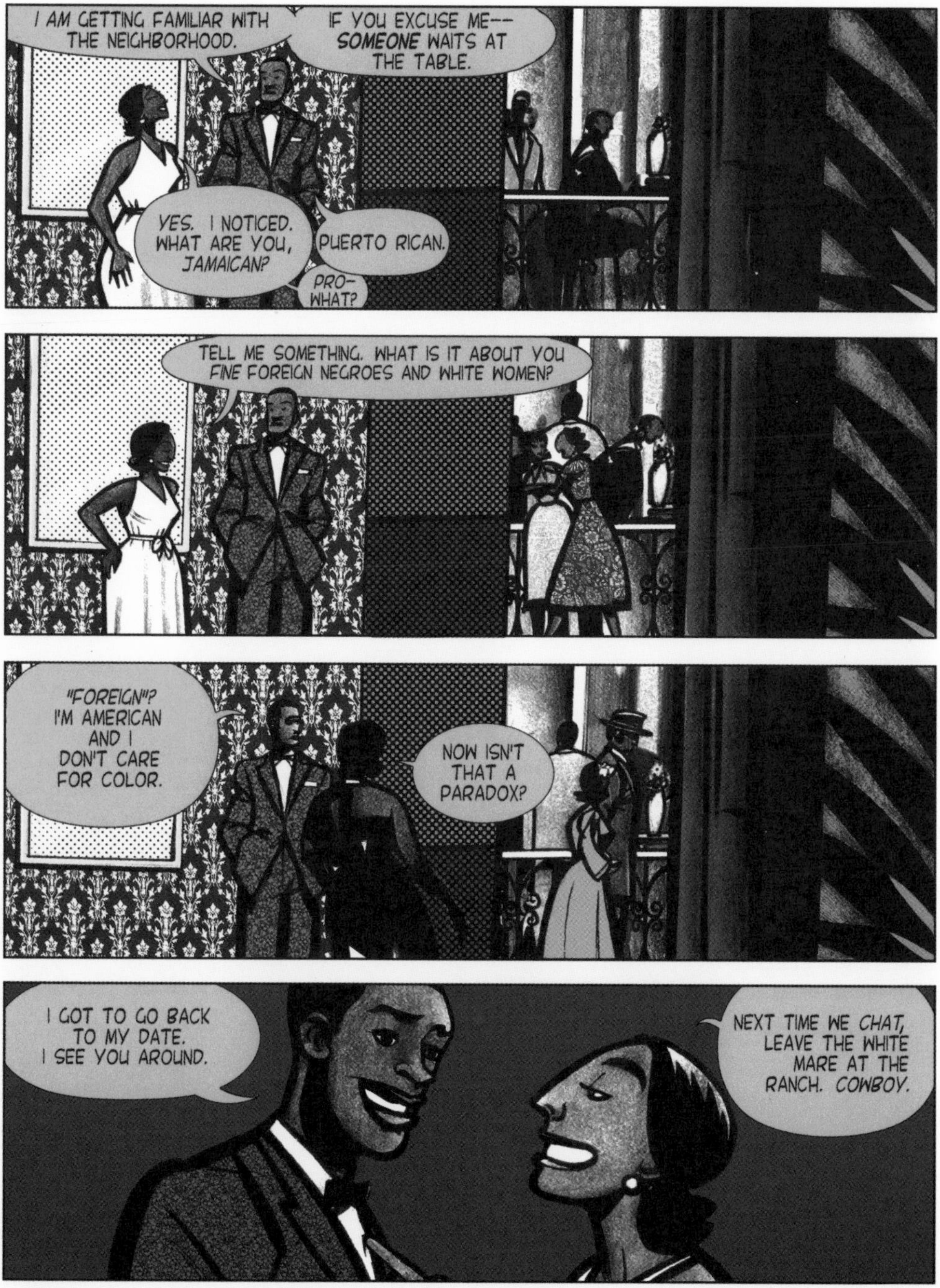
I AM GETTING FAMILIAR WITH THE NEIGHBORHOOD.
IF YOU EXCUSE ME-- SOMEONE WAITS AT THE TABLE.
YES. I NOTICED. WHAT ARE YOU, JAMAICAN?
PUERTO RICAN.
PRO-WHAT?
TELL ME SOMETHING. WHAT IS IT ABOUT YOU FINE FOREIGN NEGROES AND WHITE WOMEN?
"FOREIGN"? I'M AMERICAN AND I DON'T CARE FOR COLOR.
NOW ISN'T THAT A PARADOX?
I GOT TO GO BACK TO MY DATE. I SEE YOU AROUND.
NEXT TIME WE CHAT, LEAVE THE WHITE MARE AT THE RANCH. COWBOY.

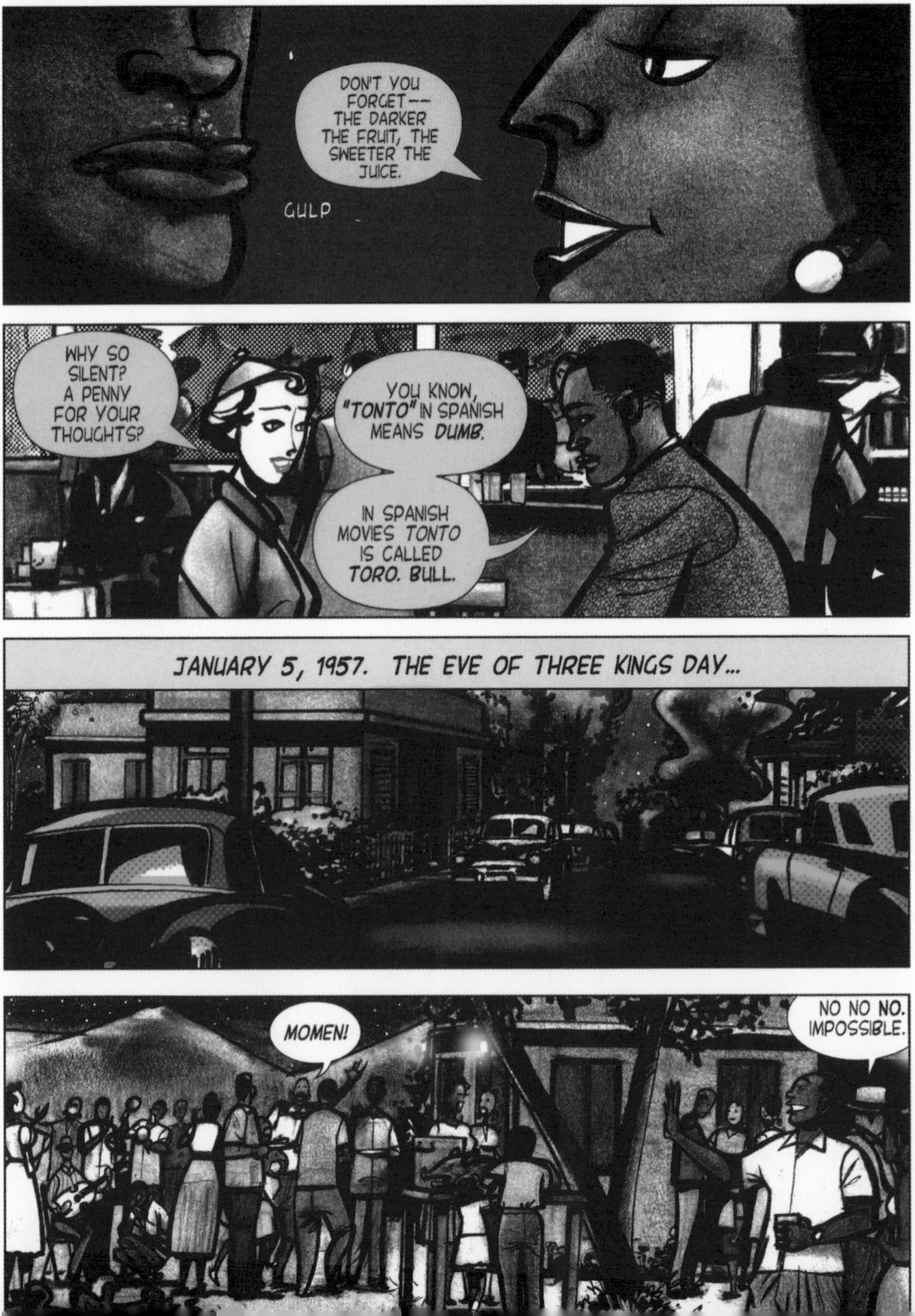
DON'T YOU FORGET-- THE DARKER THE FRUIT, THE SWEETER THE JUICE.
GULP
WHY SO SILENT? A PENNY FOR YOUR THOUGHTS?
YOU KNOW, "TONTO" IN SPANISH MEANS DUMB.
IN SPANISH MOVIES TONTO IS CALLED TORO. BULL.
JANUARY 5, 1957. THE EVE OF THREE KINGS DAY...
MOMEN!
NO NO NO. IMPOSSIBLE.

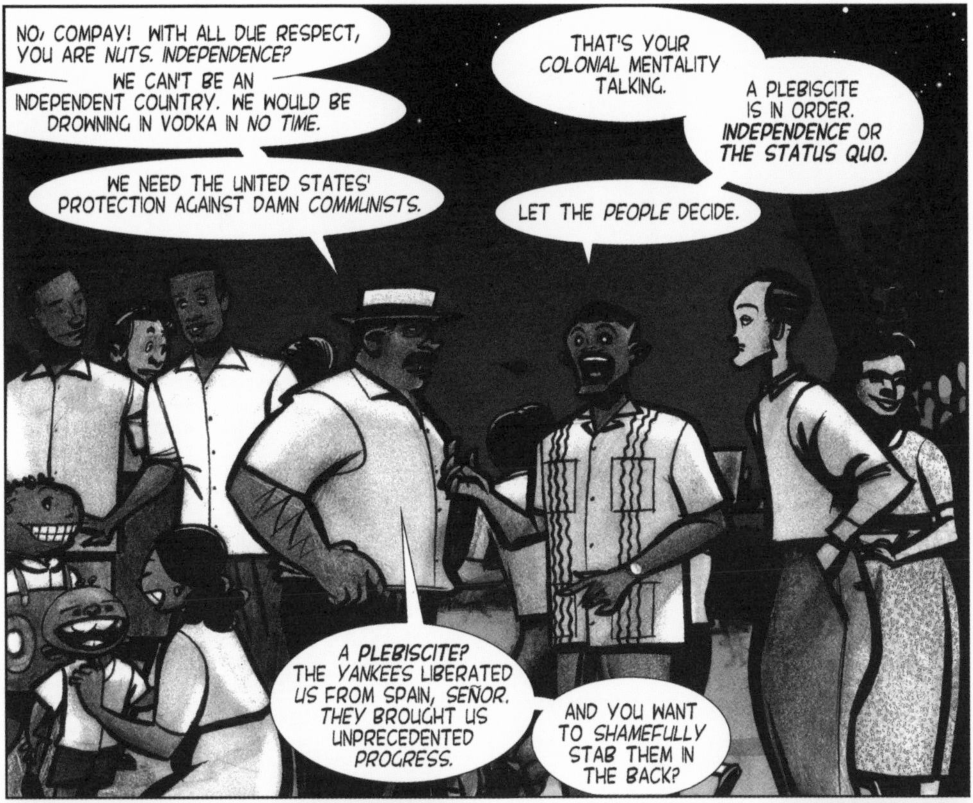
NO, COMPAY! WITH ALL DUE RESPECT, YOU ARE NUTS. INDEPENDENCE?
WE CAN'T BE AN INDEPENDENT COUNTRY. WE WOULD BE DROWNING IN VODKA IN NO TIME.
WE NEED THE UNITED STATES' PROTECTION AGAINST DAMN COMMUNISTS.
THAT'S YOUR COLONIAL MENTALITY TALKING.
A PLEBISCITE IS IN ORDER. INDEPENDENCE OR THE STATUS QUO.
LET THE PEOPLE DECIDE.
A PLEBISCITE? THE YANKEES LIBERATED US FROM SPAIN, SEÑOR. THEY BROUGHT US UNPRECEDENTED PROGRESS.
AND YOU WANT TO SHAMEFULLY STAB THEM IN THE BACK?

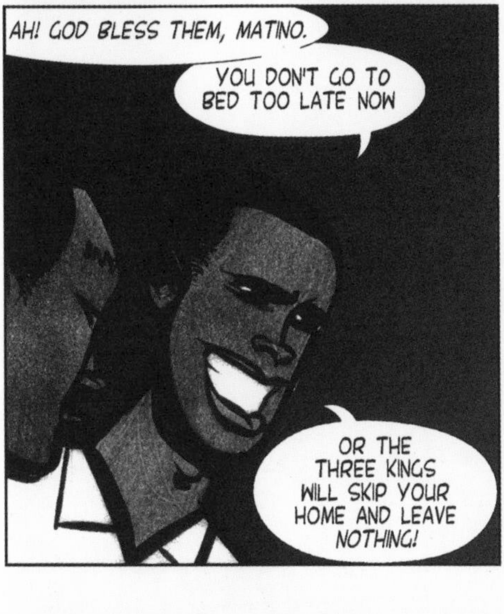
AH! GOD BLESS THEM, MATINO.
YOU DON'T GO TO BED TOO LATE NOW
OR THE THREE KINGS WILL SKIP YOUR HOME AND LEAVE NOTHING!

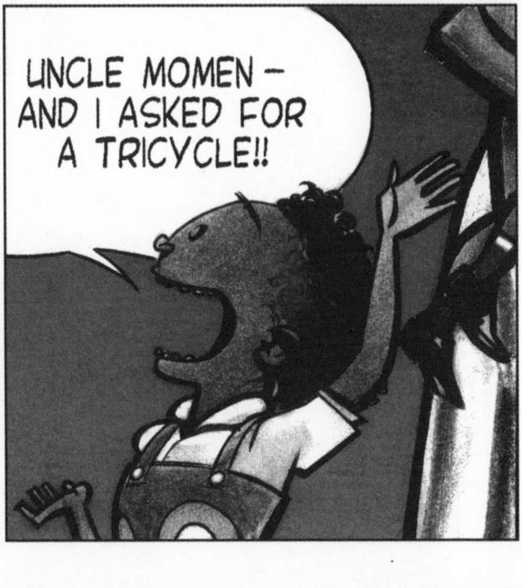
UNCLE MOMEN — AND I ASKED FOR A TRICYCLE!!

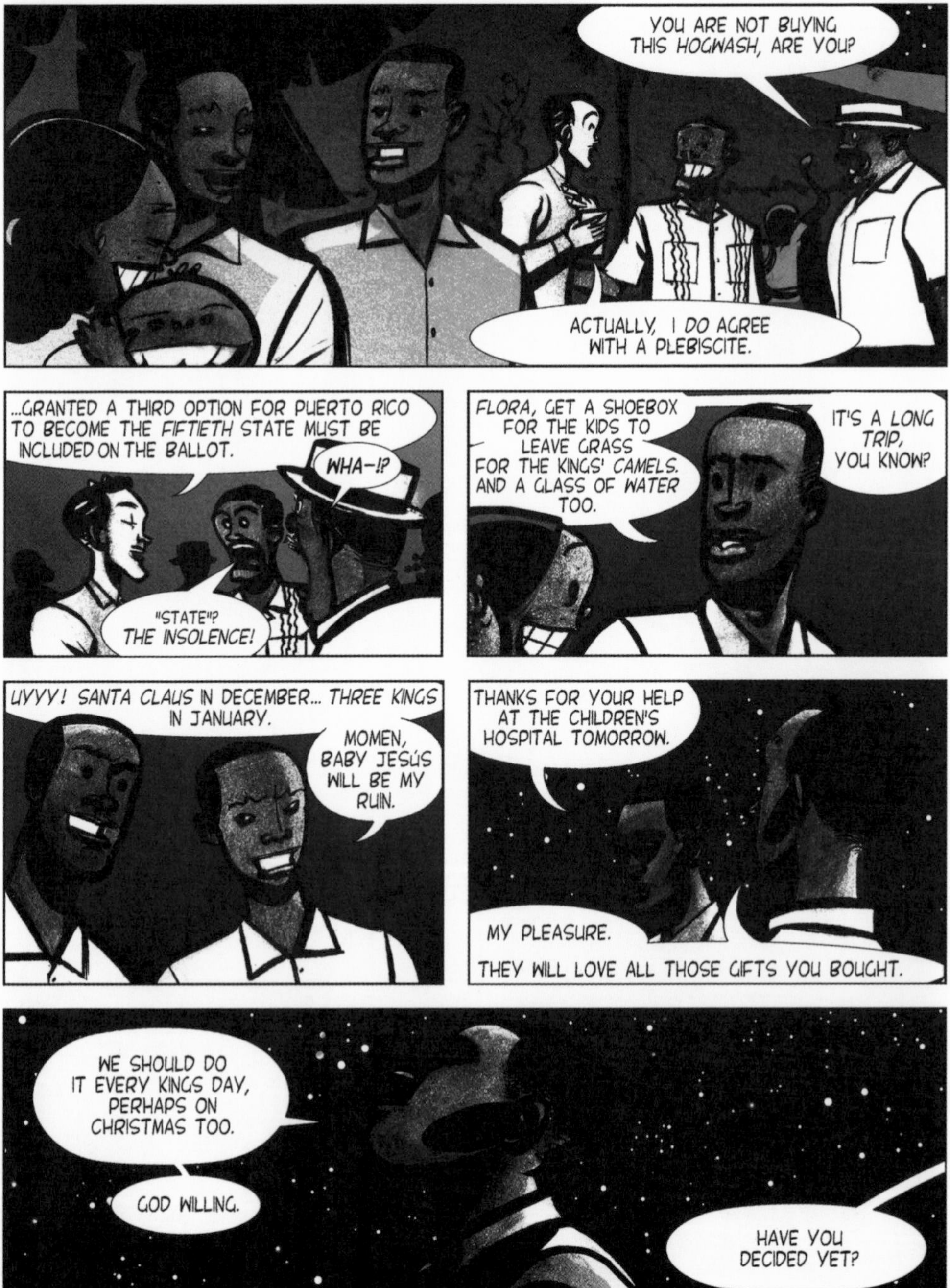

YOU ARE NOT BUYING THIS *HOGWASH*, ARE YOU?
ACTUALLY, I *DO* AGREE WITH A PLEBISCITE.
...GRANTED A THIRD OPTION FOR PUERTO RICO TO BECOME THE *FIFTIETH* STATE MUST BE INCLUDED ON THE BALLOT.
WHA-!?
"STATE"? THE INSOLENCE!
FLORA, GET A SHOEBOX FOR THE KIDS TO LEAVE GRASS FOR THE KINGS' *CAMELS*. AND A GLASS OF WATER TOO.
IT'S A *LONG TRIP*, YOU KNOW?
UYYY! SANTA CLAUS IN DECEMBER... THREE KINGS IN JANUARY.
MOMEN, BABY JESÚS WILL BE MY RUIN.
THANKS FOR YOUR HELP AT THE CHILDREN'S HOSPITAL TOMORROW.
MY PLEASURE.
THEY WILL LOVE ALL THOSE GIFTS YOU BOUGHT.
WE SHOULD DO IT EVERY KINGS DAY, PERHAPS ON CHRISTMAS TOO.
GOD WILLING.
HAVE YOU DECIDED YET?

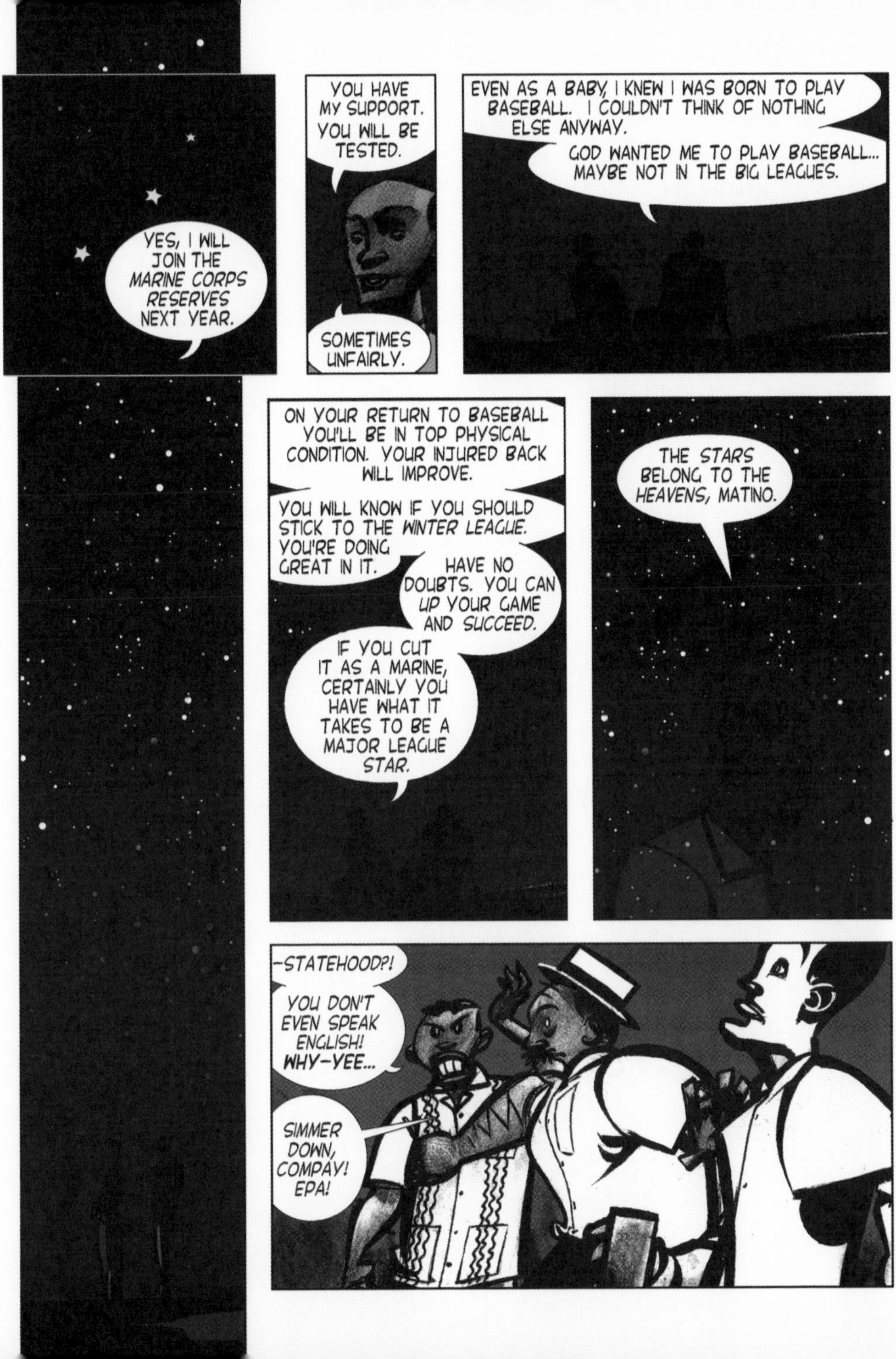
YES, I WILL JOIN THE MARINE CORPS RESERVES NEXT YEAR.
YOU HAVE MY SUPPORT. YOU WILL BE TESTED.
SOMETIMES UNFAIRLY.
EVEN AS A BABY, I KNEW I WAS BORN TO PLAY BASEBALL. I COULDN'T THINK OF NOTHING ELSE ANYWAY.
GOD WANTED ME TO PLAY BASEBALL... MAYBE NOT IN THE BIG LEAGUES.
ON YOUR RETURN TO BASEBALL YOU'LL BE IN TOP PHYSICAL CONDITION. YOUR INJURED BACK WILL IMPROVE.
YOU WILL KNOW IF YOU SHOULD STICK TO THE WINTER LEAGUE. YOU'RE DOING GREAT IN IT.
HAVE NO DOUBTS. YOU CAN UP YOUR GAME AND SUCCEED.
IF YOU CUT IT AS A MARINE, CERTAINLY YOU HAVE WHAT IT TAKES TO BE A MAJOR LEAGUE STAR.
THE STARS BELONG TO THE HEAVENS, MATINO.
-STATEHOOD?!
YOU DON'T EVEN SPEAK ENGLISH! WHY-YEE...
SIMMER DOWN, COMPAY! EPA!

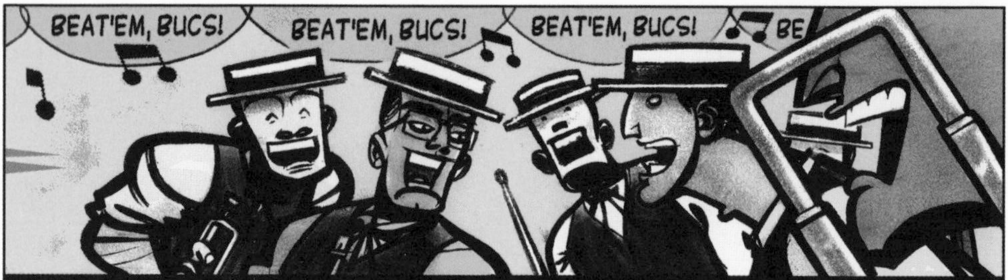
BEAT'EM, BUCS!
BEAT'EM, BUCS!
BEAT'EM, BUCS!
BE

1960

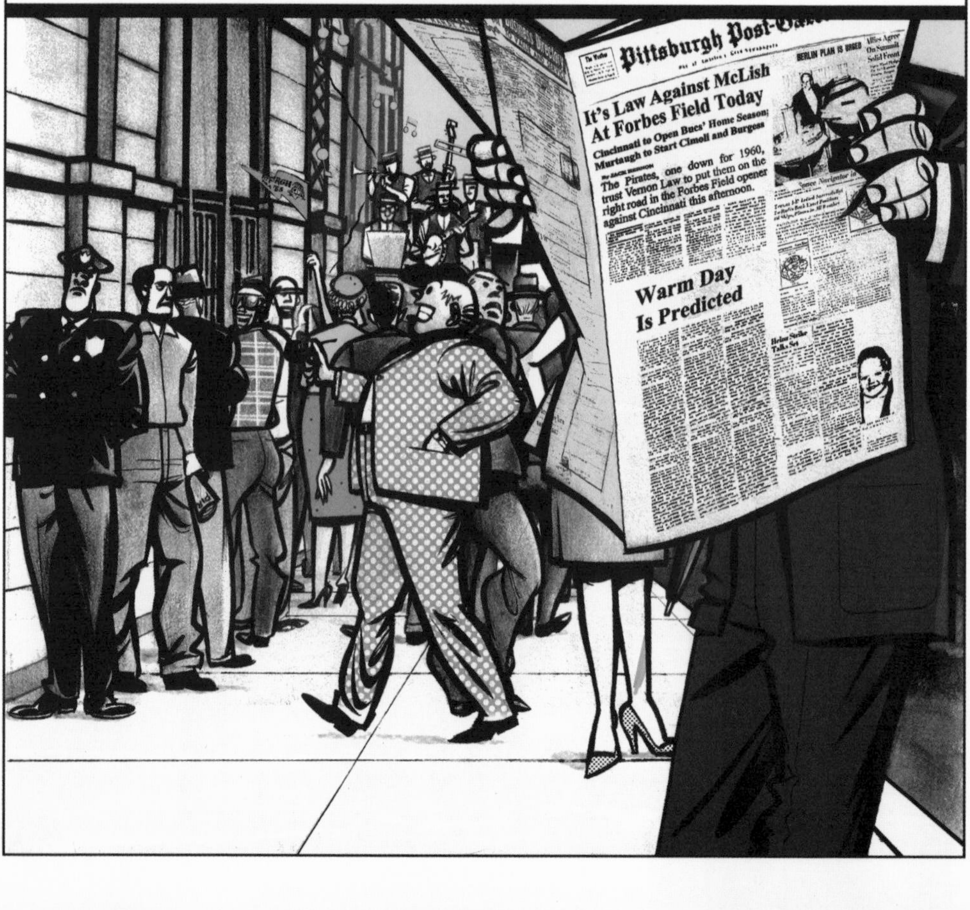
Pittsburgh Post-
BERLIN PLAN IS URGED
Allies Agree On Summit Solid Front
It's Law Against McLish At Forbes Field Today
Cincinnati to Open Bucs' Home Season; Murtaugh to Start Cimoli and Burgess
The Pirates, one down for 1960, trust Vernon Law to put them on the right road in the Forbes Field opener against Cincinnati this afternoon.
Warm Day Is Predicted

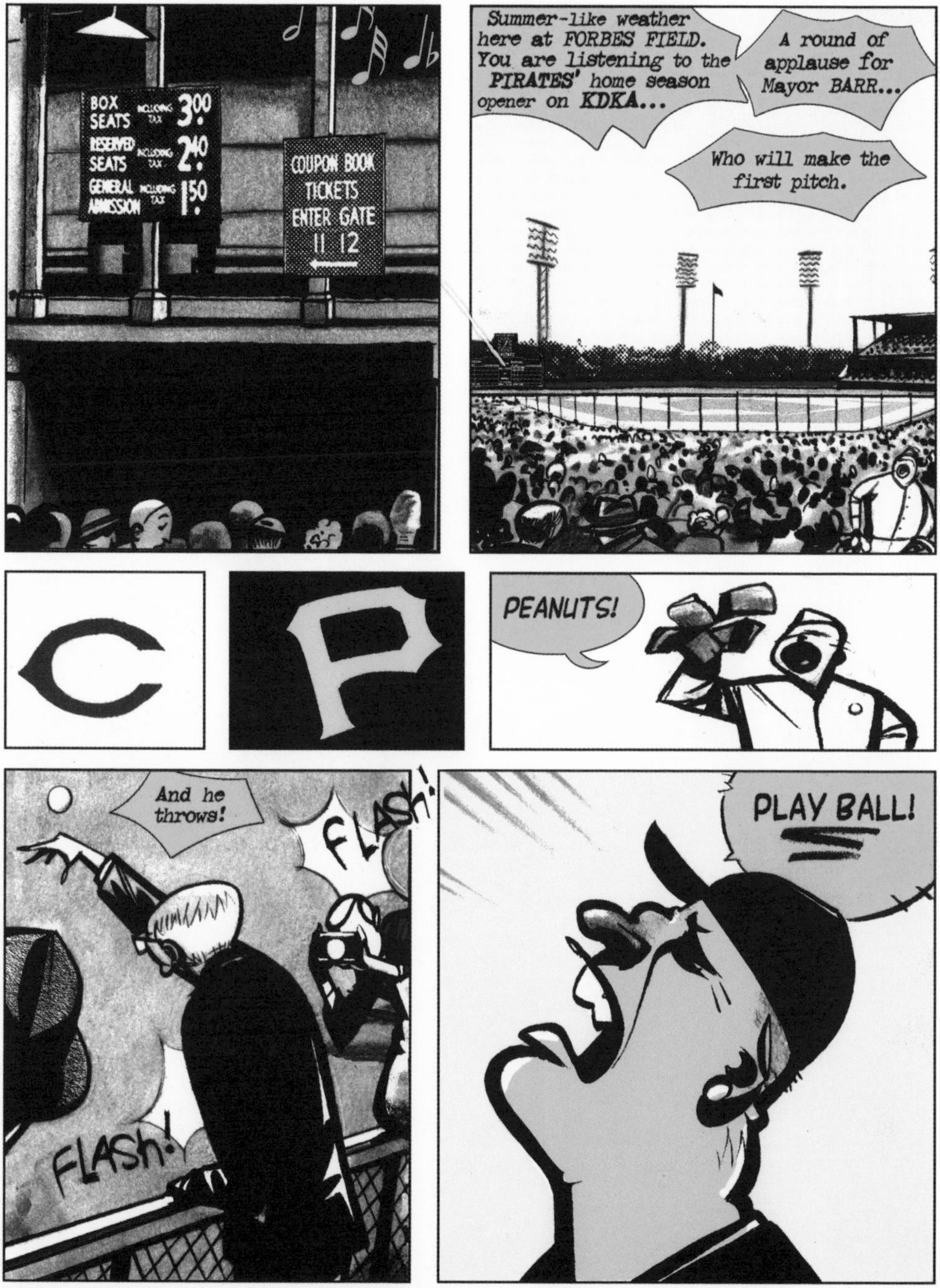

BOX SEATS INCLUDING TAX 3.00
RESERVED SEATS INCLUDING TAX 2.40
GENERAL ADMISSION INCLUDING TAX 1.50
COUPON BOOK TICKETS ENTER GATE 11 12
Summer-like weather here at FORBES FIELD. You are listening to the PIRATES' home season opener on KDKA...
A round of applause for Mayor BARR...
Who will make the first pitch.
C
P
PEANUTS!
And he throws!
FLASH!
FLASH!
PLAY BALL!

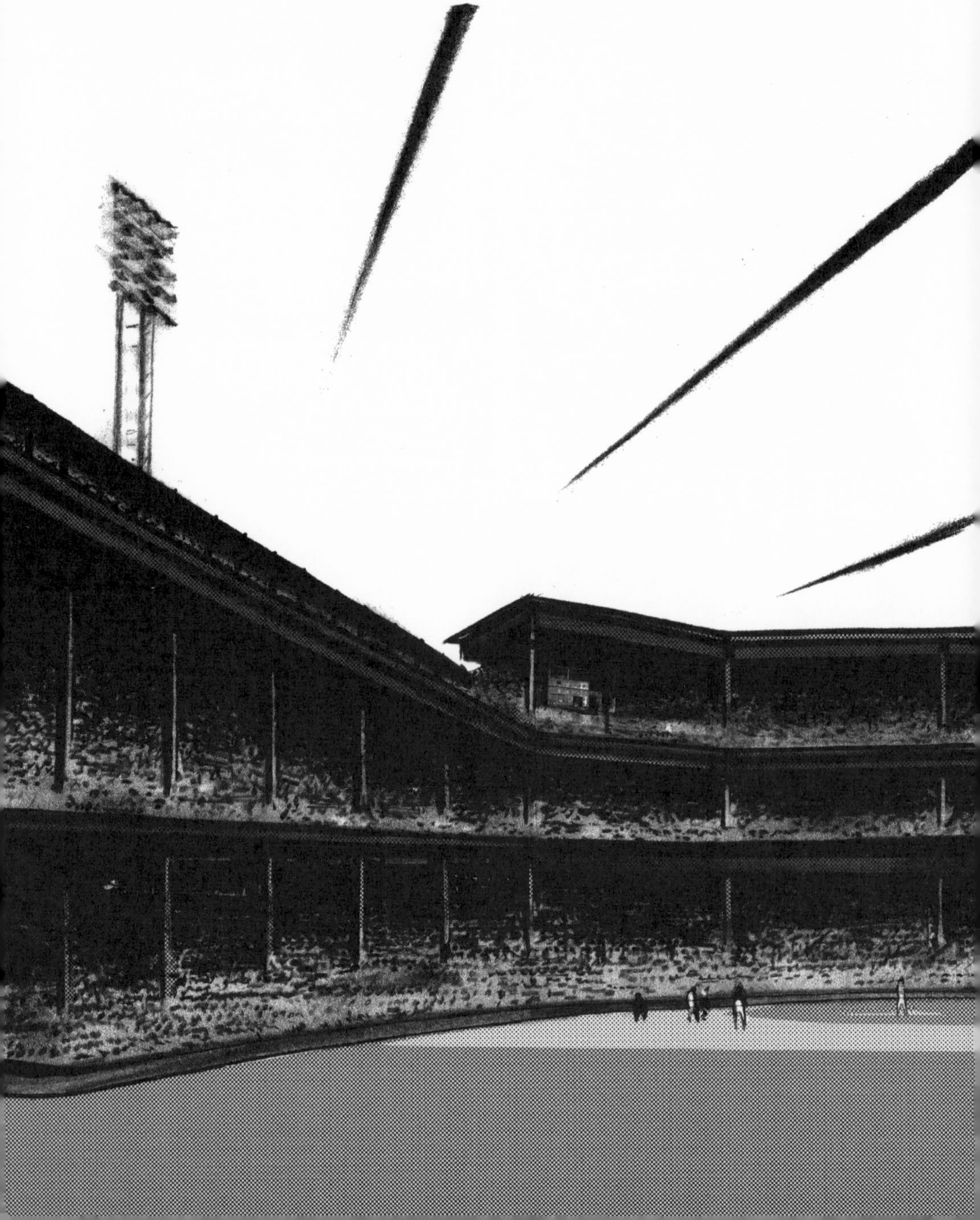

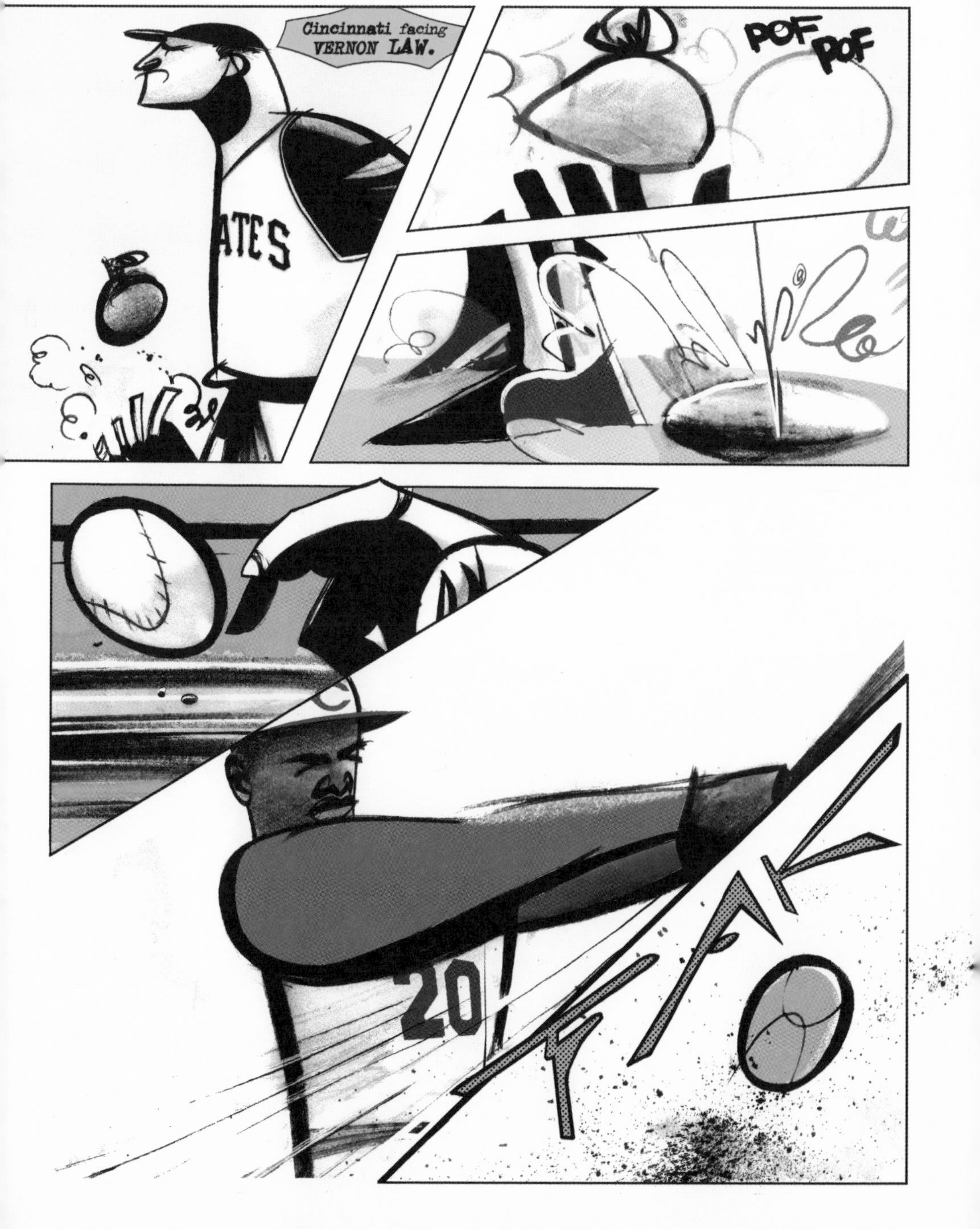
Cincinnati facing VERNON LAW.
POF POF
ATES
20

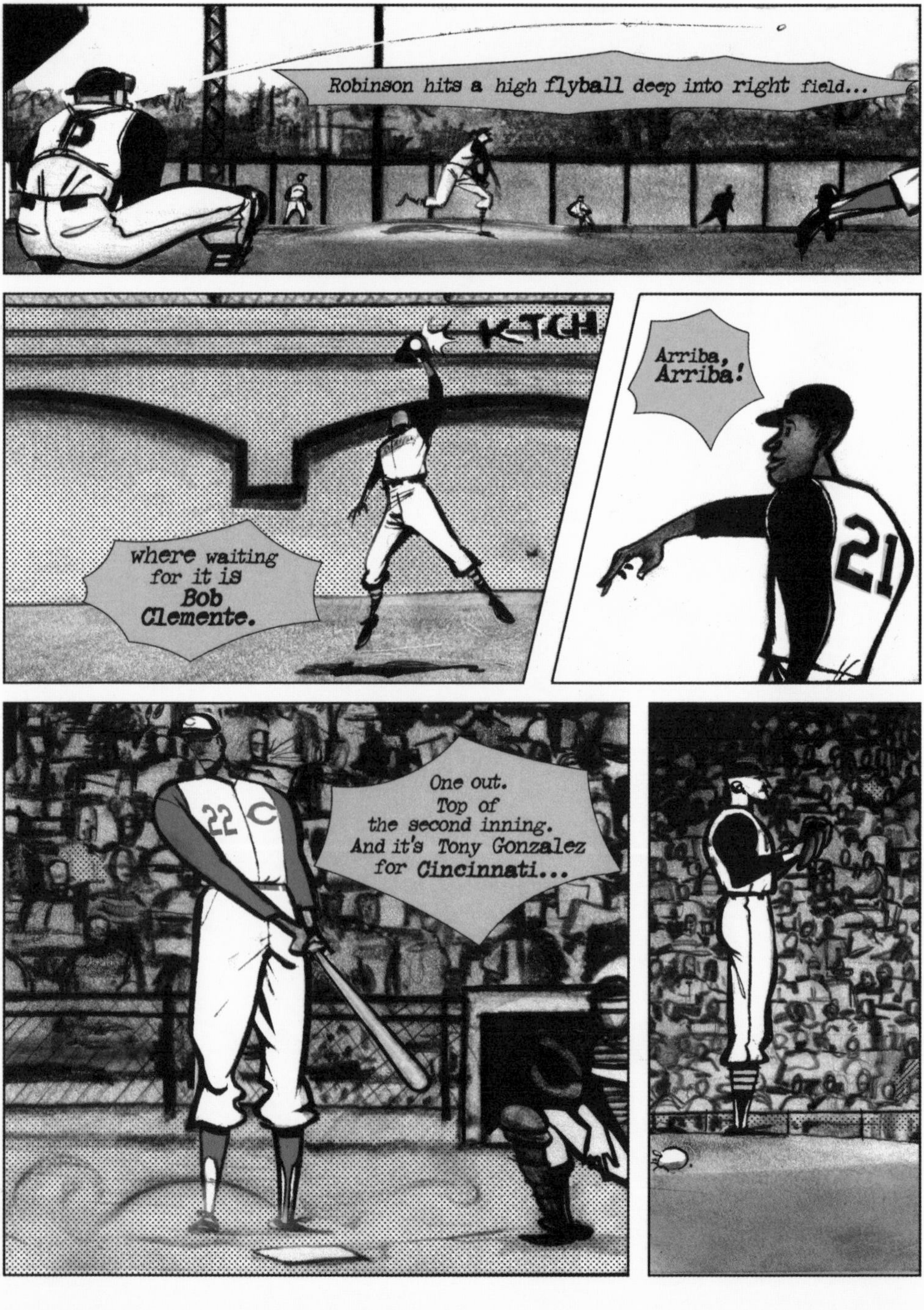
Robinson hits a high flyball deep into right field...
KTCH
where waiting for it is Bob Clemente.
Arriba, Arriba!
One out. Top of the second inning. And it's Tony Gonzalez for Cincinnati...

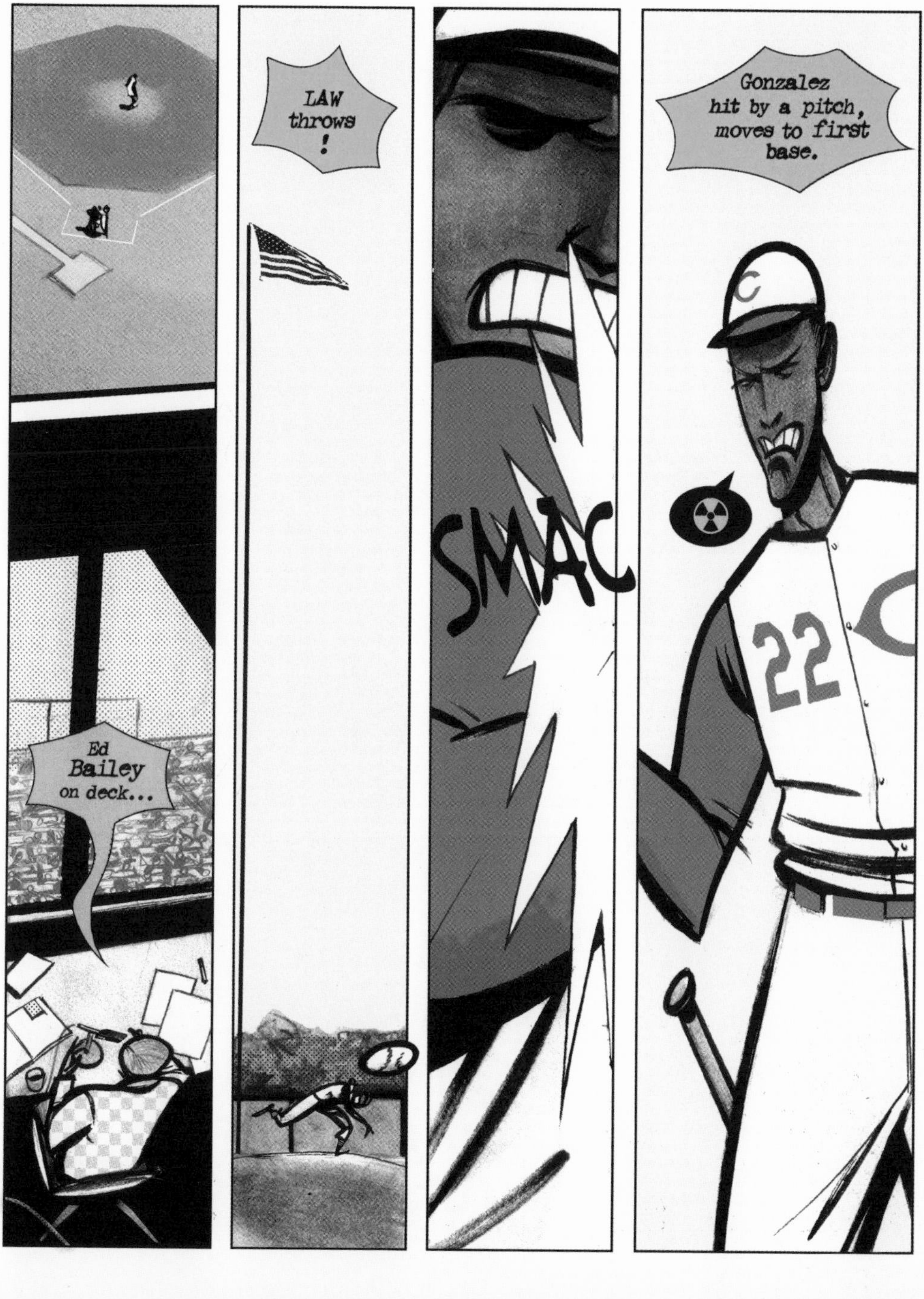
Ed Bailey on deck...
LAW throws !
SMAC
Gonzalez hit by a pitch, moves to first base.
22

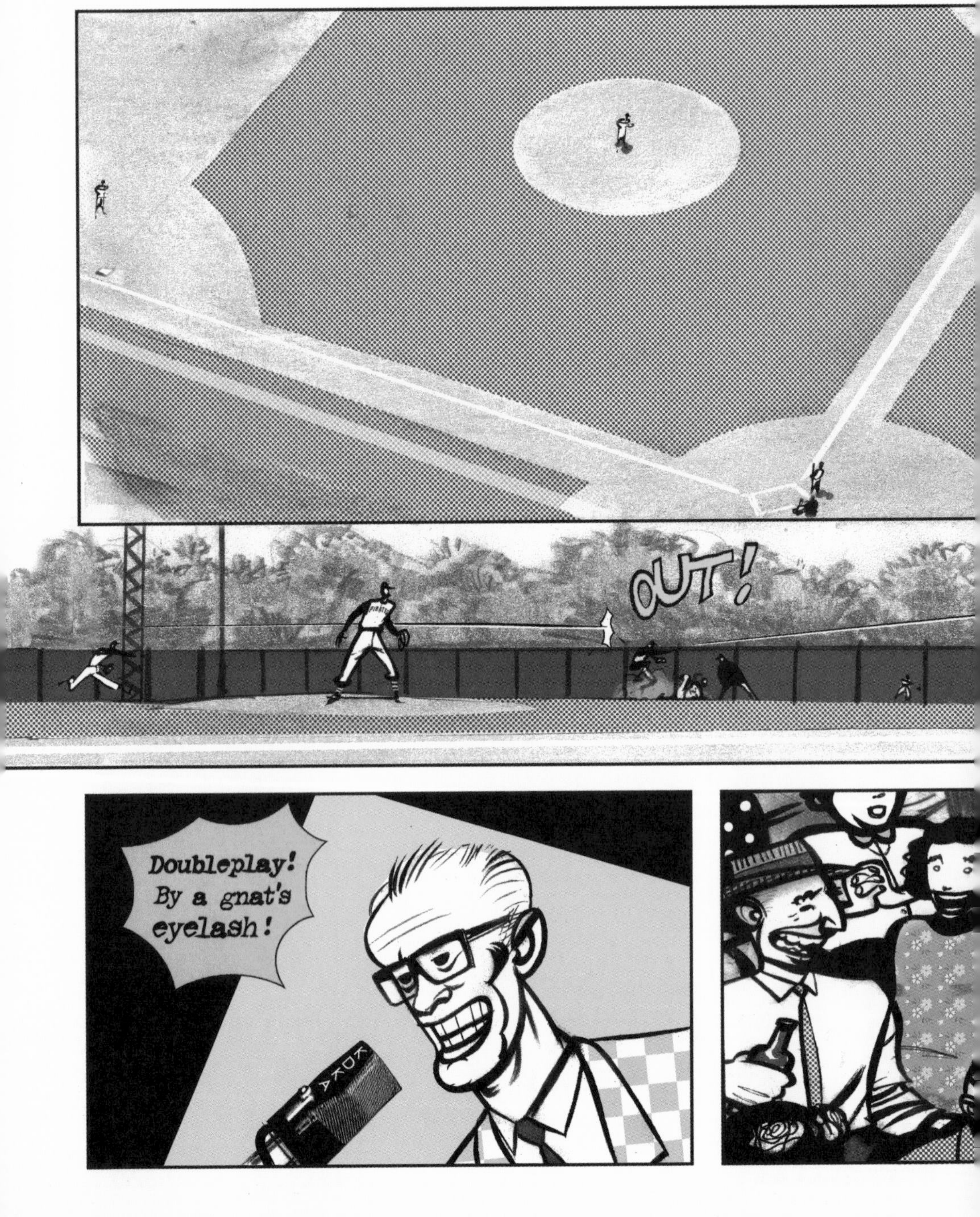
OUT!
Doubleplay! By a gnat's eyelash!
KDKA

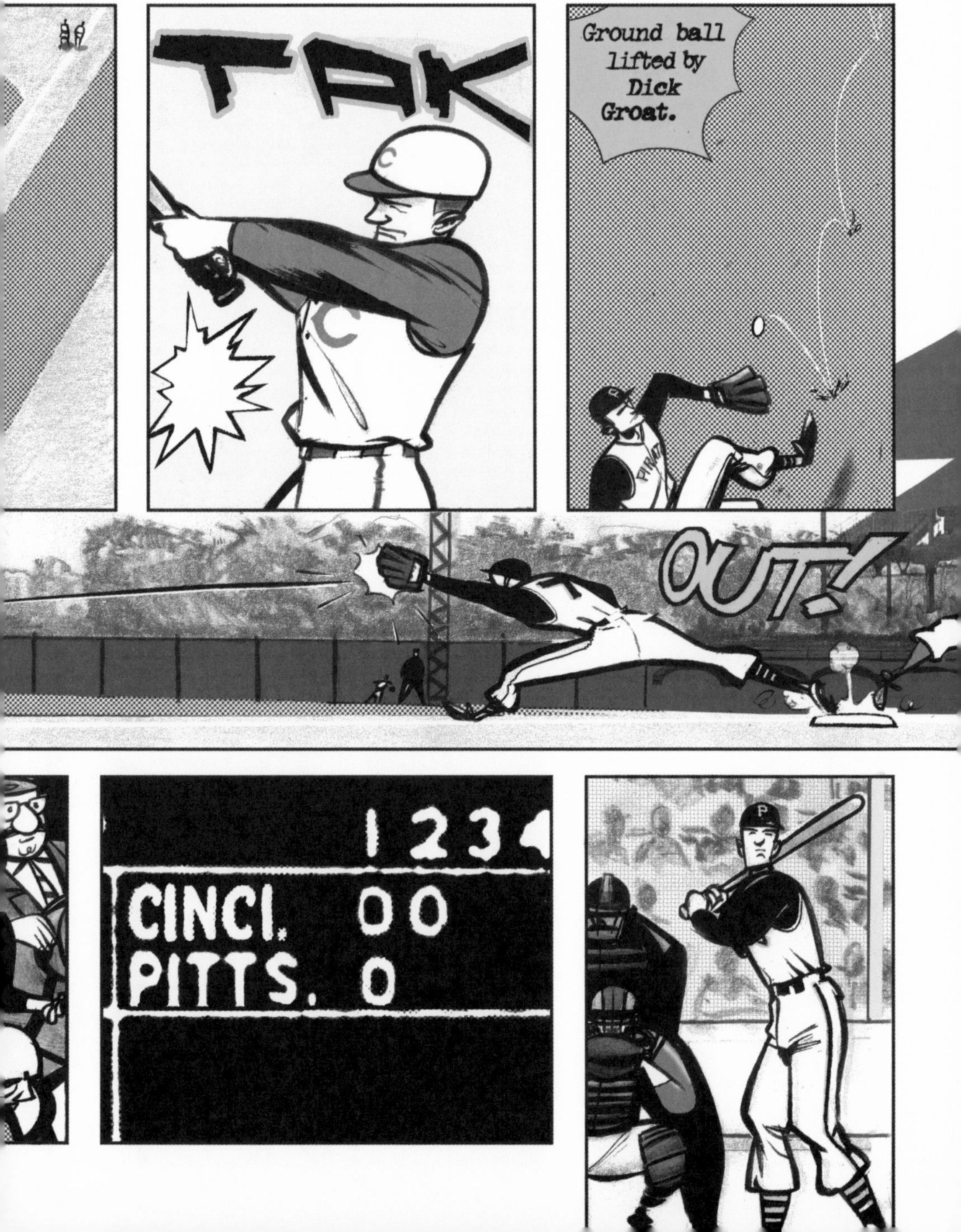
TAK
Ground ball lifted by Dick Groat.
OUT!
1 2 3
CINCI. 0 0
PITTS. 0

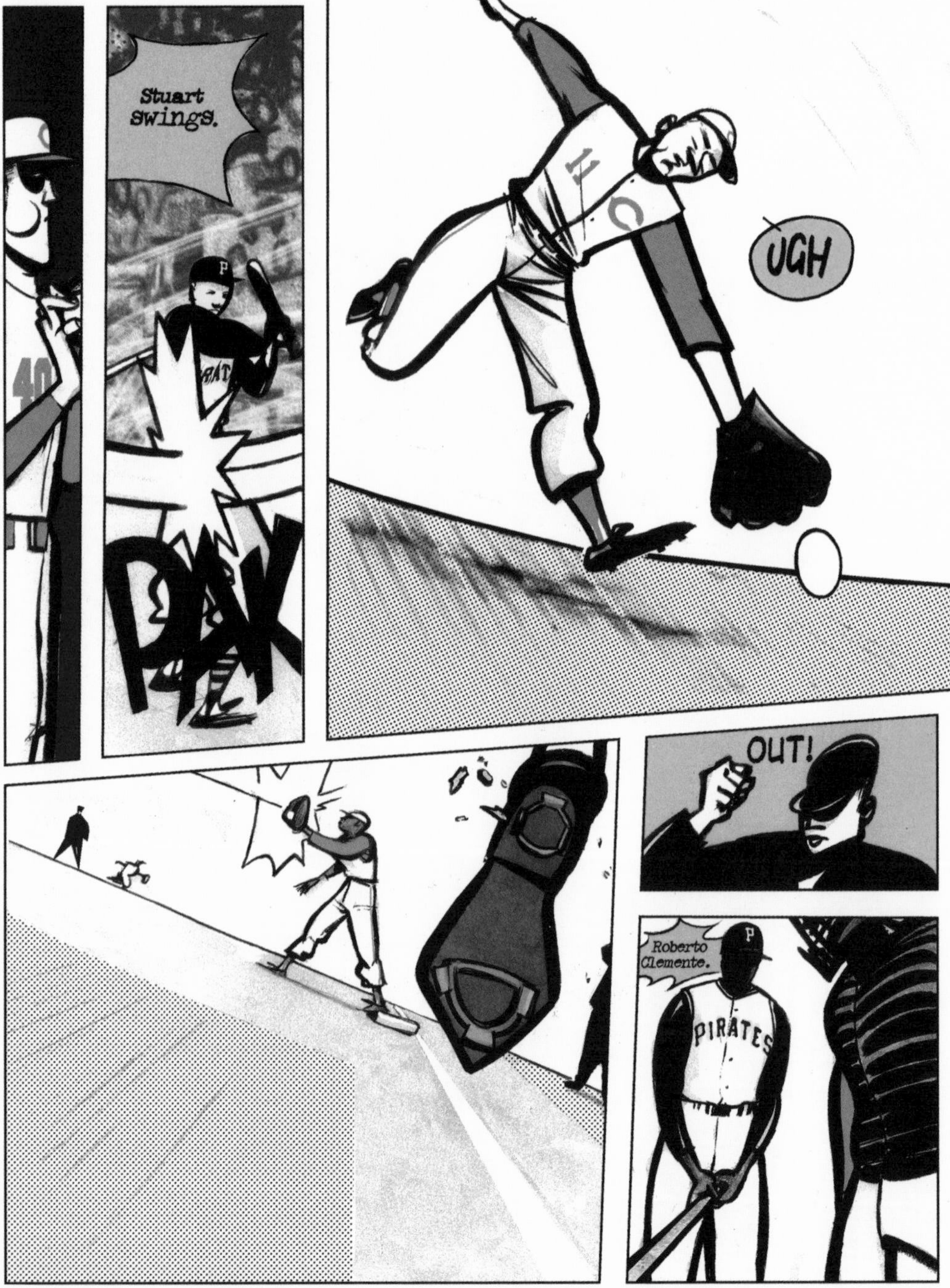
Stuart swings.
PAK
UGH
OUT!
Roberto Clemente.

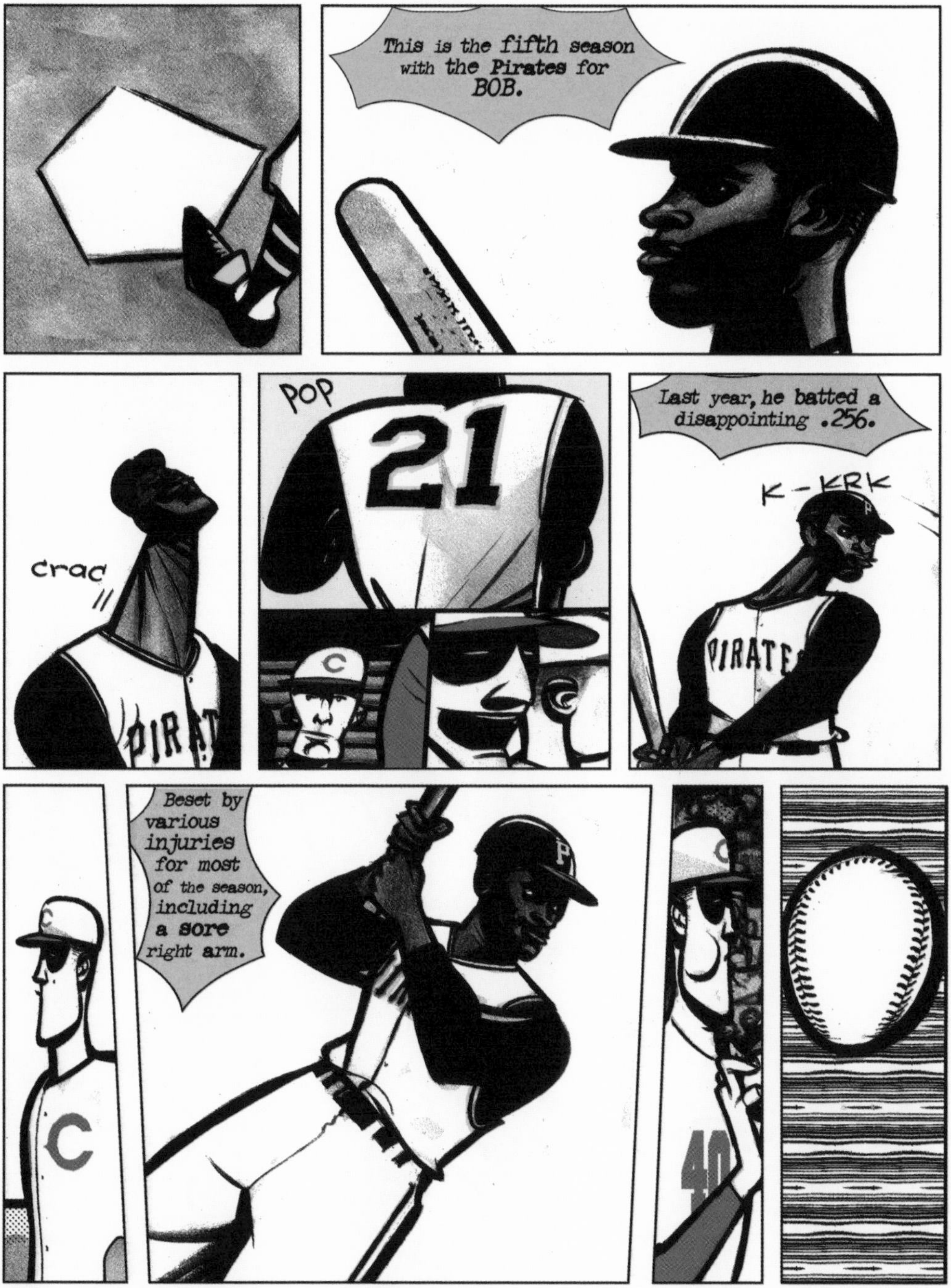
This is the fifth season with the Pirates for BOB.
crac
POP
21
Last year, he batted a disappointing .256.
K-KRK
PIRATES
Beset by various injuries for most of the season, including a sore right arm.
40

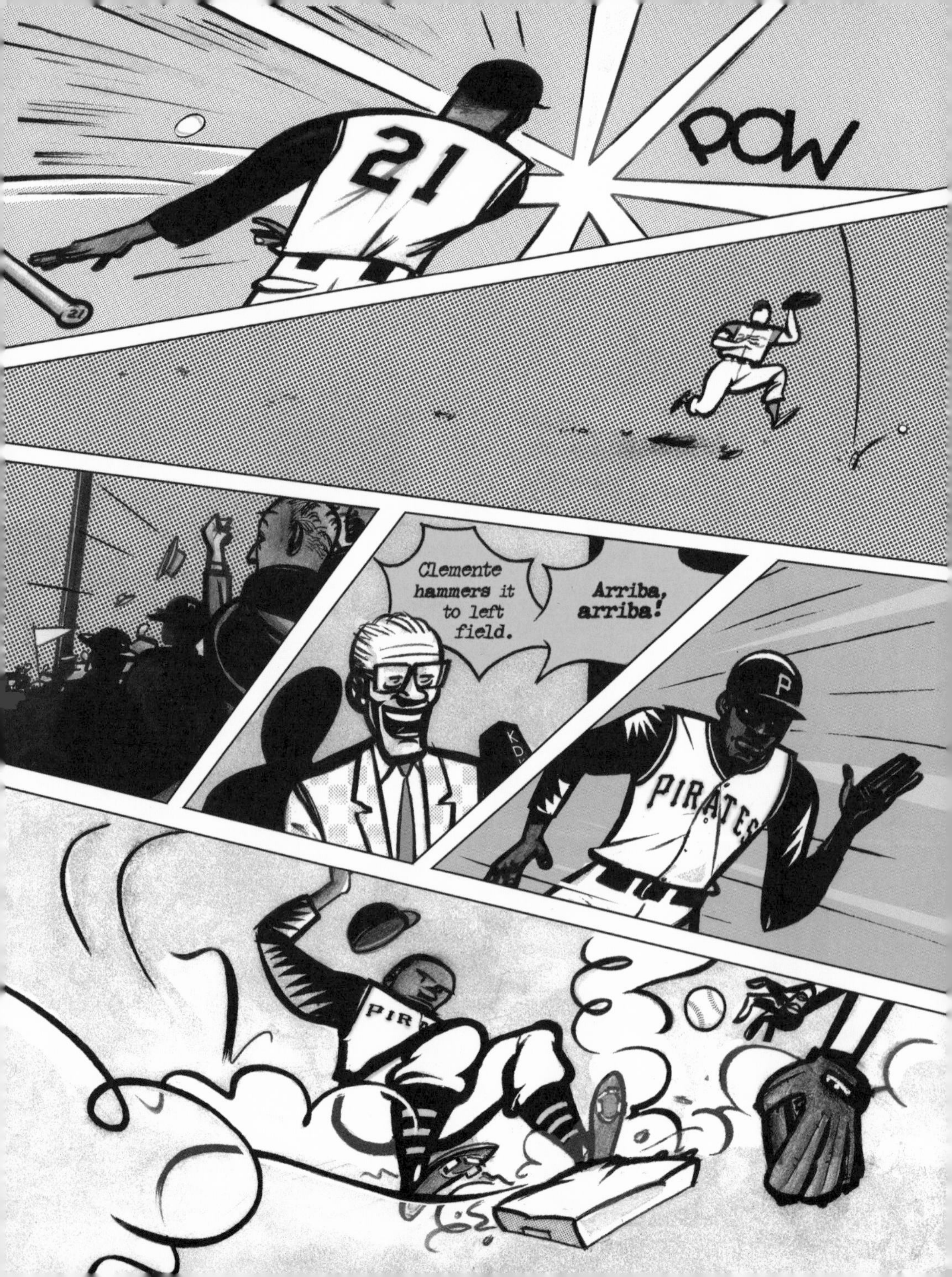
POW
Clemente hammers it to left field.
Arriba, arriba!
PIRATES
PIR

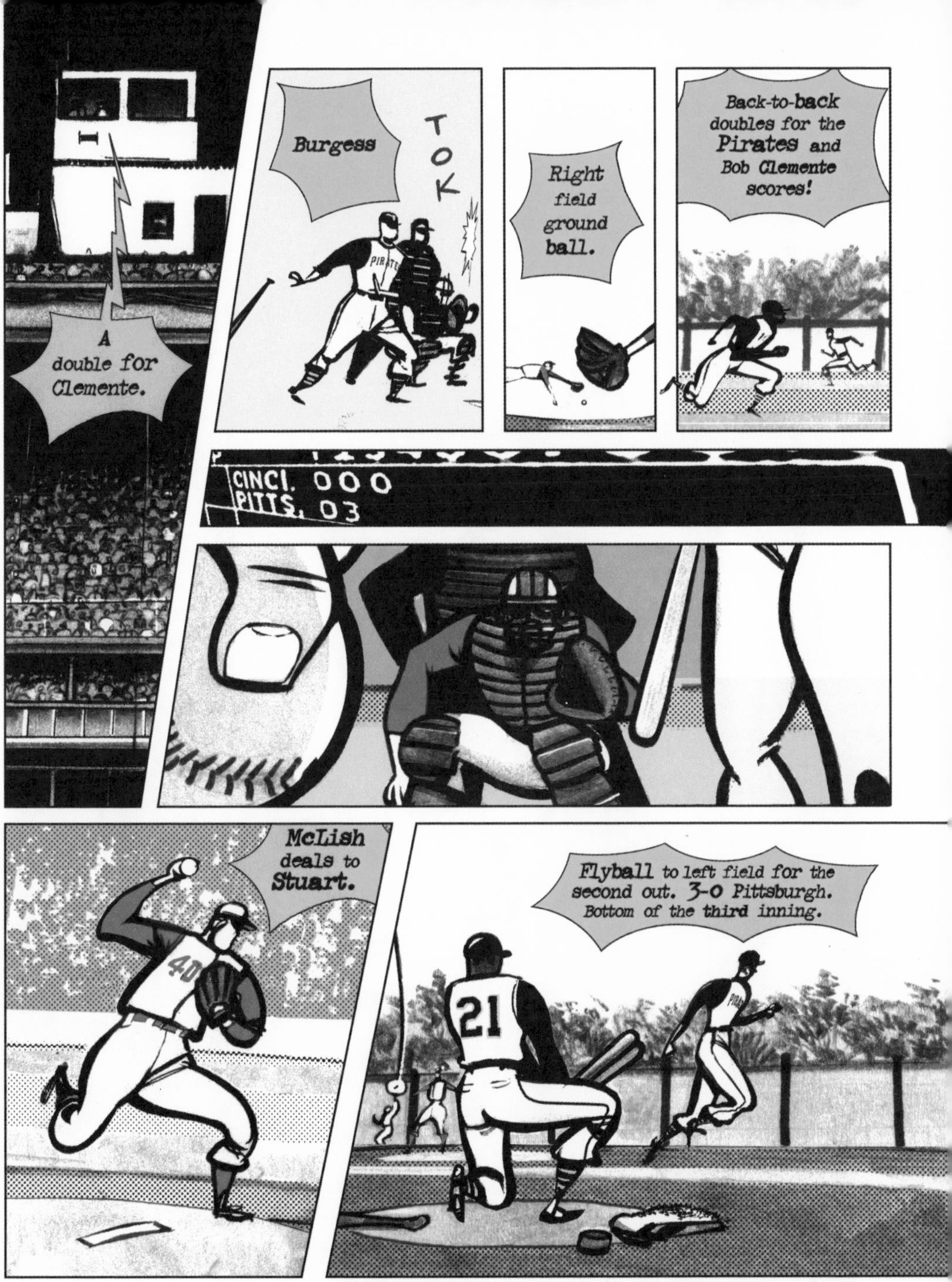

A double for Clemente.
Burgess
TOK
Right field ground ball.
Back-to-back doubles for the Pirates and Bob Clemente scores!
CINCI. 000
PITTS. 03
McLish deals to Stuart.
Flyball to left field for the second out. 3-0 Pittsburgh. Bottom of the third inning.

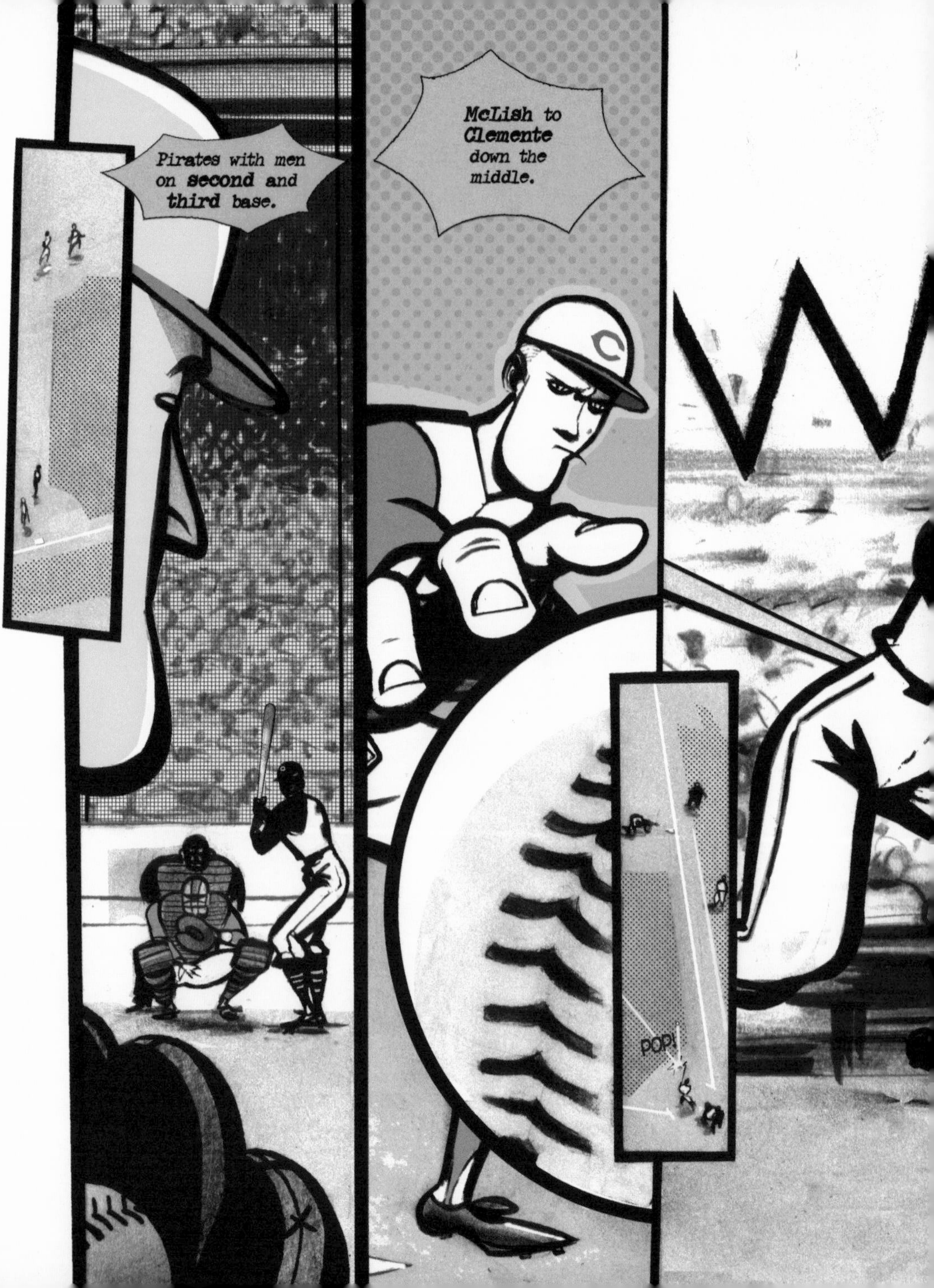
Pirates with men on second and third base.
McLish to Clemente down the middle.
POP!
W

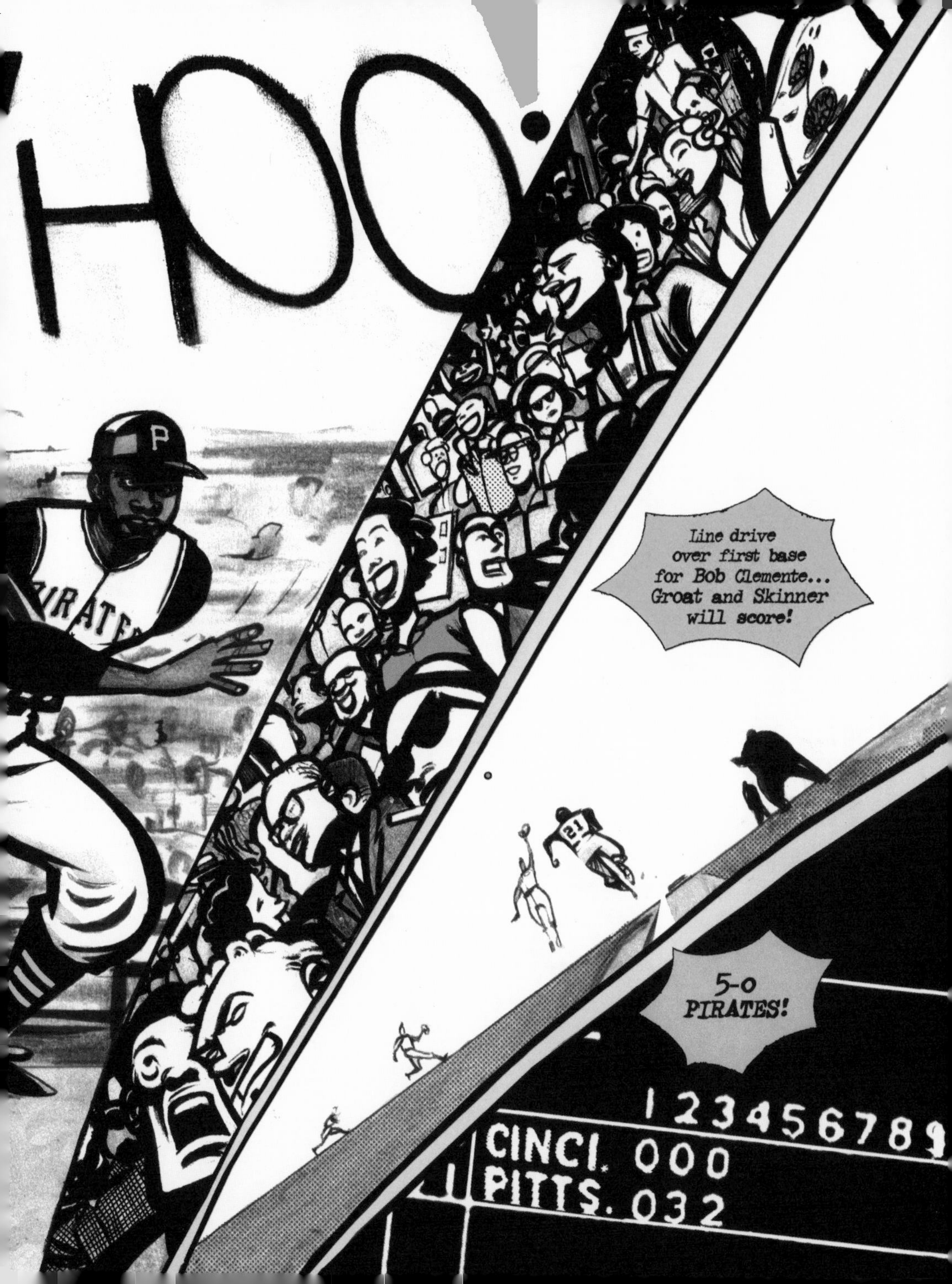

HOO!
Line drive over first base for Bob Clemente... Groat and Skinner will score!
5-0 PIRATES!
1 2 3 4 5 6 7 8 9
CINCI. 0 0 0
PITTS. 0 3 2

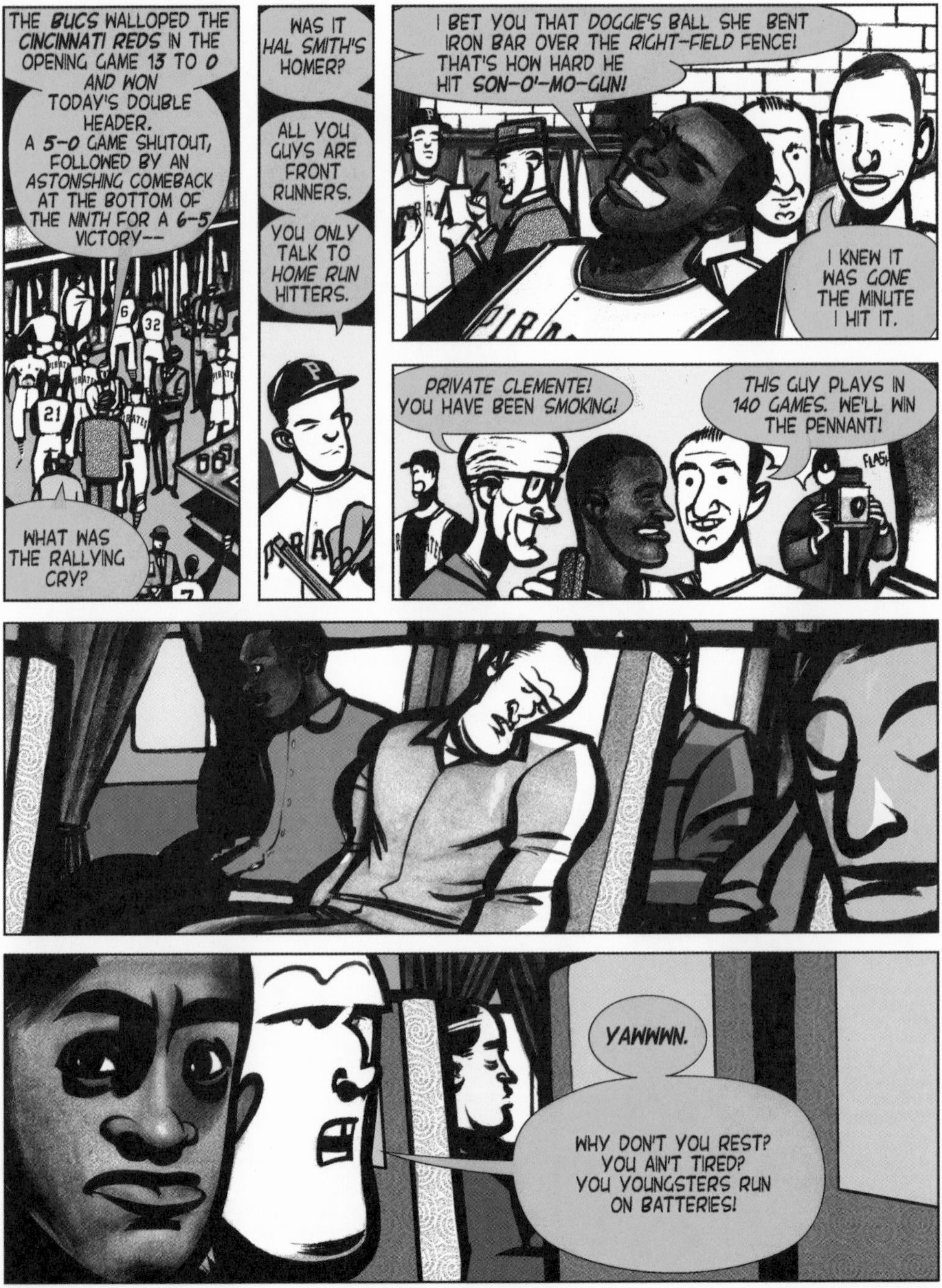
THE BUCS WALLOPED THE CINCINNATI REDS IN THE OPENING GAME 13 TO 0 AND WON TODAY'S DOUBLE HEADER. A 5-0 GAME SHUTOUT, FOLLOWED BY AN ASTONISHING COMEBACK AT THE BOTTOM OF THE NINTH FOR A 6-5 VICTORY--
WHAT WAS THE RALLYING CRY?
WAS IT HAL SMITH'S HOMER?
ALL YOU GUYS ARE FRONT RUNNERS.
YOU ONLY TALK TO HOME RUN HITTERS.
I BET YOU THAT DOGGIE'S BALL SHE BENT IRON BAR OVER THE RIGHT-FIELD FENCE! THAT'S HOW HARD HE HIT SON-O'-MO-GUN!
I KNEW IT WAS GONE THE MINUTE I HIT IT.
PRIVATE CLEMENTE! YOU HAVE BEEN SMOKING!
THIS GUY PLAYS IN 140 GAMES. WE'LL WIN THE PENNANT!
FLASH
YAWWWN.
WHY DON'T YOU REST? YOU AIN'T TIRED? YOU YOUNGSTERS RUN ON BATTERIES!

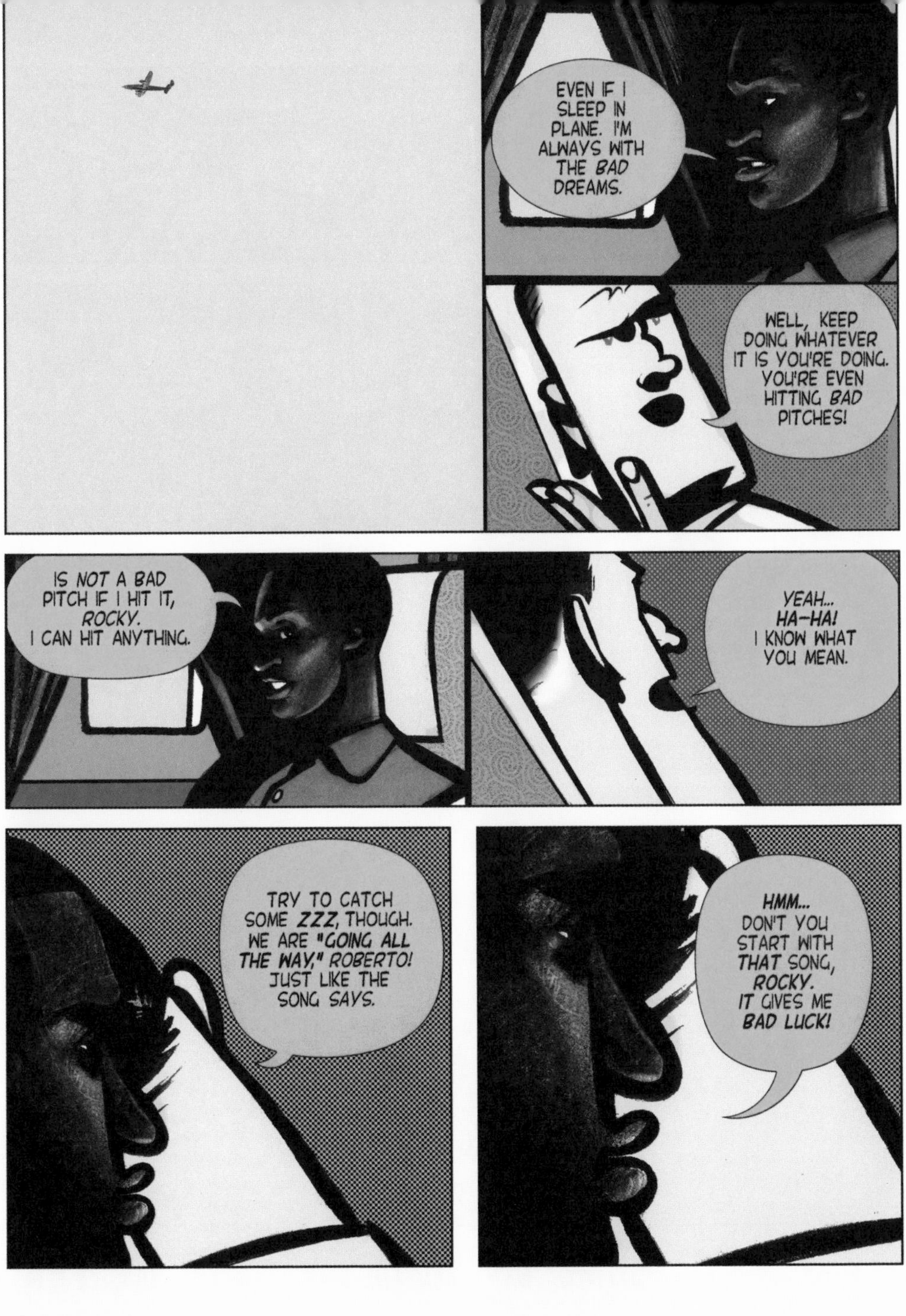
EVEN IF I SLEEP IN PLANE. I'M ALWAYS WITH THE *BAD* DREAMS.
WELL, KEEP DOING WHATEVER IT IS YOU'RE DOING. YOU'RE EVEN HITTING *BAD* PITCHES!
IS *NOT* A BAD PITCH IF I HIT IT, *ROCKY*. I CAN HIT ANYTHING.
YEAH... HA-HA! I KNOW WHAT YOU MEAN.
TRY TO CATCH SOME *ZZZ*, THOUGH. WE ARE *"GOING ALL THE WAY,"* ROBERTO! JUST LIKE THE SONG SAYS.
HMM... DON'T YOU START WITH *THAT* SONG, *ROCKY*. *IT* GIVES ME *BAD LUCK!*

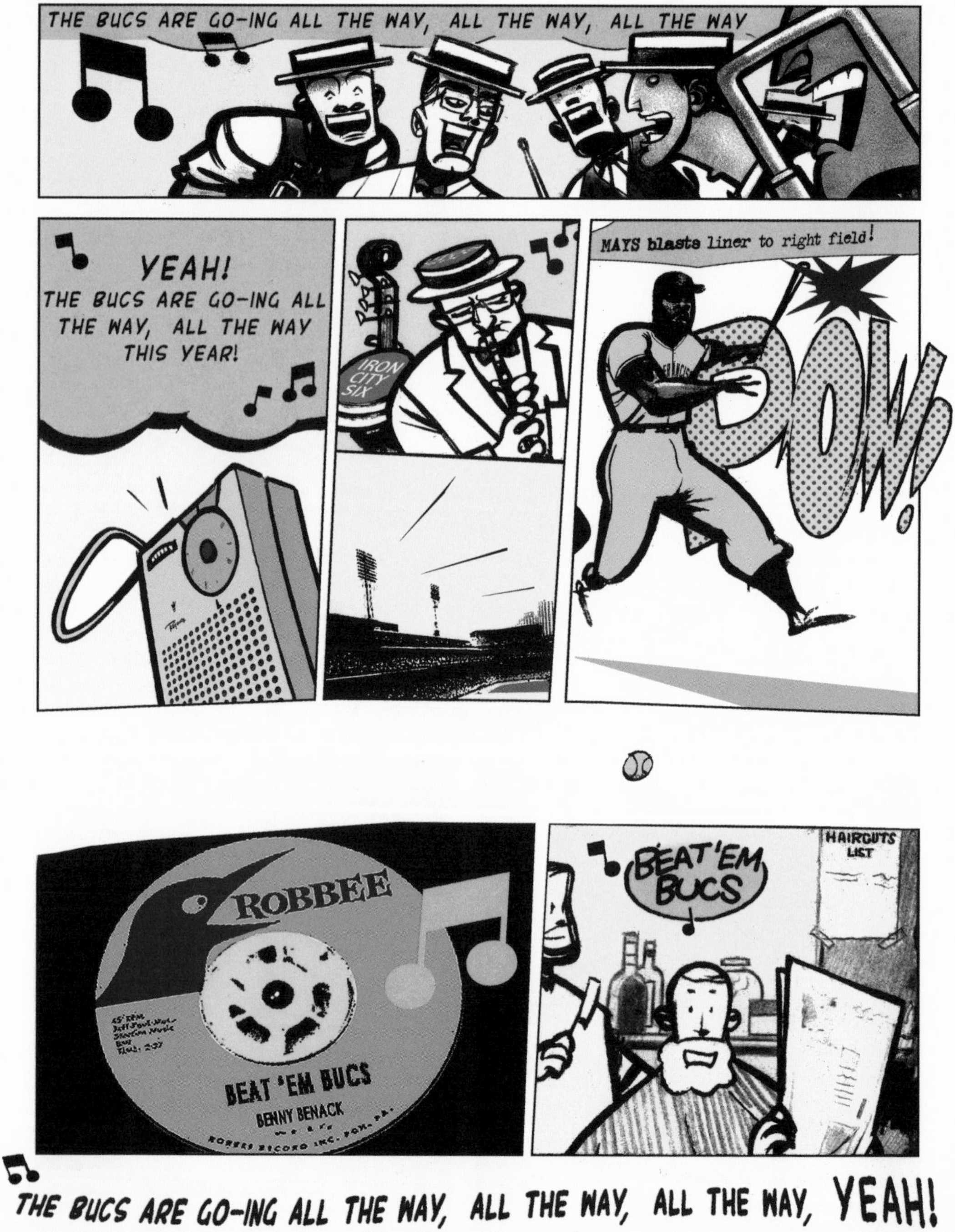

THE BUCS ARE GO-ING ALL THE WAY, ALL THE WAY, ALL THE WAY
YEAH!
THE BUCS ARE GO-ING ALL THE WAY, ALL THE WAY THIS YEAR!
IRON CITY SIX
MAYS blasts liner to right field!
POW!
ROBBEE
BEAT 'EM BUCS
BENNY BENACK
HAIRCUTS LIST
BEAT 'EM BUCS
THE BUCS ARE GO-ING ALL THE WAY, ALL THE WAY, ALL THE WAY, YEAH!

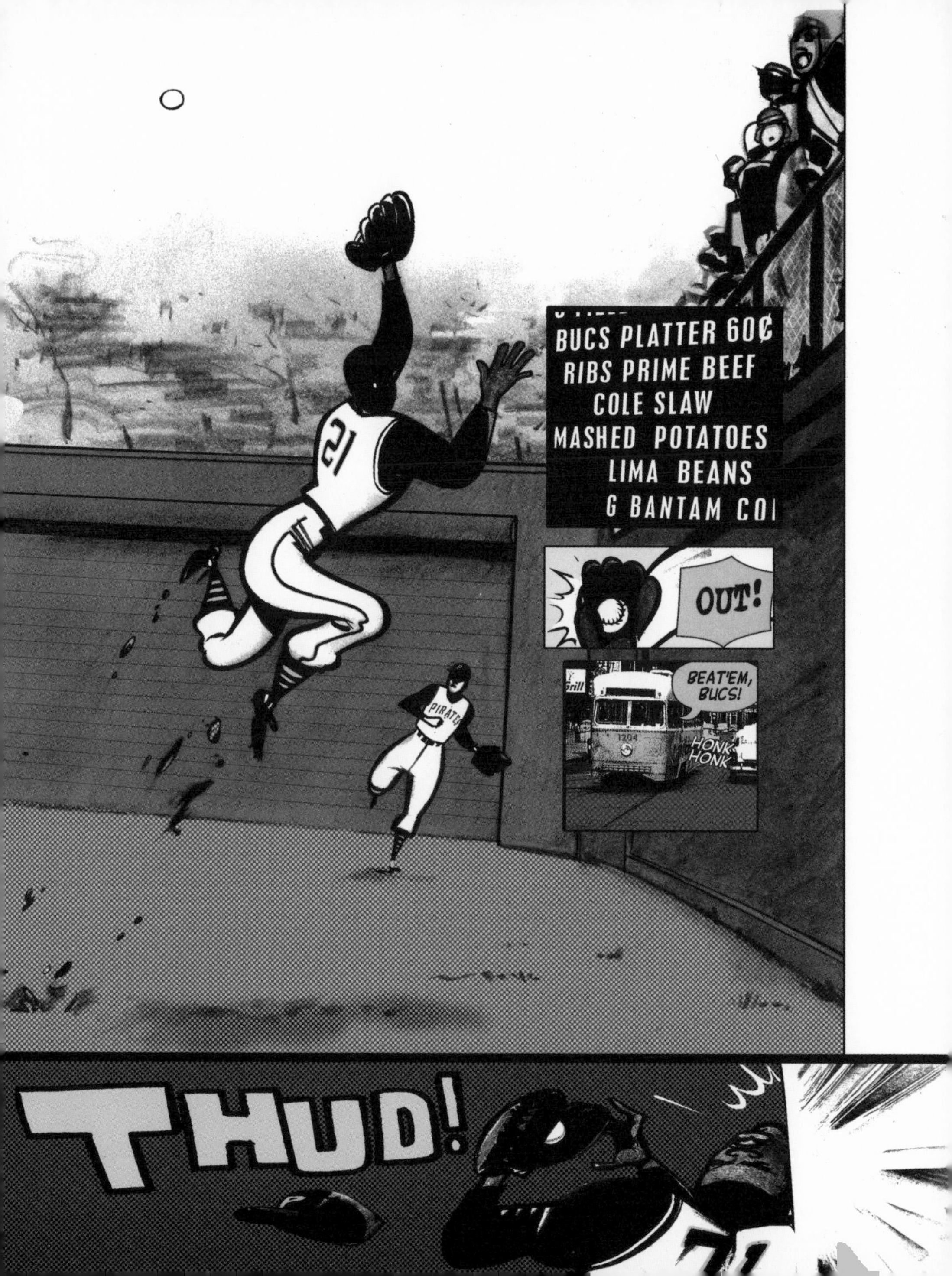
BUCS PLATTER 60¢
RIBS PRIME BEEF
COLE SLAW
MASHED POTATOES
LIMA BEANS
G BANTAM CO
OUT!
BEAT'EM, BUCS!
HONK HONK
THUD!

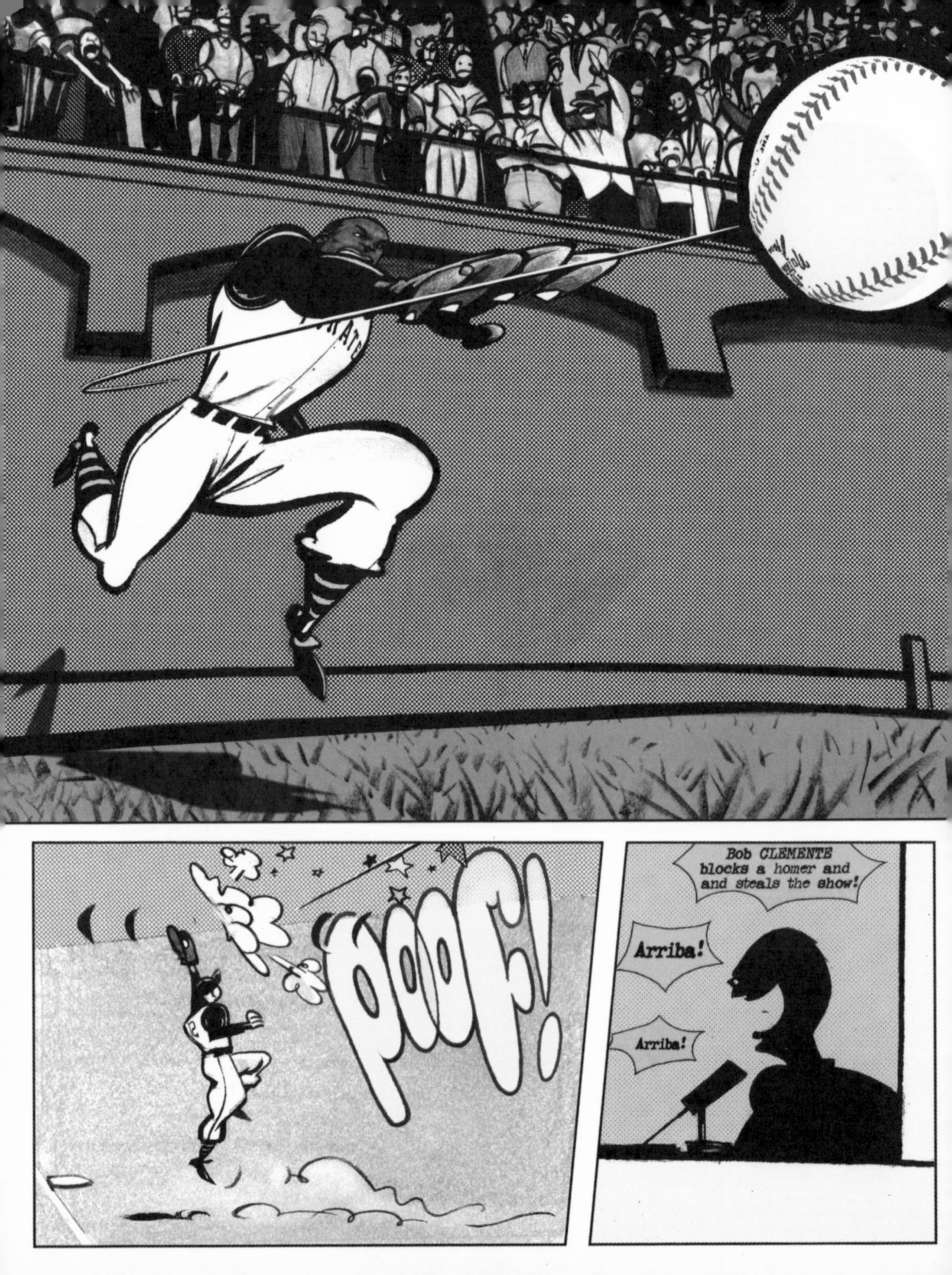
POOF!
Bob CLEMENTE blocks a homer and and steals the show!
Arriba!
Arriba!

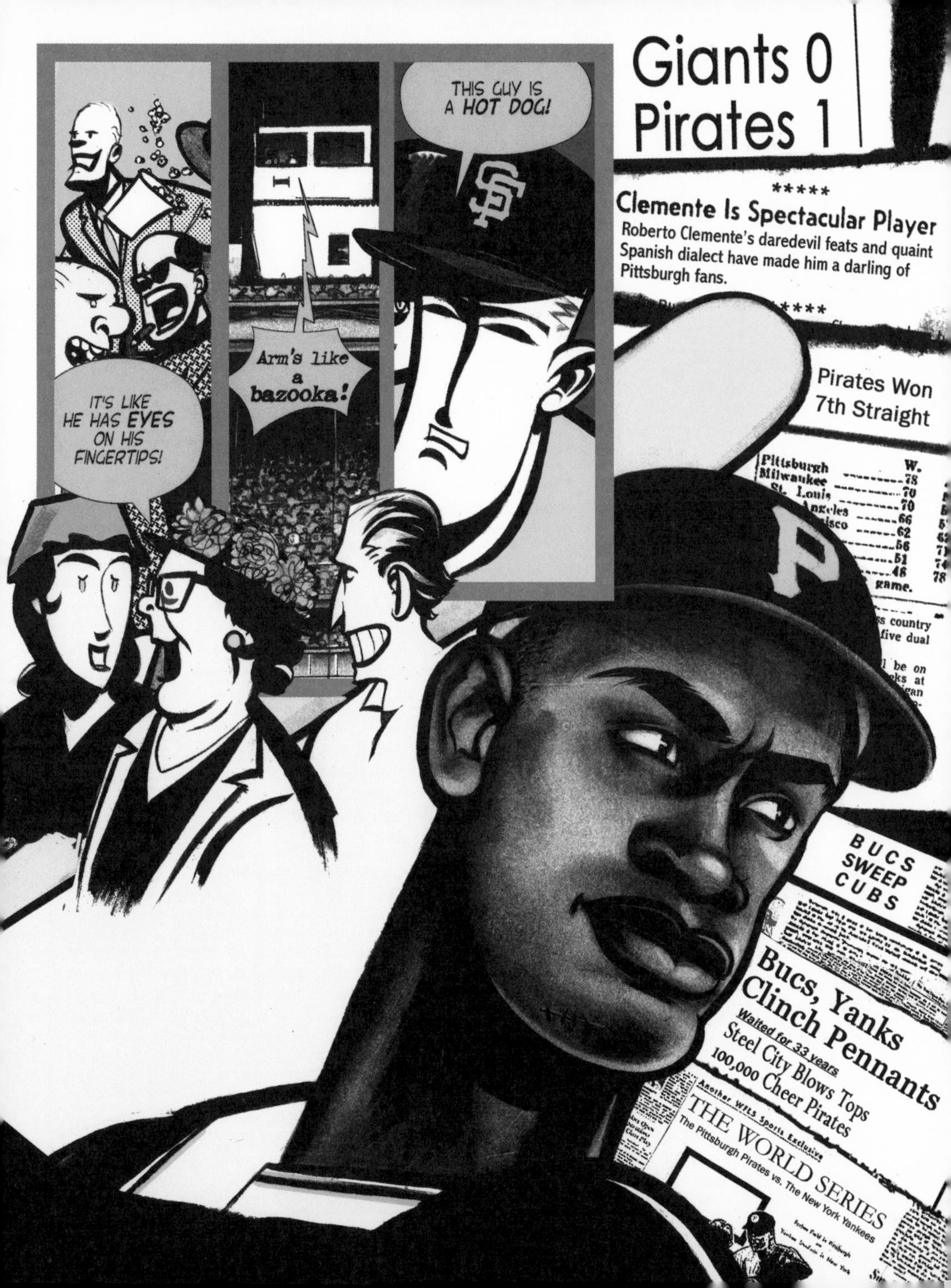
IT'S LIKE HE HAS EYES ON HIS FINGERTIPS!
Arm's like a bazooka!
THIS GUY IS A HOT DOG!
Giants 0
Pirates 1
*****
Clemente Is Spectacular Player
Roberto Clemente's daredevil feats and quaint Spanish dialect have made him a darling of Pittsburgh fans.
Pirates Won 7th Straight
BUCS SWEEP CUBS
Bucs, Yanks Clinch Pennants
Waited for 33 years
Steel City Blows Tops
100,000 Cheer Pirates
Another WFLS Sports Exclusive
THE WORLD SERIES
The Pittsburgh Pirates vs. The New York Yankees

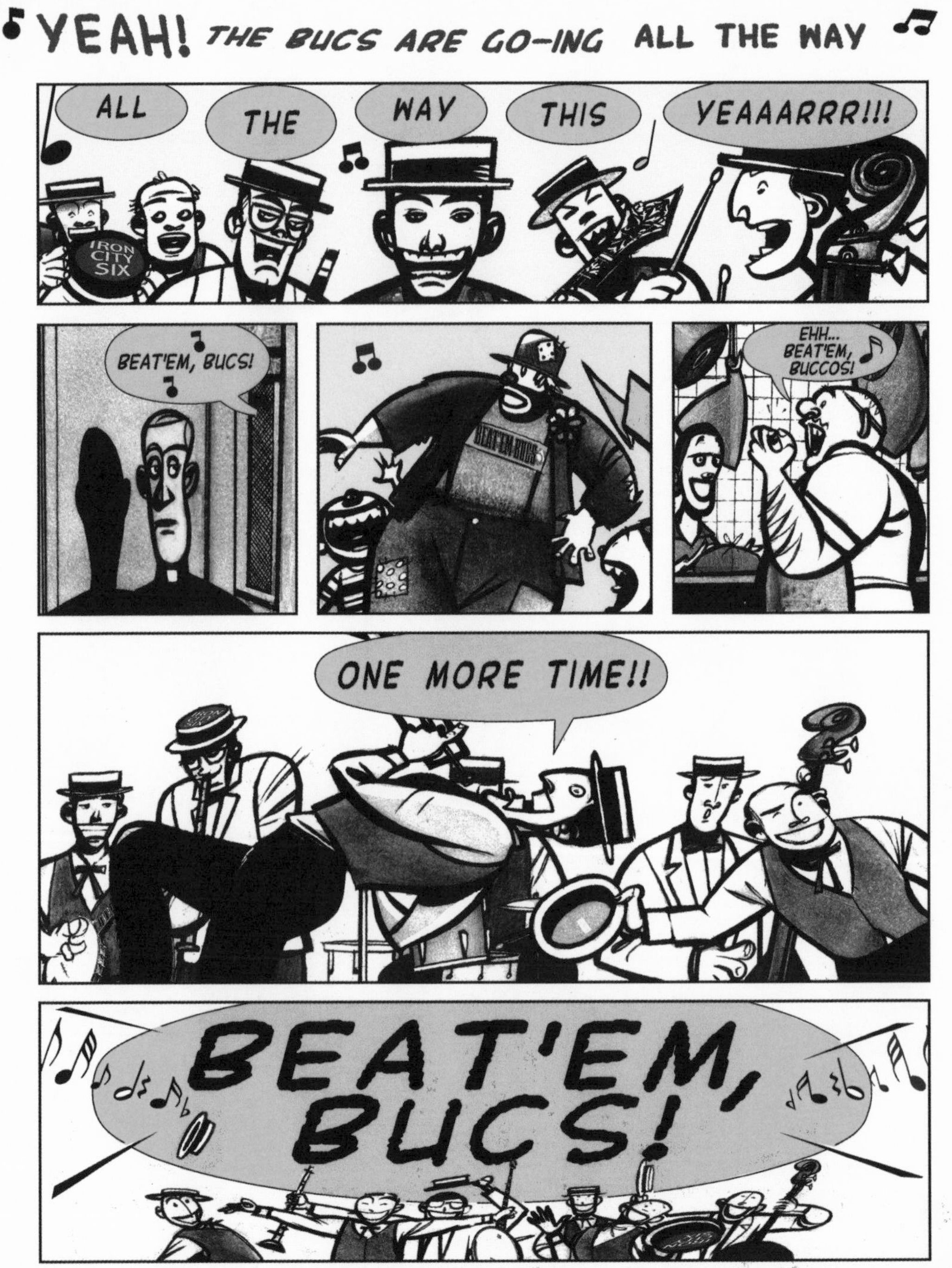
YEAH! THE BUCS ARE GO-ING ALL THE WAY
ALL
THE
WAY
THIS
YEAAARRR!!!
IRON CITY SIX
BEAT'EM, BUCS!
BEAT'EM BUCS
EHH... BEAT'EM, BUCCOS!
ONE MORE TIME!!
BEAT'EM, BUCS!

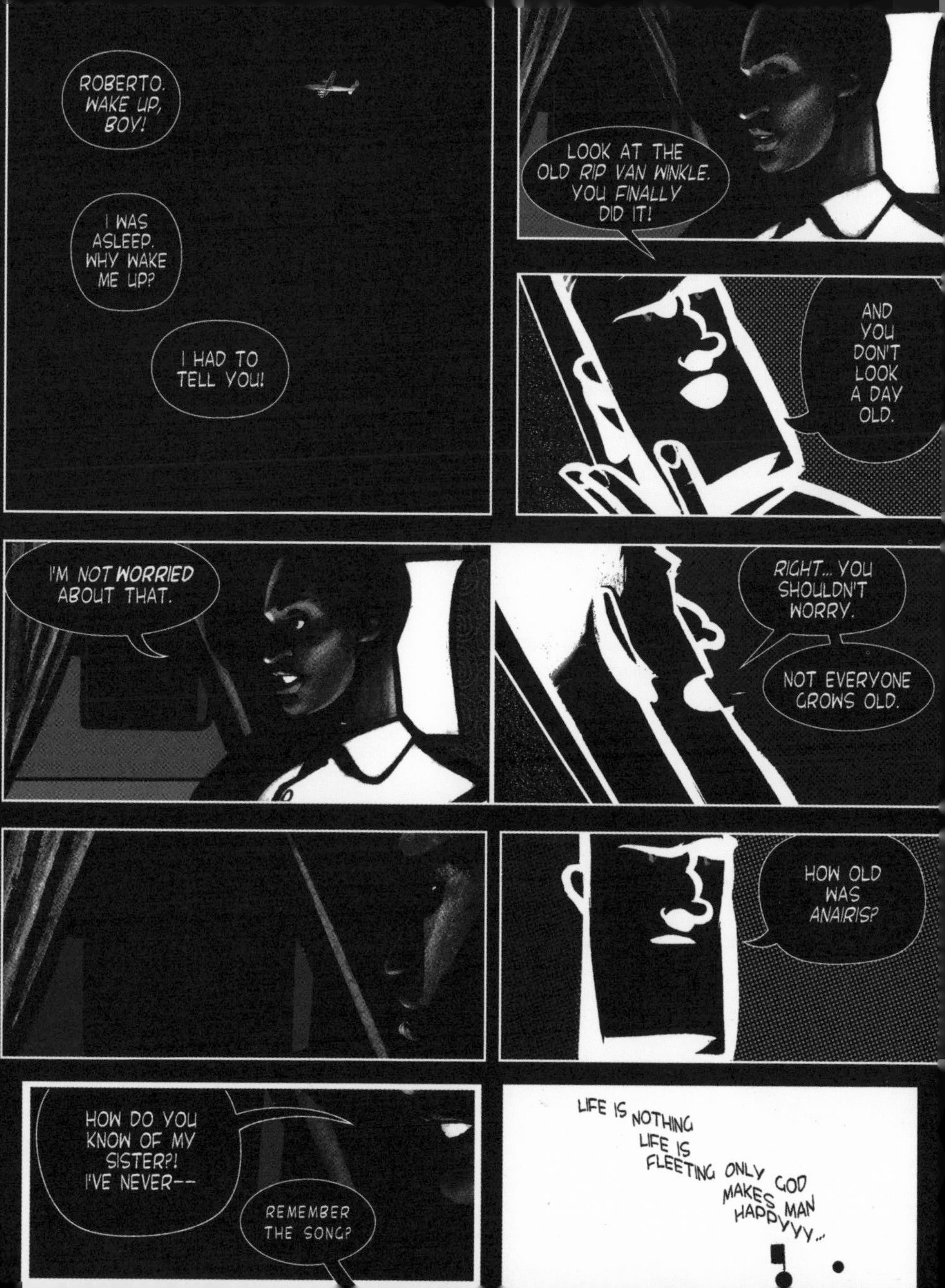
ROBERTO. WAKE UP, BOY!
I WAS ASLEEP. WHY WAKE ME UP?
I HAD TO TELL YOU!
LOOK AT THE OLD RIP VAN WINKLE. YOU FINALLY DID IT!
AND YOU DON'T LOOK A DAY OLD.
I'M NOT WORRIED ABOUT THAT.
RIGHT... YOU SHOULDN'T WORRY.
NOT EVERYONE GROWS OLD.
HOW OLD WAS ANAIRIS?
HOW DO YOU KNOW OF MY SISTER?! I'VE NEVER--
REMEMBER THE SONG?
LIFE IS NOTHING LIFE IS FLEETING ONLY GOD MAKES MAN HAPPYYY...

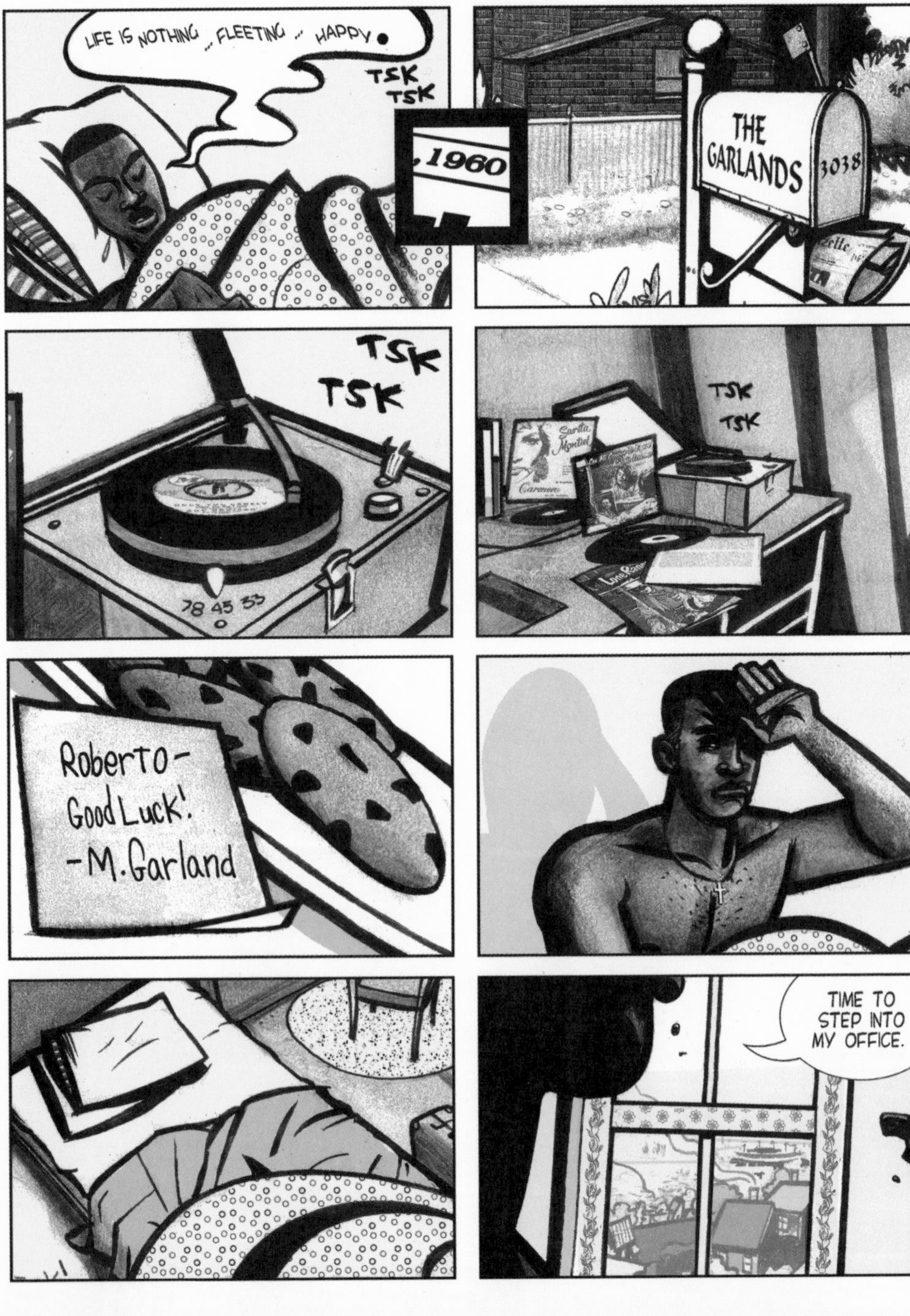
LIFE IS NOTHING ... FLEETING ... HAPPY.
TSK TSK
1960
THE GARLANDS
3038
TSK TSK
78 45 33
TSK TSK
Sarita Montiel
Carmen
Roberto-
Good Luck!
-M.Garland
TIME TO STEP INTO MY OFFICE.

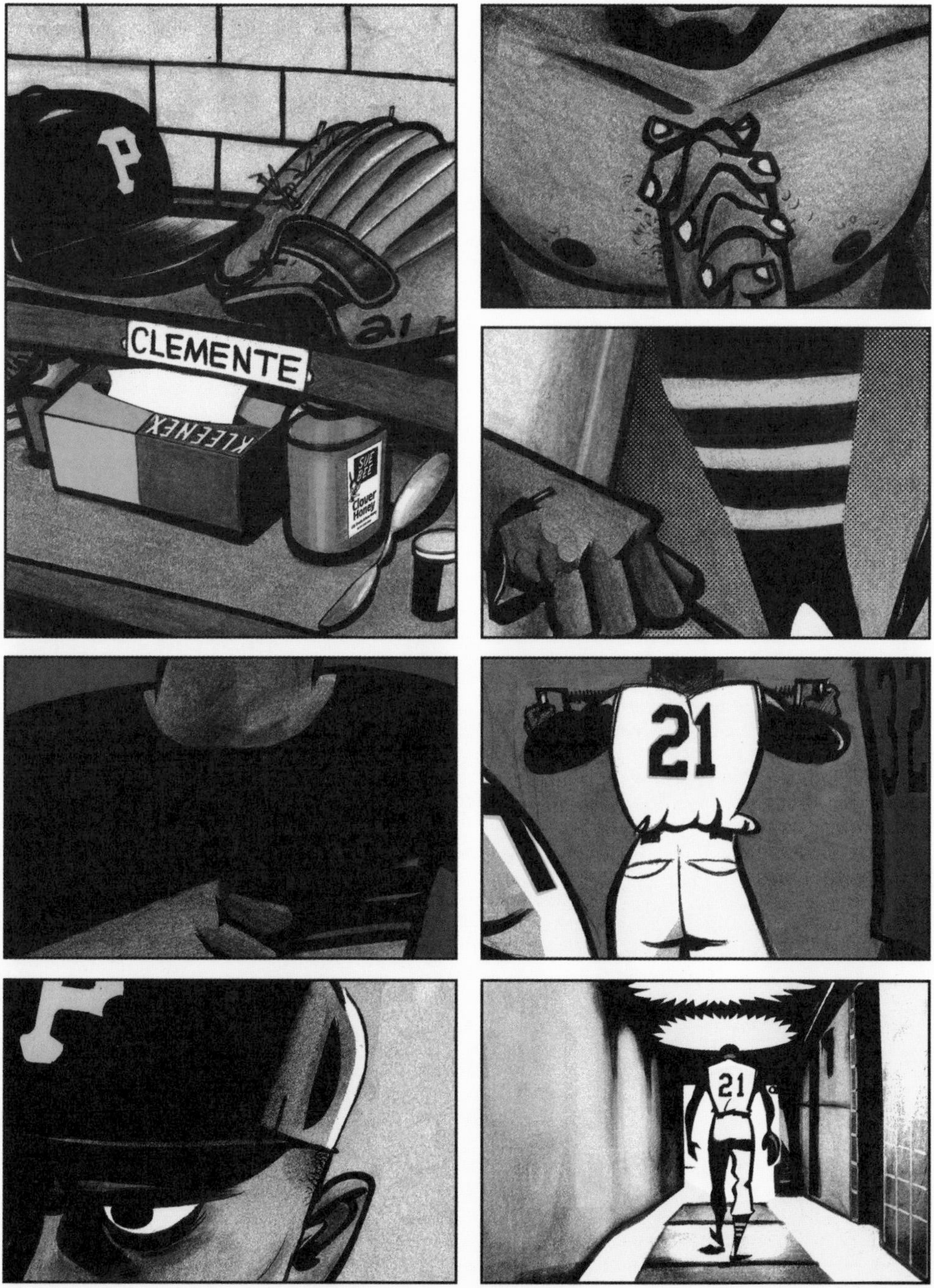
CLEMENTE
21
KLEENEX
SUE BEE
Clover Honey
21
21

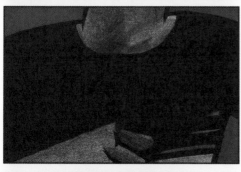

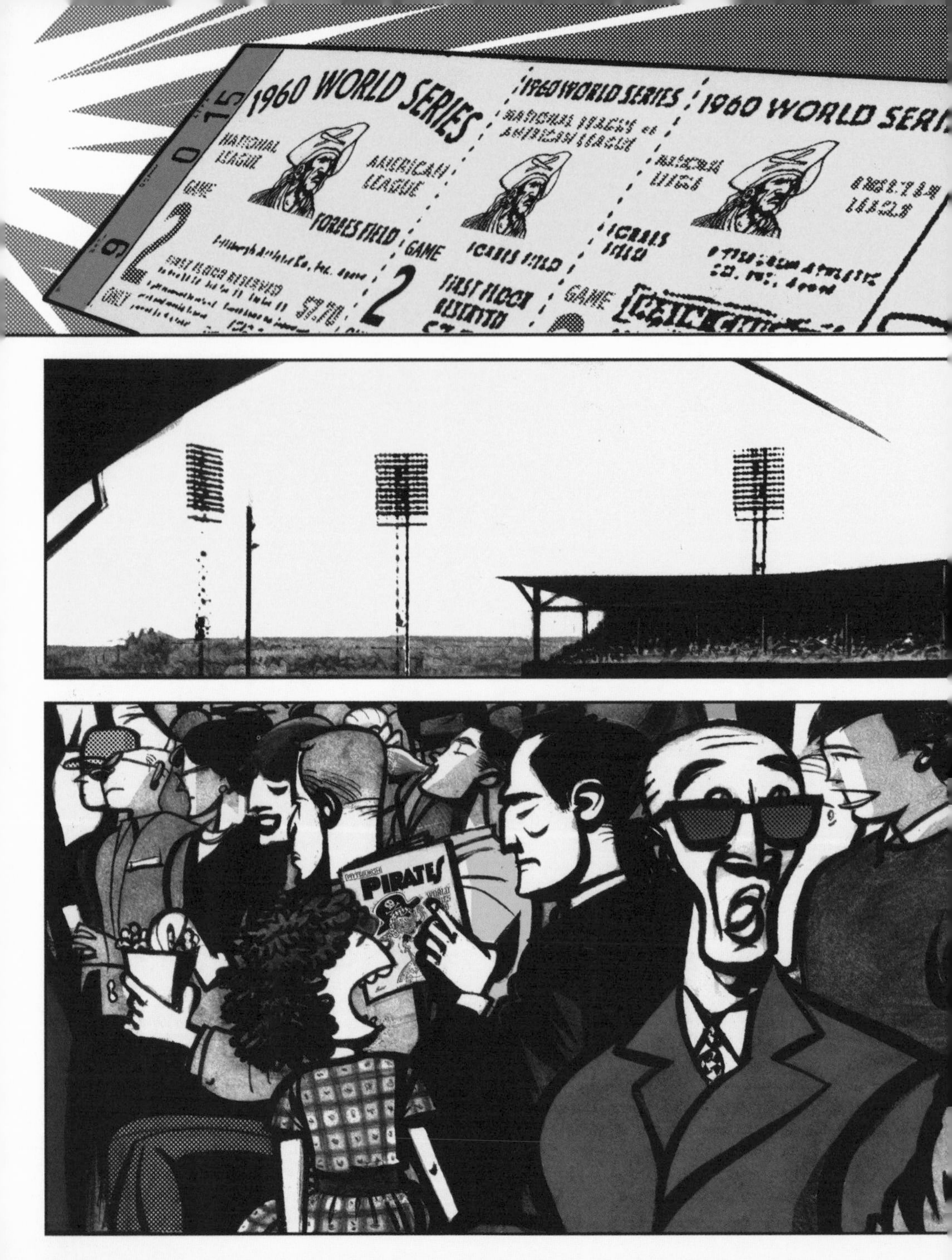
1960 WORLD SERIES
NATIONAL LEAGUE
AMERICAN LEAGUE
GAME
2
FORBES FIELD
1960 WORLD SERIES
GAME
2
1960 WORLD SERI
PITTSBURGH
PIRATES

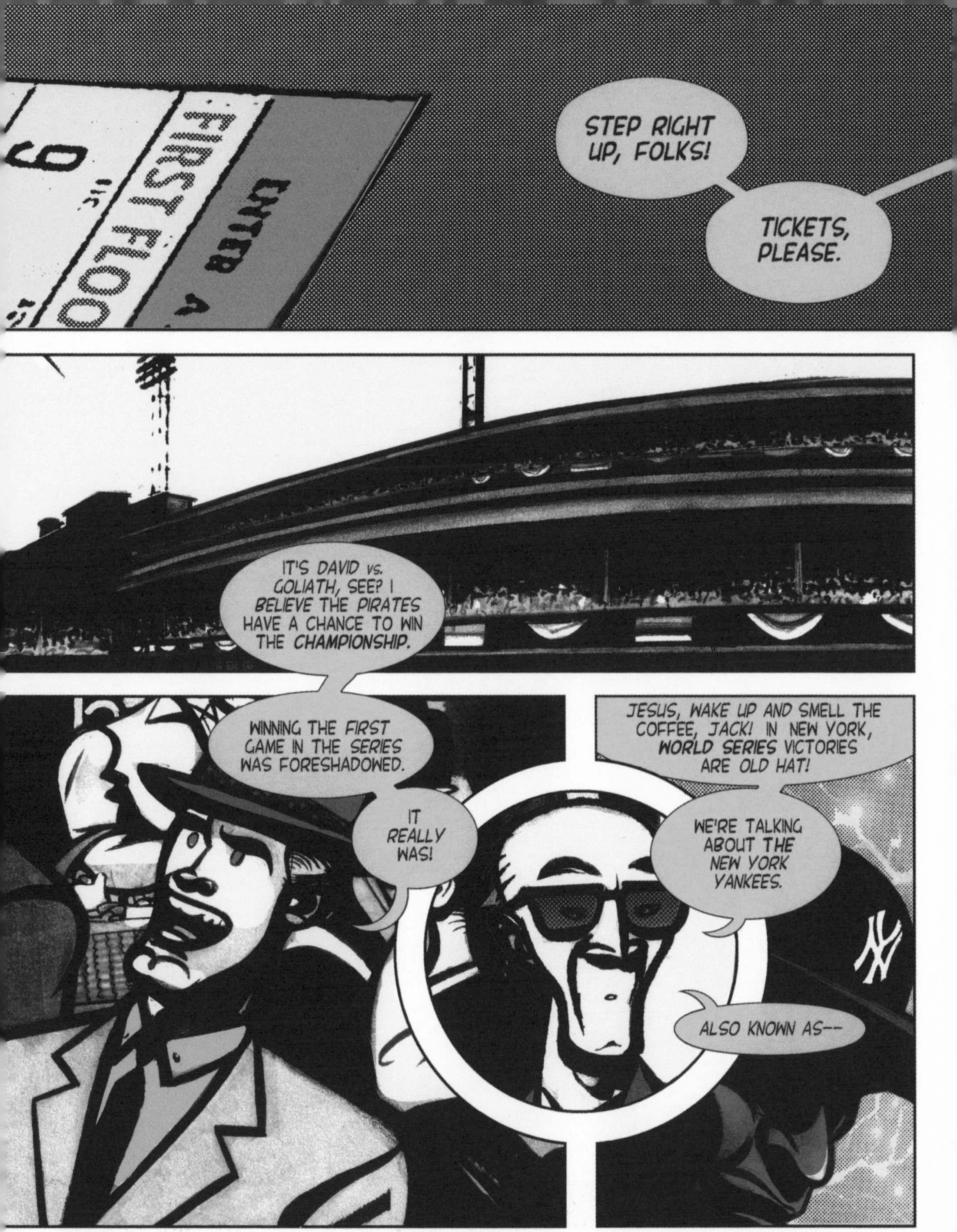
STEP RIGHT UP, FOLKS!
TICKETS, PLEASE.
IT'S DAVID vs. GOLIATH, SEE? I BELIEVE THE PIRATES HAVE A CHANCE TO WIN THE CHAMPIONSHIP.
WINNING THE FIRST GAME IN THE SERIES WAS FORESHADOWED.
IT REALLY WAS!
JESUS, WAKE UP AND SMELL THE COFFEE, JACK! IN NEW YORK, WORLD SERIES VICTORIES ARE OLD HAT!
WE'RE TALKING ABOUT THE NEW YORK YANKEES.
ALSO KNOWN AS--

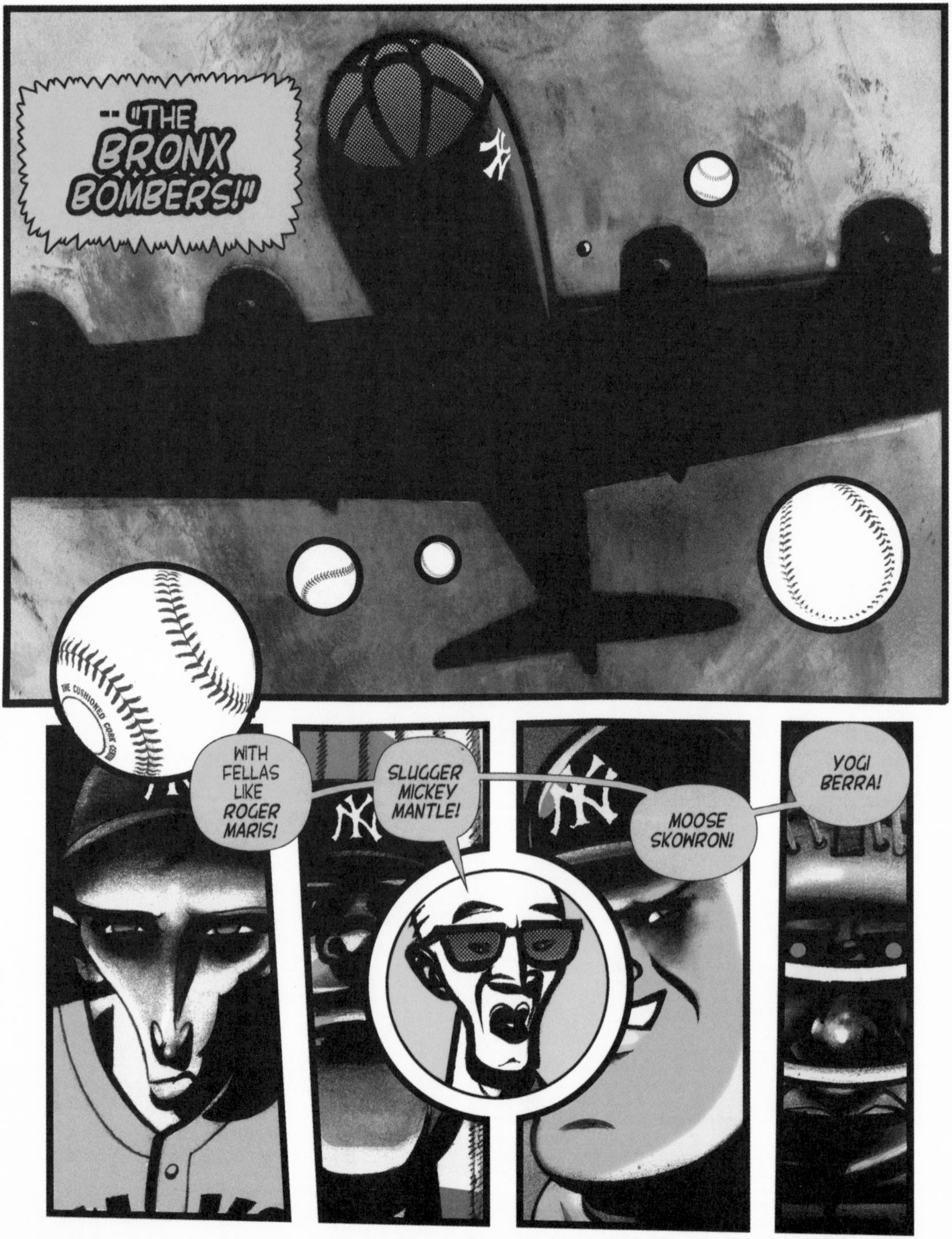
-- "THE BRONX BOMBERS!"
WITH FELLAS LIKE ROGER MARIS!
SLUGGER MICKEY MANTLE!
MOOSE SKOWRON!
YOGI BERRA!

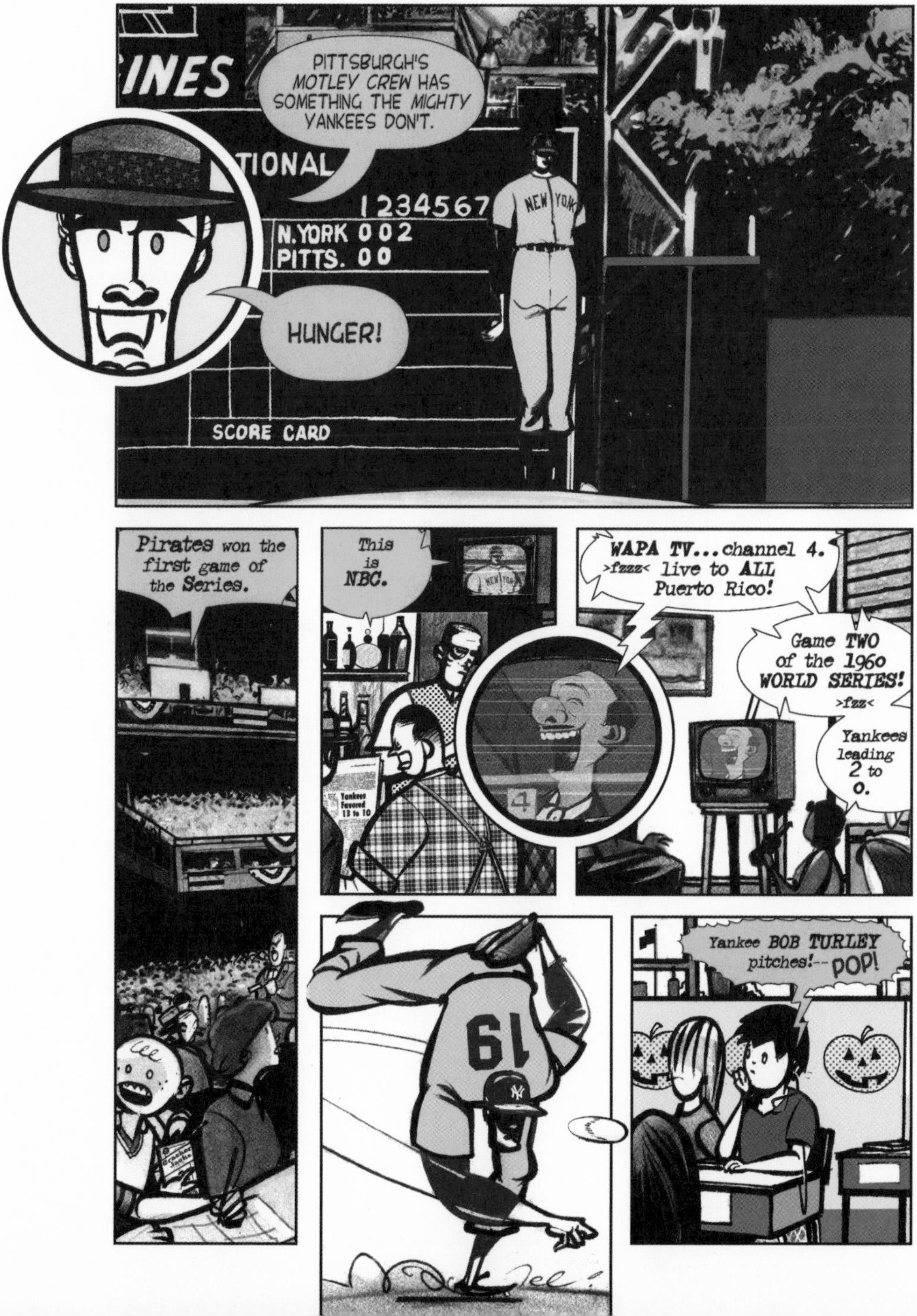

INES
PITTSBURGH'S MOTLEY CREW HAS SOMETHING THE MIGHTY YANKEES DON'T.
TIONAL
1234567
N.YORK 0 0 2
PITTS. 0 0
HUNGER!
SCORE CARD
Pirates won the first game of the Series.
This is NBC.
Yankees Favored 13 to 10
WAPA TV...channel 4. >fzzz< live to ALL Puerto Rico!
Game TWO of the 1960 WORLD SERIES!
>fzz<
Yankees leading 2 to 0.
Yankee BOB TURLEY pitches!--POP!

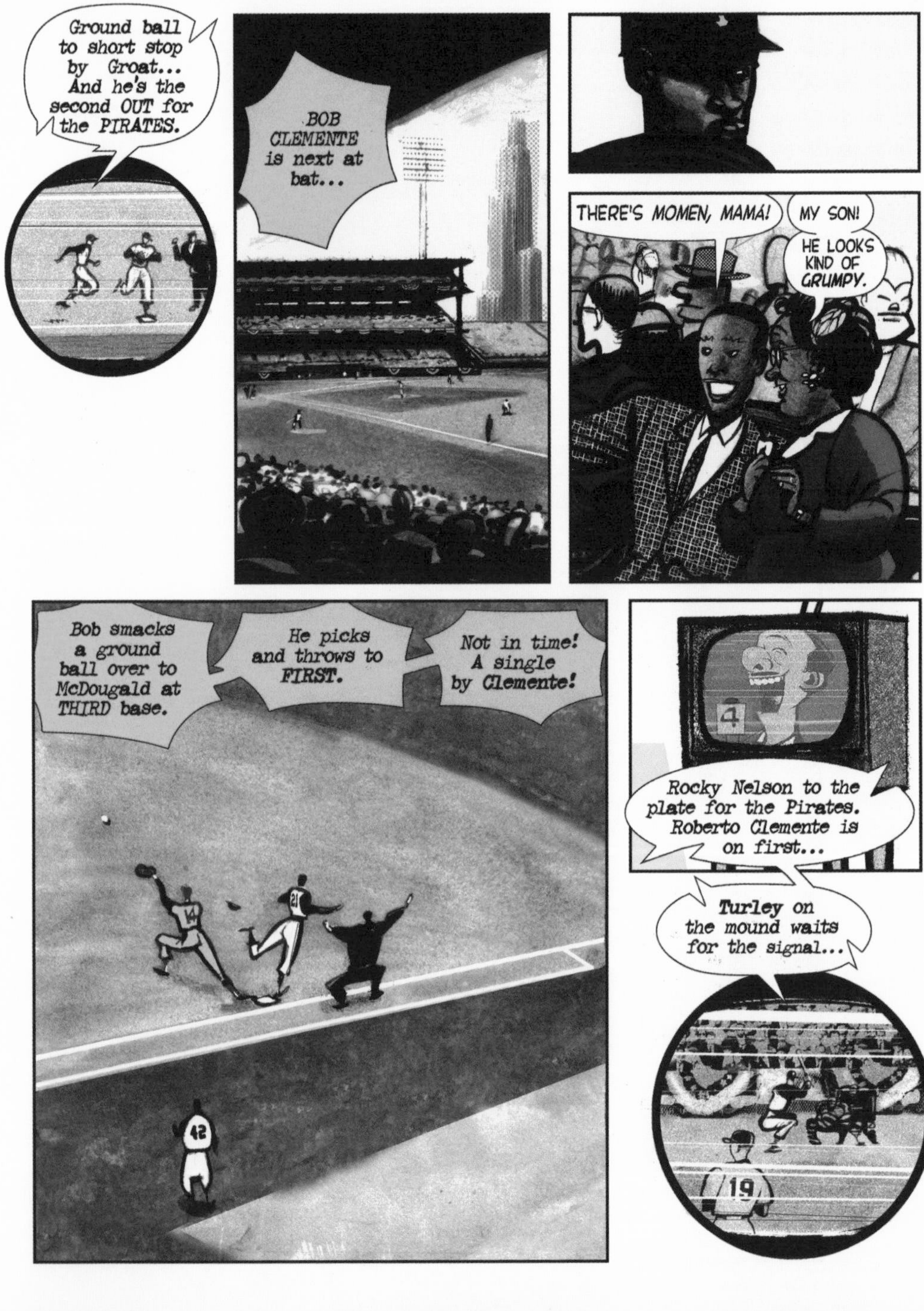

Ground ball to short stop by Groat... And he's the second OUT for the PIRATES.
BOB CLEMENTE is next at bat...
THERE'S MOMEN, MAMÁ!
MY SON!
HE LOOKS KIND OF GRUMPY.
Bob smacks a ground ball over to McDougald at THIRD base.
He picks and throws to FIRST.
Not in time! A single by Clemente!
Rocky Nelson to the plate for the Pirates. Roberto Clemente is on first...
Turley on the mound waits for the signal...

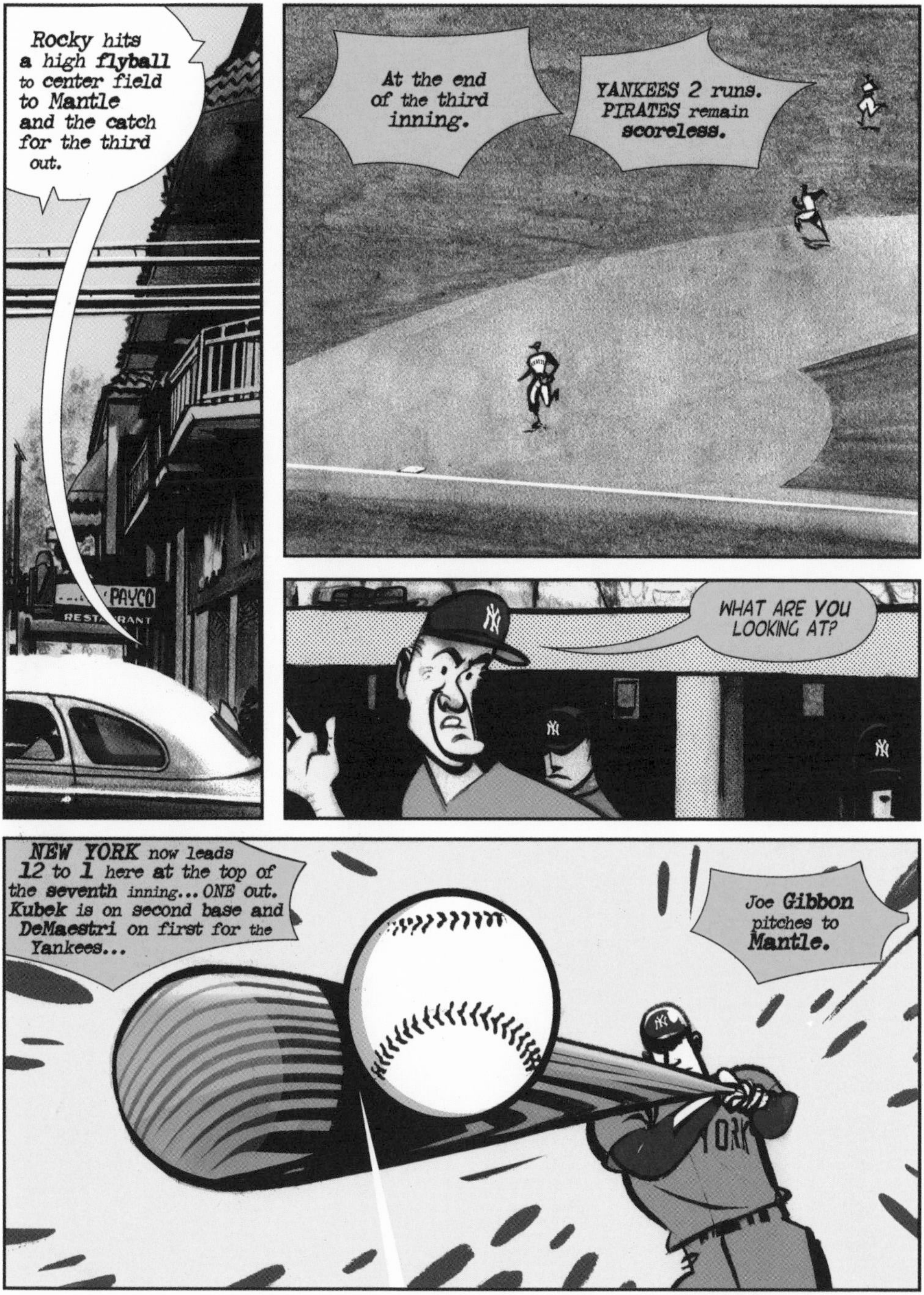
Rocky hits a high flyball to center field to Mantle and the catch for the third out.
At the end of the third inning.
YANKEES 2 runs. PIRATES remain scoreless.
WHAT ARE YOU LOOKING AT?
NEW YORK now leads 12 to 1 here at the top of the seventh inning... ONE out. Kubek is on second base and DeMaestri on first for the Yankees...
Joe Gibbon pitches to Mantle.

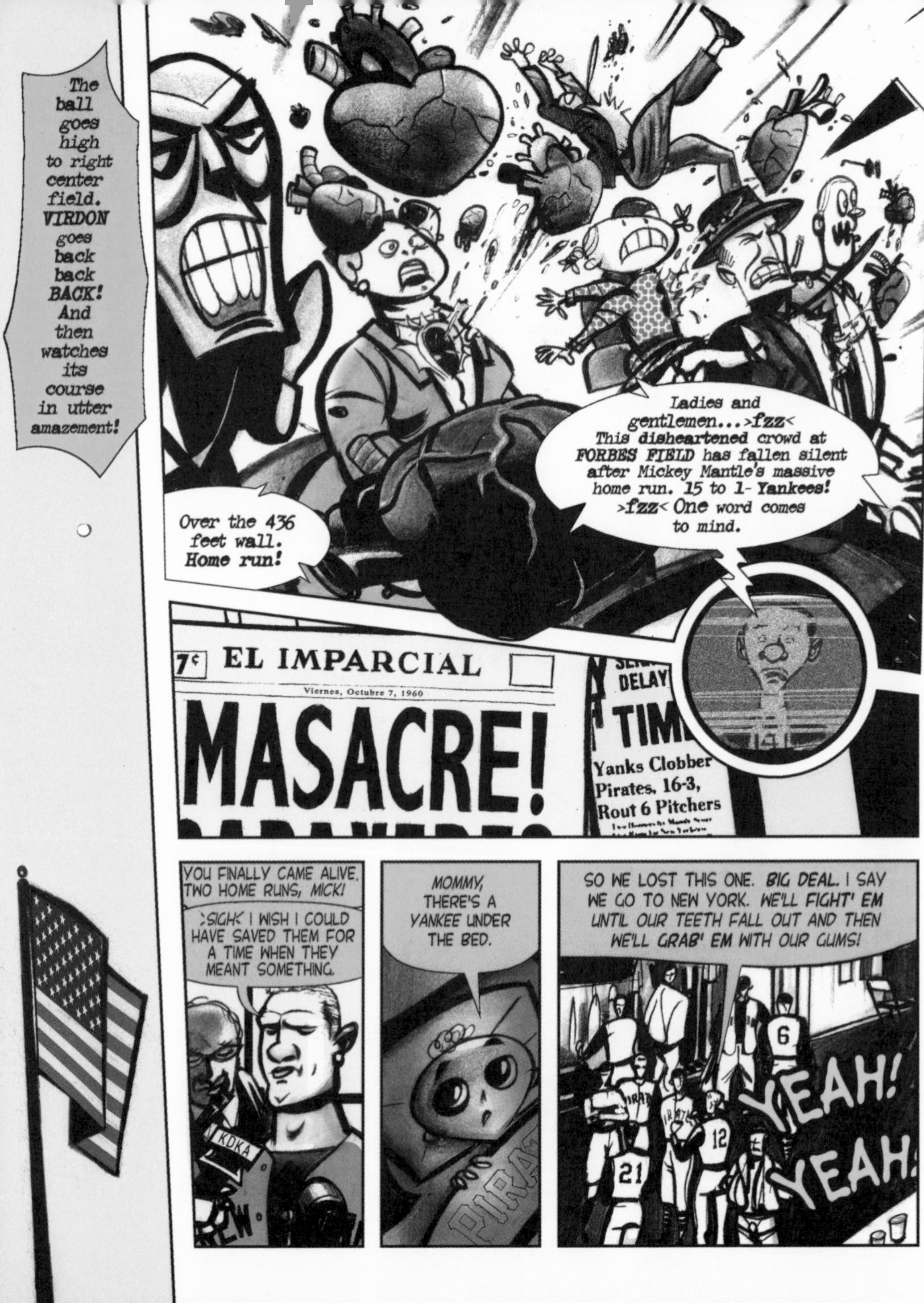
The ball goes high to right center field. VIRDON goes back back BACK! And then watches its course in utter amazement!
Over the 436 feet wall. Home run!
Ladies and gentlemen... >fzz< This disheartened crowd at FORBES FIELD has fallen silent after Mickey Mantle's massive home run. 15 to 1- Yankees! >fzz< One word comes to mind.
7¢ EL IMPARCIAL
Viernes, Octubre 7, 1960
MASACRE!
DELAY
Yanks Clobber Pirates, 16-3, Rout 6 Pitchers
YOU FINALLY CAME ALIVE. TWO HOME RUNS, MICK!
>SIGH< I WISH I COULD HAVE SAVED THEM FOR A TIME WHEN THEY MEANT SOMETHING.
KDKA
MOMMY, THERE'S A YANKEE UNDER THE BED.
SO WE LOST THIS ONE. BIG DEAL. I SAY WE GO TO NEW YORK. WE'LL FIGHT' EM UNTIL OUR TEETH FALL OUT AND THEN WE'LL GRAB' EM WITH OUR GUMS!
YEAH! YEAH!

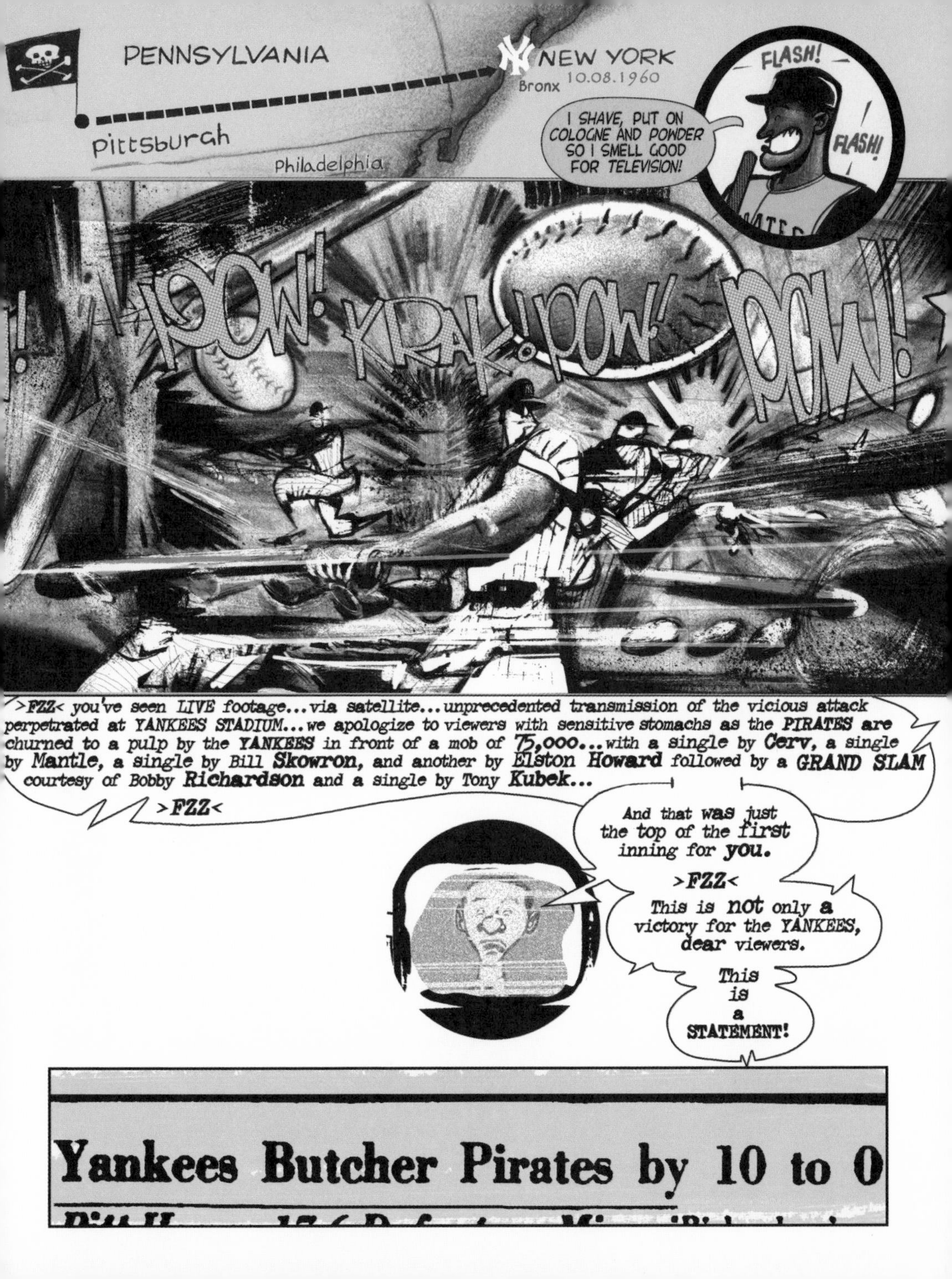
PENNSYLVANIA
NEW YORK
Bronx 10.08.1960
Pittsburgh
Philadelphia
FLASH!
I SHAVE, PUT ON COLOGNE AND POWDER SO I SMELL GOOD FOR TELEVISION!
FLASH!
POW! KRAK! POW! POW!
>FZZ< you've seen LIVE footage...via satellite...unprecedented transmission of the vicious attack perpetrated at YANKEES STADIUM...we apologize to viewers with sensitive stomachs as the PIRATES are churned to a pulp by the YANKEES in front of a mob of 75,000...with a single by Cerv, a single by Mantle, a single by Bill Skowron, and another by Elston Howard followed by a GRAND SLAM courtesy of Bobby Richardson and a single by Tony Kubek...
>FZZ<
And that was just the top of the first inning for you.
>FZZ<
This is not only a victory for the YANKEES, dear viewers.
This is a STATEMENT!
Yankees Butcher Pirates by 10 to 0

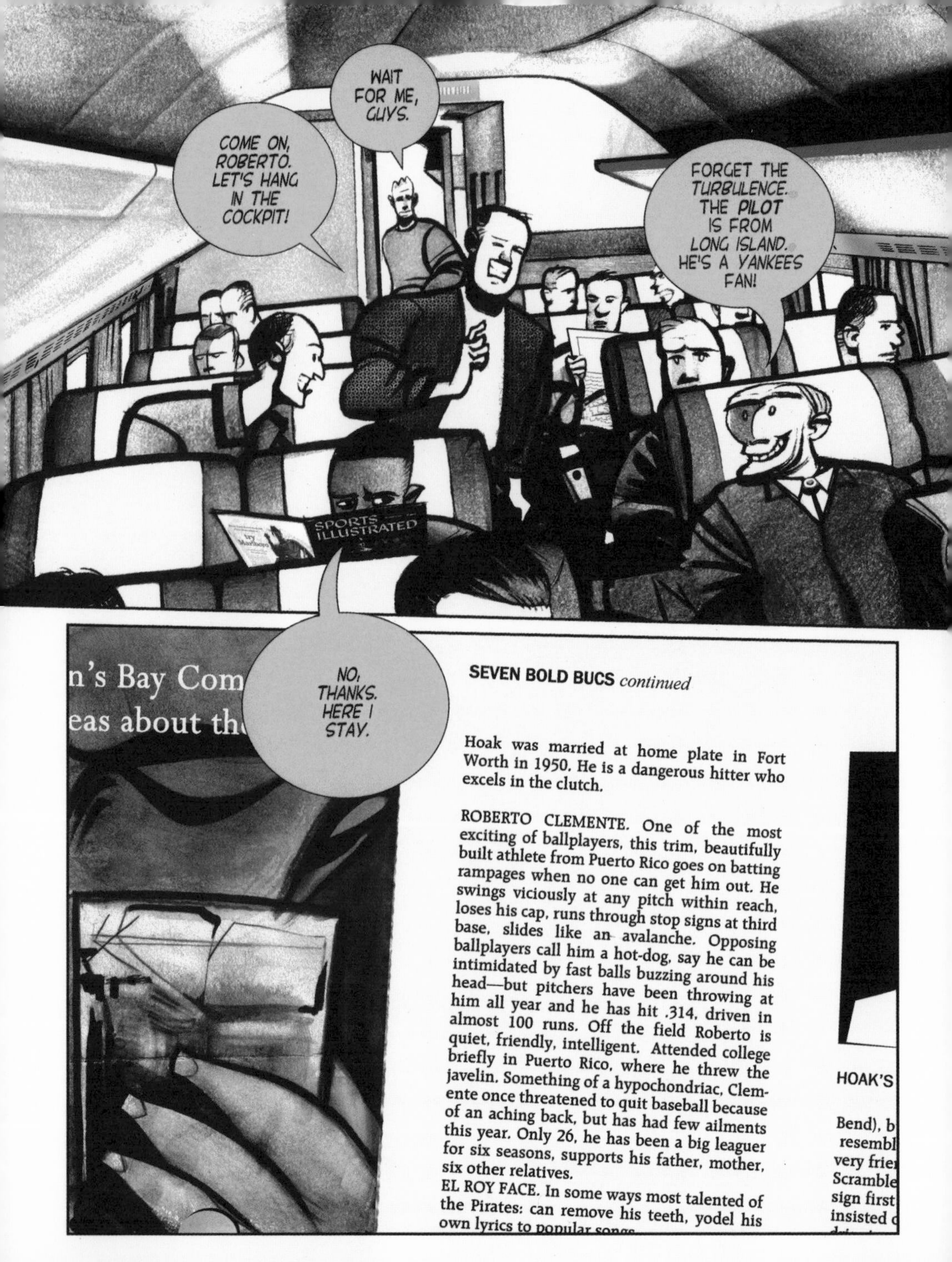
COME ON, ROBERTO. LET'S HANG IN THE COCKPIT!
WAIT FOR ME, GUYS.
FORGET THE TURBULENCE. THE PILOT IS FROM LONG ISLAND. HE'S A YANKEES FAN!
SPORTS ILLUSTRATED
NO, THANKS. HERE I STAY.
n's Bay Com
eas about th
SEVEN BOLD BUCS continued
Hoak was married at home plate in Fort Worth in 1950. He is a dangerous hitter who excels in the clutch.
ROBERTO CLEMENTE. One of the most exciting of ballplayers, this trim, beautifully built athlete from Puerto Rico goes on batting rampages when no one can get him out. He swings viciously at any pitch within reach, loses his cap, runs through stop signs at third base, slides like an avalanche. Opposing ballplayers call him a hot-dog, say he can be intimidated by fast balls buzzing around his head—but pitchers have been throwing at him all year and he has hit .314, driven in almost 100 runs. Off the field Roberto is quiet, friendly, intelligent. Attended college briefly in Puerto Rico, where he threw the javelin. Something of a hypochondriac, Clemente once threatened to quit baseball because of an aching back, but has had few ailments this year. Only 26, he has been a big leaguer for six seasons, supports his father, mother, six other relatives.
EL ROY FACE. In some ways most talented of the Pirates: can remove his teeth, yodel his own lyrics to popular songs
HOAK'S
Bend), b
resembl
very frie
Scramble
sign first
insisted

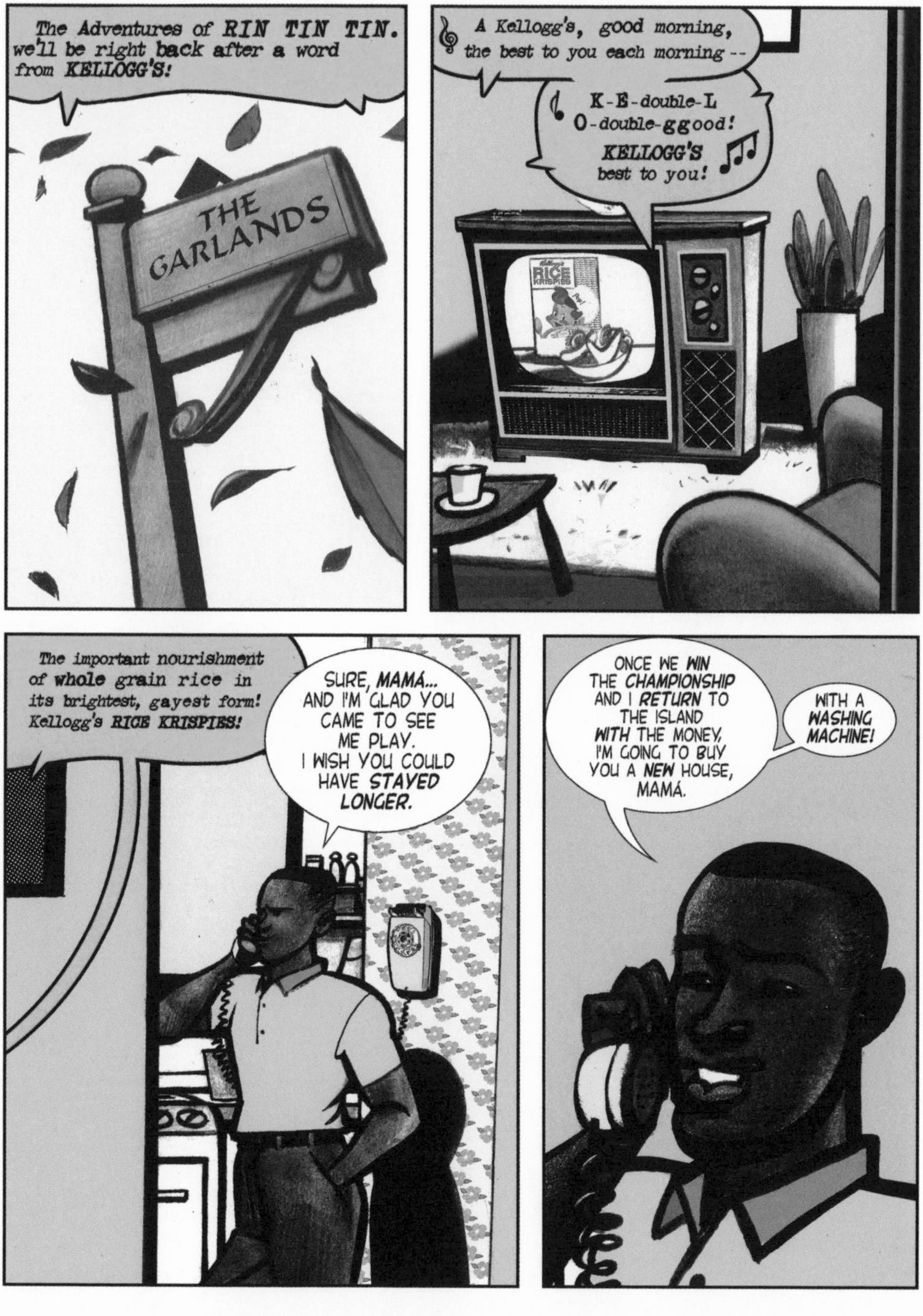

The Adventures of RIN TIN TIN. we'll be right back after a word from KELLOGG'S!
THE GARLANDS
A Kellogg's, good morning, the best to you each morning --
K-E-double-L O-double-ggood! KELLOGG'S best to you!
RICE KRISPIES
The important nourishment of whole grain rice in its brightest, gayest form! Kellogg's RICE KRISPIES!
SURE, MAMÁ... AND I'M GLAD YOU CAME TO SEE ME PLAY. I WISH YOU COULD HAVE STAYED LONGER.
ONCE WE WIN THE CHAMPIONSHIP AND I RETURN TO THE ISLAND WITH THE MONEY, I'M GOING TO BUY YOU A NEW HOUSE, MAMÁ.
WITH A WASHING MACHINE!

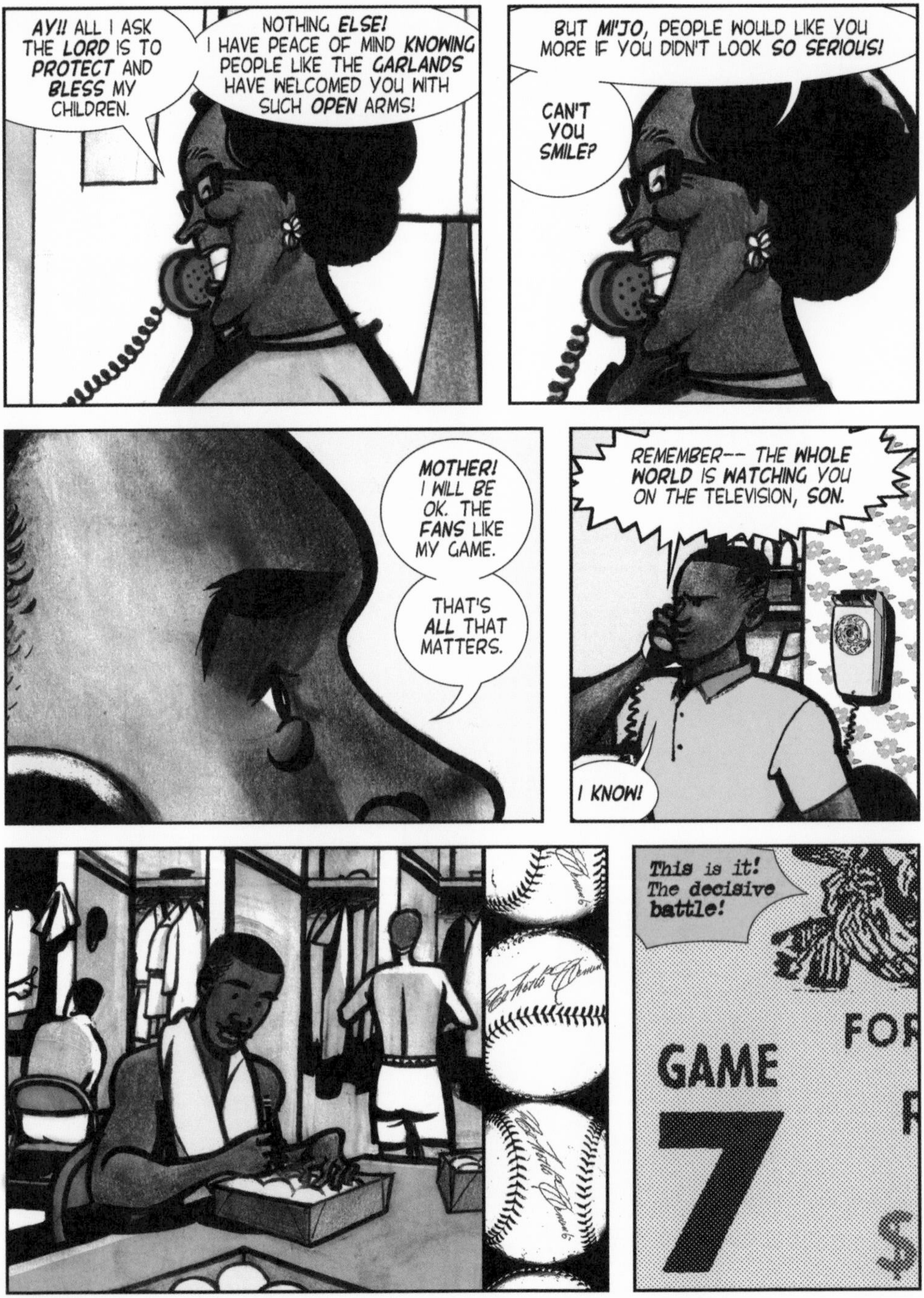
AY!! ALL I ASK THE LORD IS TO PROTECT AND BLESS MY CHILDREN.
NOTHING ELSE! I HAVE PEACE OF MIND KNOWING PEOPLE LIKE THE GARLANDS HAVE WELCOMED YOU WITH SUCH OPEN ARMS!
BUT MI'JO, PEOPLE WOULD LIKE YOU MORE IF YOU DIDN'T LOOK SO SERIOUS!
CAN'T YOU SMILE?
MOTHER! I WILL BE OK. THE FANS LIKE MY GAME.
THAT'S ALL THAT MATTERS.
REMEMBER-- THE WHOLE WORLD IS WATCHING YOU ON THE TELEVISION, SON.
I KNOW!
This is it! The decisive battle!
GAME 7

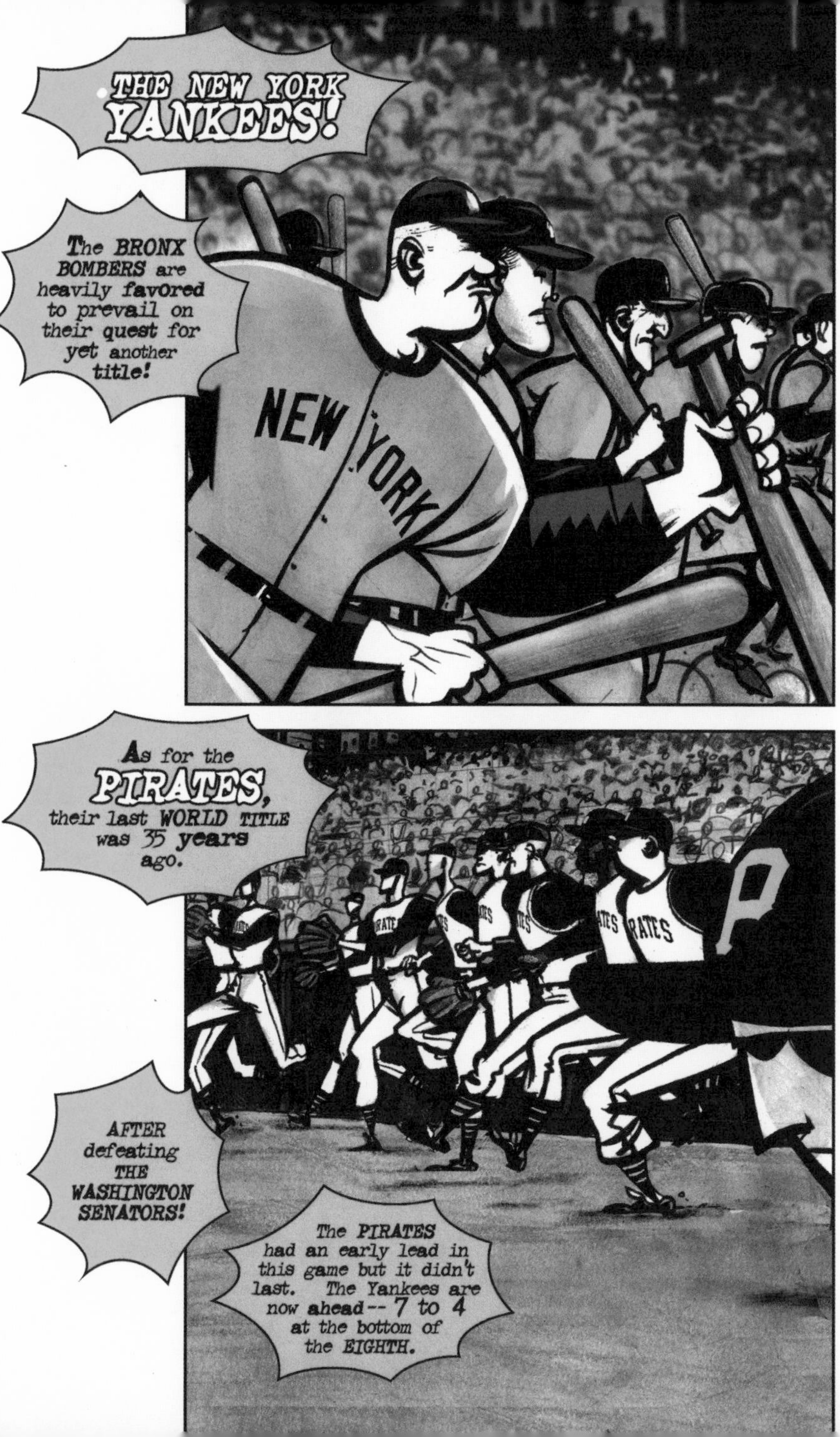
THE NEW YORK YANKEES!
The BRONX BOMBERS are heavily favored to prevail on their quest for yet another title!
NEW YORK
As for the PIRATES, their last WORLD TITLE was 35 years ago.
PIRATES
AFTER defeating THE WASHINGTON SENATORS!
The PIRATES had an early lead in this game but it didn't last. The Yankees are now ahead-- 7 to 4 at the bottom of the EIGHTH.

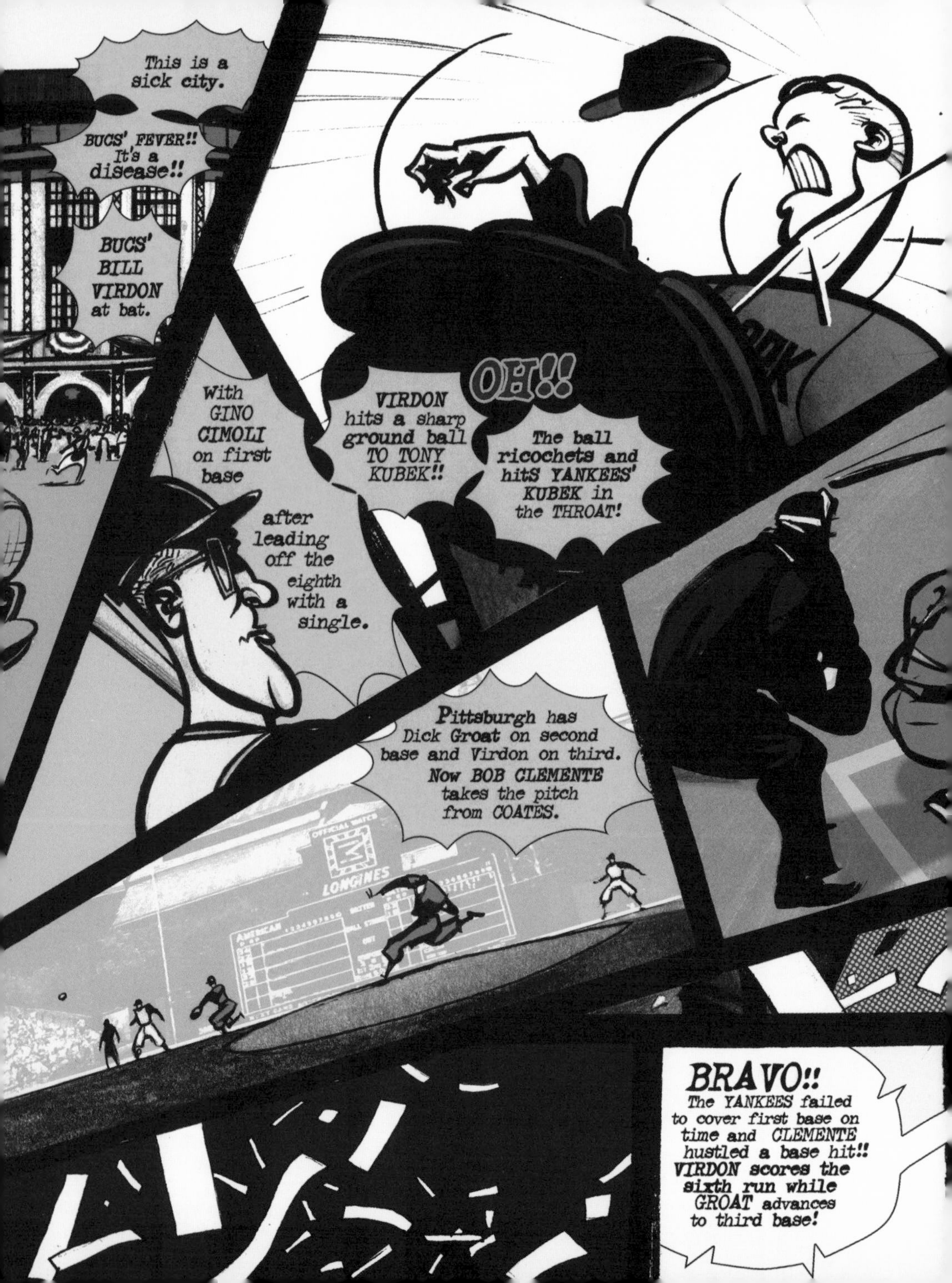
This is a sick city.
BUCS' FEVER!! It's a disease!!
BUCS' BILL VIRDON at bat.
With GINO CIMOLI on first base
after leading off the eighth with a single.
VIRDON hits a sharp ground ball TO TONY KUBEK!!
OH!!
The ball ricochets and hits YANKEES' KUBEK in the THROAT!
Pittsburgh has Dick Groat on second base and Virdon on third. Now BOB CLEMENTE takes the pitch from COATES.
BRAVO!! The YANKEES failed to cover first base on time and CLEMENTE hustled a base hit!! VIRDON scores the sixth run while GROAT advances to third base!

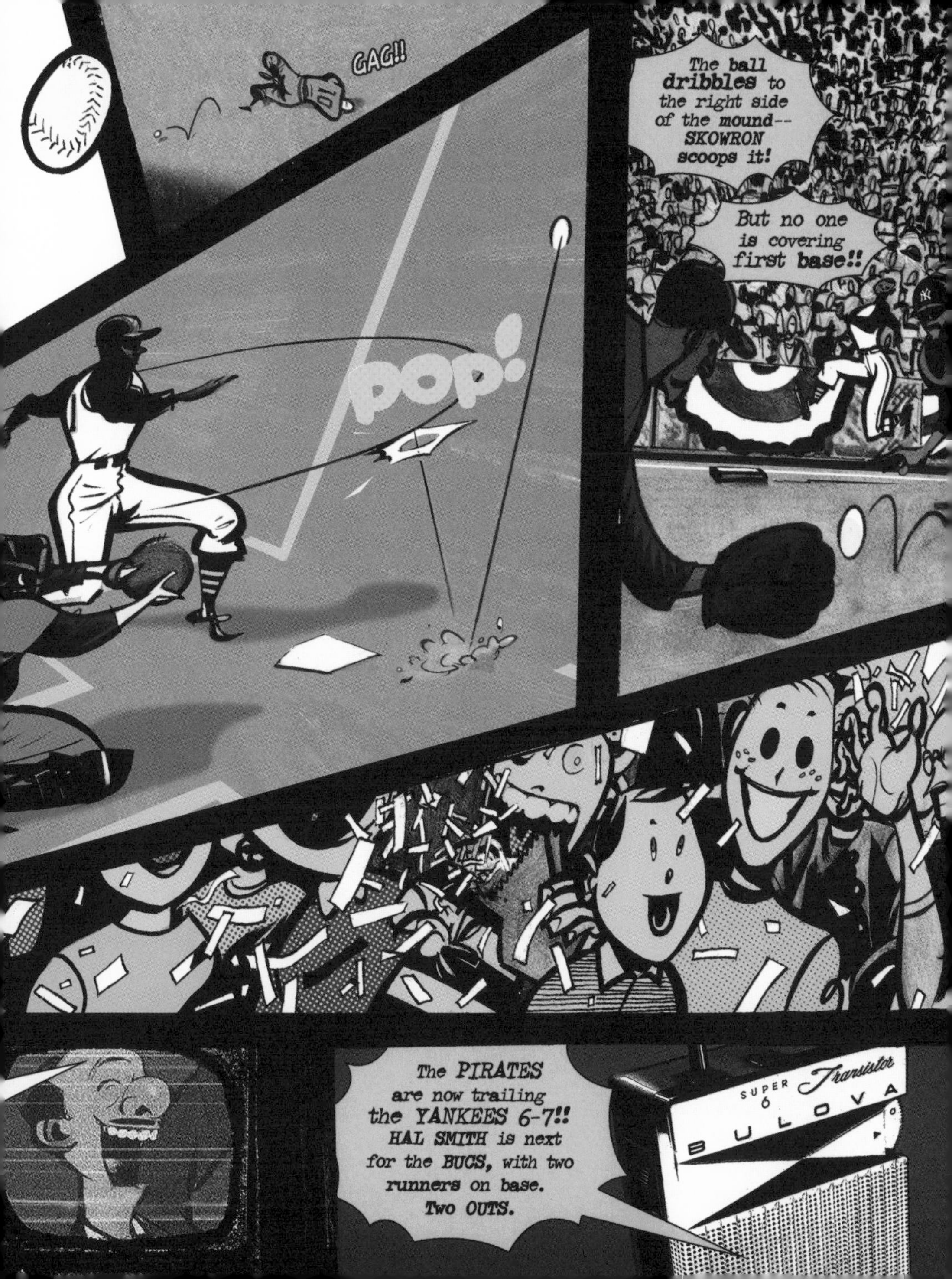

GAG!!
POP!
The ball dribbles to the right side of the mound-- SKOWRON scoops it!
But no one is covering first base!!
The PIRATES are now trailing the YANKEES 6-7!! HAL SMITH is next for the BUCS, with two runners on base. Two OUTS.
SUPER 6 Transistor
BULOVA

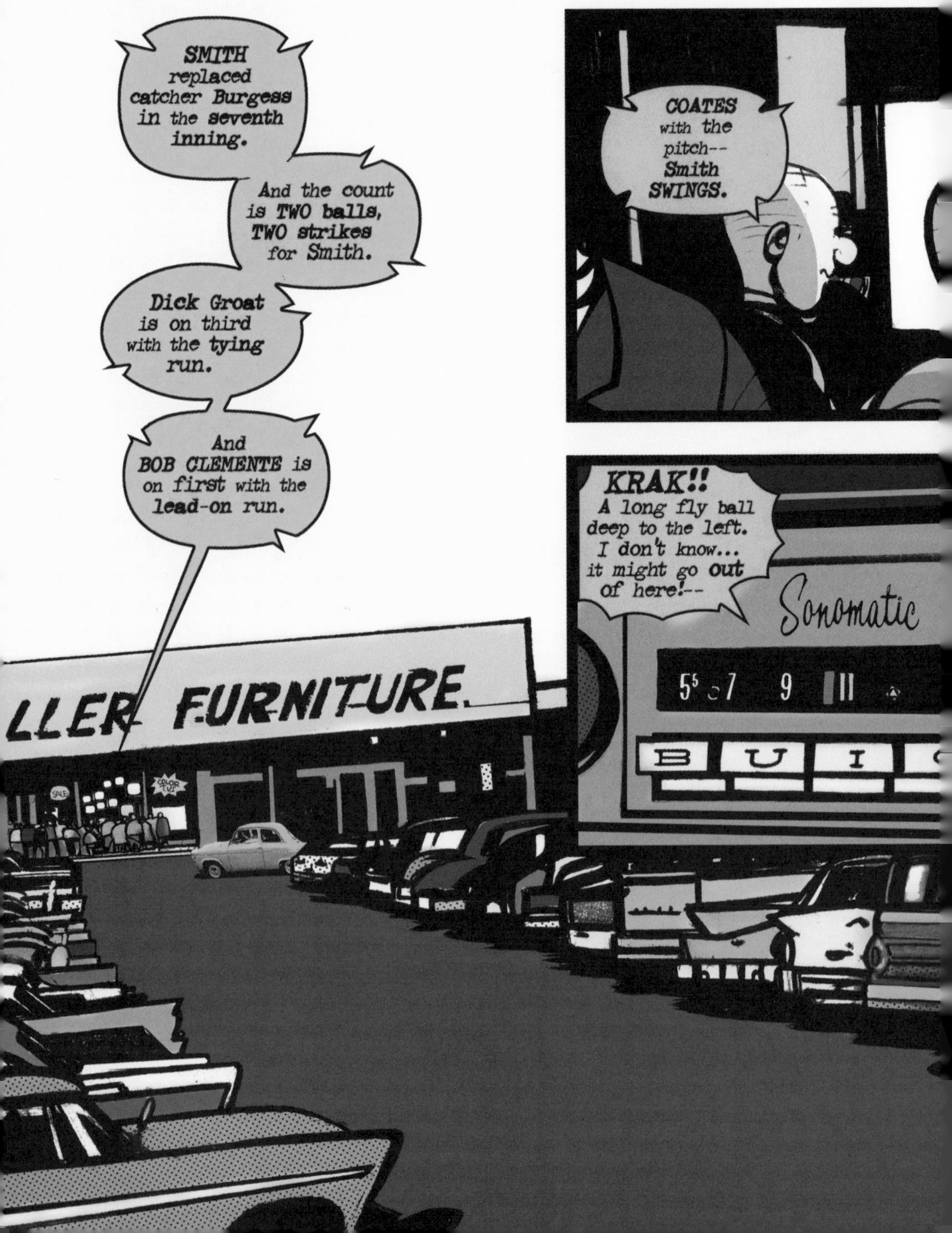
SMITH replaced catcher Burgess in the seventh inning.
And the count is TWO balls, TWO strikes for Smith.
Dick Groat is on third with the tying run.
And BOB CLEMENTE is on first with the lead-on run.
LLER FURNITURE.
SALE
COLOR TV
COATES with the pitch-- Smith SWINGS.
KRAK!! A long fly ball deep to the left. I don't know... it might go out of here!--
Sonomatic
BUI

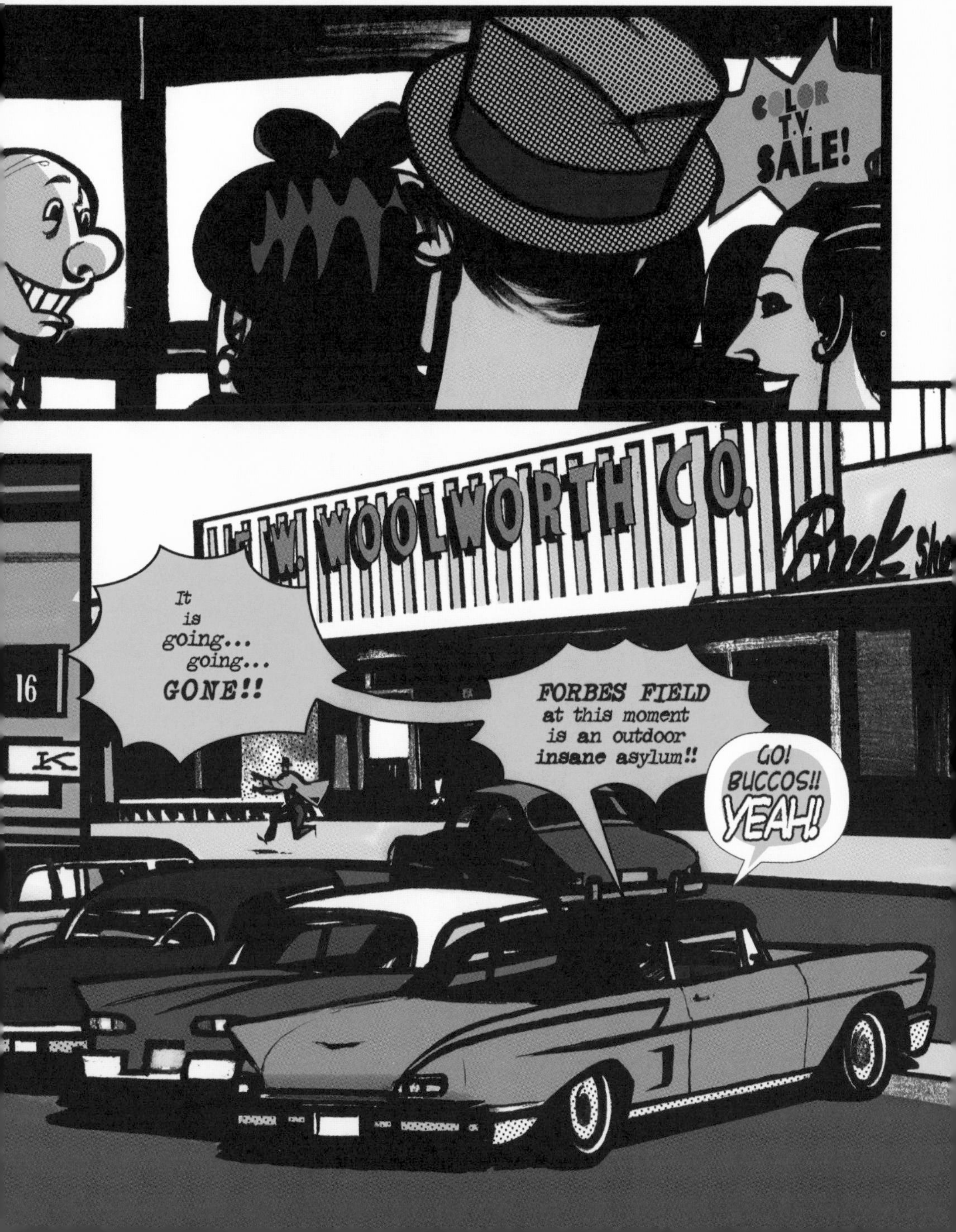
COLOR T.V. SALE!
W. WOOLWORTH CO.
16
K
It is going... going... GONE!!
FORBES FIELD at this moment is an outdoor insane asylum!!
GO! BUCCOS!! YEAH!

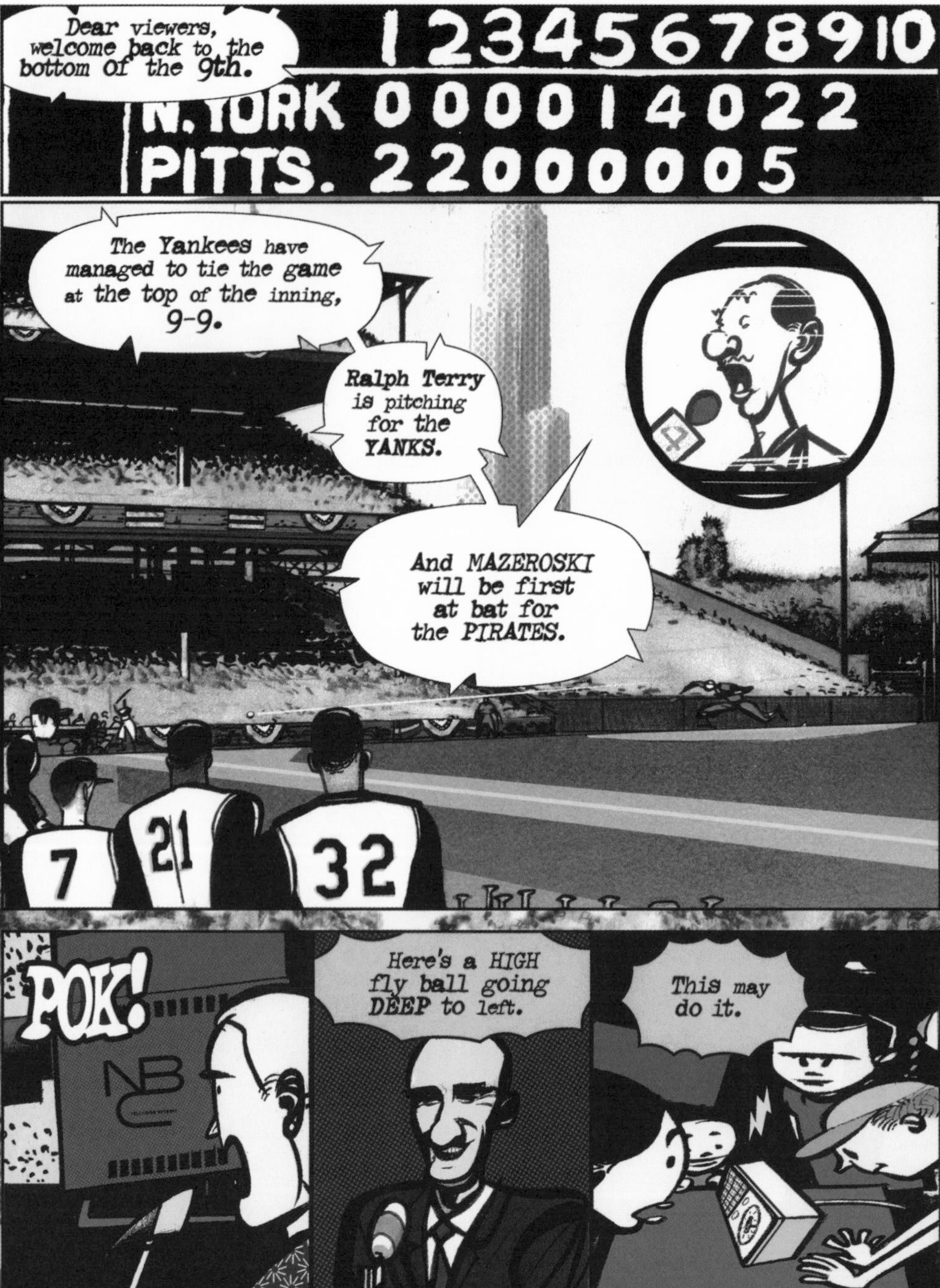
Dear viewers, welcome back to the bottom of the 9th.
1 2 3 4 5 6 7 8 9 10
N. YORK 0 0 0 0 1 4 0 2 2
PITTS. 2 2 0 0 0 0 0 5
The Yankees have managed to tie the game at the top of the inning, 9-9.
Ralph Terry is pitching for the YANKS.
And MAZEROSKI will be first at bat for the PIRATES.
7
21
32
POK!
NBC
Here's a HIGH fly ball going DEEP to left.
This may do it.

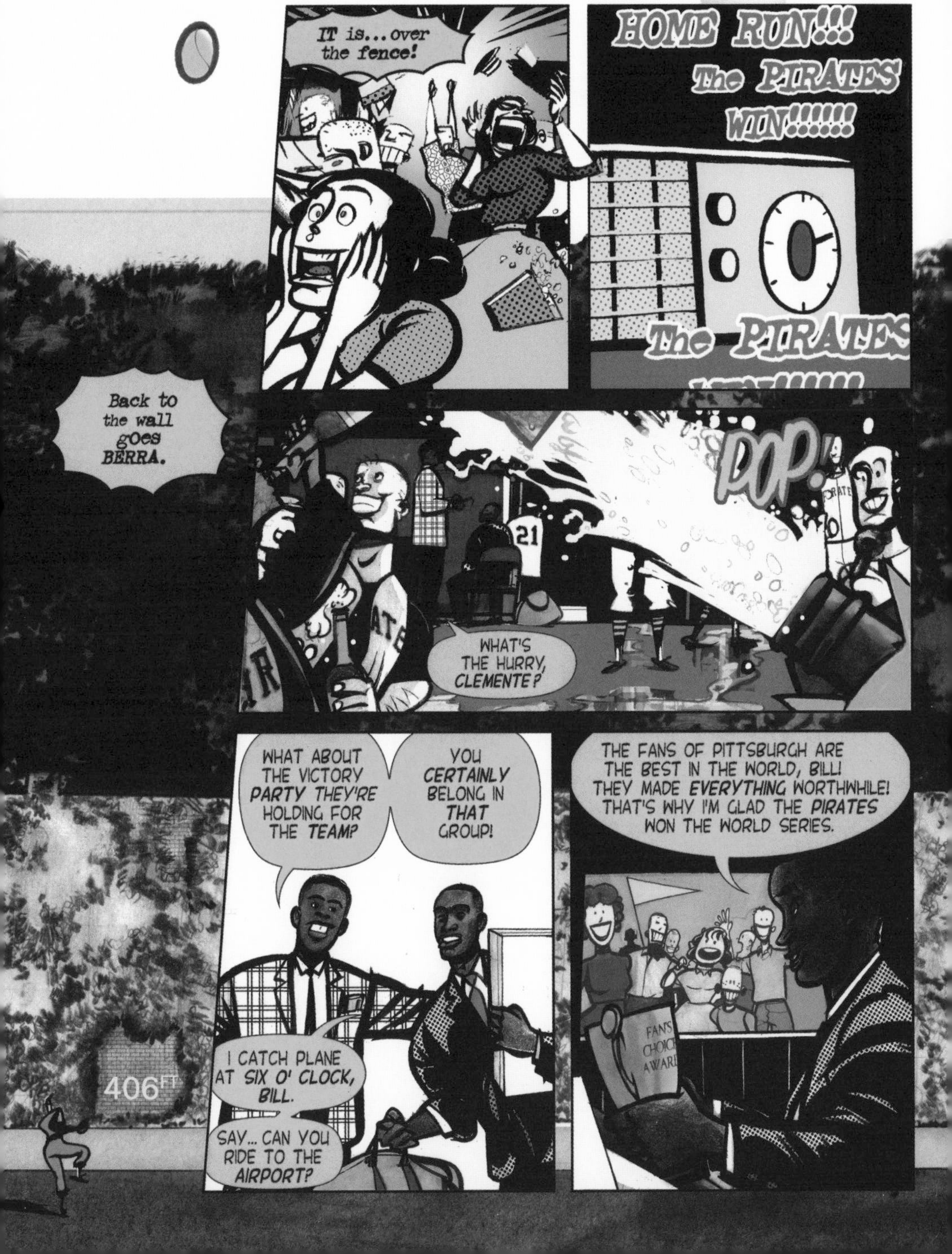
IT is... over the fence!
HOME RUN!!!
The PIRATES WIN!!!!!!
The PIRATES
Back to the wall goes BERRA.
POP!
21
WHAT'S THE HURRY, CLEMENTE?
WHAT ABOUT THE VICTORY PARTY THEY'RE HOLDING FOR THE TEAM?
YOU CERTAINLY BELONG IN THAT GROUP!
I CATCH PLANE AT SIX O' CLOCK, BILL.
SAY... CAN YOU RIDE TO THE AIRPORT?
THE FANS OF PITTSBURGH ARE THE BEST IN THE WORLD, BILL! THEY MADE EVERYTHING WORTHWHILE! THAT'S WHY I'M GLAD THE PIRATES WON THE WORLD SERIES.
FAN'S CHOICE AWARD
406FT

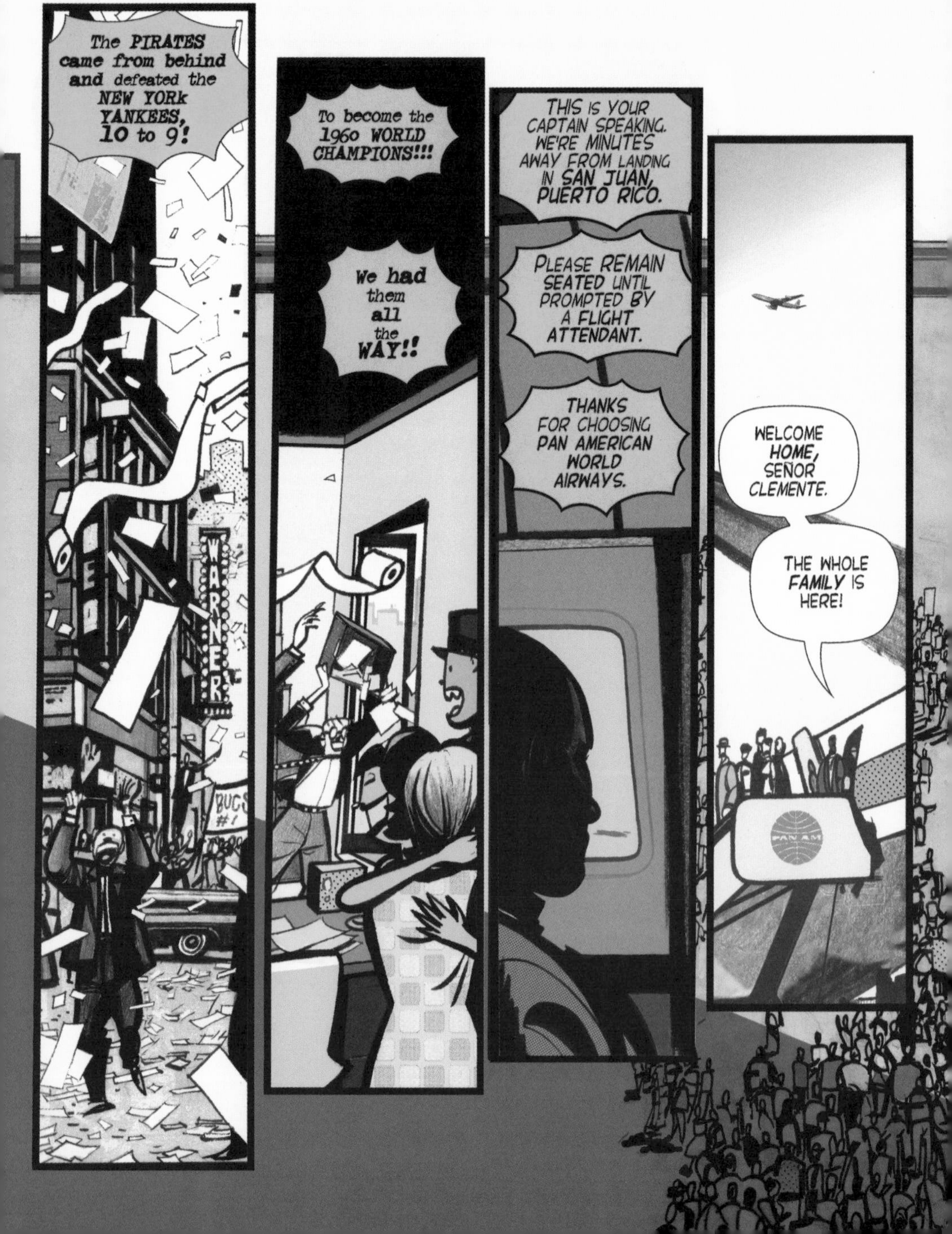
The PIRATES came from behind and defeated the NEW YORk YANKEES, 10 to 9!
To become the 1960 WORLD CHAMPIONS!!!
We had them all the WAY!!
WARNER
BUGS #1
THIS IS YOUR CAPTAIN SPEAKING. WE'RE MINUTES AWAY FROM LANDING IN SAN JUAN, PUERTO RICO.
PLEASE REMAIN SEATED UNTIL PROMPTED BY A FLIGHT ATTENDANT.
THANKS FOR CHOOSING PAN AMERICAN WORLD AIRWAYS.
WELCOME HOME, SEÑOR CLEMENTE.
THE WHOLE FAMILY IS HERE!
PAN AM

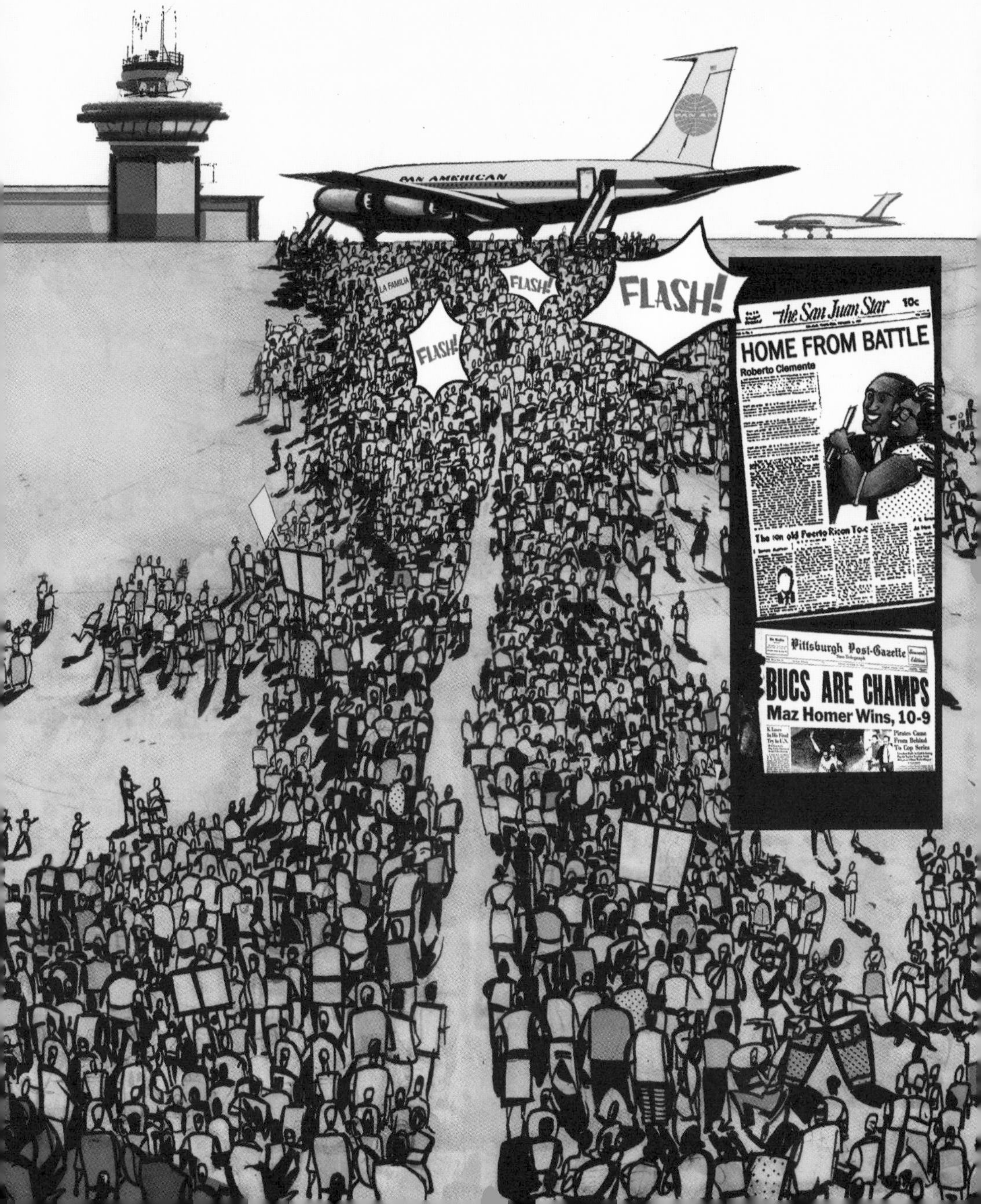
PAN AMERICAN
LA FAMILIA
FLASH!
FLASH!
FLASH!
the San Juan Star 10c
HOME FROM BATTLE
Roberto Clemente
Pittsburgh Post-Gazette
BUCS ARE CHAMPS
Maz Homer Wins, 10-9
Pirates Came From Behind To Cop Series

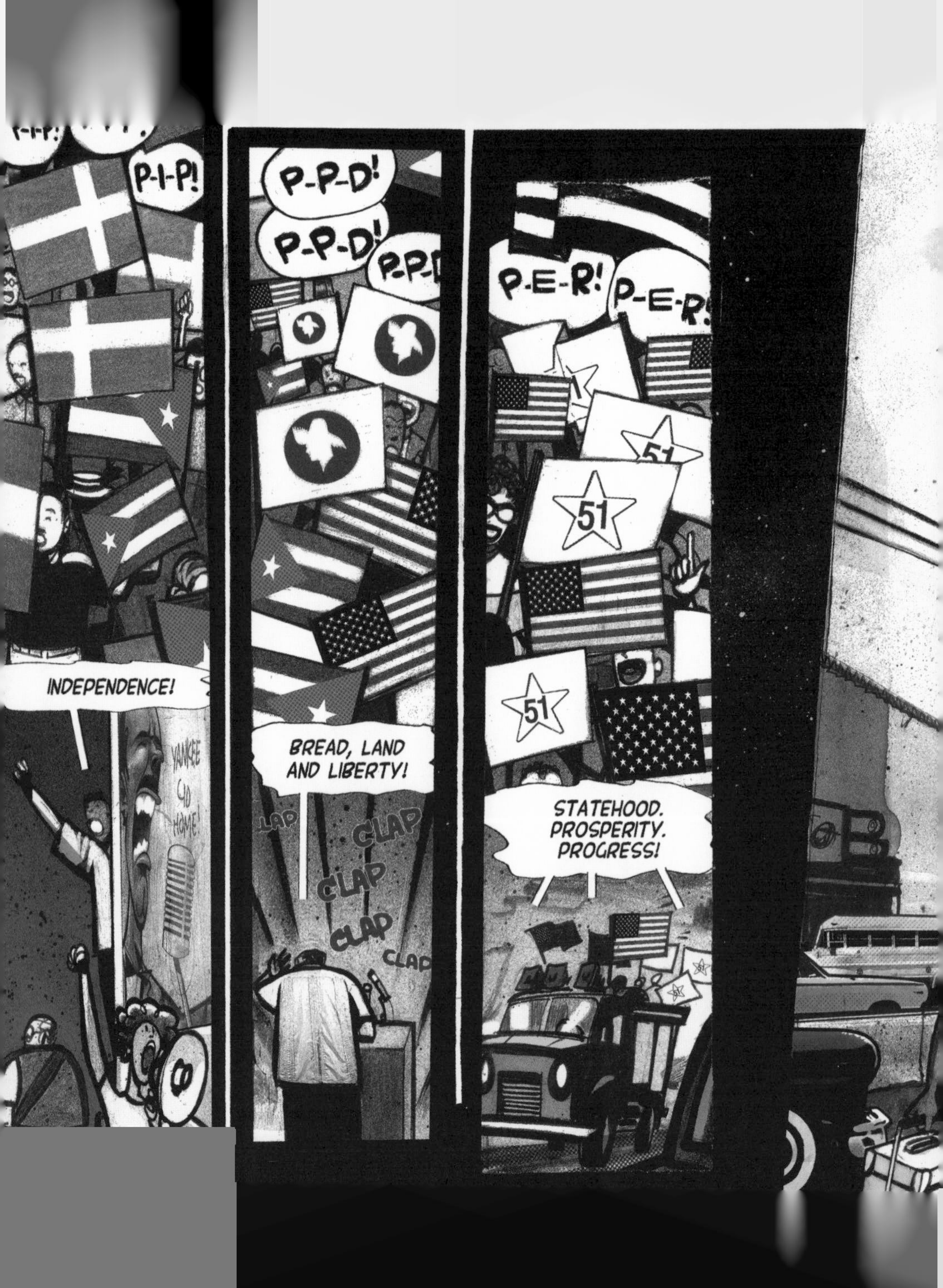
P-I-P!
P-I-P!
INDEPENDENCE!
YANKEE GO HOME!
P-P-D!
P-P-D!
BREAD, LAND AND LIBERTY!
CLAP
CLAP
CLAP
CLAP
CLAP
P-E-R!
P-E-R!
51
51
51
STATEHOOD. PROSPERITY. PROGRESS!

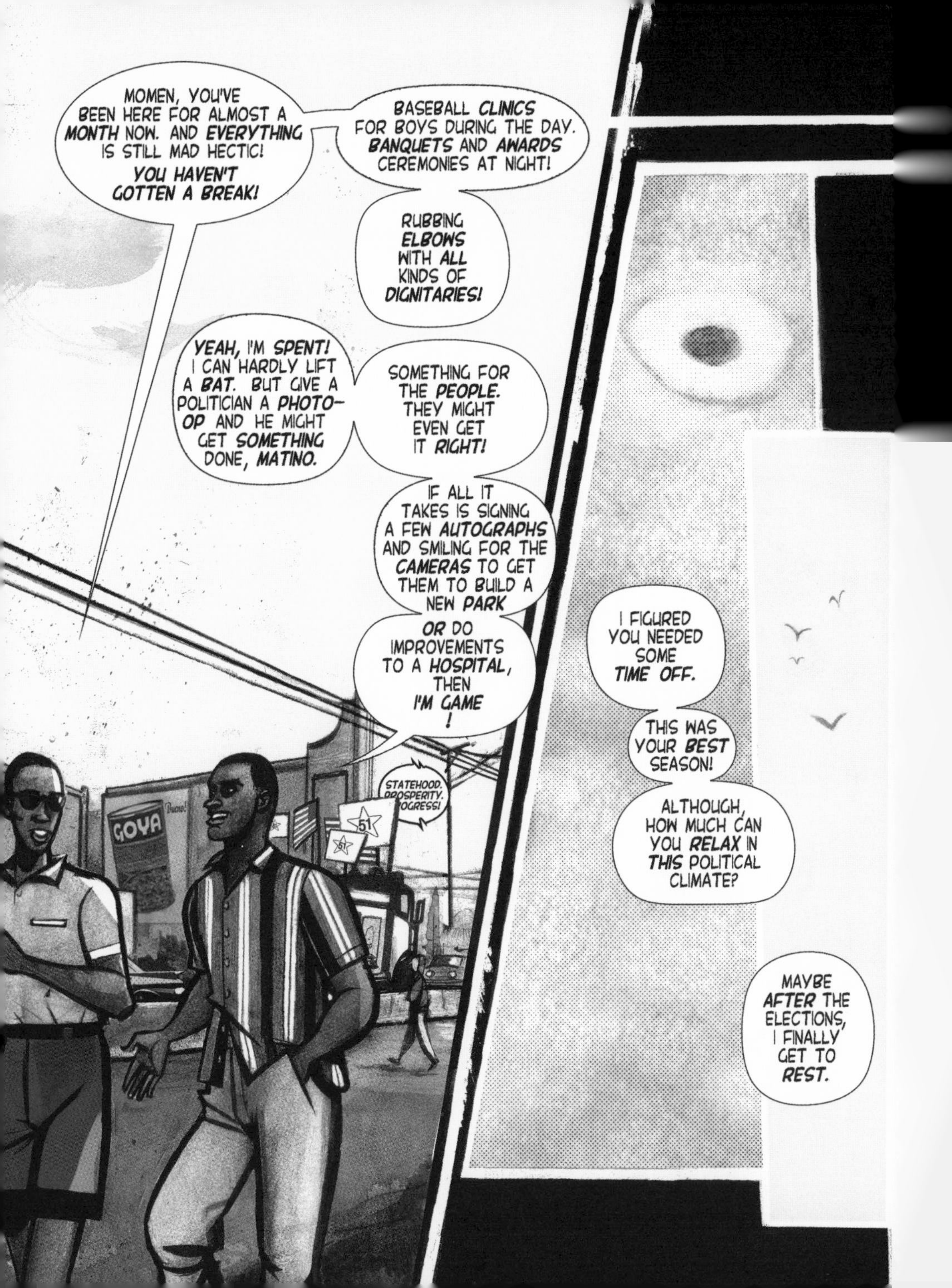
MOMEN, YOU'VE BEEN HERE FOR ALMOST A MONTH NOW. AND EVERYTHING IS STILL MAD HECTIC!
YOU HAVEN'T GOTTEN A BREAK!
BASEBALL CLINICS FOR BOYS DURING THE DAY. BANQUETS AND AWARDS CEREMONIES AT NIGHT!
RUBBING ELBOWS WITH ALL KINDS OF DIGNITARIES!
YEAH, I'M SPENT! I CAN HARDLY LIFT A BAT. BUT GIVE A POLITICIAN A PHOTO-OP AND HE MIGHT GET SOMETHING DONE, MATINO.
SOMETHING FOR THE PEOPLE. THEY MIGHT EVEN GET IT RIGHT!
IF ALL IT TAKES IS SIGNING A FEW AUTOGRAPHS AND SMILING FOR THE CAMERAS TO GET THEM TO BUILD A NEW PARK
OR DO IMPROVEMENTS TO A HOSPITAL, THEN I'M GAME!
STATEHOOD. PROSPERITY. PROGRESS!
GOYA
51
I FIGURED YOU NEEDED SOME TIME OFF.
THIS WAS YOUR BEST SEASON!
ALTHOUGH, HOW MUCH CAN YOU RELAX IN THIS POLITICAL CLIMATE?
MAYBE AFTER THE ELECTIONS, I FINALLY GET TO REST.

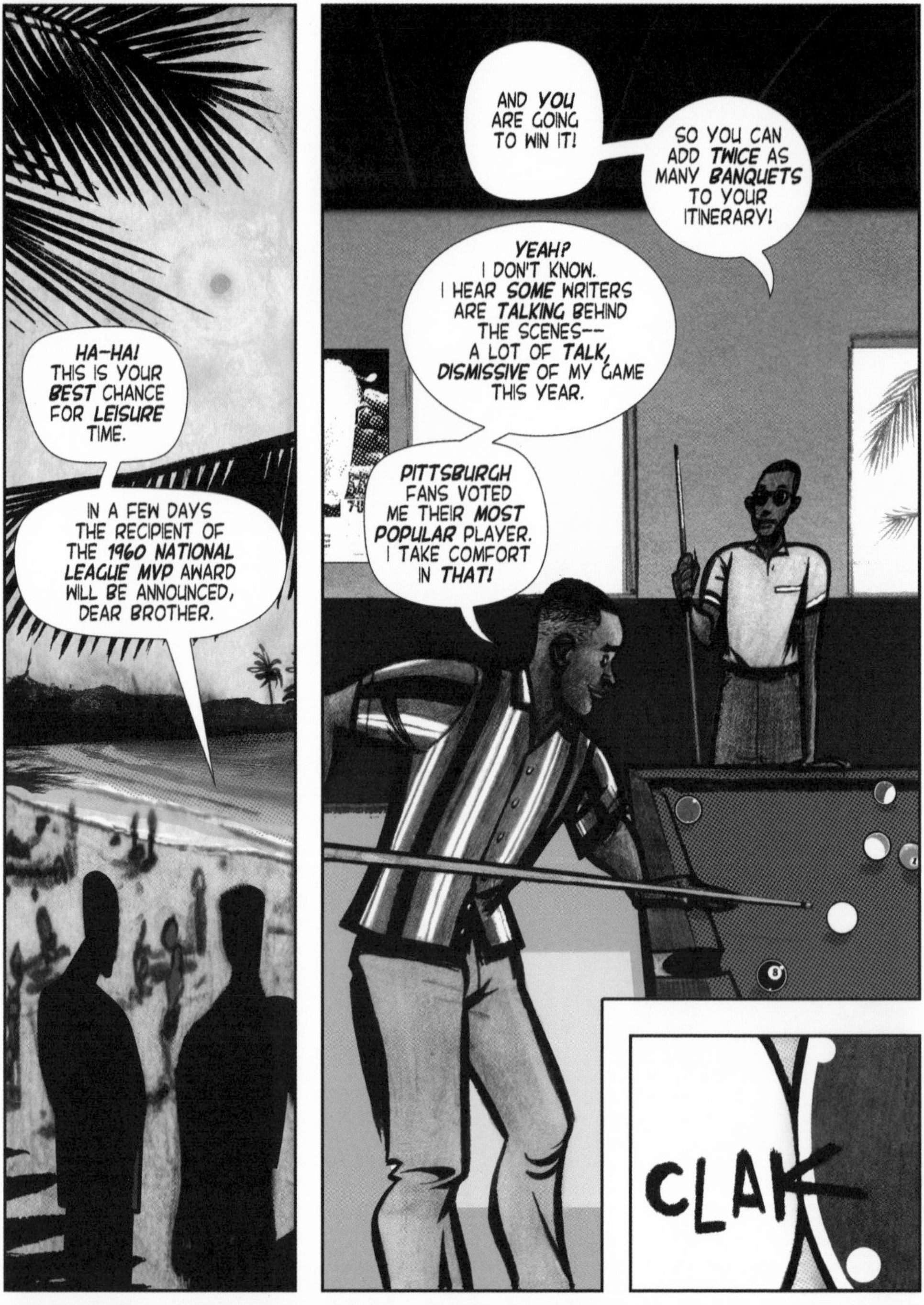
HA-HA! THIS IS YOUR BEST CHANCE FOR LEISURE TIME.
IN A FEW DAYS THE RECIPIENT OF THE 1960 NATIONAL LEAGUE MVP AWARD WILL BE ANNOUNCED, DEAR BROTHER.
AND YOU ARE GOING TO WIN IT!
SO YOU CAN ADD TWICE AS MANY BANQUETS TO YOUR ITINERARY!
YEAH? I DON'T KNOW. I HEAR SOME WRITERS ARE TALKING BEHIND THE SCENES-- A LOT OF TALK, DISMISSIVE OF MY GAME THIS YEAR.
PITTSBURGH FANS VOTED ME THEIR MOST POPULAR PLAYER. I TAKE COMFORT IN THAT!
CLAK

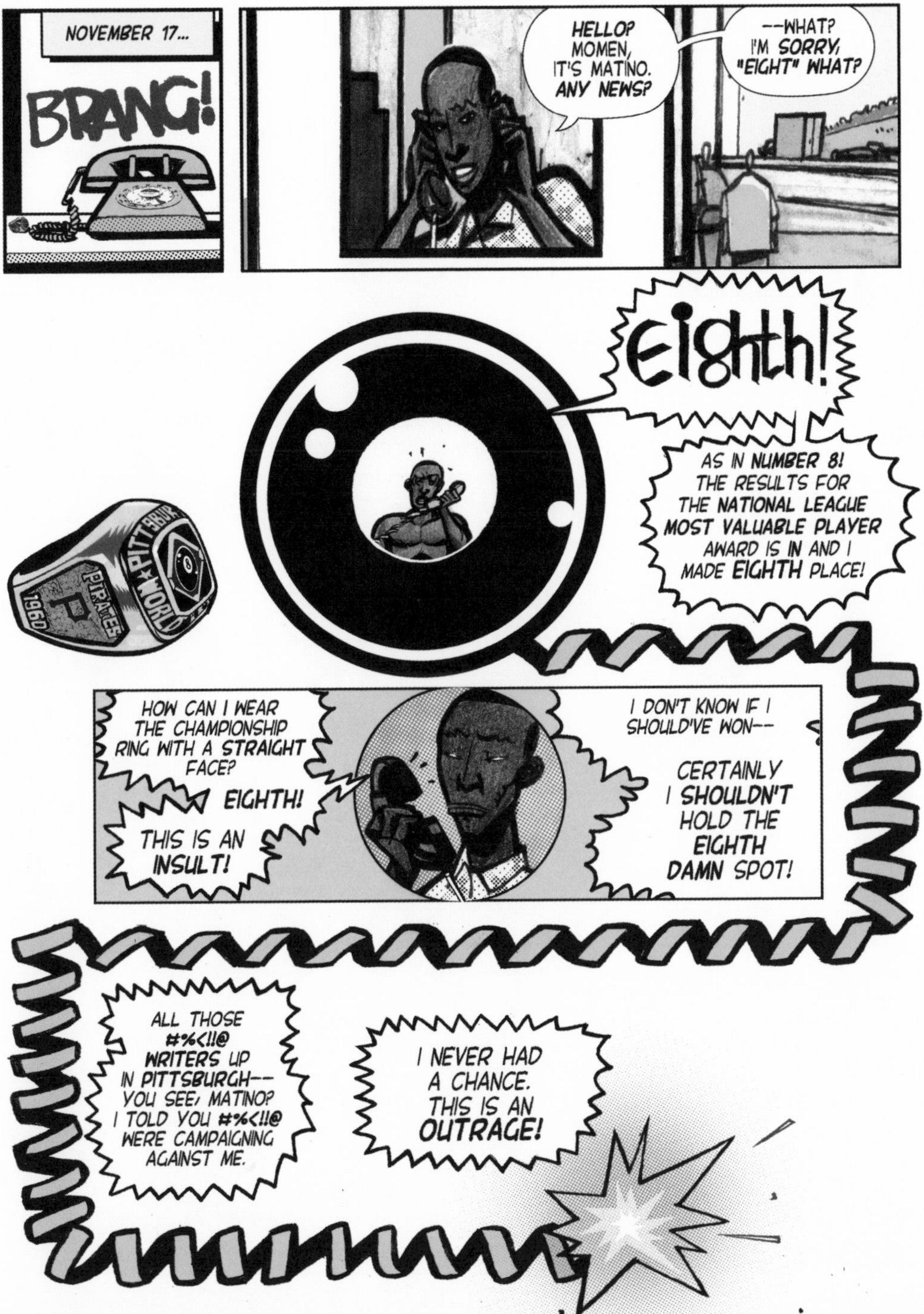
NOVEMBER 17...
BRANG!
HELLO? MOMEN, IT'S MATINO. ANY NEWS?
--WHAT? I'M SORRY, "EIGHT" WHAT?
EIGHTH!
AS IN NUMBER 8! THE RESULTS FOR THE NATIONAL LEAGUE MOST VALUABLE PLAYER AWARD IS IN AND I MADE EIGHTH PLACE!
PITTSBURGH PIRATES WORLD 1960
HOW CAN I WEAR THE CHAMPIONSHIP RING WITH A STRAIGHT FACE?
EIGHTH!
THIS IS AN INSULT!
I DON'T KNOW IF I SHOULD'VE WON--
CERTAINLY I SHOULDN'T HOLD THE EIGHTH DAMN SPOT!
ALL THOSE #%<!!@ WRITERS UP IN PITTSBURGH-- YOU SEE, MATINO? I TOLD YOU #%<!!@ WERE CAMPAIGNING AGAINST ME.
I NEVER HAD A CHANCE. THIS IS AN OUTRAGE!

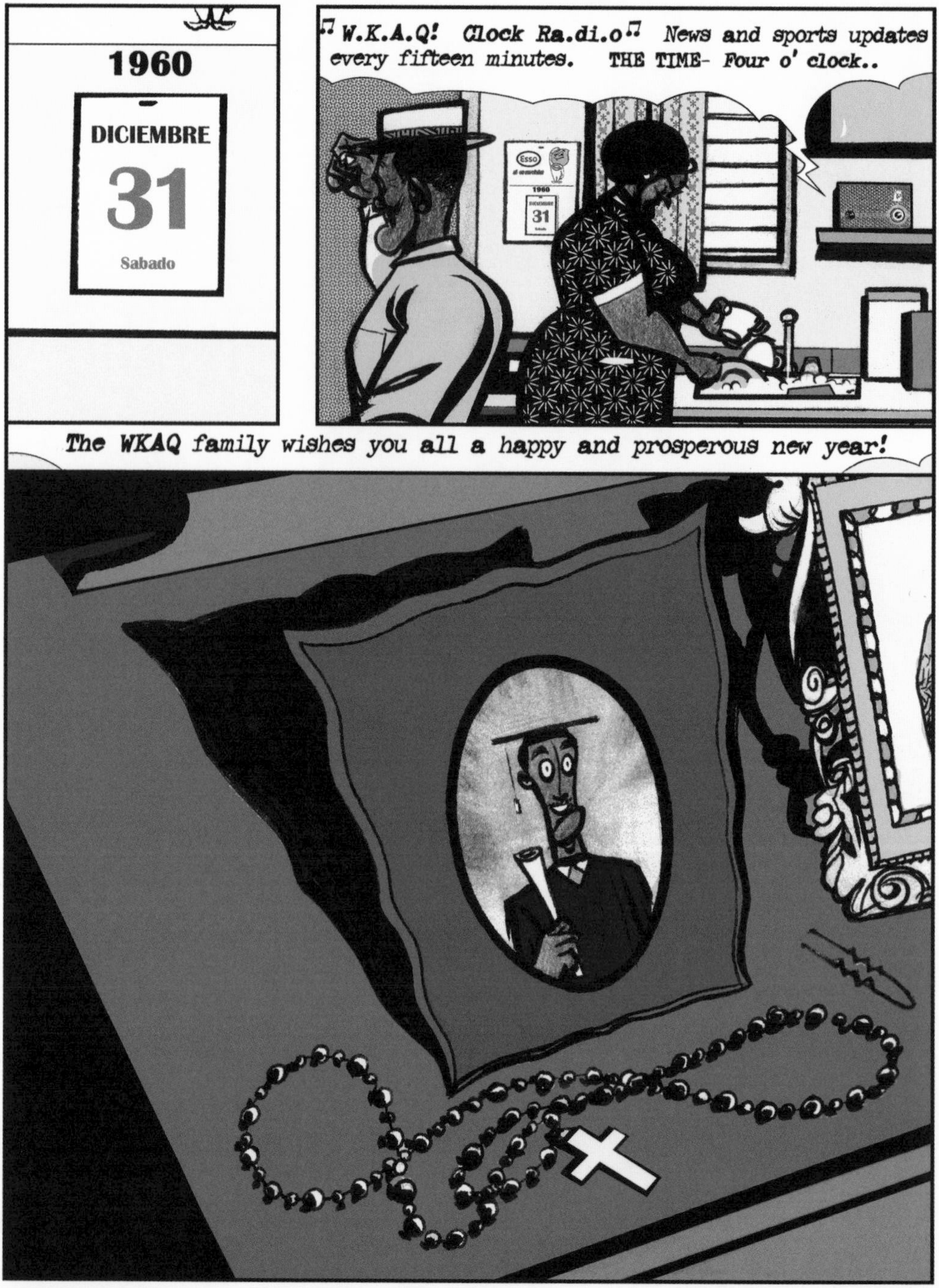
1960
DICIEMBRE
31
Sabado
♫ W.K.A.Q! Clock Ra.di.o ♫ News and sports updates every fifteen minutes. THE TIME- Four o' clock..
The WKAQ family wishes you all a happy and prosperous new year!

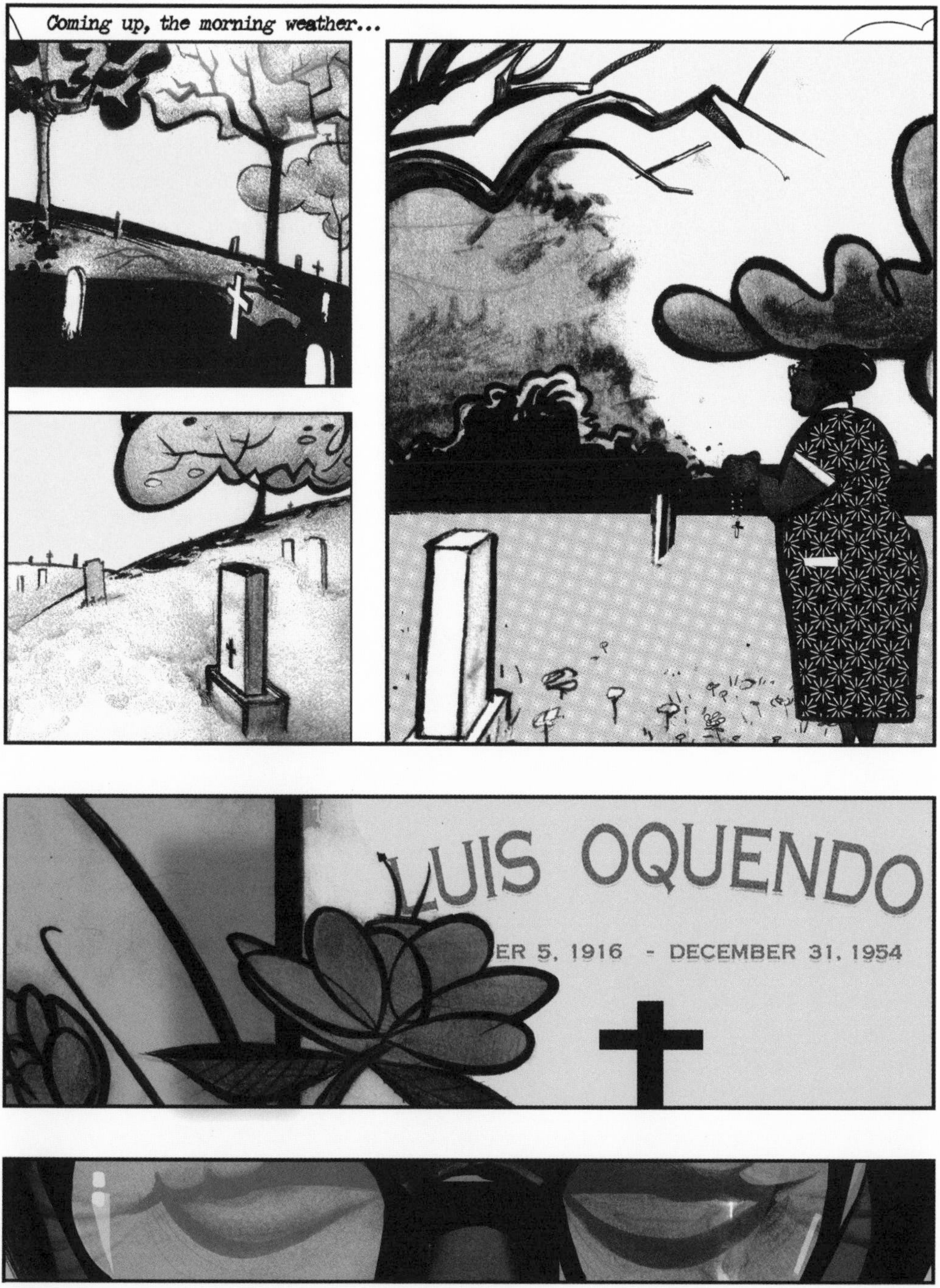
Coming up, the morning weather...
LUIS OQUENDO
ER 5, 1916 - DECEMBER 31, 1954

CHAPTER III The People of Puerto Rico

Their attitude toward the invading Americans—The proclamation of General Miles—justice and the private soldier—Depravity of the native masses—Men and women of the better class—Local attributes of life—A hint to the weary.

Before proceeding further with the story of our advance, it may interest you to know what manner of people we found the Puerto Ricans to be, and how they behaved toward us who came to them as dogs of war.

When we were first on the island, there is no doubt that the mass of the population regarded us with acute distrust, if not with dislike and fear. But the prompt measures taken by General Miles to disabuse their minds of any preconceived ideas of ensuing rape, robbery, or desecration, did much to soothe the more ignorant and childish of the natives, while the intelligent and educated class needed no further assurance than that contained in the proclamation issued by the commanding general from Ponce on the 28th of July, which was as follows:—

To The Inhabitants of Puerto Rico:

In the prosecution of the war against the kingdom of Spain by the people of the United States, in the cause of liberty, justice, and humanity, its military forces have come to occupy the island of Puerto Rico. They come bearing the banner of freedom, inspired by a noble purpose to seek the enemies of our country and yours, and to destroy or capture all who are in armed resistance. They bring you the fostering arm of a free people, whose greatest power is in its justice and humanity to all those living within its fold. Hence the first effect of this occupation will be the immediate release from your former relations, and it is hoped a cheerful acceptance of the government of the United States. The chief object of the American military forces will be to overthrow the armed authority of Spain, and to give the people of your beautiful island the largest measure of liberty consistent with this occupation. We have not come to make war upon the people of a country that for centuries has been oppressed, but, on the contrary, to bring you protection, not only to yourselves, but to your property; to promote your prosperity, and bestow upon you the immunities and blessings of the liberal institutions of our government. It is not our purpose to interfere with any existing laws and customs that are wholesome and beneficial to your people so long as they conform to the rules of military administration of order and justice. This is not a war of devastation, but one to give all within the control of its military and naval forces the advantages and blessings of enlightened civilization.

Nelson A. Miles,

Major–General, Commanding United States Army. 1898 >>>

— The promises set forth in this document were kept to the letter. Indeed, Justice sat up so straight for the people of Puerto Rico that she often toppled over backward and crushed the American soldier. To steal anything, from a kiss to a cow, was almost a capital offence; while houses and churches might have been lined with gold and jasper, or infected with the small-pox, so stringently were we kept out of them -- at least during the hostile period.

This was all a mighty good thing for somebody, no doubt, but it detracted in large chunks from the glamour of war for the soldier-boy; and I fear that the majority of us felt hurt, if not sorely cheated. Nor is it at all certain that the average inhabitant of Puerto Rico is worth coddling, protection, prosperity, "and the immunities and blessings" accorded him by his new rulers. A thick, stout cudgel or a bright, sharp axe will be more effective than honeyed words in helping him cheerfully to assimilate new ideas; though no one will believe it here at home until the hurrah is all over and some of the truth gets into general circulation.

About one-sixth of the population in this island--the educated class, and chiefly of pure Spanish blood--can be set down as valuable acquisitions to our citizenship and the peer, if not the superior, of most Americans in chivalry, domesticity, fidelity, and culture. Of the rest, perhaps one-half can be moulded by a firm hand into something approaching decency; but the remainder are going to give us a great deal of trouble. They are ignorant, filthy, untruthful, lazy, treacherous, murderous, brutal, and black Spain has kept her hand at their throats for many weary years, and the only thing that has saved them from being throttled is the powerful influence in their discipline effected by the Roman Catholic Church. When our zealous missionaries have succeeded in leading them into the confines of other creeds, we shall have all the excitement we want in Puerto Rico, and the part of our army stationed there will have no lack of exercise.

(Excerpt) FROM YAUCO TO LAS MARIAS, A Recent Campaign in Puerto Rico
by the Independent Regular Brigade under the command of Brig. General Schwan
by Karl Stephen Herrman

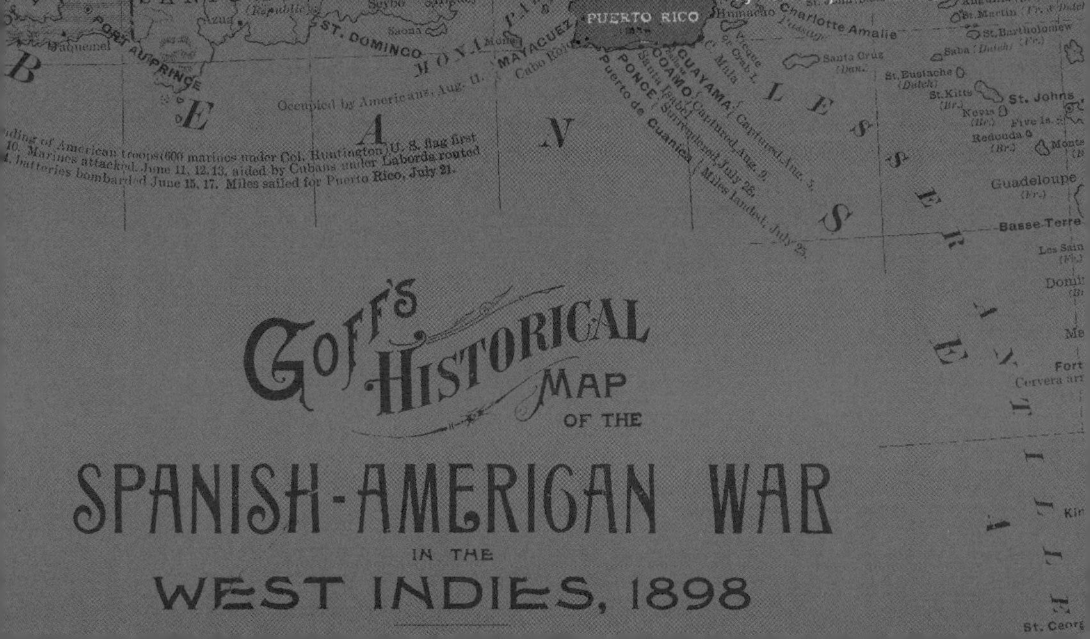

PUERTO RICO
SANTO DOMINGO
PORT AU PRINCE
MAYAGUEZ
GUAYAMA
COAMO
PONCE
Puerto de Guanica
Charlotte Amalie
Santa Cruz
Guadeloupe
Basse-Terre
GOFF'S HISTORICAL MAP OF THE
SPANISH-AMERICAN WAR
IN THE
WEST INDIES, 1898

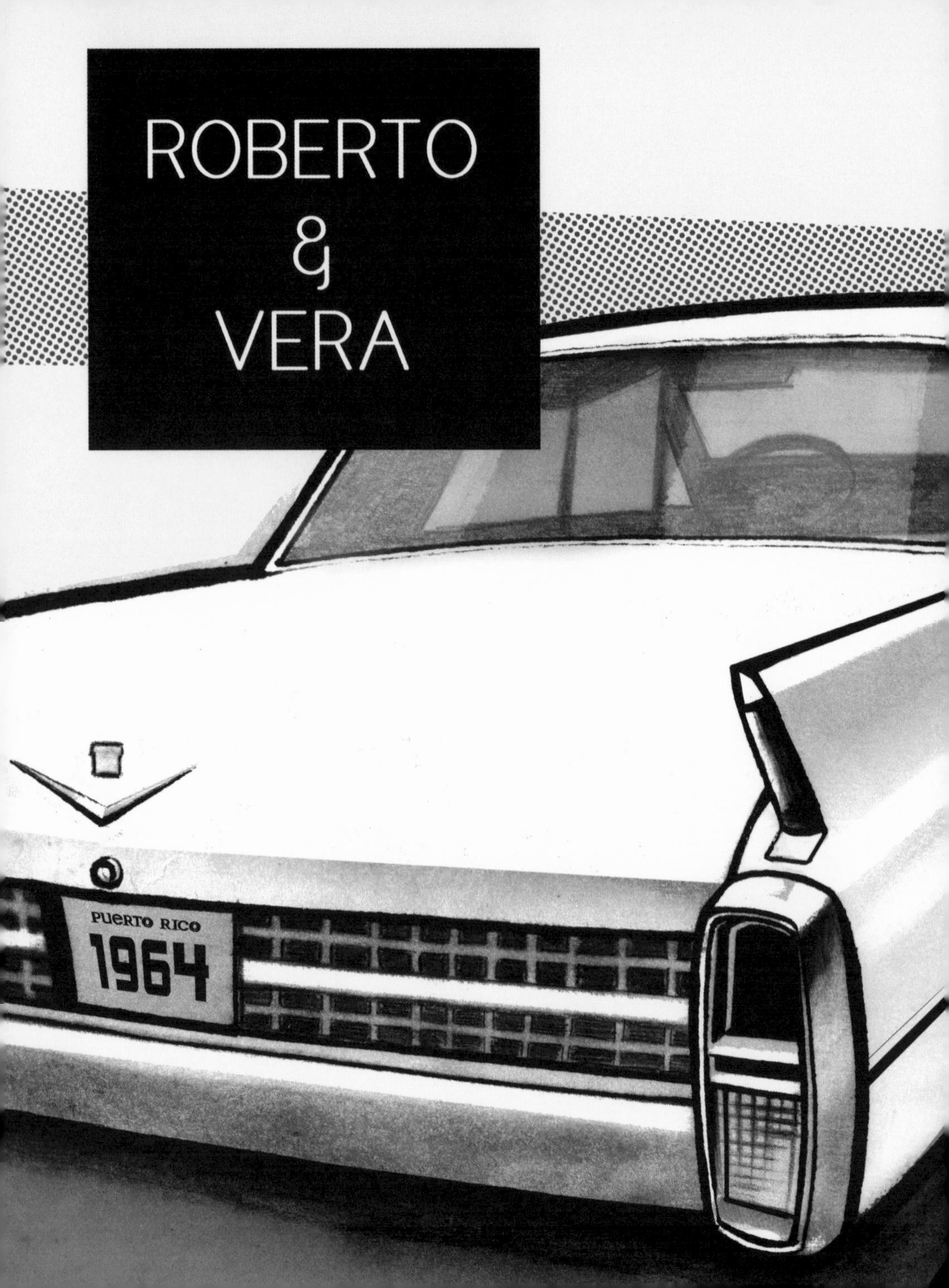
ROBERTO
&
VERA
PUERTO RICO
1964

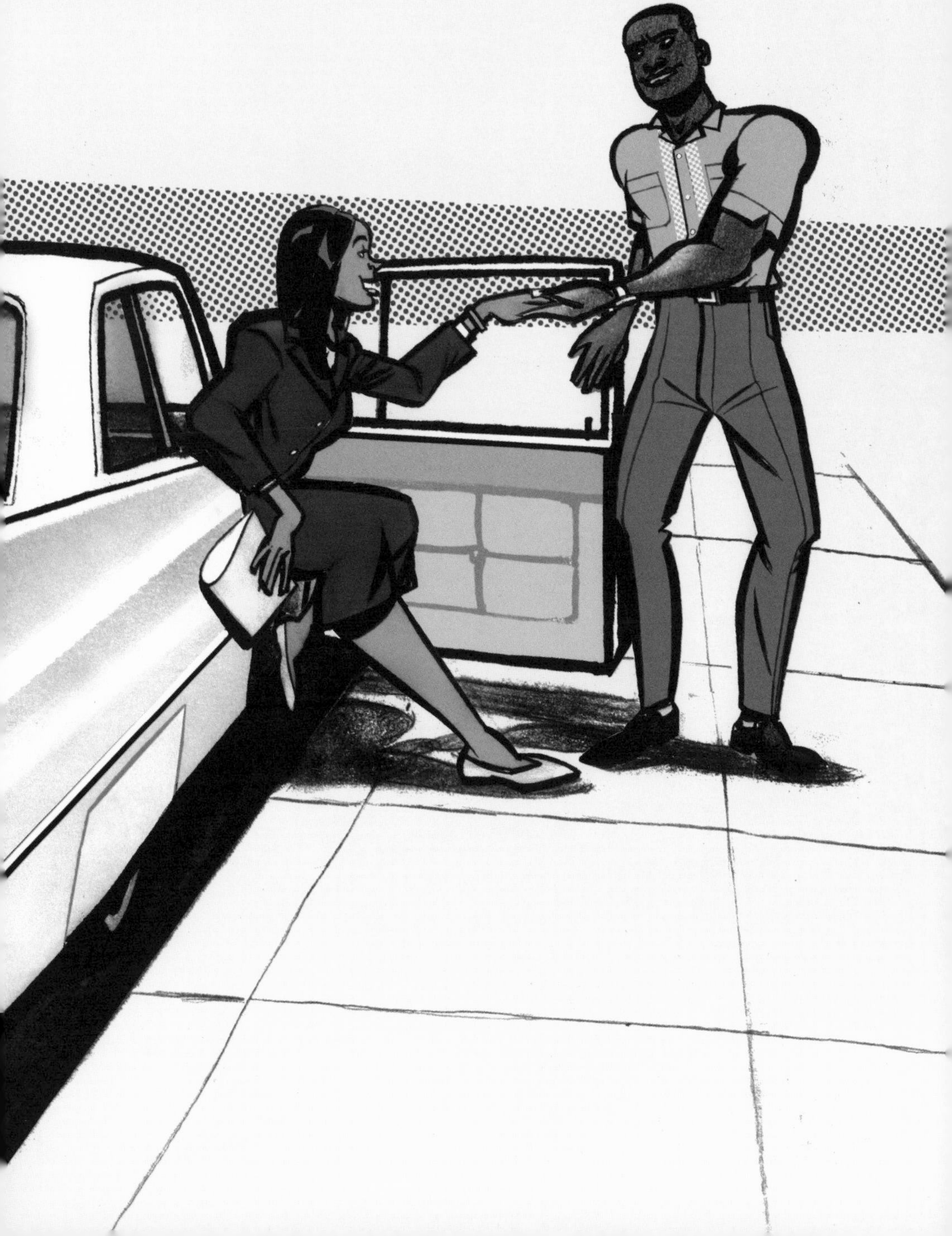

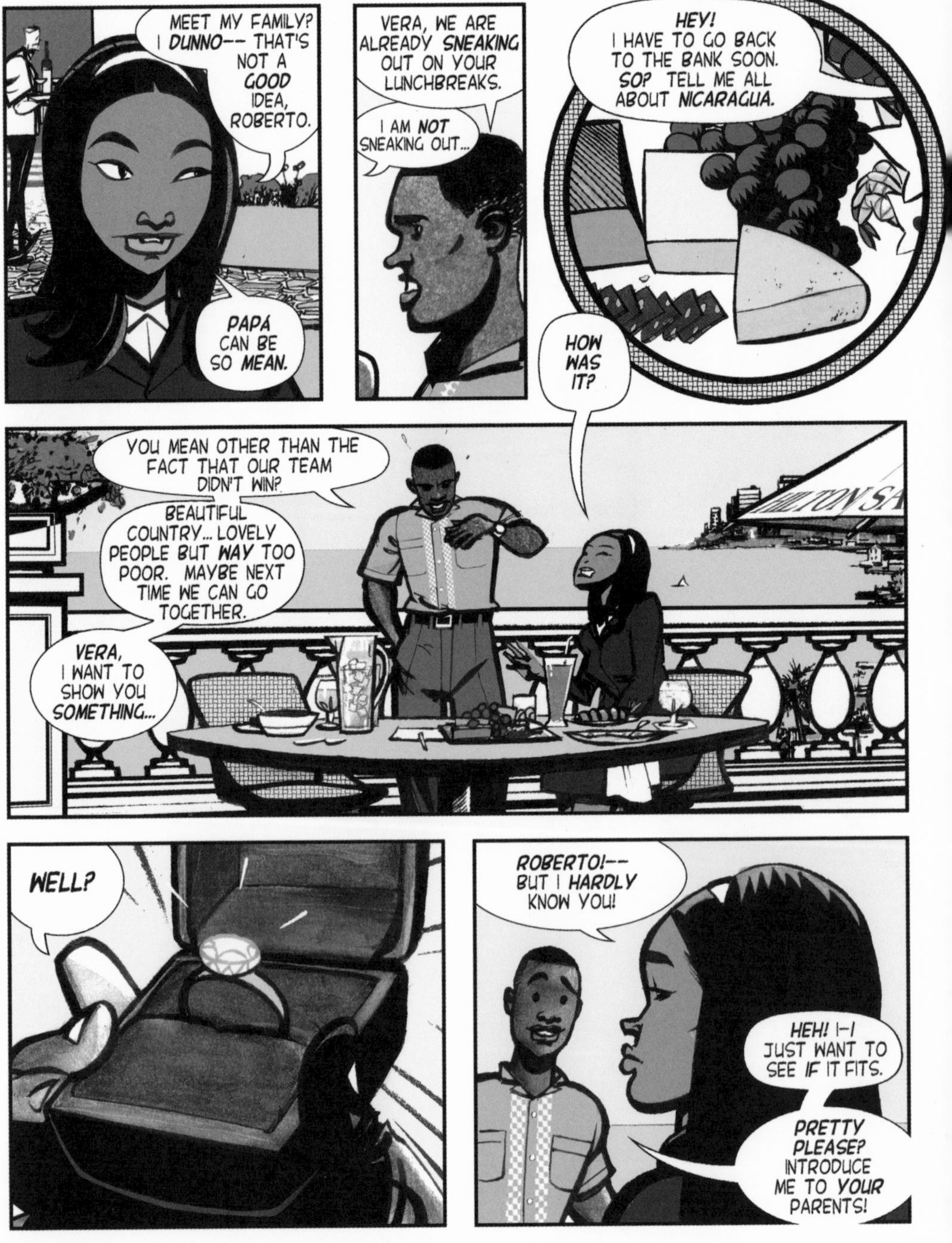
MEET MY FAMILY? I DUNNO-- THAT'S NOT A GOOD IDEA, ROBERTO.
PAPÁ CAN BE SO MEAN.
VERA, WE ARE ALREADY SNEAKING OUT ON YOUR LUNCHBREAKS.
I AM NOT SNEAKING OUT...
HEY! I HAVE TO GO BACK TO THE BANK SOON. SO? TELL ME ALL ABOUT NICARAGUA.
HOW WAS IT?
YOU MEAN OTHER THAN THE FACT THAT OUR TEAM DIDN'T WIN?
BEAUTIFUL COUNTRY... LOVELY PEOPLE BUT WAY TOO POOR. MAYBE NEXT TIME WE CAN GO TOGETHER.
VERA, I WANT TO SHOW YOU SOMETHING...
WELL?
ROBERTO!-- BUT I HARDLY KNOW YOU!
HEH! I-I JUST WANT TO SEE IF IT FITS.
PRETTY PLEASE? INTRODUCE ME TO YOUR PARENTS!

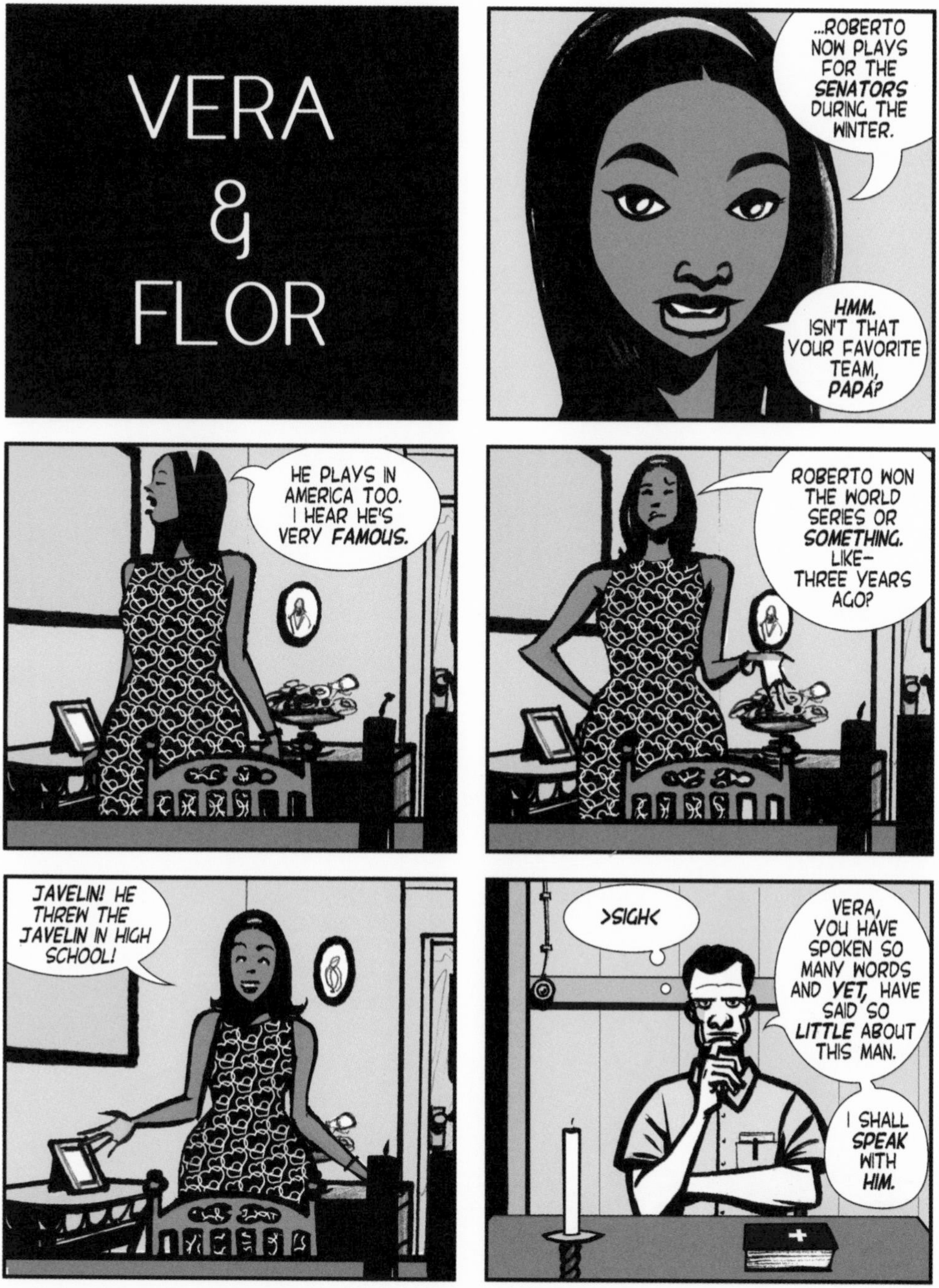
VERA & FLOR
...ROBERTO NOW PLAYS FOR THE SENATORS DURING THE WINTER.
HMM. ISN'T THAT YOUR FAVORITE TEAM, PAPÁ?
HE PLAYS IN AMERICA TOO. I HEAR HE'S VERY FAMOUS.
ROBERTO WON THE WORLD SERIES OR SOMETHING. LIKE— THREE YEARS AGO?
JAVELIN! HE THREW THE JAVELIN IN HIGH SCHOOL!
>SIGH<
VERA, YOU HAVE SPOKEN SO MANY WORDS AND YET, HAVE SAID SO LITTLE ABOUT THIS MAN.
I SHALL SPEAK WITH HIM.

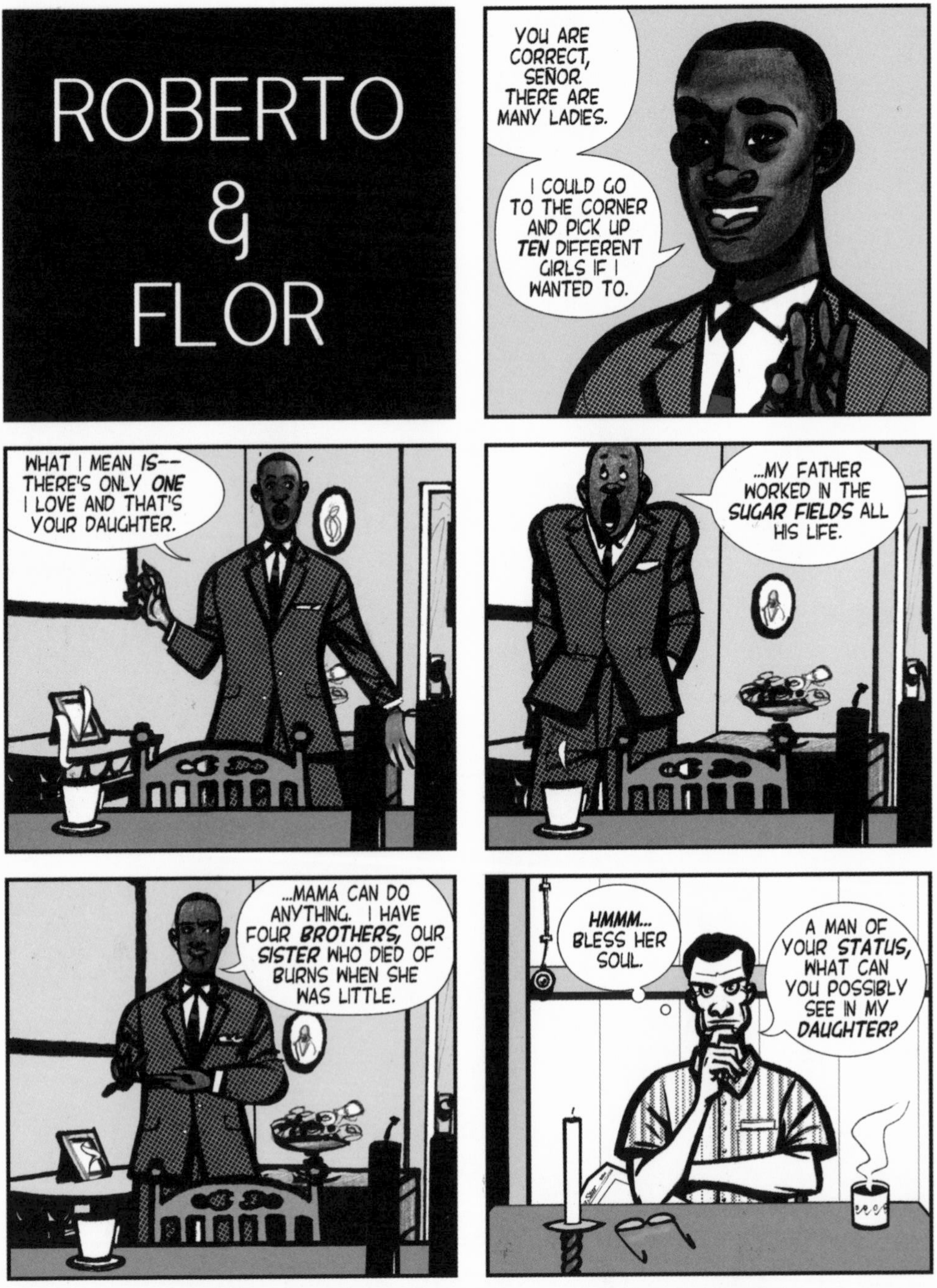
ROBERTO & FLOR
YOU ARE CORRECT, SEÑOR. THERE ARE MANY LADIES.
I COULD GO TO THE CORNER AND PICK UP TEN DIFFERENT GIRLS IF I WANTED TO.
WHAT I MEAN IS-- THERE'S ONLY ONE I LOVE AND THAT'S YOUR DAUGHTER.
...MY FATHER WORKED IN THE SUGAR FIELDS ALL HIS LIFE.
...MAMÁ CAN DO ANYTHING. I HAVE FOUR BROTHERS, OUR SISTER WHO DIED OF BURNS WHEN SHE WAS LITTLE.
HMMM... BLESS HER SOUL.
A MAN OF YOUR STATUS, WHAT CAN YOU POSSIBLY SEE IN MY DAUGHTER?

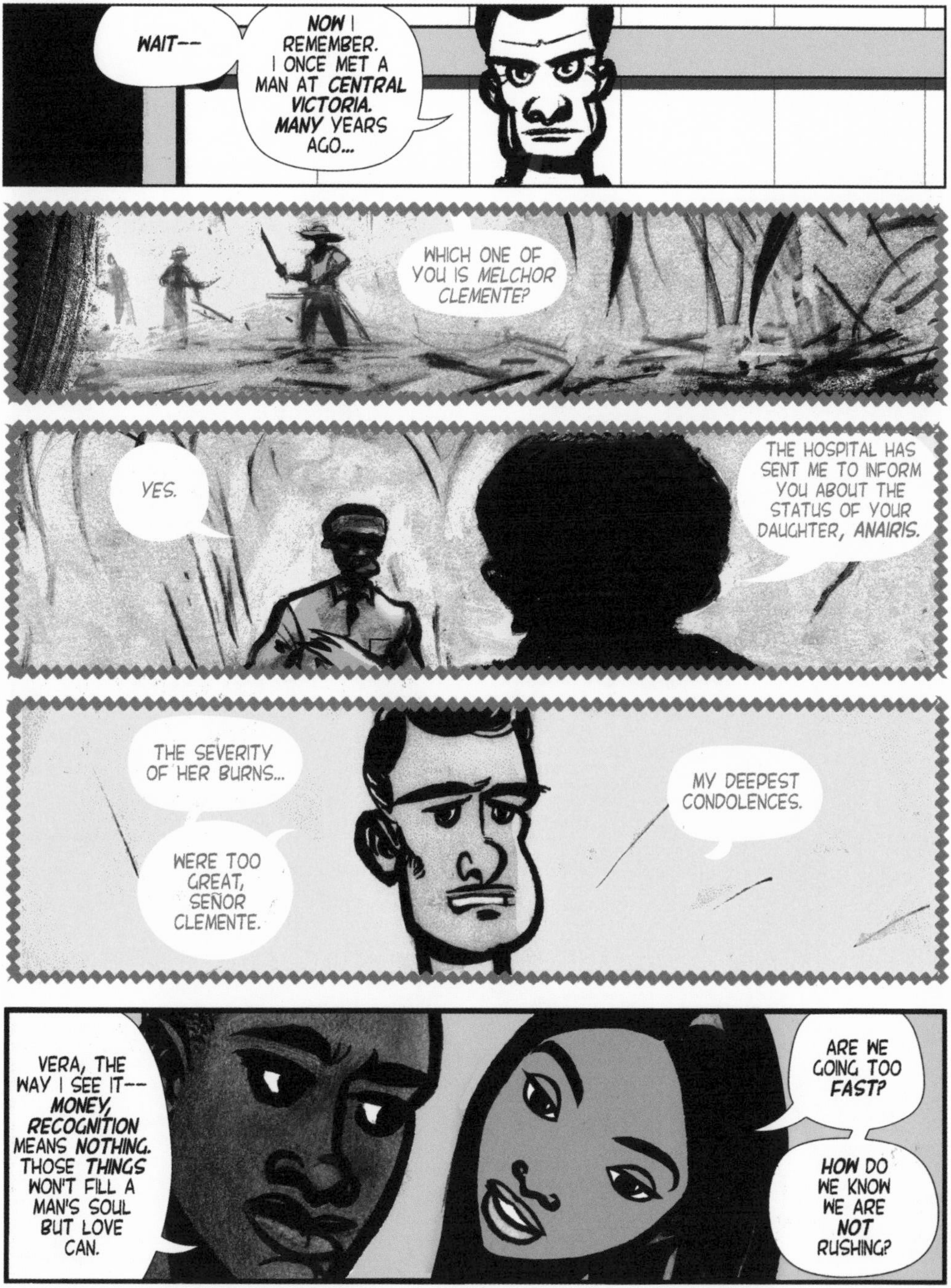
WAIT--
NOW I REMEMBER. I ONCE MET A MAN AT CENTRAL VICTORIA. MANY YEARS AGO...
WHICH ONE OF YOU IS MELCHOR CLEMENTE?
YES.
THE HOSPITAL HAS SENT ME TO INFORM YOU ABOUT THE STATUS OF YOUR DAUGHTER, ANAIRIS.
THE SEVERITY OF HER BURNS...
WERE TOO GREAT, SEÑOR CLEMENTE.
MY DEEPEST CONDOLENCES.
VERA, THE WAY I SEE IT-- MONEY, RECOGNITION MEANS NOTHING. THOSE THINGS WON'T FILL A MAN'S SOUL BUT LOVE CAN.
ARE WE GOING TOO FAST?
HOW DO WE KNOW WE ARE NOT RUSHING?

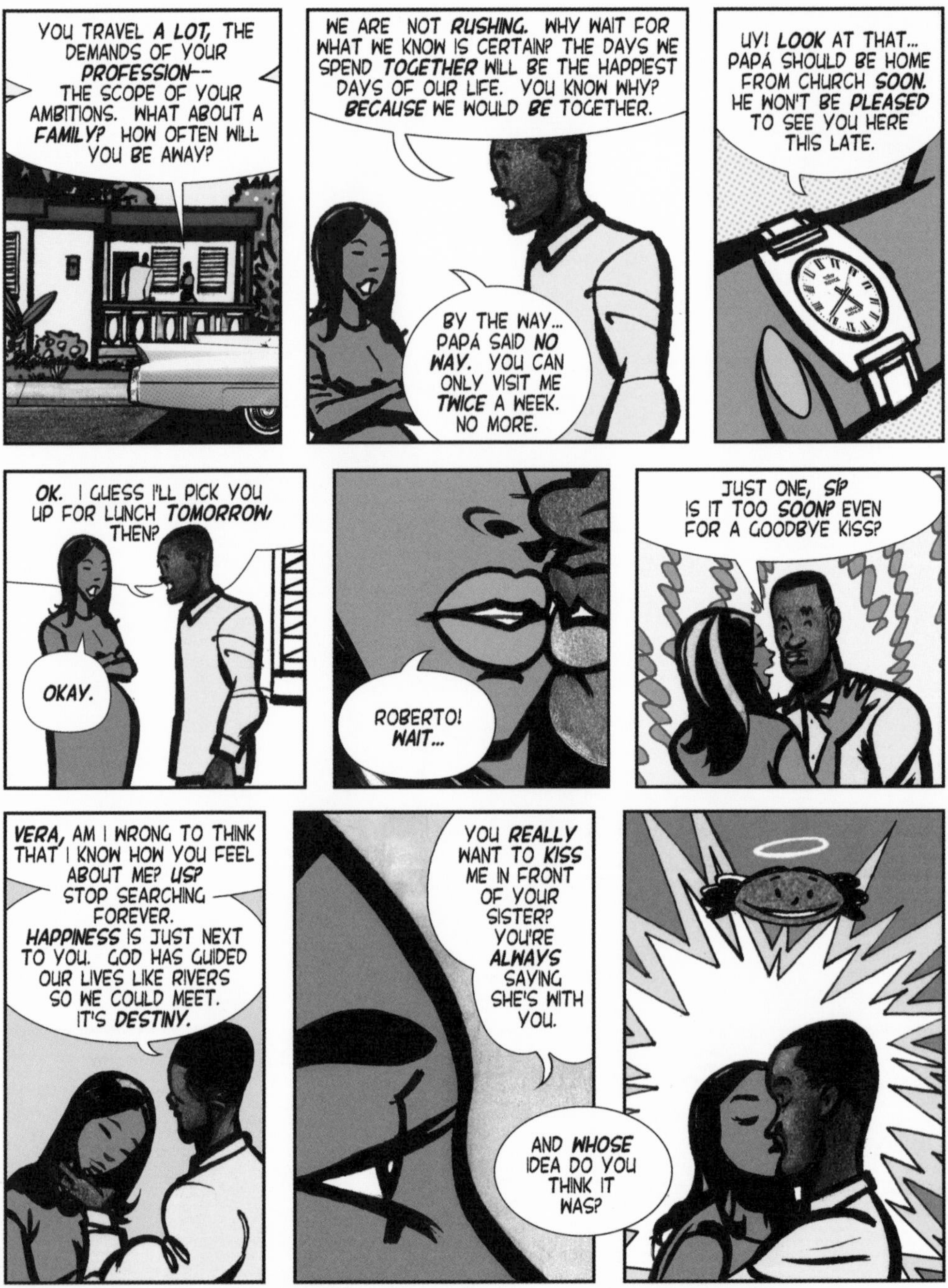
YOU TRAVEL A LOT, THE DEMANDS OF YOUR PROFESSION-- THE SCOPE OF YOUR AMBITIONS. WHAT ABOUT A FAMILY? HOW OFTEN WILL YOU BE AWAY?
WE ARE NOT RUSHING. WHY WAIT FOR WHAT WE KNOW IS CERTAIN? THE DAYS WE SPEND TOGETHER WILL BE THE HAPPIEST DAYS OF OUR LIFE. YOU KNOW WHY? BECAUSE WE WOULD BE TOGETHER.
BY THE WAY... PAPÁ SAID NO WAY. YOU CAN ONLY VISIT ME TWICE A WEEK. NO MORE.
UY! LOOK AT THAT... PAPÁ SHOULD BE HOME FROM CHURCH SOON. HE WON'T BE PLEASED TO SEE YOU HERE THIS LATE.
OK. I GUESS I'LL PICK YOU UP FOR LUNCH TOMORROW, THEN?
OKAY.
ROBERTO! WAIT...
JUST ONE, SÍ? IS IT TOO SOON? EVEN FOR A GOODBYE KISS?
VERA, AM I WRONG TO THINK THAT I KNOW HOW YOU FEEL ABOUT ME? US? STOP SEARCHING FOREVER. HAPPINESS IS JUST NEXT TO YOU. GOD HAS GUIDED OUR LIVES LIKE RIVERS SO WE COULD MEET. IT'S DESTINY.
YOU REALLY WANT TO KISS ME IN FRONT OF YOUR SISTER? YOU'RE ALWAYS SAYING SHE'S WITH YOU.
AND WHOSE IDEA DO YOU THINK IT WAS?

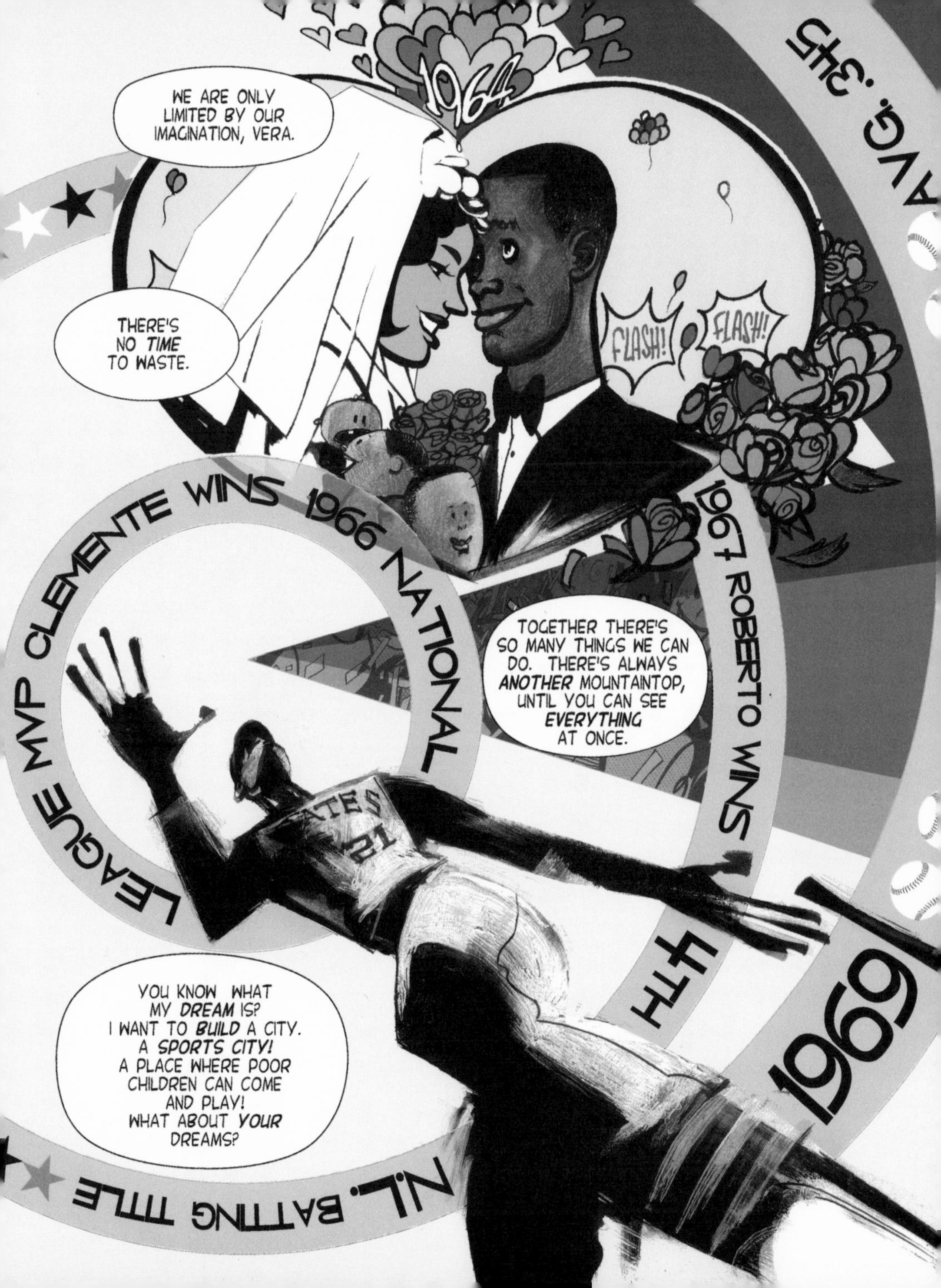
1964
WE ARE ONLY LIMITED BY OUR IMAGINATION, VERA.
THERE'S NO *TIME* TO WASTE.
FLASH!
FLASH!
AVG. .345
CLEMENTE WINS 1966 NATIONAL LEAGUE MVP
TOGETHER THERE'S SO MANY THINGS WE CAN DO. THERE'S ALWAYS *ANOTHER* MOUNTAINTOP, UNTIL YOU CAN SEE *EVERYTHING* AT ONCE.
1967 ROBERTO WINS 4TH N.L. BATTING TITLE
PIRATES 21
YOU KNOW WHAT MY *DREAM* IS? I WANT TO *BUILD* A CITY. A *SPORTS CITY!* A PLACE WHERE POOR CHILDREN CAN COME AND PLAY! WHAT ABOUT *YOUR* DREAMS?
1969

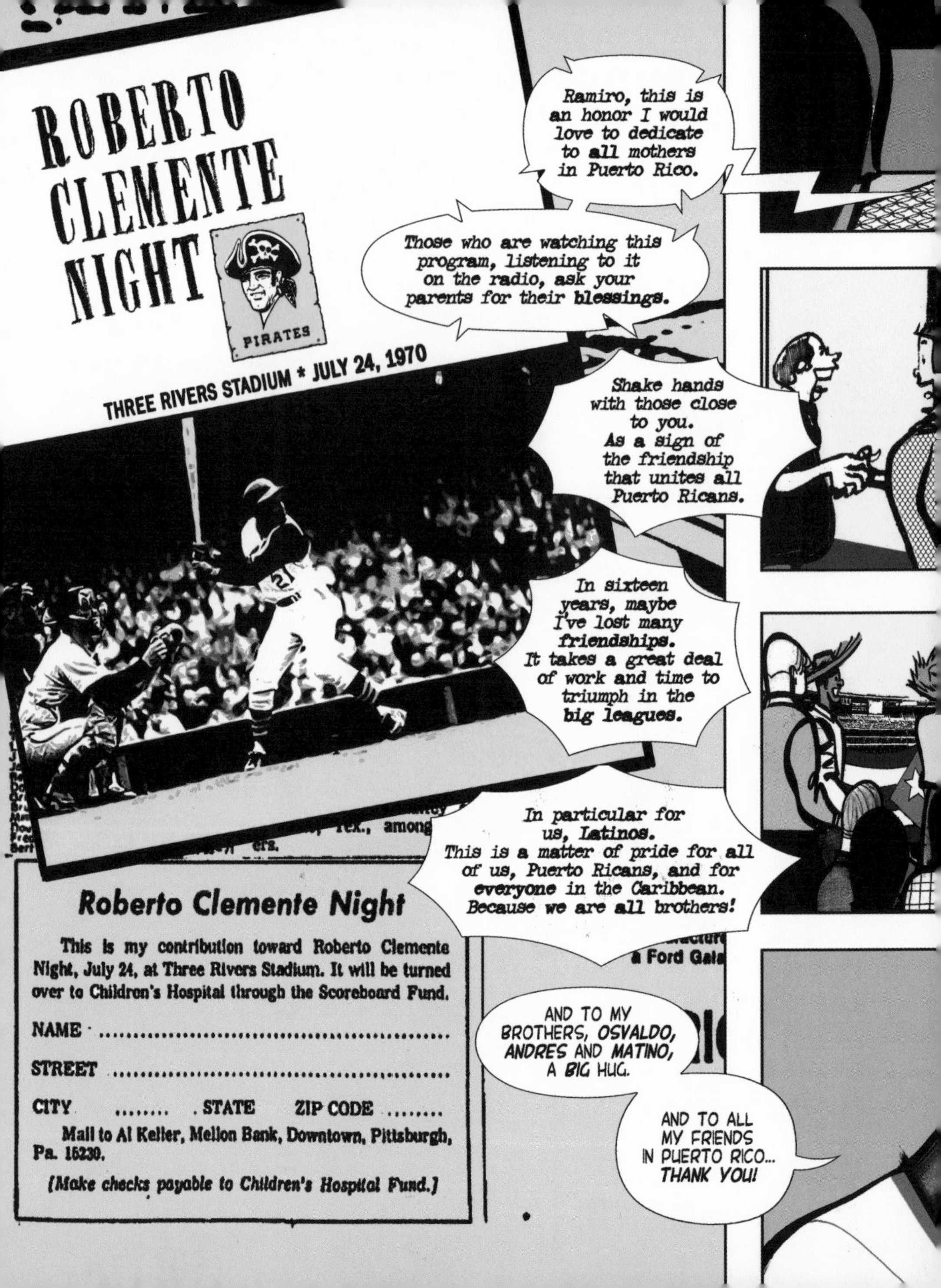
ROBERTO CLEMENTE NIGHT
PIRATES
THREE RIVERS STADIUM * JULY 24, 1970
Ramiro, this is an honor I would love to dedicate to all mothers in Puerto Rico.
Those who are watching this program, listening to it on the radio, ask your parents for their blessings.
Shake hands with those close to you. As a sign of the friendship that unites all Puerto Ricans.
In sixteen years, maybe I've lost many friendships. It takes a great deal of work and time to triumph in the big leagues.
In particular for us, Latinos. This is a matter of pride for all of us, Puerto Ricans, and for everyone in the Caribbean. Because we are all brothers!
Roberto Clemente Night
This is my contribution toward Roberto Clemente Night, July 24, at Three Rivers Stadium. It will be turned over to Children's Hospital through the Scoreboard Fund.
NAME
STREET
CITY
STATE
ZIP CODE
Mail to Al Keller, Mellon Bank, Downtown, Pittsburgh, Pa. 15230.
(Make checks payable to Children's Hospital Fund.)
AND TO MY BROTHERS, OSVALDO, ANDRES AND MATINO, A BIG HUG.
AND TO ALL MY FRIENDS IN PUERTO RICO... THANK YOU!

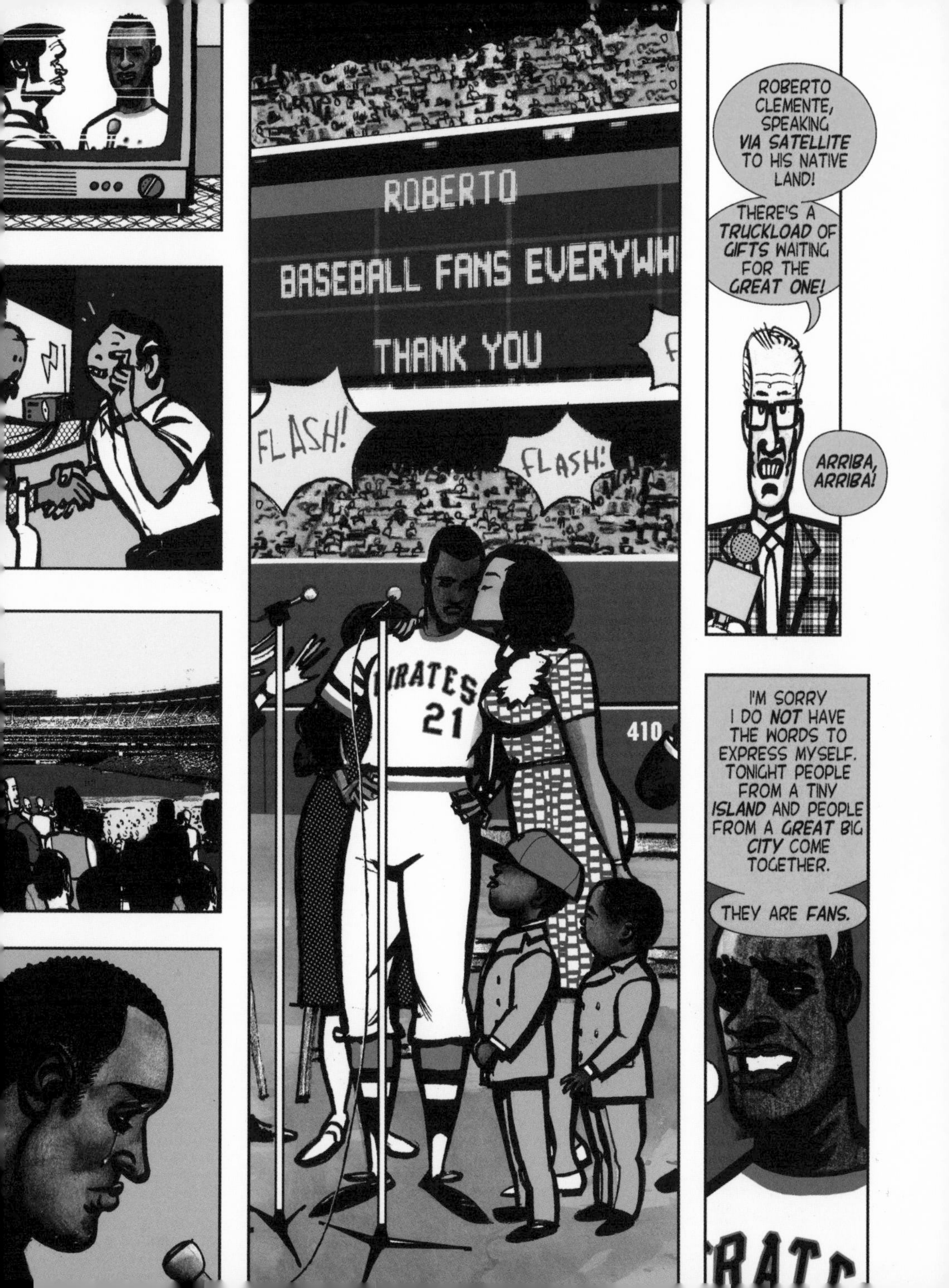
ROBERTO
BASEBALL FANS EVERYWH
THANK YOU
FLASH!
FLASH!
PIRATES
21
410
ROBERTO CLEMENTE, SPEAKING VIA SATELLITE TO HIS NATIVE LAND!
THERE'S A TRUCKLOAD OF GIFTS WAITING FOR THE GREAT ONE!
ARRIBA, ARRIBA!
I'M SORRY I DO NOT HAVE THE WORDS TO EXPRESS MYSELF. TONIGHT PEOPLE FROM A TINY ISLAND AND PEOPLE FROM A GREAT BIG CITY COME TOGETHER.
THEY ARE FANS.

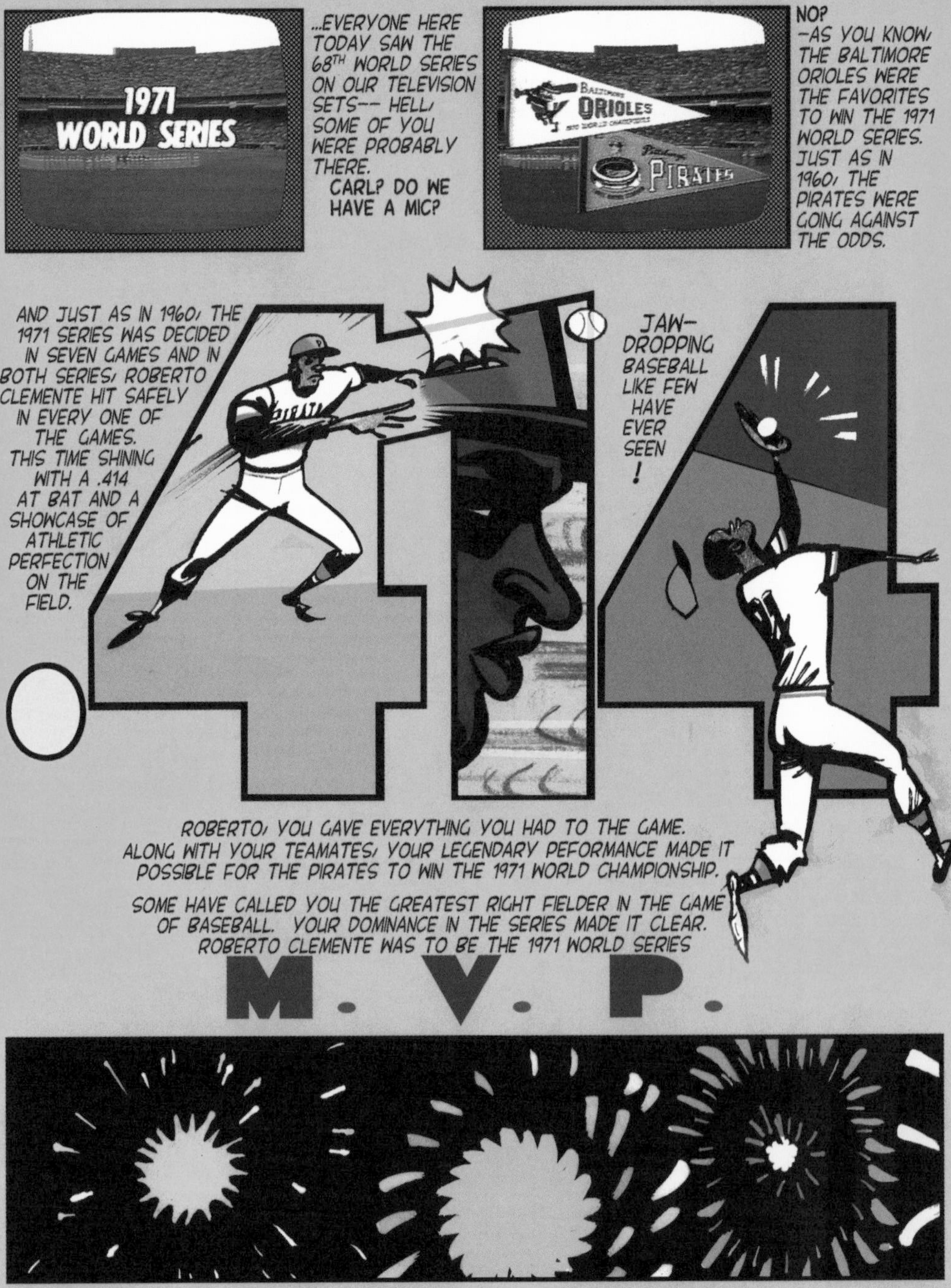
1971 WORLD SERIES
...EVERYONE HERE TODAY SAW THE 68TH WORLD SERIES ON OUR TELEVISION SETS-- HELL, SOME OF YOU WERE PROBABLY THERE.
CARL? DO WE HAVE A MIC?
BALTIMORE ORIOLES
PIRATES
NO?
-AS YOU KNOW, THE BALTIMORE ORIOLES WERE THE FAVORITES TO WIN THE 1971 WORLD SERIES. JUST AS IN 1960, THE PIRATES WERE GOING AGAINST THE ODDS.
AND JUST AS IN 1960, THE 1971 SERIES WAS DECIDED IN SEVEN GAMES AND IN BOTH SERIES, ROBERTO CLEMENTE HIT SAFELY IN EVERY ONE OF THE GAMES.
THIS TIME SHINING WITH A .414 AT BAT AND A SHOWCASE OF ATHLETIC PERFECTION ON THE FIELD.
JAW-DROPPING BASEBALL LIKE FEW HAVE EVER SEEN!
ROBERTO, YOU GAVE EVERYTHING YOU HAD TO THE GAME. ALONG WITH YOUR TEAMATES, YOUR LEGENDARY PEFORMANCE MADE IT POSSIBLE FOR THE PIRATES TO WIN THE 1971 WORLD CHAMPIONSHIP.
SOME HAVE CALLED YOU THE GREATEST RIGHT FIELDER IN THE GAME OF BASEBALL. YOUR DOMINANCE IN THE SERIES MADE IT CLEAR. ROBERTO CLEMENTE WAS TO BE THE 1971 WORLD SERIES
M.V.P.

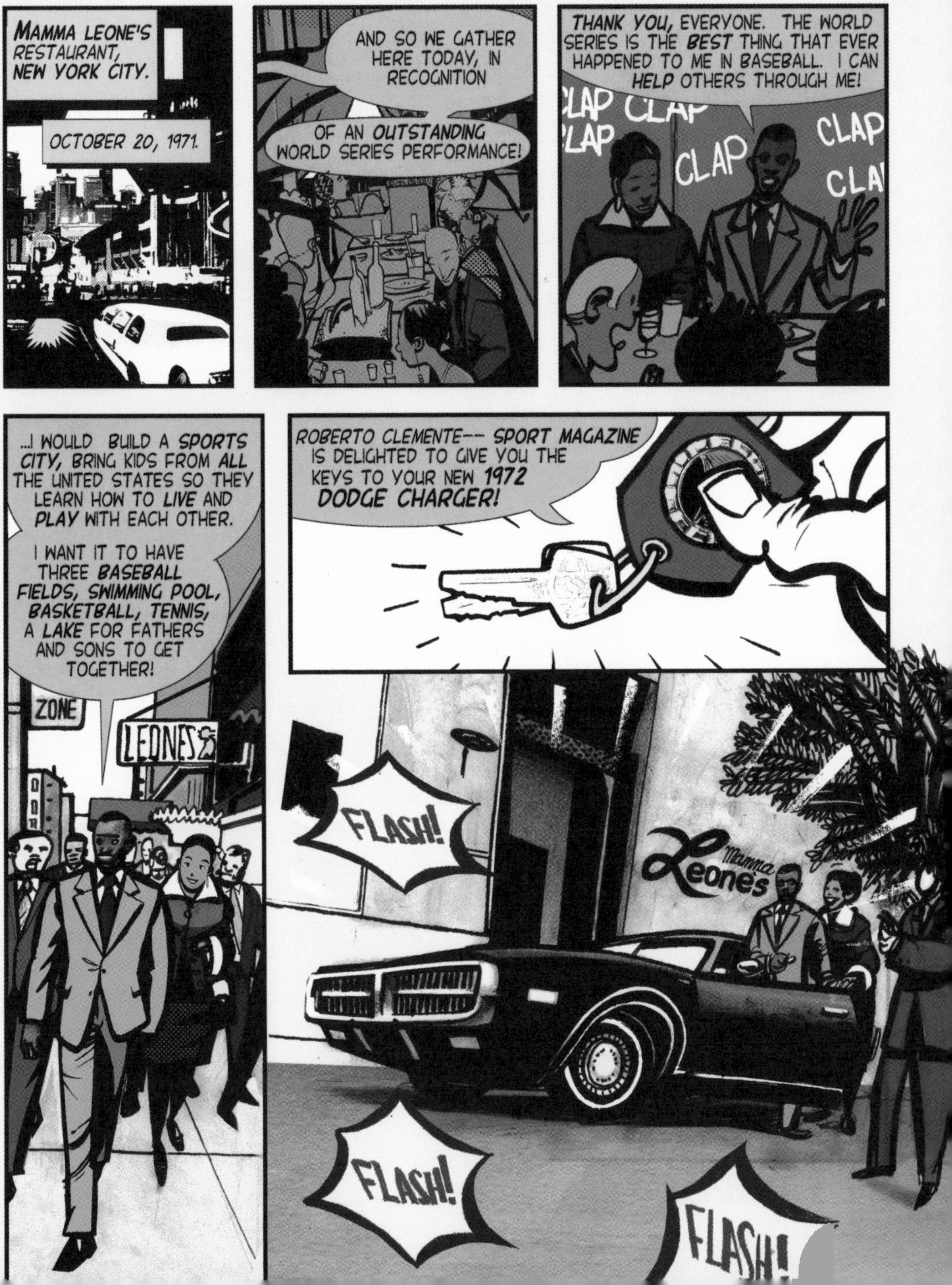
MAMMA LEONE'S RESTAURANT, NEW YORK CITY.
OCTOBER 20, 1971.
AND SO WE GATHER HERE TODAY, IN RECOGNITION
OF AN OUTSTANDING WORLD SERIES PERFORMANCE!
THANK YOU, EVERYONE. THE WORLD SERIES IS THE BEST THING THAT EVER HAPPENED TO ME IN BASEBALL. I CAN HELP OTHERS THROUGH ME!
CLAP CLAP
CLAP
CLAP
CLAP
...I WOULD BUILD A SPORTS CITY, BRING KIDS FROM ALL THE UNITED STATES SO THEY LEARN HOW TO LIVE AND PLAY WITH EACH OTHER.
I WANT IT TO HAVE THREE BASEBALL FIELDS, SWIMMING POOL, BASKETBALL, TENNIS, A LAKE FOR FATHERS AND SONS TO GET TOGETHER!
ZONE
LEONES
ROBERTO CLEMENTE-- SPORT MAGAZINE IS DELIGHTED TO GIVE YOU THE KEYS TO YOUR NEW 1972 DODGE CHARGER!
FLASH!
Mamma Leone's
FLASH!
FLASH!

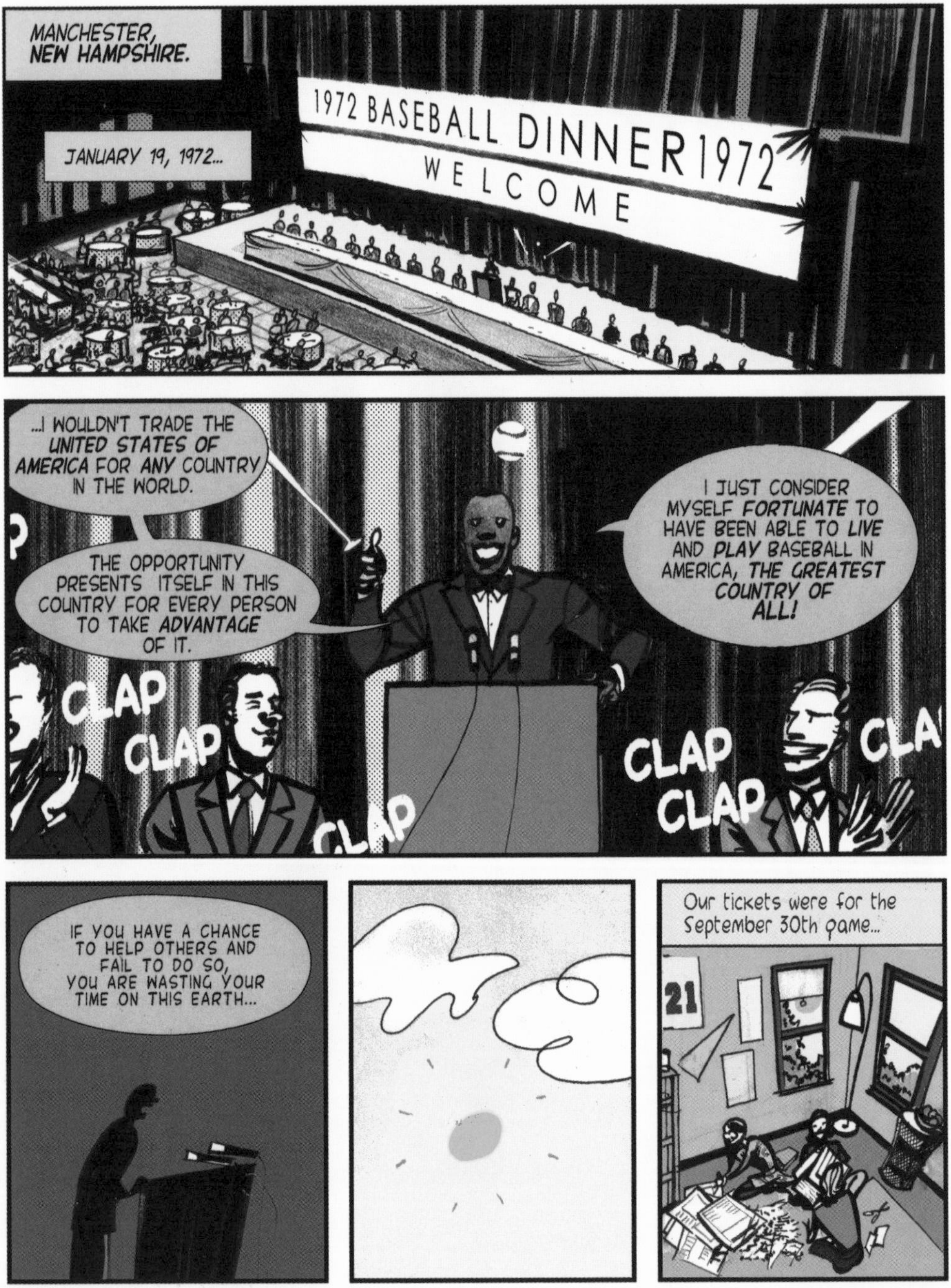
MANCHESTER, NEW HAMPSHIRE.
JANUARY 19, 1972...
1972 BASEBALL DINNER 1972
WELCOME
...I WOULDN'T TRADE THE UNITED STATES OF AMERICA FOR ANY COUNTRY IN THE WORLD.
THE OPPORTUNITY PRESENTS ITSELF IN THIS COUNTRY FOR EVERY PERSON TO TAKE ADVANTAGE OF IT.
I JUST CONSIDER MYSELF FORTUNATE TO HAVE BEEN ABLE TO LIVE AND PLAY BASEBALL IN AMERICA, THE GREATEST COUNTRY OF ALL!
CLAP
CLAP
CLAP
CLAP
CLAP
CLAP
IF YOU HAVE A CHANCE TO HELP OTHERS AND FAIL TO DO SO, YOU ARE WASTING YOUR TIME ON THIS EARTH...
Our tickets were for the September 30th game...
21

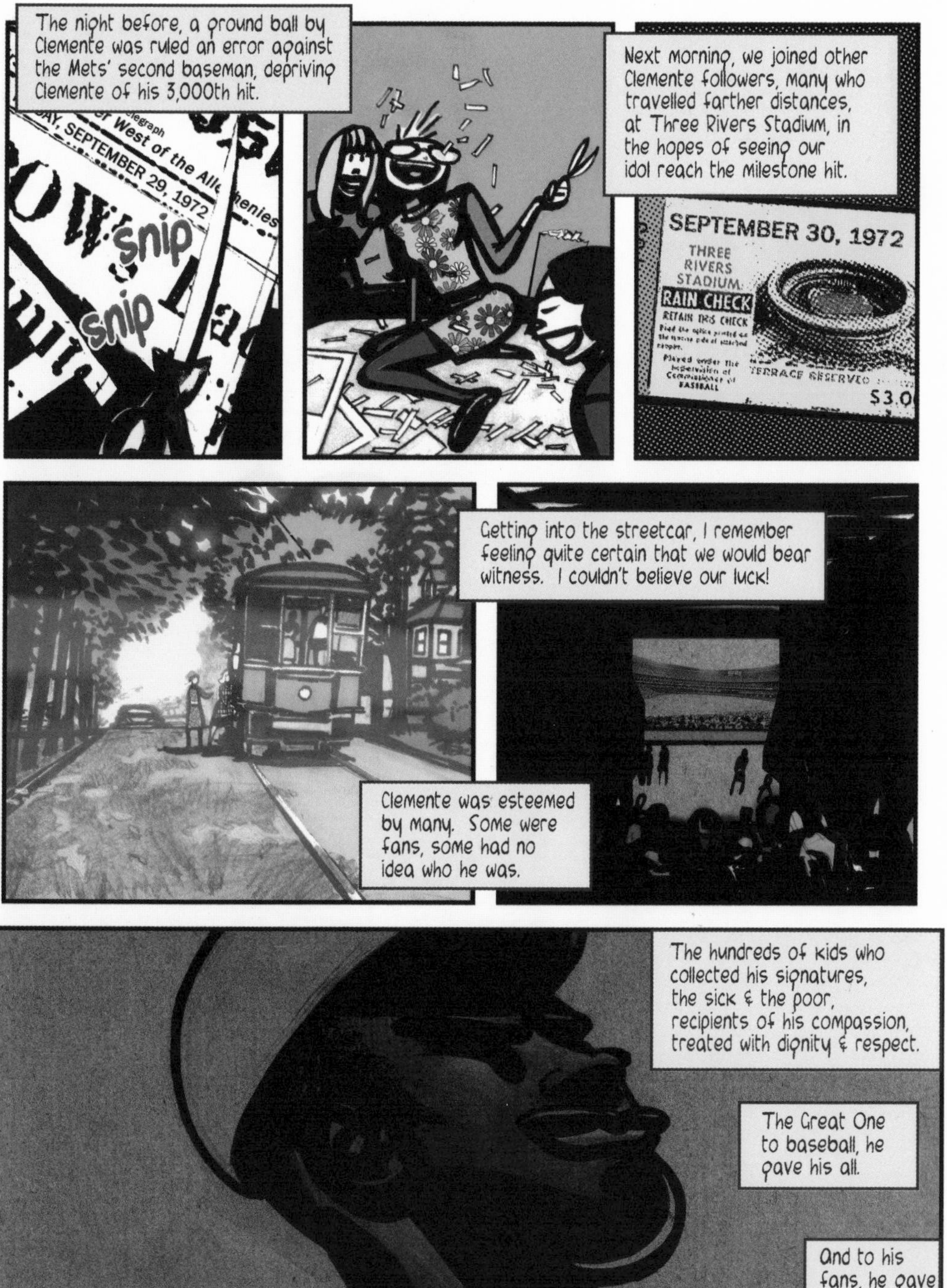

The night before, a ground ball by Clemente was ruled an error against the Mets' second baseman, depriving Clemente of his 3,000th hit.
West of the Allegheni
SEPTEMBER 29, 1972
snip
snip
snip
Next morning, we joined other Clemente followers, many who travelled farther distances, at Three Rivers Stadium, in the hopes of seeing our idol reach the milestone hit.
SEPTEMBER 30, 1972
THREE RIVERS STADIUM
RAIN CHECK
RETAIN THIS CHECK
Getting into the streetcar, I remember feeling quite certain that we would bear witness. I couldn't believe our luck!
Clemente was esteemed by many. Some were fans, some had no idea who he was.
The hundreds of kids who collected his signatures, the sick & the poor, recipients of his compassion, treated with dignity & respect.
The Great One to baseball, he gave his all.
And to his fans, he gave us pride.

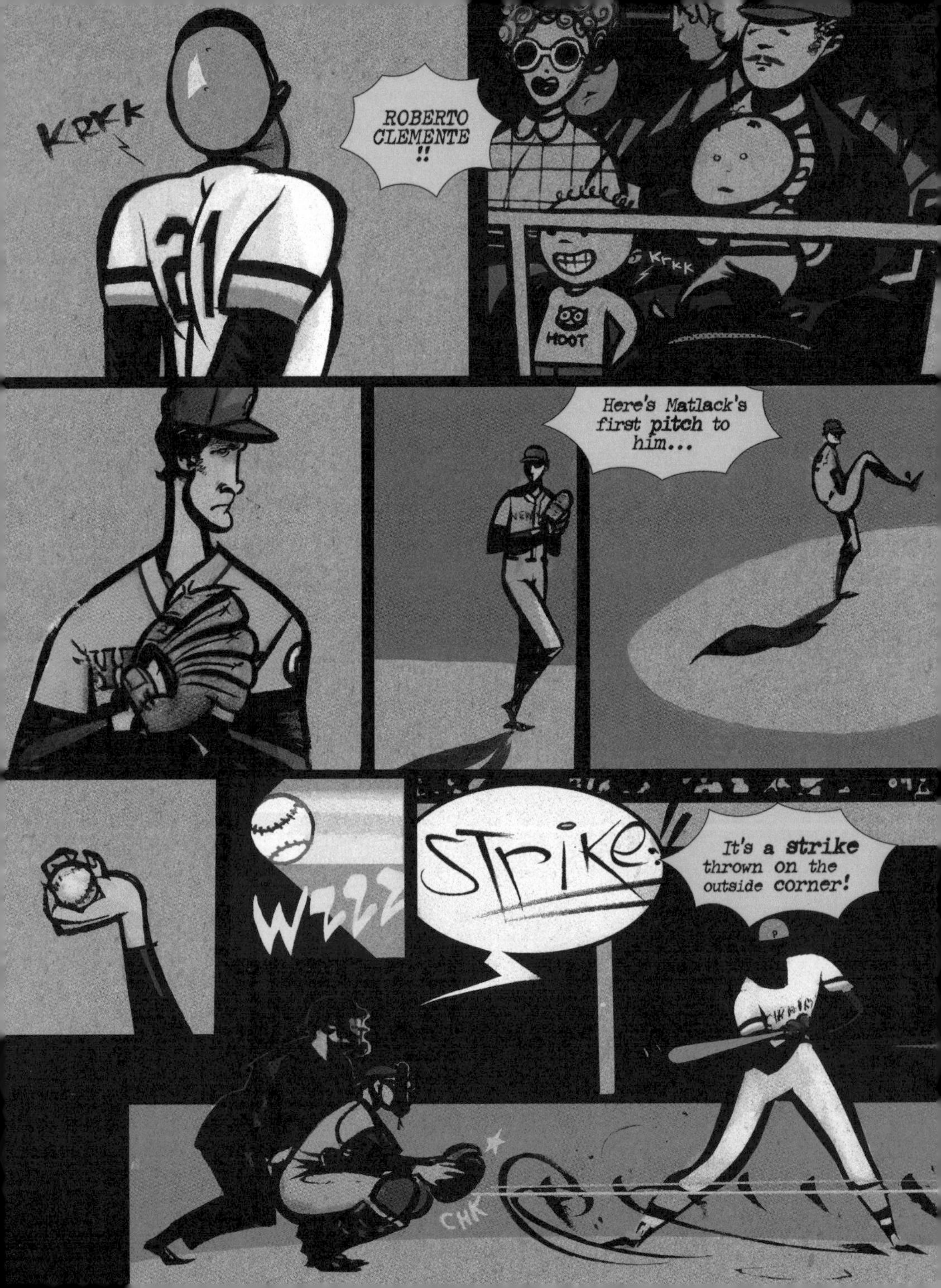

KRKK
ROBERTO CLEMENTE !!
HOOT
KRKK
Here's Matlack's first pitch to him...
WZZZ
STRIKE!
It's a strike thrown on the outside corner!
CHK

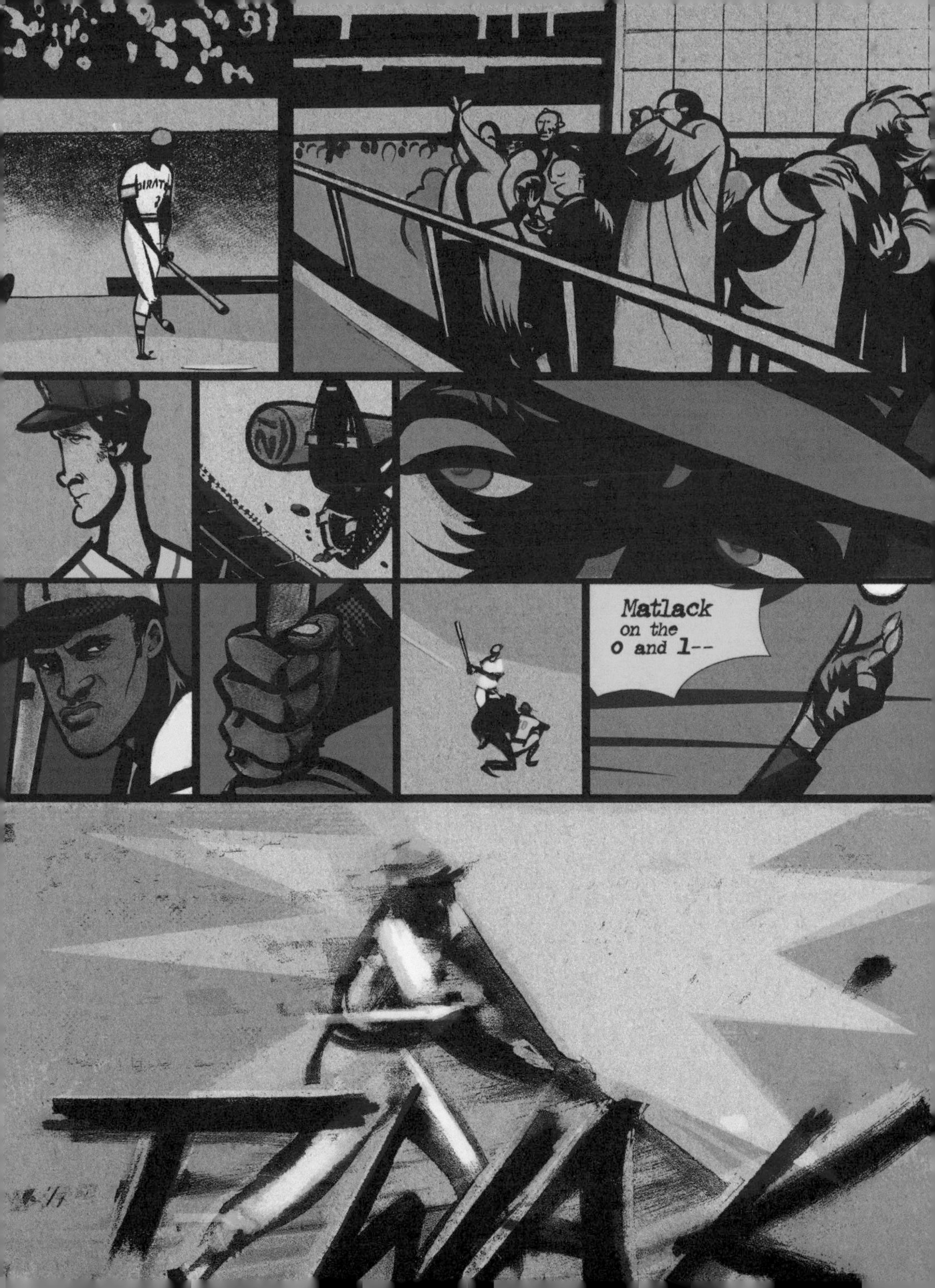
Matlack on the 0 and 1--
TWAK

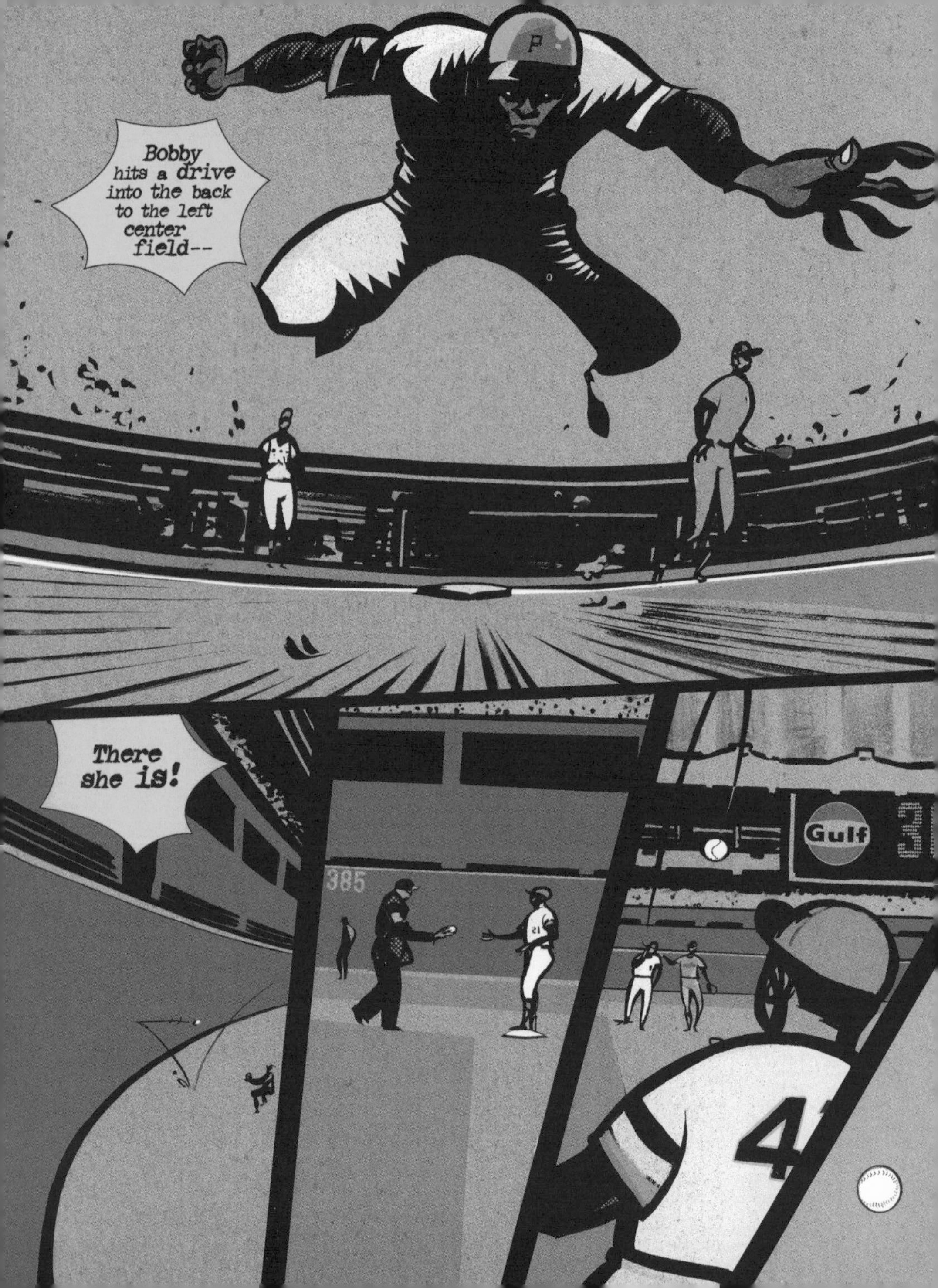
Bobby hits a drive into the back to the left center field--
There she is!
385
Gulf
21
4

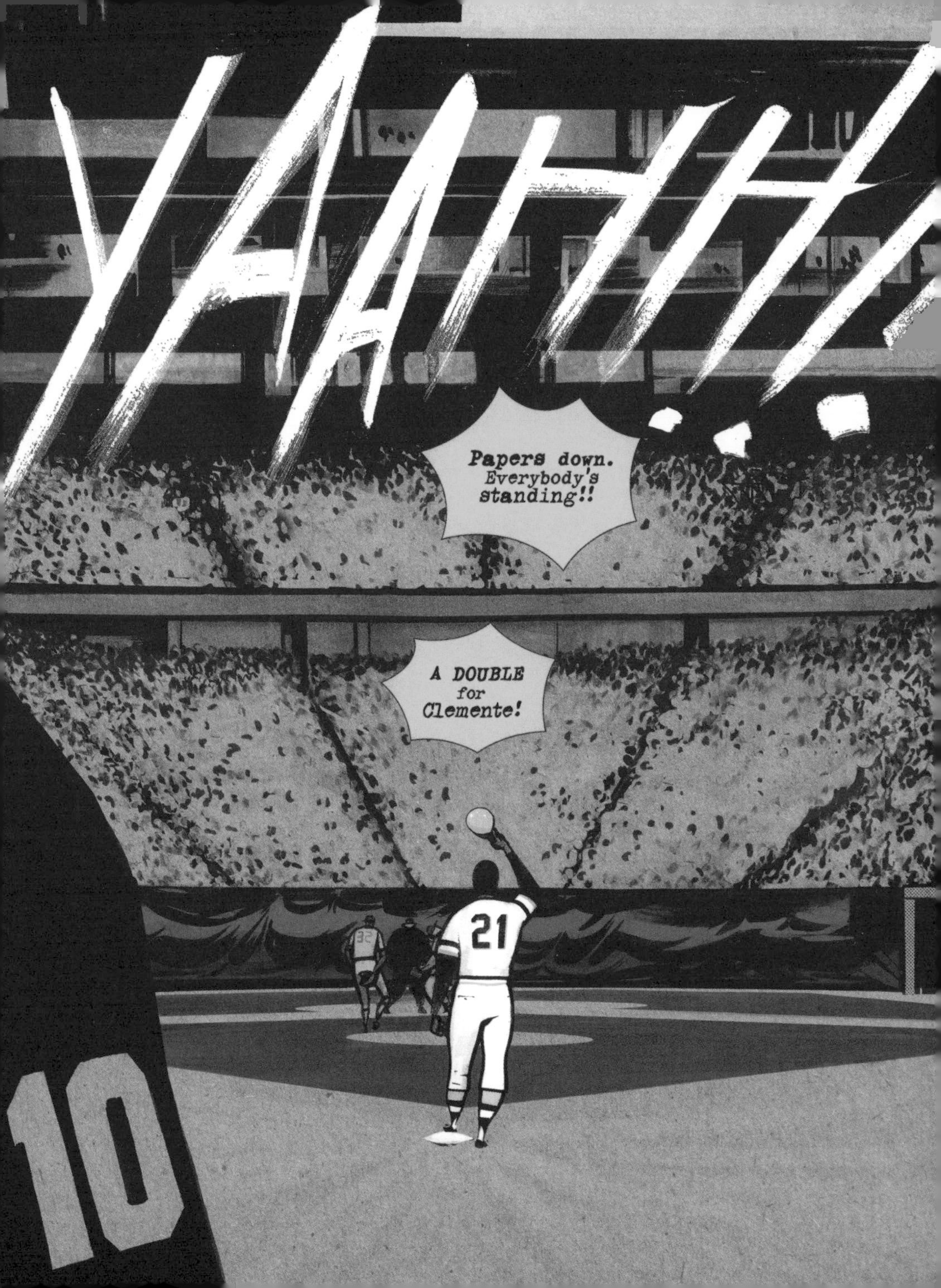
YAAHHH...
Papers down. Everybody's standing!!
A DOUBLE for Clemente!
21
10

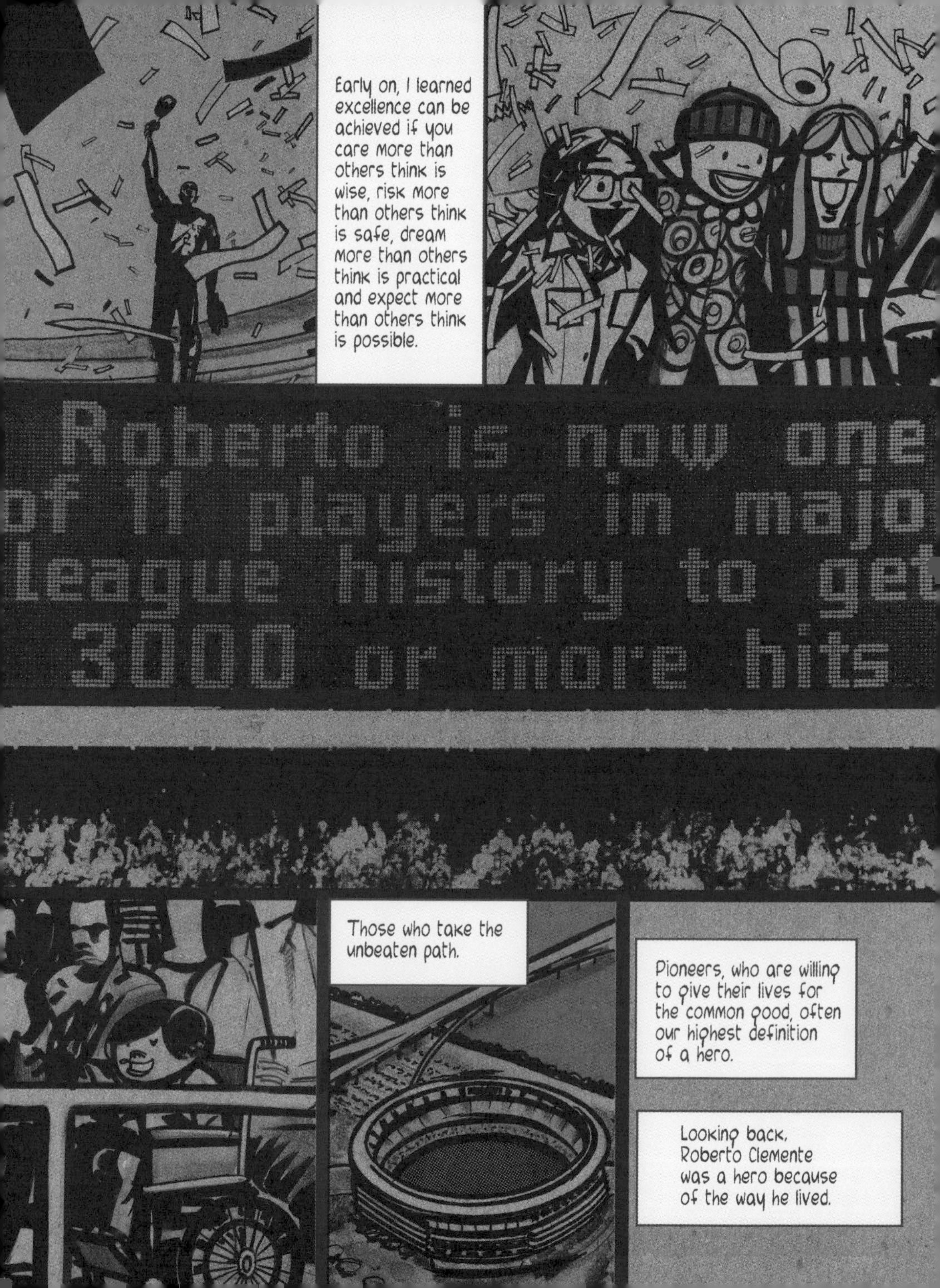
Early on, I learned excellence can be achieved if you care more than others think is wise, risk more than others think is safe, dream more than others think is practical and expect more than others think is possible.
Roberto is now one
of 11 players in majo
league history to ge
3000 or more hits
Those who take the unbeaten path.
Pioneers, who are willing to give their lives for the common good, often our highest definition of a hero.
Looking back, Roberto Clemente was a hero because of the way he lived.

♪ W-K-A-Q - Clock Radi-o... ♪

The time:
4:2o AM

In international news--
Nicaragua continues in
a state of chaos after
last week's earthquake
that killed thousands
and left thousands more
homeless. In the capital
city of Managua, there
were reports of looting.
The smell of unrecovered
bodies permeates the scene.
Rescue teams are starting
to fear disease outbreaks
and Red Cross volunteers
complained that supplies
weren't getting into the
hands of the population.

Accusations of
supplies being seized
by soldiers at
delivery points
and rerouted to
goverment warehouses
has been denied
by Nicaragua's
Supreme Commander
of the Armed Forces,
Anastasio Somoza.

More relief will be shipped from
Puerto Rico on the freighter,
San Expedito, carrying 246 tons
in food and aid.
The National Guard was advised
to provide transportation for
the cargo from dockside to
Masaya, a town near Managua,
according to Roberto Clemente.

Clemente also said his committee has another
planeload in the works.
This is the fourth cargo sent to Nicaragua since
the catastrophe.

RIO PIEDRAS.

...WE ARRIVED AND I MADE SURE THE AID DIDN'T GET *LOST.* THEY DON'T WANT BAD *PUBLICITY.* YOU SAW HOW IT WAS WHEN WE WERE THERE.

THANKS FOR GOING WITH ME, *VALDY.*

EVEN IN SUCH SAD CIRCUMSTANCES. *TOMORROW,* THEN. YOU'RE A GOOD FRIEND. >CLICK<

CAROL? *YES,* IT IS CLEMENTE. VERA AND A FAMILY FRIEND WILL BE WAITING AT THE *AIRPORT* IN SAN JUAN. I CAN'T BE THERE. I HAVE TO FLY TO *NICARAGUA.*

YOU'RE ALL COMING, *RIGHT?*

I WILL RETURN ON *NEW YEARS* AND MEET YOU ALL.

WE'RE GOING TO CELEBRATE WITH A BIG, *JUICY,* ROASTED PIG! IT'S *GREAT* YOU ARE COMING TO SPEND *NEW YEARS* IN *PUERTO RICO* WITH US!

...YOU'RE WELCOME. *GOOD NIGHT!*

ROBERTITO-- WHAT ARE YOU DOING THERE?

>CLICK<

NOTHING.

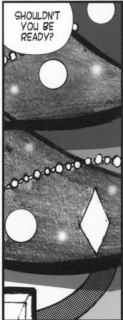

SHOULDN'T YOU BE READY?

GET YOUR SANDALS. WE HAVE TO TAKE YOU AND YOUR BROTHERS TO *GRANDMA...*

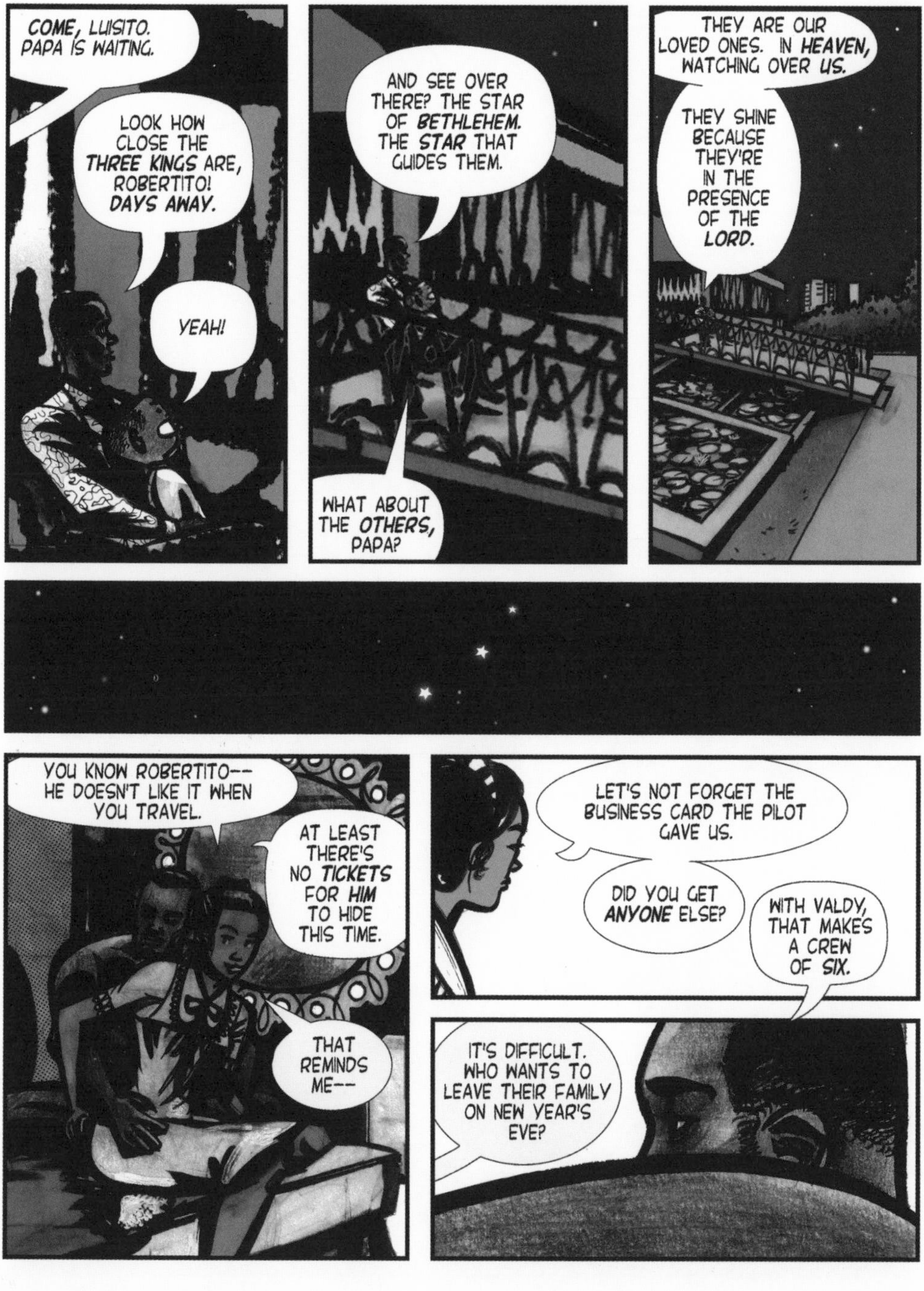
COME, LUISITO. PAPA IS WAITING.
LOOK HOW CLOSE THE THREE KINGS ARE, ROBERTITO! DAYS AWAY.
YEAH!
AND SEE OVER THERE? THE STAR OF BETHLEHEM. THE STAR THAT GUIDES THEM.
WHAT ABOUT THE OTHERS, PAPA?
THEY ARE OUR LOVED ONES. IN HEAVEN, WATCHING OVER US.
THEY SHINE BECAUSE THEY'RE IN THE PRESENCE OF THE LORD.
YOU KNOW ROBERTITO-- HE DOESN'T LIKE IT WHEN YOU TRAVEL.
AT LEAST THERE'S NO TICKETS FOR HIM TO HIDE THIS TIME.
THAT REMINDS ME--
LET'S NOT FORGET THE BUSINESS CARD THE PILOT GAVE US.
DID YOU GET ANYONE ELSE?
WITH VALDY, THAT MAKES A CREW OF SIX.
IT'S DIFFICULT. WHO WANTS TO LEAVE THEIR FAMILY ON NEW YEAR'S EVE?

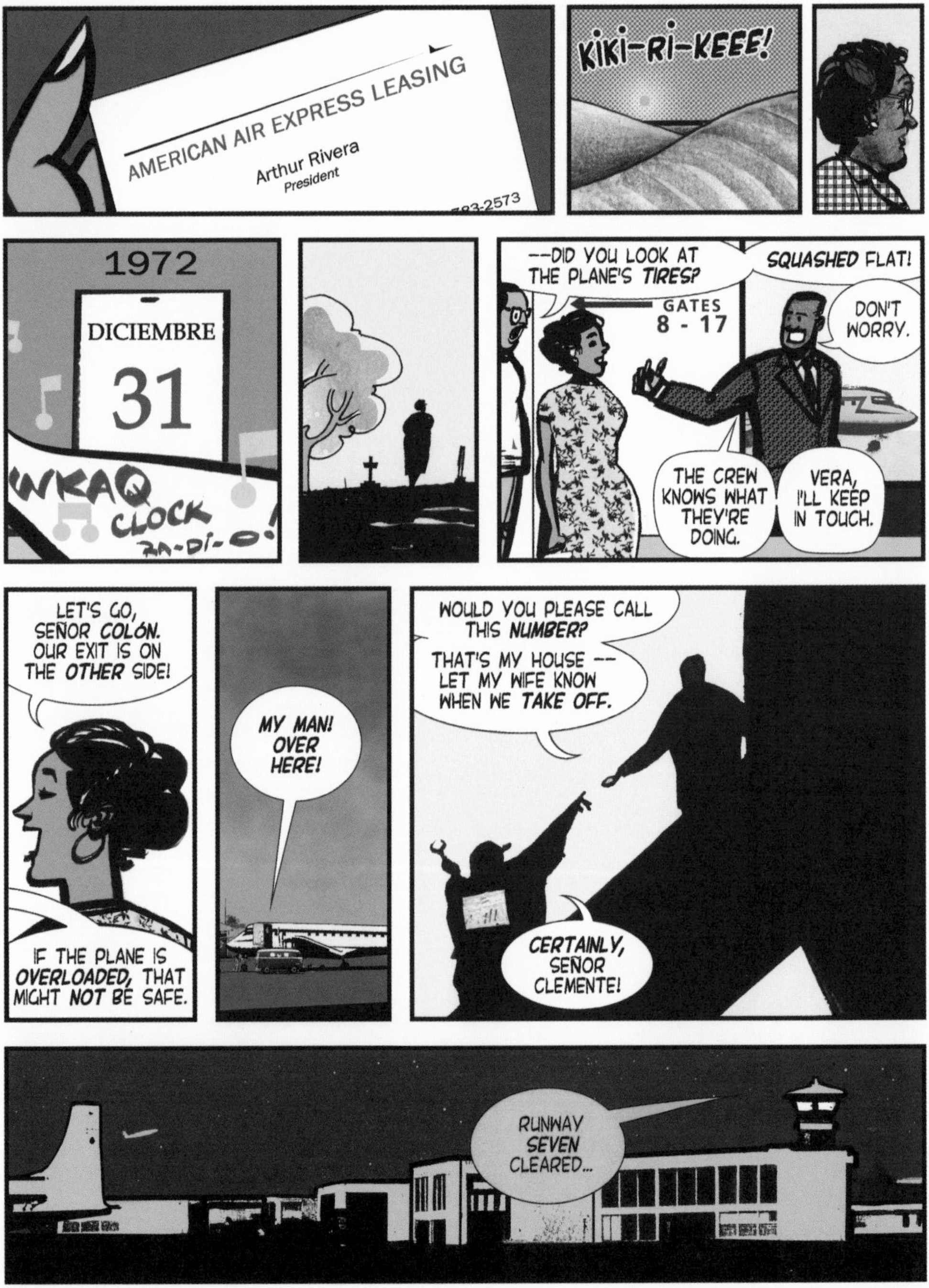
AMERICAN AIR EXPRESS LEASING
Arthur Rivera
President
KIKI-RI-KEEE!
1972
DICIEMBRE
31
WKAQ
CLOCK
--DID YOU LOOK AT THE PLANE'S TIRES?
SQUASHED FLAT!
GATES 8 - 17
DON'T WORRY.
THE CREW KNOWS WHAT THEY'RE DOING.
VERA, I'LL KEEP IN TOUCH.
LET'S GO, SEÑOR COLÓN. OUR EXIT IS ON THE OTHER SIDE!
IF THE PLANE IS OVERLOADED, THAT MIGHT NOT BE SAFE.
MY MAN! OVER HERE!
WOULD YOU PLEASE CALL THIS NUMBER?
THAT'S MY HOUSE -- LET MY WIFE KNOW WHEN WE TAKE OFF.
CERTAINLY, SEÑOR CLEMENTE!
RUNWAY SEVEN CLEARED...

DOUGLAS FIVE HUNDRED ALPHA ECHO... RUNWAY SEVEN CLEARED FOR TAKEOFF.
Alpha record, roger.
Tower... this is five hundred alpha echo coming back around bzz~
FIVE HUNDRED... UHH... ALPHA ECHO... SAY AGAIN.
FIVE HUNDRED ALPHA ECHO, SAY AGAIN....

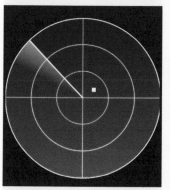

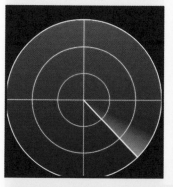

At 9:23 PM, the aircraft crashed near the coast of San Juan.
Roberto Clemente's body was never recovered.

In August 1973, Clemente became the first Latin American
to be inducted into the National Baseball Hall of Fame.

In 1974, the Roberto Clemente Sports City opened its doors in
Carolina, Puerto Rico.

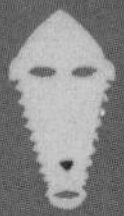

BOMBA

Created on Puerto Rico's colonial sugar plantations by African slaves and their descendants, bomba is the most purely African music genre of Puerto Rico and one of the oldest, dating back to the 1680s. Bomba's roots may trace back to the Akan people of modern Ghana, the original ancestors of much of the black population of Puerto Rico. Performing and dancing the bomba provided a social and political outlet for a people burdened with the hardships of slavery; bomba was danced at the sugar plantations on Saturday nights and holidays, usually in open areas in the sugarcane fields or in the plazas of the town square. Although the bomba developed as a secular dance form, it provided an outlet for spiritual expression and release as well. Forbidden from worshiping their ancient African gods, the African communities fused their customs onto the worship of St. James. During festivals that honored the Christian saint, bomba music was played and a traditional mask, called "vejigante" in Spanish, was worn. The mask was supposed to scare away the evil spirits and pirates that populated the Caribbean.

Bomba dances were performed during important social or community events. As with other music traditions that originate in West Africa, dance and music are inseparable counterparts in a bomba performance. Some historians say that the bomba was first developed in Loíza, a town on the Northeast coast of Puerto Rico with a strong African presence. Regardless of its original birthplace, the genre continued to develop in coastal towns such as Ponce, Loíza Aldea and Mayaguez where in the 1800s large communities of black workers gathered around sugar cane mills. As the workers moved to San Juan and other urban areas, bomba became a part of urban cultural life.

Traditional bomba ensembles featured two or three differently pitched drums, typically made from rum barrels and called barriles, a single maraca, a pair of sticks ("palitos") called cuá or fuá that tap out a fixed organizing rhythmic timeline on the side of the drum or another resonant surface. A solo singer is answered by a chorus call-and-response style, singing over the great variety of rhythmic patterns that comprise the bomba. The lyrics are generally of topical nature, revolving around the life of the community and island history, and include improvised parts referring to the dance and music performed. Lyrics are delivered in alternating stanzas and responsory parts. Traditionally, a bomba started with a female solo voice called "laina", singing a phrase that evoked a primitive call, answered by the chorus, and supported by the musicians who provided the 2/4 or 6/8 rhythm with various percussion instruments.

The barrel shaped drums or barriles are covered with tightly stretched skins and played by hand. The lower pitched drum is called the buleador, and it plays a supporting fixed rhythmic pattern.

The smaller, higher pitched drum is called the subidor, primo or repicador. The drums are accompanied by the rhythmical beating of the sticks and maracas. There are many rhythmic patterns and variations that comprise the bomba family, and some bombas have names that reflect their African origin, such as cocobale, babú, belén, cunyá, yubá and sicá, which is the bomba rhythm most often adopted by modern orchestras.

Other bomba styles are named for the type of dance it is associated with, such as the bomba Holandes or the leró, which is a French derivative of the word "rose", referencing the formation of the dancers that symbolized a rose.

Traditionally bomba is danced by a mixed couple who take turns showing off their skills, competing with each other and with the drummer. The dancers proceed in pairs and without contact. The excitement and sensual tension in the music is generated by the often improvised interactions of the singer and chorus, the drummers' rhythmic exchanges, and the suggestive "conversation" between the highest pitched drum and the dancer. The drummer follows the movement of the dancer; dancer and drummer cajole, tease and challenge each other to what appears to be a sensual dual, which lasts as long as the dancer's stamina continues. The effect is that of an intimate visual and musical exchange between singer, drummer and dancer.

~Nili Belkind

NATIONAL GEOGRAPHIC

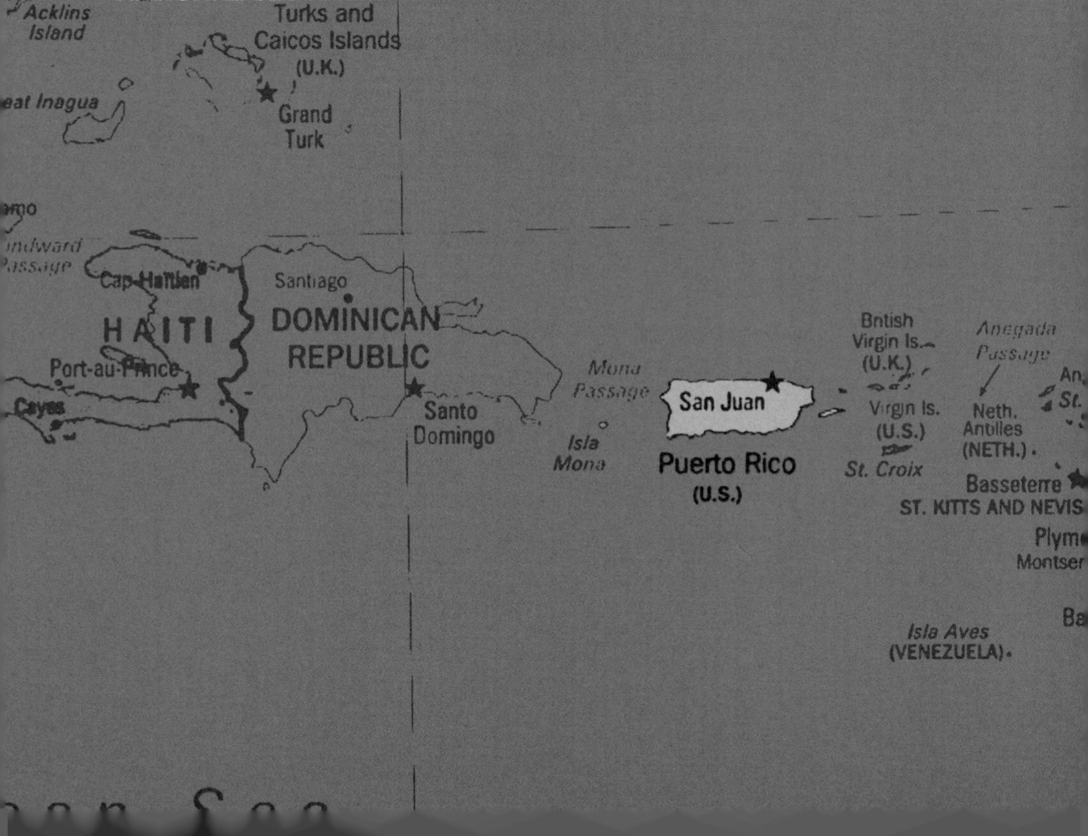

North Atlantic Ocean
San Salvador
Samana Cay
Acklins Island
Turks and Caicos Islands (U.K.)
Grand Turk
Great Inagua
Windward Passage
Cap-Haïtien
HAITI
Port-au-Prince
Cayes
Santiago
DOMINICAN REPUBLIC
Santo Domingo
Mona Passage
Isla Mona
San Juan
Puerto Rico (U.S.)
British Virgin Is. (U.K.)
Virgin Is. (U.S.)
St. Croix
Anegada Passage
Neth. Antilles (NETH.)
Basseterre
ST. KITTS AND NEVIS
Montserrat
Isla Aves (VENEZUELA)

sanlida cheng
EDITOR

gary groth
EDITORIAL LIAISON

eric reynolds
ASSOCIATE PUBLISHER

Designer> wilfred santiago
Proofreader> conrad groth

21> Fantagraphics Books INC,
7563 Lake City Way N.E., Seattle,
WA, USA 98115.

Visit the official 21 website at
21comix.com

You may survey Fantagraphics'
line of comics, graphic novels,
prose novels, criticism, and coffee
table art books including other
fine books by Wilfred Santiago
and make purchases by calling
1-800-657-1100, or visit

www.fantagraphics.com

First Edition: 2011

ISBN> 978-1-56097-892-3

Distributed in the USA by W.W. Norton &
Company, Inc
(212.354 5500)

Distributed in Canada by the Canadian Manda
Group
(416.516.0911)

Distributed in the UK by Turnaround Distribution
(208.829.3009)

Distributed to comics stores by Diamond Comics
Distributors
(800.452.6642)

Printed in China
10 9 8 7 6 5 4 3 2 1

Summary> "The story of baseball star Roberto Clemente and his journey from an impoverished
childhood to baseball-sized fortune and fame, as he strives to go the distance for respect."

PUBLISHERS
gary groth & kim thompson

acknowledgments

For their advice, patience and expertise, a very short list. And that's why it's special.
 I'm most thankful to Gary Groth, Eric Reynolds, Kim Thompson, the FB staff, Mark McVeigh, Anthony Cheng, Ivan Velez Jr., Alt 0209 & David Katzman.

21

Since 1976

Seattle
u s a

www.fantagraphics.com

For Sanlida

SELECTED BIBLIOGRAPHY

WWW

BASEBALL-ALMANAC.COM ° BASEBALLLIBRARY.COM ° BASEBALL-REFERENCE.COM FOIA.FBI.GOV ° FOLKWAYS.SI.EDU ° LATINOSSPORTSLEGENDS.COM ° LOC.GOV MLB.COM ° NATIONALGEOGRAPHIC.COM ° PBS.ORG ° QUEBEC.SABR.ORG ° RCSC21. COM ° RETROSHEET.ORG ° USMC-MCCS.ORG

NEWSPAPERS

THE MIAMI NEWS> July 26, 1960, THE NEVADA DAILY MAIL> June 8, 1960, THE NEW PITTSBURGH COURIER> January 13, 1973. PITTSBURGH POST-GAZETTE> June 8, 1960, October 14, 1960, September 19, 1972, THE NEW YORK TIMES> October 18, 1971, October 1, 1972, January 2, 1973. THE TIMES-NEWS> June 8, 1960, THE PITTSBURGH PRESS> July 25, 1970, January 2, 1973, February 4, 1973. THE SAN JUAN STAR> December 30, 1972, SARASOTA HERALD TRIBUNE> July 26, 1970, THE VALLEY INDEPENDENT> October 11, 1960.

MAGAZINES

ESQUIRE> March, 1985, August, 1958, May 1963. LIFE> April 14, 1961, May 24, 1968, June 5, 1970. LOOK> February 21, 1967. SPORTS ILLUSTRATED> February 28, 1955, August 6, 1956, April 30, 1960, October 10, 1960, March 7, 1966, July 3, 1967. TIME> September 26, 1960, October 25, 1971, November 25, 1971.

BOOKS

ATLAS PUERTO RICO Bilingual Edition> By Angel David Cruz Baez & Thomas D. Boswell, Cuban American National Council, 1997.
CLEMENTE The Passion & Grace of Baseball's Last Hero> By David Maraniss, Simon & Schuster, 2006.
FROM YAUCO TO LAS MARIAS> By Karl Stephen Herrmann, Richard G. Badger & COMPANY, 1900.
KING: The Photography Of Martin Luther King Jr.> By Charles Johnson & Bob Adelman, Viking Studio, 2000.
LAS LEYENDAS DEL BEISBOL CUBANO 1878-1996> By Angel Torres, Angel Torres Pub Co, 1997.
THE NATIONAL PASTIME Volume 26> By Society for American Baseball Research, University of Nebraska Press, 2006
THE NEW DICKSON BASEBALL DICTIONARY> Paul Dickson, Harcourt Brace & Company, 1999.
PRIDE OF PUERTO RICO: The Life of Roberto Clemente> Paul Robert Walker, Harcourt Brace & Company, 1988.
REFLECTIONS ON ROBERTO> By Phill Musick, Pittsburgh Associates, 1994.
ROBERTO CLEMENTE: Baseball's Humanitarian Hero> By Heron Marquez, Carolrhoda Books Inc., 2005.
ROBERTO CLEMENTE: Baseball Leyend> By Carin T. Ford, Enslow Publishers, 2005.
ROBERTO CLEMENTE: THE GREAT ONE> By Bruce Markusen, Sports Publishing LLC, 2001.
THE SANTURCE CRABBERS> By Van Hyning, McFarland & Company INC., 1999.
THE SUMMER GAME> By Roger Angell, Bison Books, 2004.

OTHERS

AMERICAN EXPERIENCE: Roberto Clemente> Director Bernardo Ruiz, PBS Home Video, 2008.
FREEDOM OF INFORMATION/Privacy Acts Section> Federal Bureau of Investigation, Subject: Roberto Clemente File Numbers: 62-12188, 92-6347.
ROBERTO: The Roberto Clemente Story> Producer, Joe Lavine, Phoenix Communication Group, 1993.